AVON STREET

PAUL EMANUELLI

The
Mystery
Press

'It was a much safer place for a gentleman in his predicament –
he might there be important at comparatively little cost.'

Jane Austen, *Persuasion*
(referring to Bath)

First published 2012

The Mystery Press, an imprint of The History Press
The Mill, Brimscombe Port
Stroud, Gloucestershire, GL5 2QG
www.thehistorypress.co.uk

British Library Cataloguing in Publication Data.
A catalogue record for this book is available from the British Library.

ISBN 978 0 7524 6554 8

Typesetting and origination by The History Press
Printed in Great Britain
Manufacturing Managed by Jellyfish Print Solutions Ltd

Prologue

Thomas Hunt left his home in the early hours of that February morning in 1850 and made his way through the maze of Avon Street alleyways. Nestled in his arms was his three-year-old daughter, still drowsy from the beer that he had fed her earlier. As he walked, he rocked her gently and sang a lullaby; the same song over and over again.

Memory led him without thought through gaps and passageways half-hidden in the dark rookery of huddled buildings. He strode, unthinking, through the filth-filled gutters that ran beside rank after rank of windowless hovels. His senses were oblivious to the stench; his bare feet numb to the cold, his mind conscious only of the small, warm body in his arms, and the words of the song that bound them together. Still he walked on, stopping for nothing, his eyes registering nothing, until he reached the muddy banks of the River Avon. Only then did he pause for a moment to kiss his daughter's forehead, before wading out into the river.

When the ice-cold waters began lapping at her body, she struggled against the imprisoning cradle of his arms. He held her tightly then and whispered softly until she was submerged. Her body arched and fought against him. Still he held her under the water, resisting her struggle for life, until he could feel no more movement.

Only when her body was still and limp did the reality of what he had done explode in his mind. He had wanted to protect her from his life, from the struggle to survive in Avon Street, from the inevitable loss of hope and faith. Now he understood that he had robbed her of her chance to *be*.

Holding her tight, he willed her back to life, willed the warmth of his body to pass to her. He held her tighter still, kissing her forehead time and again, holding her cold hand in his, and trying to call out for help and forgiveness. No prayer-words came. Instead he screamed, like an animal in the night, and buried deep within the formless sound he cursed the name of 'Nathaniel Caine', the only man he hated more than himself. Then, in the sudden peace of the silence that followed, he surrendered his life to the water.

Thomas Hunt was found later that morning, fifty yards downstream. The river carried his daughter's body almost twenty miles away from him and through five battering weirs.

Map of central Bath circa 1850 by Cotterill.
(Bath and North East Somerset Records Department)

Chapter 1

Eyes were watching him. James Daunton could sense them, probing and picking at his spine, like a surgeon's scalpel. He turned and looked back down the deserted road that ran alongside the River Avon, but all he could see were the dark shapes of people moving to and fro across North Parade Bridge; faceless ghosts in the night, too far away to pose any threat. He turned back again, scrutinising every window and shadowy recess in the nearby Institute Building, but still he could see no one. Pulling his coat tighter, he walked on.

James dismissed his sense of foreboding as best he could, put it down to tiredness. The moon was full and low and bright; much brighter than the gaslights that glowed at intervals along the road. Its shifting white light was playing shadow-tricks with his mind, he told himself; conjuring ghosts where none existed. On instinct he reached inside his coat, checking that his money was safe. The back of his hand brushed against the letter. Searching for a distraction, he took the pages from his pocket. He already knew the letter's contents by heart. Just holding it between his fingers was enough to send its sentences spilling again through his mind. It would be so easy to let it go, he thought; let the wind take it from his hand and carry it away, but that would solve nothing. He struggled to decide who had betrayed whom, and yet was left wondering if it even mattered?

Shivering, he returned it to his pocket and quickened his pace, anxious now for the company of friends. He turned before reaching the row of ugly factories and warehouses that blocked his view of Pulteney Bridge beyond and crossed through the shadow of the Abbey church. As the sounds of people drew louder, so his mind became easier. He smiled to himself, surveying the bustle of ramshackle, makeshift shops that hugged the Abbey's side. Each stall looked as if a good shove would bring it tumbling down, and yet they survived.

In front of the shops, the air was rich with the scent of potatoes baking on smoking braziers. James struggled through the usual throng of beggars and street-sellers, with their trays of combs and pins, nutmeg graters and cutlery. He tried to avoid their eyes and outstretched hands. Then he noticed the girl, hidden at first in the crowd; a pale girl of seven or eight years. There was nothing unusual in her appearance. She wore a sacking dress and was playing on one of the penny whistles from the tray that hung around her neck. He saw that she wore no shoes, but then many of the children of the poor went shoeless. Everyone said it was to appeal to the sympathy of those they begged from, but he knew in his heart that it was more often from necessity. She shivered as she played, and yet she seemed oblivious to the cold, oblivious to the people around her; perhaps that was what made her seem so vulnerable. He found himself reaching into his pocket, shuffling coins. 'This is for you,' he said, pushing his way past the others and giving the girl a shilling.

She smiled at him, her eyes shining bright. 'Are you buying them all?'

'No,' James replied. 'You must keep them. You can sell them tomorrow. The money is a gift, a payment for your beautiful playing.'

She grinned and took a whistle from the tray, polishing it on her dress. 'This one sings sweet as any bird,' she said, holding it out towards him with a broad smile.

He accepted it and returned her smile. 'Run home now, and get out of this cold night air.' As he turned to walk away, he reached inside his pocket, grasping another coin, but when he turned back she had already disappeared from sight, lost in the crowd.

When he reached the Abbey churchyard it was busy and flooded with light from the tall windows of the Pump Rooms. He could see the people inside, taking their seats for the concert. The musicians were tuning their instruments, the discordant notes doing battle as they filled the air. Slowing occasionally, he acknowledged various acquaintances in the square with a nod of the head. He even exchanged greetings with one or two, but did not break his stride until he saw the person he was looking for.

Frank Harcourt was standing beneath the honey stone colonnades which formed an entrance to the churchyard from Union Street.

A tall man of about thirty with a wiry, angular body, he stood head and shoulders above most of those around him. His face was striking, in both its strength and warmth; the always ready smile, displaying perfect white teeth, offsetting the harder aspects of his features. He was of course impeccably dressed, as usual, everything tailored to his own precise requirements, everything perfectly matched.

'You're late, James,' Frank said. 'It seems to have become your custom of late.'

James held out his hand. Frank was never late of course, though he never seemed to hurry anywhere; always composed and at his ease, always so sure of what he wanted from life. James envied him that certainty of purpose and resolute optimism. 'My apologies Frank, I needed to walk for a while and clear my mind.'

Frank laughed. 'Don't look so concerned. I arrived only a few moments ago myself.' He reached out and shook James' offered hand. 'And what do you have there, hidden in your coat?'

James brought out the whistle with a smile and placed the tips of his fingers, with elaborate precision, on its finger holes. He pursed his lips several times, in preparation, his face overly serious, as though he was readying himself for a solo concert performance. 'I would like to play, for your enjoyment, a lesser known piece by Mr Mozart.' He put the mouth-piece to his lips and produced a short cacophony of random, tuneless notes to the obvious displeasure of several passers-by.

Frank laughed. 'Mr Mozart would never recognise his composition.' He turned, smiling, and made to leave. 'You are a gentleman of many talents, James, but playing the tin whistle is not one of them.'

'We are not due to meet your friends for hours yet,' James said, putting the instrument in his pocket. 'Why did you wish to meet so early? Where are we going?'

'If I told you our destination you would probably provide a hundred reasons not to go there. Trust me and I will show you where some excitement can be had in this tedious city.'

'I take it we are going to Avon Street?'

Frank laughed. 'You know me too well James. Avon Street has so much to offer, provided one knows where to seek it out.' He paused, his expression questioning for a moment. 'Correct me if I'm wrong, but I thought that you had enjoyed our recent forays to the place?'

'They were entertaining, yet not without a certain amount of guilt.'

Frank smiled. 'Ah yes, guilt – a much wasted use of a man's time in my opinion. Something best kept for old age, when one has little else to do. Besides we're only going as far as Westgate Buildings. You can barely smell Avon Street from there.'

With Frank leading the way they soon reached a busy Kingsmead Square. Two constables stood beneath the bare trees at its centre, chatting and nodding occasionally to passers-by. The tops of their tall stovepipe hats and the silver buttons on their long tunic coats glistened in the light of the nearby street lamp. James noticed that they kept their gaze resolutely diverted from the open doors of the nearby warehouse, in Westgate Buildings; the doorway to which the crowd was so obviously drawn.

James shielded his eyes in the light from the doorway of the massive warehouse and, like all the others, handed over a shilling to one of the burly men guarding the entrance. The smell that greeted him as he entered the building was as pungent as a dose of smelling-salts. The sweat of the crowd mingled with the reek of stale beer, and did battle with an overpowering stench of sewage.

James hesitated for a moment, and held his hand up by reflex to his nose. At the side of the door, crowds jostled to get near to a table loaded with barrels, though the place could hardly have had a liquor licence. He considered buying a drink, but thought better of it and followed Frank, who was already making a path for them through the mass of bodies.

In his desperation to keep up, James pushed by a man standing, drinking in the crowd. The push caught the man off balance, sending him stumbling forward. When he turned, the effects of his shove were all too apparent; the man's waistcoat and trousers were stained with dark patches of spilt beer. James tried to smile, stumbling over words of apology, but half suspecting that it was pointless before the words were spoken. He watched as the man passed his now largely empty mug to one of his friends. The man was grinning, but it was a cold grin. He reached out suddenly and James felt the man's fingers around his throat, pushing him backwards into the crowd. It took him by surprise. He could smell the beer on the man's hand as he tried to pull his hand away, but his hold was too strong and the more he struggled the tighter became the grip. 'I apologised,' James said, struggling for breath.

'Did you now?' The man laughed and drew back his other fist to strike, just as Frank stepped out of the crowd to the man's side.

'Enough of this!' Frank said. 'My friend meant you no harm. It was a simple accident.'

'Wait your turn,' the man replied, half-looking in Frank's direction, his cold hand retaining its grip on James' throat. 'I'll sort you out later.' Then he looked towards his friends. 'Or do you want him, lads?' They moved forward in response.

Frank moved to James' side. Using the diversion, James brought his arm up with force and broke the man's hold on his neck and stepped back. He knew now that there was no escape.

'We want none of this,' Frank said. 'Reconsider!'

The man took a step forward, laughing. Then his expression changed. James followed the frightened stare of his eyes and saw the man who had pushed his way through the crowd, behind Frank. He was a bewhiskered giant of a man with an ugly scar running across the width of his cheek. Everyone around them seemed suddenly quiet in his presence.

His opponent took a step backwards, pushing his friends to one side, a strained smile on his now ashen face. 'Just a misunderstanding,' he said, looking at the man with the scar. 'I meant no offence Mr Caine.' His words trailed off as he lowered his gaze and then turned, trying to smile in Frank's direction. 'I was just larking about. I wouldn't have hurt him.'

Frank stared back at the man. 'You should apologise to my friend.'

'I'm sorry,' the man said, turning to James.

James nodded and then turned away, looking around him for the scar-faced man, but his vast frame was already some distance away and he was fast disappearing into the crowd. Frank threw an arm around James' shoulder. 'Follow me, James,' he said, ushering him through the crowd. 'There's money to be won.'

'Did you know that man?' James asked.

'No more than you did. Let's be grateful that he saw reason before something came of it. They might have beaten us senseless, or had us ejected before we had a chance to lay a bet.'

'No, you misunderstand,' James said, 'I was referring to the large man standing behind you, the man with the scar. The one he called Caine.'

Frank brushed the sleeve of his coat with the back of his hand. 'Perhaps he was one of the organisers, or one of the thugs they employ to keep the peace. Now let's find a bookmaker and relieve him of some money.' He tidied his collar and walked on.

Robbed of the promised fight, the crowd surged forward and James felt himself propelled ever closer to the rough wooden amphitheatre in the centre of the warehouse. All around him men were standing on benches and tables, all looking in the direction of the arena. James could now see into the circular wooden pit. It must have been twelve feet in diameter, he estimated. Within seconds he found himself pushed up against the stout, rough wooden fence, felt it digging into the bottom of his ribcage.

At the far side of the arena was a small mound of hard-packed red earth where twenty or so rats were gathered, scrabbling at the wooden walls. The rest of the circular floor was littered with the bodies of dead rats. The stench was appalling. Above the pit, lanterns were suspended, lighting every inch of the bloodied ground below, and every crevice in the fence surrounding it.

He watched as a young boy with a broom walked up to the arena, through a wide gap between the benches at the far side of the room, and unbolted a gate in the fence. Entering, he took the stave, hooked to a cord around his trousers, and began, with incredible accuracy and dexterity, to dispatch any rats that showed signs of wounds. Then, taking up his broom, he swept the torn bodies into a pile, before picking them up in bunches, by their tails, and flinging them into the corner of the room, counting the corpses out loud as he threw them. On the corner walls, behind the growing heap of bodies, James could make out rows of collars and several stuffed heads of dogs, with staring glass eyes and torn fur.

When the arena was clear the Master of Ceremonies, a squat man with a pockmarked face and a booming voice, stepped to the gate. 'Let's have some quiet now,' he roared, 'and all of you who has dogs, keep they quiet too.' Men scrabbled to get a view, fighting to get to the tiered platforms at the sides of the room; standing on tables and benches in the centre. 'The next dog is the third of the six we have before you tonight,' the fat man continued. 'You've all seen him before. His name is Captain. His owner is Caleb Brown and he hails from Wiltshire. The bookmakers will be pleased to take bets on first and second for the night, and on the individual kill for each dog. Please place your bets, gentlemen. The rules be the same for every match, fifty rats in the arena, and as many rats as he can kill stone dead, not wounded, in fifteen minutes, is what the dog scores.

The winner tonight will take away a silver collar and three gold sovereigns. Now, let's have the rats and only the girt big uns mind.' The crowd cheered.

James grabbed hold of the nearest bookmaker. 'How did the first two dogs fare?' he asked.

'They was just to make up numbers; novice dogs getting their first blooding,' the man said. 'The first had twelve and the second twenty-three.'

'What odds will you give me on Captain to take the night?'

'Captain's the favourite. You won't get better than evens anywhere in the house.'

James held out four notes to the man. 'Twenty pounds on Captain to win then.'

'I can't take that,' the bookmaker said. He muttered under his breath, 'Bloody gentry . . . All the same . . . throwing their sodding money about.'

'Damn me!' Frank interjected loudly, staring intently at the man, before bursting into mocking laughter. 'Has the world gone mad? You must forgive us, my man. We thought your livelihood depended on the taking of bets. We hadn't realised that you were selective in your choice of customers. Is there perhaps something wrong with our money?'

James smiled, but the bookmaker's words had taken him by surprise, made him think. He could see now, all too well, that the stake was excessive. He needed a win and a sizeable win, but he knew nothing of the sport, nothing of the dog's form, and he had wagered far more than he could afford.

'There's no need for that,' the bookmaker said. 'It's just as I can't carry a bet that big on the favourite. I haven't got time to lay it off.'

James looked at Frank. 'The bet was too large. We have the night ahead of us and the card game in a few days time.' He turned to the bookmaker, 'Five pounds then. Will you take the bet?'

'I'll take it,' the bookmaker said, as he passed the marker to James. 'And you?' he asked, looking in Frank's direction. 'The clever one – do you want Captain?'

'No, I'll have five pounds on the sixth dog; if you'll give me odds of three to one or better. I believe he goes under the name of King George.'

The bookmaker snatched the note from Frank's hand. 'I'll give you three to one, but I can't do better.'

James smiled at Frank and then turned his attention back to the arena, trying to forget his impetuousness. The Master of Ceremonies had left the ring and the young lad had taken his place again. This time he had no broom, but was carrying two wire cages in his scarred hands. They were filled with new rats, enough to replace each of the corpses he had thrown from the arena. The stench from the cages left no doubt as to their origin.

His duties done, the boy bowed, acknowledging the roars of approval from the crowd. One or two threw coins into the ring, which the boy quickly seized on, brushing the rats aside, wincing, but feigning indifference at the occasional bite.

James watched as the rats ran towards the raised mound at the side of the fence, heaping body upon body as they fought to escape, until the mound of earth was covered by a living, moving heap of rats, scrabbling over each other to climb the barrier. The boy walked nonchalantly to the gate and tossed the cages over the fence. Captain's owner passed the small brown and white terrier to the boy by the scruff of the neck and clambered over the fence into the arena. Then the boy handed the dog back to him and vaulted the fence. The man moved to the centre of the arena holding Captain and as the Master of Ceremonies called out that the time had begun, he released the dog. The rowdy gathering let out a huge roar and money began to change hands quickly.

The crowd chorused, as though with one voice, 'Blow 'em! Blow 'em!' and James watched as those leaning on the fence, above the mound of rats, stretched over and blew furiously. It seemed to unnerve the rats, causing them to scatter from their defensive mass, making them easier prey for the dog. Bodies flew from the pack as the dog tore into them. Each rat shrieked its own death, as the dog's jaws snapped and shook.

Then one of the rats bit into the terrier's nose and clung on, blood soaking its coat and the ground around. A second took hold of the dog's upper lip. Captain yelped with pain and tried to toss the rats free, but they clung on, and the bleeding increased as the wounds grew deeper. James willed the dog to free himself.

By the time he was free, the dog had lost precious seconds. Urged on by his owner, Captain again tore into the rats, seemingly oblivious to the pain. When the whistle blew, the dog's owner seized him by the leather collar around his neck. Thirty-nine dead rats were counted in the arena.

A good result, despite the set-back, James thought, but the sport was not to his liking. The dogs and rats might only be following the dictates of their nature, yet there seemed little natural in taking pleasure, and even profit, in such a staged and bloody slaughter. He could see the dog was still bleeding from his nose and mouth and watched as his owner took a bottle from his pocket and poured it over the dog's face. For a few seconds the scent of peppermint masked the smell of the sewers.

'I fancy a dousing in peppermint water will do little to help the dog,' Frank said. 'The sewer rats have a habit of giving dogs the canker from their bites, and that dog is badly bitten.'

The words made James feel uncomfortable. He tried to brush his thoughts aside, reaching into his pocket for more money, but his hand found the letter again and the old concerns came flooding back. Looking at the faces around him, grinning and laughing and noisy, he felt uneasy. He longed for the cool night air outside and some quiet, and time to think. The voices of his conscience and the expectations of others, normally mute when he gambled, were suddenly loud. He counted his remaining money and then thrust it back into his pocket, unable to shake his feelings.

'You look somewhat ill at ease,' Frank said.

'I've had enough of this place,' James replied.

'Was it that oaf who upset you earlier? Or is it the stink of the sewer rats? I know it isn't to everyone's taste, but they put up a better fight than barn rats. It strikes me as a damnably good event.'

'It feels more like butchery to me, than sport. I am tired and there's work I need to complete tomorrow, business that I should have attended to long before now.'

'You can't leave me to my own company so early in the evening.' Frank laughed. 'And if the work has waited this long it can always wait a little longer.'

'It's fine for you. You don't need to work, but work is an increasing necessity for me.' James held out the marker for the bet. 'Could you collect anything due me?'

Frank shook his head and put both hands behind his back, smiling. 'A good stiff brandy will soon set you right.' He took a hip flask from his pocket and drank, before passing it to James. 'You can't desert me, in such an ungentlemanly manner. Stay, at least until we know the result.'

James took a drink and handed the flask back. Frank put his left arm around his shoulder and laughed, and James felt compelled to return his smile. 'I'd never have suspected when we first met that you would become such a good friend and such valued company,' Frank said. 'You spend too much time with people like Dr Wetherby. How such a dreary man attracted such a beautiful wife, or a friend like you, remains a mystery to me.'

'Richard is a good man,' James replied. 'It's a pity that there is no liking between the two of you.'

'It is as it is,' Frank said. 'Now have another wager, while we see how my dog fares and then we'll move on.'

'No,' James replied, 'I have gambled enough. The more I try to make good my losses, these last few months, the greater they grow.'

'You've just had a run of bad luck,' Frank said. 'It must end soon. At least stay until we know the result. You cannot leave me alone in this mob and I have friends waiting in The White Hart Hotel, influential friends. I promised I would introduce you to them.' He smiled. 'I'm sure that one of us will win tonight and whoever wins will pay for the remainder of the evening.'

'Very well,' James said. 'I will stay, but I'll not wager more.'

Chapter 2

Belle Bennett waited in the wings for the others to arrive, as she did every night. It had begun years ago, become a habit, and then grown into a superstition. She had to be in place before she was called, as though if she was ever late her performance might suffer. Those few minutes between curtain-call and taking her place on stage were when she felt most alive. She drank in the heady mixture of apprehension and exhilaration, more intoxicating for her than any wine.

As the others joined her, Belle smiled at them. This too was instinctive, the mutual giving and exchanging of reassurance and support before the show commenced. One or two looked, at first, as though they might return the gesture, but as Cauldfield pushed his way past them, their expressions froze and their smiles died, only half-formed.

Cauldfield winked as he passed her. His breath was rank in her nostrils, as he pressed his body hard against her. 'I'm sorry that you have such a meagre part again, my dear, but the peasant dress is very becoming.' He grinned and put his hand on her shoulder for a moment, before sliding it slowly, down her bare arm. The sweat of his palms felt clinging and oily on her bare skin. 'Your life could be so much easier,' he whispered. Then he drew back, as if waiting for her to react. Belle struggled to keep the emotion from her face, biting back her words, saying nothing as she scrubbed instinctively at her arm. 'Everyone is going to The Garrick's Head for a drink afterwards,' he resumed, speaking loudly enough for the others to hear; almost loudly enough for the audience in the front row of the auditorium to hear. 'Will you be joining us?'

She turned and looked at the others. She knew what was expected of her; expected of them all. Actors and actresses had to be seen around town, promoting their current production, bringing in the paying crowds. She was torn for a moment, wanting to join them, wanting to laugh and forget for a while, but she knew she would not be allowed to forget, because Cauldfield would be there. 'I think not,' she said. 'I'll more than likely go straight home tonight.'

Cauldfield seized immediately on her words, with his by now familiar superior smile, addressing the others as though he was already on the stage with a captive audience. 'Perhaps Miss Bennett is too consummate an actress to be seen with mere players, such as ourselves.' He laughed. 'Though one might have thought that she could at least try to make use of what looks she has, to bring the gentlemen in.' He turned to her. 'Or do you think they come to see you act?'

He smirked, as though it had been some innocuous joke. The ever doting Daisy draped herself around his shoulders. He kissed the girl's cheek and smiled. 'Don't prize yourself too highly, Belle, or you'll only have further to fall.' Two months ago, or even one, and she might have matched his words, but not now. Cauldfield turned to the others. 'Our little Belle thinks herself better than us. She truly believes that she has an exceptional talent.' Then, grinning at her, he said it. 'I believe it was the very same belief that deluded your father and mother.'

She wanted to rake the smug smile from his face with her fingernails. Instead she said and did nothing. As she turned away their quiet laughter stung her tired mind, yet it did not hurt as much as her own silence. She realised now the extent of the power he held over her.

When Belle emerged from the Theatre Royal it was almost midnight. She busied herself fastening the bottom buttons of her coat, resisting the urge to run, as she watched the others troop into The Garrick's Head. The wind was strong and threatened to tear the bonnet from her head. She took the white glove off her right hand. The cold air stung her fingers and numbed her body. She noticed her hands were shaking as she pushed the strands of windblown hair back into the confines of the bonnet and struggled with the ribbons, pulling them tighter, before retying them beneath her chin.

As the door to The Garrick's Head swung closed, the square fell back into a dark silence. She listened to her own solitary footsteps, echoing in the emptiness, as she crossed the deserted, cobbled square. Saw Close was flanked by stables and hauliers' yards and a cattle market had taken up much of the square when she had walked to the theatre that afternoon. Now that the wind had dropped, the air was full of the sweet, sickly stench of the animals. She feared for her shoes and the hem of her dress, but, looking down, she saw that the cobbles had already been swept clean by the scavengers, with their carts and buckets, collecting the cowpats and horse droppings; wasting nothing that could be used or sold.

Walking past the Bluecoat School, she entered the darkness of Bridewell Lane. The top of the alley was poorly lit and one of the houses there was derelict. Its doorway was boarded up; the number 'nine' gouged into the wood of the central plank, as though visitors might still be expected at some time. An involuntary shiver shook her body. She struggled to understand. It had happened on previous nights, this feeling of evil, haunting that doorway, as though it still carried the memory of some violent act. She quickened her pace, drawn ever faster, like a moth, to the well-lit lower end of the lane, where the houses were new and all their portals intact and secure.

As soon as she saw the door of number two Bridewell Lane, she felt its comfort. She opened it quietly and crept carefully up the creaking staircase. Turning the knob of the door at the top of the stairs, she silently eased it open. Jenny's voice greeted her softly. 'Don't be concerned,' she said, 'Molly's fast asleep. With any luck she shouldn't wake now until morning. I knew you'd be home soon, so I put some coals on the fire. Warm yourself, you must be freezing.'

Belle gazed down at Molly's tiny frame as she lay sleeping, lost in the vastness of the bed. She seemed so peaceful, a blissful three year old, wrapped in the comfort of child-dreams. Belle leant forward and kissed Molly on the forehead, enjoying the scent of childhood innocence. 'She grows more like her mother, each day,' she whispered.

'She's far prettier than I ever was,' Jenny replied.

Belle took off her coat and gloves and sat on the corner of the bed, tugging at her boots. The left boot had begun letting in water recently. As she turned it over in her hands she noticed the stitching was coming apart on one side. The sole was worn as thin as paper at its centre, but at least there were no holes, no need for patching yet.

The warmth of the room wrapped itself around her like a soft blanket, enveloping her in its sanctuary. She looked around, breathing in the reassurance of familiar surroundings. It was a simple room; not large, but comfortable enough for the three of them, dominated by the large bed at its centre. Two chests of drawers stood in the recesses on either side of the fireplace; one for herself and one for Jenny and Molly. There were three upright chairs, one on either side of the bed and the one on which Jenny was sitting at the small work table beneath the window. The only other furniture was a small dressing table and a wash-stand and between them stood her travelling chest.

She walked over to Jenny and put a hand on her shoulders. 'If Molly grows to be half as pretty as her mother, then she will be a true beauty.'

'It's you who turns all the heads, whenever I've been out walking with you.'

'Nonsense,' Belle replied, embarrassed yet enjoying the compliment.

She studied Jenny's face, deep in concentration, the tip of her tongue protruding slightly between pursed lips, as she threaded tiny jet beads onto the cotton, and sewed them with intricate precision into the neckline of the bodice she was finishing. 'You make me feel guilty. I wish you would stop working. You were sewing when I woke this morning and you're still at it now. Your eyes must be tired, working in the candlelight.' Jenny was in her early twenties, as was she, but her face seemed older. Belle watched her stand, her spine at first refusing to straighten, until, hands on hips, she arched her back into comfort again and stretched, before tidying her work.

'I'm not the only one who looks tired.' Jenny said, studying her. 'You look worried. Has that Cauldfield been bothering you again?'

'No.' The lie came without thinking. 'I'm just tired. Cauldfield's too busy with one of the other girls now, to pay much attention to me.'

'Not that Daisy girl from Wells, her with the big chest?'

Belle smiled. 'She's the one. And whatever she may lack in wit, she more than makes up for in the willingness of her disposition, as I'm sure several members of the company could vouch – the men, that is. But, if she keeps him occupied and meets his needs, it's all to the good.'

Jenny grinned. 'Would you mind if I left my work things out, so I can start first thing in the morning?'

'Don't worry on my account.'

'I washed your grey dress and hid the fraying hem with some ribbon I'd saved.'

'You do too much for me. I don't deserve it.'

Jenny walked over to the bed, undoing her dress. 'You do deserve it and more, but still, we must be grateful for what we have, and help each other how we can.' She leant over and kissed Molly's forehead. 'I heard today of a poor young girl who was drowned the other night in the river, and her father with her. He must have been trying to save her.'

Belle shivered. 'How awful, and you're right of course. We should be grateful.' She hesitated, wondering if she had the energy to say what needed to be said, and to deal with its inevitable effect. She took off her earrings and placed them on the dressing table, catching her reflection for a moment in the mirror. Tired, blue-grey eyes stared back at her, as though it was a stranger she was looking at. She remembered sitting with her mother, talking, and taking it in turns to brush each other's hair, the silk, auburn strands caught in the bristles of the brush, mother's and daughter's indistinguishable. Now her hair was a mess of shapeless tangled knots, but she did not have the energy to brush it, though she knew she would regret it in the morning. Turning away, she poured water into the bowl on the wash-stand, and dabbed what she could of the surplus powder from her face. 'I'd hoped we might talk for a while,' Belle said, 'but we're both probably too tired.'

'You talk while I get ready for bed.'

'The theatre was half empty tonight,' Belle said, trying to lay the ground. 'There was a concert in the Pump Rooms and some awful ratting contest in Avon Street. And I've no work tomorrow either. There's a touring operetta company appearing in the theatre.' She hesitated, feeling her way. 'I may not have enough to pay all my share of the rent this week.'

'We'll manage somehow. You've paid more than your share when I've been short. Have you seen anything recently of that gentleman friend of yours?' Jenny asked, getting into the bed. 'You never speak of him.'

'No,' Belle replied, 'and I hope I never shall again.' The time for saying what she really needed to say had gone in that moment. It would have to wait. The sudden feelings of anger and pain had taken her by surprise. She had struggled to keep the emotion out of her voice, but knew that she had failed.

'I'm sorry,' Jenny said, 'I'm a fool for mentioning him. I should have understood. I don't know where Molly and me would be without you, and I don't just mean you helping with the rent.' She pulled the sheet up to her chin. 'Goodnight, Belle.'

Belle blew out the candle on the worktable. 'Goodnight Jenny.' She moved the chair noiselessly to a place by the fire and sat, bathing in the flickering warm glow of the fire. Though she fought it, the image of his face would not leave her mind now. He had won their game; a game she had not even been aware that they were playing. She wondered how she could have been so stupid as to love him. If she needed another reason for leaving, the prospect of meeting him again certainly provided it. She searched inside for warmer memories; looked around the room, willing friendly ghosts into existence, but all she saw were the flickering shadows. There was no doubt in her mind now. She had to leave Bath.

Chapter 3

Sitting in the armchair by the fireplace, in the large basement kitchen, Nathaniel Caine struggled to pull off his fine boots. He grimaced at their resistance; a film of sweat and grime binding skin to leather. Still, they looked good and that was the main thing; did him justice, as the man of means he now was. Perhaps they were too tight, but then again they had cost him nothing.

Caine massaged the life back into his bare, aching feet, rubbing the corns and blisters, raised and red, against blackened blotchy skin. When he had finished, he cupped his hands to his face and inhaled with quiet satisfaction. Smiling to himself, he remembered how the boots had come to him. He'd had much less of a struggle removing them from the feet of the gentleman who used to own them than he had just had taking them off his own feet; but then the gentleman in question had been unconscious at the time.

Caine sat back in the chair, allowing himself a moment of satisfaction. In here he had nothing to fear from the outside world. The house in Hucklebridge's Court dwarfed its neighbours in strength and size. Its doors were solid oak, and always kept locked and bolted. Most of the windows had been bricked or boarded up, and behind each of the windows that still held glass was a row of strong iron bars. It was a fortress amongst the ramshackle Avon Street hovels that surrounded it. No, Caine reflected, he feared no one outside those walls. Yet his companions inside the house were a different matter.

Unfolding the old newspaper that had been lying on the seat, Caine scanned over the front page, filled with notices and advertisements. They were of little interest to him. He was proud of his learning.

It set him apart. He'd had to pay for it of course, and not just in money. Admitting his ignorance to another man, and one who had been younger than him, had hurt. To have that man look down his nose at him for month after month, treating him like a child, had hurt even more, but he'd never reacted, never once given way to his temper.

His teacher had overcharged him. He had known that even then, but silence always comes at a price. Still it had been worth the money and the trouble. He could still remember how good it felt when he paid him that last time. His instincts had told him to kick him up the arse, but instead he had wished him good day and said, 'Your services are no longer required.' The look on his face was worth the restraint. There had been no need to warn him about keeping their secret. He knew the tables had turned.

Lowering the paper for a moment, Caine switched his attention to his companions, playing cards, sitting at the long mahogany table in the centre of the room; swirls of smoke rising from their pipes and circling above their heads. None of them can read properly, he thought, gazing at the bovine faces gathered around the table. One or two of them knew enough to master the lists of names he gave them, lists of debtors to be collected from; but he was the only one who could truly read, and make sense of numbers; the only one who knew exactly who owed what, and when they were due to pay. It was a profitable business, money lending, especially when he had seen off all of his competitors. Then there were those who paid for his protection, he needed to keep records of those too, to make sure they got visited regularly, got reminded who was in charge in Avon Street.

Caine stretched his tired legs, feeling his age for a moment, yet he was not that old, he told himself. The card game was getting noisier. Jeb was shooting his mouth off again, trying to intimidate the others; bluffing as usual. Caine smiled to himself, knowing all too well that the louder Jeb shouted, the worse his hand would be. It was when he was quiet that Jeb was dangerous. If ever a man had earned his appearance it was him; a permanent sneer etched into every line and twist of his features.

As Jeb added to the already tidy pot of money in the middle of the table, three of the men stacked their cards, swearing various oaths in the process. It was now between Jeb and the Wood brothers, Harry and Tommy. 'Don't get too bloody comfortable!' Caine shouted. 'There's business to be discussed.'

'Did we do well at the ratting tonight?' Jeb asked, putting his cards flat on the table for a moment and turning around.

'Aye we took a good cut,' Caine said, 'and there was no trouble – thanks to me.' There were a few grunts and groans around the table, but no one spoke back. Caine studied Harry Wood's face. He would win, no doubt about it, you could see it in his eyes. Jeb could bluff for as he long as he wanted, but Harry was a cold piece of work. Caine watched him. He never seemed to look at his own cards, never arranged or ordered them in his hand; just watched Jeb's face, like a fox playing with a chicken.

Jeb did not have many allies amongst the crew, but there were some that would pitch in with him out of fear, if they thought the time was right. He might not be as hard as Harry, but he was just as dangerous. Show him any weakness and he picked away at it, like a sore. Jeb would remember a grievance and let it fester for weeks, till you thought it was forgotten. Then he'd have you.

Jeb picked his cards up again and stared at Tommy Wood, willing him to back down. Tommy grinned from ear to ear, but Caine guessed he would throw his hand in sooner rather than later. No killer instinct in that lad, never took anything serious. Still, you couldn't help liking the lad. There was a spark of something in him that set him apart. Everyone liked the boy, apart from Jeb.

Caine smiled as he watched Tommy, sitting there grinning, making jokes at Jeb's expense. No one else would get away with it, Caine thought, but Jeb knew all too well that if he took Tommy on, he'd have Harry to deal with, and in cold blood not one of them could beat Harry in a fight. But when Harry lost his temper his blood boiled and he lost all sense. He'd come at you then like a bull at a gate. That was when he was vulnerable. It was then he could be beaten.

Yes, it was Jeb and Harry Wood that needed careful watching now, but Caine had their measure. He stroked the deep scar that curved around from his left ear and disappeared into the whiskers, at the corner of his mouth, grinning to himself. If they were both threats, it was no bad thing. Keep them set against each other; keep them uncertain, fighting for favour. That was the way. Like people said; divide and rule. 'Did you collect from Rickman at the Kingston Mills, Jeb?' Caine asked. The room fell silent.

Jeb looked uneasily towards him. 'No, Nat. We went there but he still won't pay and he got a bunch of his lads to see us off. If I'd had more men with me . . . ' He broke off the sentence and spat on the floor. 'There was just too many of them.' The silence grew deeper.

Caine knew they were waiting for him to react. 'Fine,' he said, 'torch the warehouse tomorrow night. He's got a thousand pounds worth of flour and wheat in there. Let's see how he likes saving the few pounds he should have paid us, compared to what it's going to cost him. Maybe it'll learn a lesson to anyone else who's thinking of being brave.' They all laughed.

It wasn't meant to be like this, Caine thought. His partner had told him how easy it would be in Bath, how there was more money to be made from selling protection to the factories and warehouses than from farmers. He had been right, but only in part. The gentlemen didn't bend as fast as farmers. They thought the law was there to protect them. Maybe they'd bend better now when they saw what he could do, or perhaps he was overstepping himself? Only time would tell. Still it was easy enough making money out of the poor. He'd been right about that. Lending to those who couldn't afford to borrow was a very profitable business.

Caine looked at Harry Wood and then at Tommy again. A few years separated the brothers in age though they might still have been mistaken for twins. They were both tall and stocky in build and both had the same curly brown hair. Their features, too, were similar, though Tommy had a plump face whilst Harry's face was thinner and slightly jaundiced. The real difference between them though was in their characters. Tommy was always cheerful and full of humour. Harry was given to brooding and much darker in his moods. He had been the head in their family since the day the man who called himself their father had run off to God knows where. Harry must have been about thirteen then, Caine thought. It had made him strong, but it had also given him a weakness. 'He's getting too bloody soft, that brother of yours, Harry,' Caine shouted. 'People won't pay if he's always smiling at them.'

Harry looked up. 'It's just his nature. Don't worry yourself; they'll pay, while I'm with him. We balances each other out.' He turned to his brother and winked.

'This bain't be something to laugh at,' Caine spat back. 'You'm getting behind with your collections Tommy.'

Tommy winced. 'I'll back you up against anyone, and thieve for thee as good as the next, but it goes against the grain, taking from them who has nothing. I don't like this lending business. You charge so much and then they can't pay.'

'If you don't like it you can allers move on.' Caine watched as Harry stood and put a hand on his brother's shoulder. He wondered if this was the right time. He watched as Jeb put his cards on the table and reached slowly down towards the hilt of the knife that protruded from his boot. There was nothing Jeb would like better than to see the Wood brothers off.

He sized up Harry Wood again, letting the silence grow. He didn't need to take him on, not now. It was enough just to stir the pot a bit between Harry and Jeb, remind them who was boss. Caine smiled. 'Settle down Harry. Just get the lad in order.' He smiled at Tommy. 'You're a good lad, Tommy – just a bit too soft for your own good.'

Tommy smiled back. 'But I make you laugh don't I Nat?'

'Aye, you do that,' Caine said.

Harry smiled and sat. 'Leave it to me, Nat. You know you can trust us.'

Caine nodded discretely at Jeb, acknowledging his support. Jeb nodded back and smiled to himself as he picked up his cards again. Caine went back to his paper. He'd done all that he wanted and never once had to move from his chair.

For a few minutes the room was quiet except for the sound of money being thrown into the pot, and his own occasional turning and folding of the paper. The piece about the drowning was the last thing he expected to see.

Caine leapt to his feet without thinking and the room fell silent. 'Bastard,' he shouted, 'that bastard Tom Hunt! It's all in the paper about him and his brat drowning.' He tore and ripped at the newspaper, before hurling the crumpled mass into the fire. 'He'll be more trouble dead than he was alive, if we don't do something about it.' Then as he watched Harry raking in his winnings Caine began planning his next move, and the one after that.

Chapter 4

As soon as she awoke, Belle was aware of the whispering voices on the other side of the room. It was obvious that Jenny was working hard at distracting Molly in an effort to keep her quiet. Belle kept her eyes closed for a moment, enjoying the quiet chatter of mother and daughter. For a moment she allowed herself to share in their enjoyment of being together, knowing how much she would miss them when she left. When, finally, their conversation was punctuated by Molly's laughter and Jenny's shushes, Belle stretched and sat up in bed. 'You should have woken me.'

As if in answer, Molly climbed down from her chair, ran across the room and threw herself onto the bed, wrapping her small arms around Belle's neck; hugging her with all the strength that her three-year-old body could muster. 'Big kiss for Belle,' she said.

'Don't strangle your Aunt Belle,' Jenny called to Molly. 'Sorry, she's wanted to wake you for ages, but you were sleeping so soundly I didn't want to disturb you. Besides it's still early, and pitch black outside. There's a mug of tea there on the chair beside you. It should still be warm.'

Belle tickled Molly into a fit of giggles and then turned to Jenny. 'It's best I get this over with quickly. I wanted to tell you last night, but we were both tired and it seemed best left until the morning. I'm afraid I have some bad news.'

Jenny looked up from her work. 'What is it?'

'I told you that the theatre was half empty last night and that I have no work today, and that I was short of money.'

'And I told you that we'll manage somehow.'

'That's not the worst of it,' Belle said, preparing herself, watching the concern growing in Jenny's expression. 'Cauldfield's starved me of work, these last two weeks or so, given me only minor parts to play. And he's made it clear I was lucky to get even those.' She hesitated. 'I think I'm going to have to leave Bath. I've no money and he's slowly killing any confidence I had.'

'Come away, Molly,' Jenny said. 'Let Aunt Belle drink her tea in peace.'

Belle dabbed at her eyes with a corner of the sheet and then put her arm around Molly's shoulders. 'No let her stay,' she said. 'Molly's no bother, are you?' She tickled her again and kissed her cheeks repeatedly, until Molly buried her head under the bedclothes.

'You can't leave,' Jenny said. 'You're part of our family. You have been since the beginning. That first morning when you came to see the room above, it was no accident that I bumped into you on the stairs. I saw you from the window when you arrived and Molly and I both liked the look of you. We waited by the door for ages, waiting to hear you on the stairs, and we didn't invite you in from the goodness of our hearts, though I wanted you to think so. I needed to see how Molly took to you, but I needn't have worried. We both liked you from the start. Please don't leave.'

'You schemer, and there was me thinking it was coincidence.' Belle smiled. 'I don't want to leave, but if I were to stay I'd just be a burden.'

'You would never be a burden. We'll manage somehow. Perhaps I could borrow a little more.'

Belle shivered. 'That's what I mean. I knew that would be your first thought.' She found herself picturing the two debt collectors who had called last Friday as she was leaving for the theatre; the one smiling and friendly, the other expressionless and cold. It had been the first she had known of Jenny's debts. 'Please promise me you won't borrow from them again,' Belle said.

Jenny came over to the bed and retrieved Molly before walking over to the window and pulling the curtains to one side. 'Look Molly, it's a misty old day,' she said, sitting her at the table. 'Finish your milk now.'

She returned and sat on the edge of the bed, her expression thoughtful; her smile somewhat distant. 'They're not so bad, the Wood brothers. I know Harry can be frightening, but Tommy's always been a nice lad. He wouldn't let Harry hurt us.'

'But what if you can't pay?' Belle asked.

'They've always let me borrow a little more in the past, if I haven't had enough to pay them. Besides, I had no choice. There is no one else I can borrow from.'

'But your debts keep growing, even when you pay,' Belle said. 'Promise me you won't go to them again.' She leant forward and put a hand on Jenny's shoulder. 'I still have some things of my mother's that I can sell, if the worse comes to the worst.'

'It needn't come to that,' Jenny said, 'and I won't borrow more. If you can look after Molly, I'll go to the shops in Milsom Street. I've finished three bonnets and I've been plucking up the courage to try to sell them.' She smiled at Belle. 'You've helped me so much.'

'But I gave you no help in making the bonnets. I don't have your skill with needle and thread.'

'No, but you've taught me how to present myself and how to behave with others. You made me see that they're no better than me, the ladies and the shop-keepers in Milsom Street. I'm not afraid of them any more, when they look down their noses at me. Perhaps, for once, I can help you a little, as you've helped me in the past. Just promise you'll stay and I promise I won't borrow.'

'Very well,' Belle said. 'I'll stay for a while longer.'

'You look dreadful James!' Richard exclaimed, as soon as he had closed the drawing room door behind him. 'Perhaps I should be visiting you as your doctor, rather than as your friend.'

James gestured for him to sit. Richard Wetherby was every inch the successful doctor, decidedly smarter in appearance now than when they had first met. His wife, Charlotte, had seen to that of course. His fine black worsted jacket and waistcoat were well tailored. The sand brown trousers were of the same quality, braided with black silk. The ensemble went some way to disguise the fact that he had become noticeably thinner in recent months, but could not completely hide it.

'It's true, I do feel unwell, but it's of my own doing,' James replied, trying to shake some life back into his body.

'Forgive me,' Richard said, 'but I see too many patients suffering from conditions that might have been avoided. I really have no wish to see you become one of them. I take it you were out again with Harcourt and his friends and that this is the outcome.'

James studied his pale reflection in the gilt-framed mirror above the fireplace. He hesitated, trying to clear his mind, struggling to bring some order to the events of the previous evening. He could remember, well enough, planning their strategy for the coming card game, with Frank, over dinner at The White Hart. Then Frank's friends had arrived, a group of well-connected people. He could even recall some of their names.

They had all been in good humour, he recalled, when they had set off together for Southgate Street but when he tried to picture what had happened there, his memory flooded with hazy faces, and half-remembered conversations, until he could not be sure what was real and what was imagined. Of the thirty pounds he had taken with him, he had found only a few coins in his pocket that morning, yet Frank had paid for dinner, with his winnings from the ratting contest. It was as though the night had become some half-remembered dream.

James sat and turned to Richard. 'We went to The White Hart Hotel and then a group of us to some ale house, in Southgate Street. I don't recall its name.'

'That explains your condition,' Richard said. 'Have you any idea of how they adulterate the beer in the ale houses around Avon Street? It's full of foxglove, henbane, opium and God knows what other concoctions. They use chemicals so that they can water down the beer, keep its taste and appearance, but make it stronger, and still sell it cheaply. It's little wonder that you look so poorly.'

'The ale was strong,' James said, 'and it certainly seems to have affected me badly. But what's done is done, and now I must pay the price.' Inside he felt a sense of relief that Richard had offered at least some explanation of why he should feel as he did; that there was some rational explanation of his condition. Yet still the lost hours worried him.

'I don't think you realise how much you have changed of late,' Richard said.

It was half statement, half question and it took James by surprise. Yet he knew all too well that it was true. He shrugged. 'And I don't think you realise, my friend, how difficult it was to be accepted into Bath society, as an "Oirishman", or how hard it was to find work and achieve some standing. The law is a profession seemingly favoured by bigots. I am not by nature so outgoing as you might think me.'

'But you have no trace of an Irish accent.'

'Thanks to a good education, and years of disciplining my speech.' Where else but Bath, James wondered, could his transformation have been so easily executed, or so readily accepted? One could be whoever one chose to be in Bath, with the correct manners, and upbringing, and opinions, and enough money to maintain the façade. It was a city of wealthy migrants where the right address, and furnishings, and

tableware, and servants, could all be hired for the season, or for as long
as they were required, a city where appearance was all, and substance
mattered little.

'You make too much of your ancestry. I never thought any less of
you, because you are Irish,' Richard said.

'But you are not like others,' James replied.

'It's a wonder that you can support yourself from your work, with
your socialising and gambling, but of course you have your annuity;
six hundred pounds a year, is it not?'

'Perhaps I've been somewhat distracted of late. But I have always
taken pride in my work, particularly when I believe in the justice of a
case. I am a good advocate.'

'But half of them never seem to pay. Has that housebreaker Maggs
paid you yet?'

James resented the question. 'You know damn well that drawing up
deeds and contracts holds little appeal to me; and no, Charlie Maggs
has not yet paid me, though I'm sure he will. He was innocent and I
proved him so. He visits sometimes and we play chess together, and
when he has the money, he will pay me.'

'He has charmed you out of your fee,' Richard interrupted. 'I hope
you do not keep money in the house.'

'Charlie Maggs would not rob me,' James said. 'He is too old for
house-breaking now, and besides he is an honourable man, in his way.'

'Well, it's not for me to tell you how to live your life.'

James laughed. 'You've done little else lately, though rarely perhaps
to this extent. What's put you in this mood?'

Richard looked a little embarrassed and seemed to stumble
over his words for a moment. 'I'm truly sorry, James. I say what I
do, because you are my closest friend and because I care about your
wellbeing.' He paused as though ordering his thoughts, rubbing his
eyes and forehead vigorously. 'You think it a gentleman's adventure, to
explore the dens around Avon Street, but I see what that place does
to those who struggle to survive there. There are houses, less than half
the size of your own, with half a dozen families living in them, and
hardly a wage between them. Children sleep on floors, with straw
for a bed, and rats, and mice, and cockroaches for company. When
they're not working for a few pennies a day they're sent out begging,
or rummaging in the river or in piles of rubbish to find something
to eat, or something they can sell. When they have time to play it is
in streets that flood each time the river rises, and where the gutters

run with effluent and waste from overflowing cesspits. There are flop-houses where old people and itinerants sleep standing up, with their arms hung over a rope and they pay for the privilege of hanging there. And you think you know Avon Street?'

'I have no illusions concerning the place,' James answered, his mind still busy trying to digest what Richard had said.

Richard stared at him for a moment, and then looked distractedly into the flames of the fire. 'I had to examine a man and his daughter in the morgue of the Mineral Hospital on Sunday morning. They had drowned in the river on the previous night.' His words were slow and soft spoken and he paused, as though lost in thought, for a moment. 'I surprise even myself, sometimes.'

'In what way?' James asked.

'I've seen so much death, yet its cruelty still has the power to shock me. God knows why it should be so. Perhaps because it forces me to realise my own limitations, and reminds me how tenuous the hold we have on life truly is.' He hesitated as though looking for the right words, but unable to find them.

From where he sat in the brocade, wing-backed armchair, James caught sight of the portrait of his mother, reflected in the mirror above the fireplace, as though she was watching him, just out of sight across the room, a face so full of youthful compassion and hopes for the future. 'I understand your feelings, better than you might think,' he said.

'Some have the ability to see only what they want to see, yet the more I perceive of the world, the less I understand.'

'But you're a doctor. The truth of life and death confronts you every day.'

'You've always been a good friend,' Richard said, smiling. 'I am sorry that I preach to you sometimes, like some pious vicar.' He paused and his expression became serious again. 'The girl was the same age as my own little Charity. Underneath all the river mud and weeds, her hair looked just like hers. When I washed her clean, her face was disfigured and bruised beyond recognition, and I kept seeing Charity's face. How could any God allow such a thing to happen?'

'I have a friend who knows the Avon Street area well and all that goes on there,' James said. 'Shall I try to discover more?'

'Stay away from Avon Street, James,' Richard said. 'I'll discover soon enough all I need know. I'm to give evidence to the Coroner's Court on Thursday. All I needed from you was a sympathetic ear, and that you have given me. It's best you don't involve yourself.'

Chapter 5

When Belle and Molly returned from the park, Jenny was already sitting at her work- table sketching vigorously. A small pile of coins sat in front of her and she was still wearing her best Sunday dress. Pieces of fabric lay scattered around her feet undisturbed from the morning. The flames in the fireplace roared up the chimney, as if in celebration of the unaccustomed feast of good fuel, never normally lavished on the fire in the middle of the day.

Belle took off her own gloves and then helped Molly take off her woollen mittens. The two of them began warming their hands in front of the fire. 'I take it you sold a bonnet?' she said, and then smiled.

Jenny laughed. 'Jolly's took all three and paid a good price.' She picked up the coins, jingling them in her cupped hands. 'And they said they would take as many as I could make. I wonder now if I should have asked for more.'

'That's wonderful news. It's a well respected shop, too.' Belle picked Molly up and sat her on the corner of the bed to take off her coat and shoes, before tucking her under the bedclothes. She was asleep, almost before she had lain her down. 'I'm afraid Molly wore herself out running about the park,' she said, as she crossed to the window. 'It's just begun snowing again.'

Jenny stooped and began hurriedly picking up the discarded pieces of blue silk brocade, scattered around the base of the table on which she had been working. 'I should have cleaned up this mess before I went out.' In her excitement, some of the fragments of material spilled from her hands as she ran to the window and smiled at the sight of the swirling snowflakes.

'Don't be silly,' Belle said, 'it's spotless, as usual. I don't mind the cloth. It's your living.' Belle knew the ritual well by now. Jenny cut and tacked, layered and pleated material, with the precision of an engineer and the skill of an artist. No matter how strictly the materials were issued to her, or how rigorously they checked the remnants she returned, Jenny always managed to spirit away some material for future use. She would work twice as long, if at the end of the day she was left with precious material for her bottom drawer.

'I hate scrimping like this,' Jenny said. 'When I was a daily dressmaker I used to earn two or even three shillings a day and I wasn't short of customers willing to pay. There was none of this mess then, I'd visit them at home, making their dresses and doing the difficult work, while they passed part of the day doing the simple sewing themselves, so they could boast about their dressmaking skills and how much they had saved their husbands or fathers.'

Belle watched as Jenny dutifully folded each remnant and placed them in a pile on the table before selecting the preferred piece, and placing it in the bottom drawer of the chest which stood beside the window. The remnant would re-appear as trimmings on a simpler dress bought second-hand, or as the decorative fabric of a bonnet or hat which she would then sell.

The bottom drawer of 'rescued' fabrics was Jenny's provision for the bad times; her escape and Molly's future. It seemed only fair, Belle mused. Jenny was paid little more than a shilling a day now to take work in and that was when she could get the work. If it wasn't for her skill and reputation she'd have got no work at all.

'Molly looks so well,' Jenny said, 'she spends too long shut up in this room with only me for company. It's good to see her with roses in her cheeks. Thank you for this morning.'

'I enjoyed it,' Belle said, 'and it cost us nothing. Besides all I did was give you an hour or two to sell your hats.'

'It's a long time since I day-dreamed,' Jenny said. 'I walked the length of Milsom Street, looking in at the displays in the shop windows and seeing the outfits that the young ladies were wearing as they paraded up and down. I realised that there wasn't a dress that I couldn't make myself and in most cases, make better.' She blushed and fidgeted nervously with her hands.

'Then why don't you?' Belle asked, although she already knew the answer.

'I can't afford the materials and even if I could, it would take me weeks.

I would need someone to do the cutting and the basic sewing so that I could spend time on the patterns and the finishing and how would I sell what I made? But that doesn't matter. I have something I can dream about. That will do well enough for now.'

Belle looked around the room, taking in all the drawings on the walls, admiring their skill; a few simple lines and loops and light shading and yet each was the perfect reproduction of the look of a dress or hat. Sometimes when a ball or concert was held, Jenny would stand outside the Assembly Rooms or the Guildhall, studying the outfits, working out in her mind how the materials were cut and layered, flounced and pleated, stitched and finished, until she knew how she would have made each of them and how each could be improved. The drawings, she did from memory, or imagination.

'We both have dreams,' Belle said. 'I want more than anything to be a great actress.'

'And to be rich and famous and courted by the nobility,' Jenny said, with a barely controlled giggle.

'No. It would be enough to know that my talent is real, and not just a delusion.'

'But you are a good actress. You have shown me the pieces from the newspapers, saying how good you are.'

'Yet I know I can do more. The applause is like a drug that satisfies you for a moment and then leaves you hungry for more, but sometimes the applause is in your heart and you know that it is real.'

'Don't you dream about meeting a nice young man and having a family?' Jenny asked.

'Perhaps,' Belle said, 'in time. But I need to prove myself first and I don't believe I could ever give up acting for a man. Besides, my choice of men has not been good in the past.'

'You tell me to believe in myself and yet you find it just as difficult,' Jenny said. 'Who do you need to prove yourself to? You look for the good opinion of those who you don't even respect. I wish you could reject the insults as easily as you reject the praise. We both recognise the truth in our minds, yet we cannot accept it, we look for reasons why we should fail. But my reasons are real; yours are your own imaginings.'

The hard knock on the door took them both by surprise. They had heard no step on the stairs. No one was expected. They looked at each other, and then at the money on the table. Jenny crossed to the door, looking over her shoulder. Belle ran to the table and covered the coins with a piece of cloth from the floor.

As Belle turned, Jenny opened the door. 'Tommy Wood,' she said. 'But it's not collection day today. Why are you here and where's your brother?'

Tommy walked into the room, closing the door quickly behind him. His jacket looked damp where snow was melting into the thin fabric. Belle recognised him at once. He was one of the men who had called last Friday; one of the debt collectors. He nodded to her, seeming a little disconcerted at her presence, as he had been on the last occasion she had seen him. Belle nodded back.

'I've come to warn you,' Tommy said, to Jenny. 'Harry don't know I'm here. No one knows.'

'Warn me of what?' Jenny asked.

'It's my boss, Nat Caine. He says we've got too friendly with our customers, and he's moving us all around, changing who we collect from.' Tommy looked over at Molly asleep in the bed. 'I'd hate anything to happen to you, or little Molly.'

'You've always been good to us,' Jenny said, touching Tommy's arm with her hand, allowing her fingertips to rest for a moment on his sleeve. 'You've given me more time to pay when I've needed it, even let me off a few pennies now and again. Don't think that I haven't noticed, or that I haven't been grateful.'

Tommy smiled. There was genuine warmth in his smile, Belle thought.

'But I've let you borrow more, when I should have said no,' he said.

'That was only because I asked you,' Jenny interrupted.

'Aye, but I did you no service,' Tommy said, 'and now it haunts me. They're not all like me and my brother, the others. I know Harry can seem cold at times, but he'd never hurt young 'uns or women.' He paused, brushing his damp hair back with his hand. 'But Jeb's a different kettle of fish, and he's the one who'll be collecting from you next time. I just needed to know as you've got enough to pay. Jeb's a bad sort.'

'Don't worry,' Jenny said. 'I've enough to pay this week. Perhaps then we'll have to move.'

'They'll find you wherever you move to, in Bath.'

'I don't mean to run and hide,' Jenny said, 'just that we might need to find somewhere we can better afford.'

'I must go,' Tommy said, opening the door. 'Harry will be looking for me. Have this,' he said, before adding, 'for Molly.' He pressed something into Jenny's hand. 'Don't tell anyone I've been here or it'll come back on me with a vengeance. Take care.'

'What did he give you?' Belle asked, as soon as Tommy had closed the door behind him.

'He gave me two shillings.' Jenny smiled. 'He's such a good lad, not a bit like his brother.'

'Did you mean what you said about moving?' Belle asked.

'It's always been a struggle affording this place,' Jenny said. 'Now that your wages are cut, perhaps we should give up and look for a new place, as long as it's nowhere near Avon Street.' She paused, looking around the room. 'But this place holds so many memories. Molly's father set us up here. He made me stop work when I was expecting her, rented this room for us and furnished it and bought me pencils and paper for my drawing. When he stopped coming, I didn't know what to do.'

'Was he married?' Belle asked. 'It's just that you usually avoid talking about him.' She felt embarrassed, uncertain for a moment if she had said too much. 'I don't want to pry.'

Jenny's expression was distant for a moment. 'No, he wasn't married, though he might as well have been. When he stopped coming, and I had no money left, I plucked up courage to go to his home.' She sighed, a long sigh, and glanced towards Molly. 'He wasn't there and I was surprised when his mother agreed to see me. She was all smiles and pleasant at first. She took me into the morning room where I used to work, where I first met her son. She told me he had been sent to the Indies and that he would settle there. Then she told me that the room was paid for, for a year and she gave me a sovereign and began showing me advertisements she had cut out from the newspaper. All the advertisements were from homes offering to adopt a baby; some for fifteen pounds others for twenty pounds. She said she would pay to have Molly adopted.'

'I've heard of those places,' Belle interrupted, seeing the distress on Jenny's face. 'Baby farms, they call them.'

'So had I,' Jenny replied, 'they feed the babies with watered down milk, doctored with lime, until they are too weak to survive and when they die they pocket the money. She knew that too. She preferred to see her grand-daughter dead than recognise her.'

'What a dreadful woman,' Belle said. 'What did you say to her?'

'I told her I would take care of Molly myself, and she became angry. "You will receive nothing then from my family and should you ever return to my home, I will summon a constable," she said. She never once saw Molly, or she'd never have been so heartless.' Jenny stopped speaking and looked over towards Molly again, her eyes liquid-bright. 'The worst thing is that I kept the sovereign she gave me.'

'Come here,' Belle said, seeing the tears welling. She hugged her tightly, feeling the dampness of Jenny's cheek against her neck. 'You've had such a struggle, and you've always worked so hard, but how did you get so deep in debt?'

'It was long before you came here,' Jenny replied. 'I've always taken in work and it brought in enough to feed and clothe us, but I could never make enough for a nice place like this. I had to have someone to share the room and help pay the rent.'

'Yes, I remember you telling me of Millie, the girl who was here before me,' Belle replied. 'She seemed like a nice girl.'

'She was,' Jenny said, 'but I've never told you of the others.'

'There were others, before me?'

'Two,' Jenny said. 'I caught the next girl shaking Molly, because she was crying, and then the one after that robbed me. She took the rent money and everything else I had, of any value. It was then I started borrowing, but I still couldn't manage. I suppose I should have moved, but it's such a nice place, and then you came along. You mustn't leave, not yet.'

Chapter 6

The men looked uneasy as Caine walked into the kitchen. He looked at each of them in turn, watching them squirm, letting his strength feed on their apprehension. They expected him to speak, so he chose to remain silent for a while. There was power in silence. He knew now was the time; the time to wake them up and teach them some respect. He just had to find some excuse.

Caine watched their vacant faces, feeling the acid anger burning inside him. Not one of them had a thought of owing him anything; not a grateful feeling between them. They'd take it all away from him in the blink of an eye, if they thought they could get away clean. He smiled to himself, forgetting his anger for a moment and moved to his armchair. 'So you took my absence as an excuse for idleness?'

'We've been out all morning,' Harry Wood snapped. 'We just came in for something to eat.'

'And stayed to play cards,' Caine said, working on the uncertainty.

'It's only a couple of hands,' Jeb replied. 'Anyways, where've you been, all dressed up like that?'

'I've been to the Coroner's Court,' Caine replied. 'Not that any of you have the wit to understand why.'

'To see what they decided about Tom Hunt killing himself and his daughter?' Harry Wood asked, tentatively.

'Do you think I care about that?' Caine spat back. 'I went so that I'd be seen there. So no one would open their big mouths about Hunt owing us money. I don't want the authorities nosing about in our business, because some strutting Irishman starts blabbing his big Oirish mouth off.'

'We should have come with you,' Tommy Wood said, smiling.

'If we'd gone in like a mob, it would have drawn attention,' Caine said. 'Besides the day's not come yet when I need you lot behind me to put respect in people. They saw me there and that was enough. They all kept their mouths shut about Hunt owing us.' He smiled. 'The jury said he was a murdering lunatic.'

'How much did he owe us when he died?' Harry Wood asked.

'It's not the money,' Caine shouted. 'It were only three pounds, but his dying has stirred things up. They'm all saying that he topped his self because of debts, even if they were too scared to say so in court.'

'Maybe it was his debts,' Tommy Wood said. 'He never struck me as being a lunatic, and Jeb did give him a deal of grief, threatening what he'd do to his wife and kids.' He turned to his brother and then to Jeb. 'You said as much yourself, Jeb.'

'If you're soft they don't pay,' Jeb said, 'and if one of 'em gets away with it then the others stop paying, and word spreads fast in Avon Street. Besides, he knew what to expect.'

'You don't know where to draw the line,' Tommy said, looking again to his brother for support.

'I wasn't any harder than he deserved,' Jeb spluttered, watching Harry Wood. 'I only hit him a few times and I even give the bastard extra time. He told me he knew someone who would give him the money. They must have let him down or else he were lying.'

'Jeb's right,' Caine said, watching the man smile at the unaccustomed recognition. 'Hunt shouldn't have borrowed what he couldn't pay back. He knew the rules. Anyways, it came out in court that he still had enough money for drink.'

'I heard his wife got arrested for shop-lifting,' Jeb interrupted. 'That's why he did it, because he had to look after his brats on his own.' He laughed and a few of the others joined in, but not the Wood brothers, Caine noticed. 'Anyways, what's done is done, who cares why he did it?' Jeb said, staring at Harry Wood.

'He's dead and we won't get paid,' Harry said. 'But three pounds isn't much of a set-back. It's over and best forgotten.'

'But it won't be that quickly forgotten,' Caine spat back. 'There's someone who won't let people forget. Think who our best customers are for money lending?' He waited, making it clear he expected an answer, needing them to understand.

'The Irish,' Harry replied. 'They'm breeding like rabbits. There's more of they now in Avon Street than in Dublin, and they'm always short of money, now there's no work on the railways.'

'That's right, the Irish in Avon Street,' Caine said, measuring his words. 'And Hunt's wife is as Irish as they come and that papist priest, Brennan, keeps telling his bloody flock not to borrow from us.'

Jeb laughed 'There's nowhere else they can borrow. We've driven everyone else out.'

'Brennan's already talking about lending to them himself,' Caine spat back, 'setting up some sort of Friendly Society, as he calls it. Mark my words, it'll be worse now because of Thomas, bastard, Hunt. The priest will use his death to turn the Irish against us, if they needed any more turning.'

'Why don't we get rid of Brennan?' Jeb asked.

'Don't be stupid,' Caine spat back. 'There'd be hell to pay if we kill him. The Irish think he's a saint. But we need to do something, and quick before he gets them organised.' Caine stood. 'It needs thinking about.' Deep down he wondered if he was getting too old to keep up with it all, but he needed more put by; enough so he wouldn't end up like his father.

The thought took him by surprise. He hadn't given the briefest thought to his father for years. He could barely remember him, but he remembered well enough that his father never went short of food, even if it meant his wife and son going without. That hunger still haunted Caine's stomach, always complaining and paining him.

He had still been a child when his father had headed the old Cockroad gang, 'feared throughout the West Country', his father used to tell him on the few occasions he was drunk enough to be happy, but not that drunk that he wasn't. He was certainly feared by his wife and his son. Caine could not picture his face now, but he remembered his bull-neck and heavy hands well enough. He'd ended his days on the gibbet at Gloucester jail, swinging with a rope around that bull-neck, for the whole world to laugh at, like so many other Caines before him. It wasn't going to happen to him though; he would make sure of that. He'd been there that day, watching with the others. He tried to remember if he had laughed like them, but the memory was buried and he preferred not to resurrect it.

The others had returned to their game of cards as Caine paced the length of the kitchen, feeling the anger growing inside him. 'Let's have a reckoning,' he said, and immediately picked up on Jeb's uneasy expression.

Caine walked to the far end of the table and began sifting through the contents that had been placed there. By the side of the large tin cash box stood a number of neat columns of coins, mainly copper, but some silver and gold and next to them a few notes. He took the small black, leather-bound book from under the tin, scanned the names and ran his eyes down the columns of dates and amounts, stopping when he reached the entry for Thomas Hunt. He obliterated the name with thick black pencil lines. That was the good thing about learning, he thought, half the time those who borrowed forgot what was owed and tried to argue over when it was due, but he always had it here, written down in his book, as good as any bank manager. What was to be paid and when and how much each of the lads had collected.

He began calculating what should have been collected that morning, from those who were due to pay. He knew he would find something wrong, and, if he did not find it, he could always invent some reason. By the side of the coins was a small heap of silver items, cutlery, snuffboxes, card cases, matchboxes and silver household plate and when he had finished writing he sifted through the objects. He looked up at the men again. Jeb was watching him, but he looked back at his cards as soon as he knew he'd been spotted. Caine knew now what had to be done.

'The small silver and the bank notes was all brought in by pickpockets and the silver plate from a burglary you agreed up at The Circus,' Harry Wood said. 'I paid four sovereigns and ten shillings for the £5 pound notes and eight sovereigns for the £10 notes, like you said, and I got the silver for next to nothing. I put the reckoning in the cash box.'

'That's good,' Caine replied. 'We'll smelt the silver plate down tomorrow. It's too easy to recognise as it is.' He noticed Jeb watching him from the corner of his eye. 'One of you can take the watches and the small silver into Bristol at the end of the week,' Caine said, not letting on that he'd noticed Jeb's interest. 'But spread them around, I don't want to depend on a couple of fences and have they cutting prices on us.'

Caine counted the banknotes and sovereigns before taking them over to the safe in the corner of the room. He bent forward and unlocked it with the key he kept on the thick gold chain around his neck. Then he returned to the table and began counting the other coins into the tin cash box. He checked his book again. He was sure now. He readied himself quietly. 'There's enough in the tin here for buying whatever comes in this afternoon and tomorrow,' Caine said.

He kept his tone soft and measured. They paid little attention as he walked slowly down the length of the table, until he was standing behind Jeb's chair. 'What you collected today ain't right,' he said, watching as Jeb's body froze.

'Nothing to worry about, Nat,' Jeb said. 'I borrowed a bit for the cards. I was going to put it back from my winnings.'

Jeb kept his eyes averted and showed no reaction when Caine placed his left forearm on his shoulder and pushed down hard, and then harder, until he felt the pain bite. 'They's good cards, Jeb,' he said, 'best be sure they'm not marked.'

'We're all friends Nat,' Jeb stuttered. 'We wouldn't play with marked cards.'

Caine took the knife from its sheath on the belt under his jacket and held it under Jeb's ear. 'But they'm bound to get marked when I take off this ear, Jeb.' He kept his voice low, hiding the exhilaration he felt.

'Don't, Nat, please don't,' Jeb said. 'I was going to put the money back.'

'You've let me down, Jeb,' Caine said. 'You've disrespected me. You know you never steal from your own.' He could feel the tension in Jeb's body now; sensed him preparing to make his move. 'And don't try for that knife in your boot,' he said, 'I'll have both your ears off and slit your throat before you reach it.'

'I'm sorry,' Jeb said. 'I was just borrowing the money.'

Caine drew the razor-sharp knife back slowly towards him, slitting through Jeb's earlobe, watching as the blood began first to drip and then to trickle like a scarlet stream onto his shoulder. All the time he leant harder with his left arm on Jeb's body, pushing him down further with all his force.

'Keep your ear,' he said, when he was satisfied with his work. He wiped the knife's blade on the back of Jeb's shirt, before sliding it back into its sheath. 'Put the money back, with a bit added, and have some respect in future, or it'll be your head I take off, not just your ear.'

Jeb grabbed a rag from his pocket and held it to his ear. His earlobe was no longer attached to the side of his head and the rag quickly drenched a vivid red with blood.

Caine went back to his armchair and was about to sit. The room was still and though Jeb was careful to move quietly, Caine sensed his approach. He whirled round to face him, pulling his knife as he turned.

'Ready for it, Jeb?' Caine pulled himself up to his full height. He was forty, Jeb was closer to twenty, but Caine was still the more powerful of the two and he could see the uncertainty in Jeb's eyes. 'Sit down now and I'll let you live, but you ever face me with a knife again and you'll be dog's meat.'

Jeb backed away, tucking his knife into his boot as Caine knew he would. He sheathed his own knife, smiling, knowing that order had been restored for a while. At the table, he saw Harry Wood looking at Jeb's cards, before replacing them where Jeb had left them. He smiled to himself, confident now that they understood who was master, and who was servant.

Moving the old Cockroad gang to Bath had been the making of them. It had been only eighteen months and they already ruled the city or at least the Avon Street quarter and it was all his doing. Yet he knew that wasn't quite true. In fairness it had never really been his idea. His good luck was all down to chance, to stopping the London coach that night and robbing its single passenger.

You could have knocked him down with a feather when that same man tracked them down to The Blue Bowl, a month later; came in bold as brass asking for his watch back and his money. Everyone laughed at him, dressed fit for a gentleman's club, like a lawyer, or a doctor, or one of the landed gentry, but he walked in, as if he hadn't a care in the world, with only a thin wooden cane to defend himself.

'If I can track you down the law will do it someday soon,' he'd said and the words had rung true. Highway robbery had become a dangerous business, what with the peelers on horses, and the drivers carrying more guns with them than an infantry regiment. Besides the pickings were getting thin, with more and more of the gentry travelling by train. He had thought the stranger a bit simple at first, risking his life for a few sovereigns and a watch. But then he made his proposal and it had been a good one.

That's when they took up working together and it had been very profitable for them both from the start. He was a clever man and knew things as only a gentleman could. It was him who supplied the information on the best places to rob and the things worth taking. It was even him who came up with the idea of moving the gang to Bath and got them started up with the money lending, and lending was the most profitable robbery of all.

The best part of it was he was never greedy in the cut he took, not compared to the money they were making. And he had no ambitions to take over, knowing full well that the lads would never accept him, being a gentleman and all. He stayed the sleeping partner, knowing his place, providing the ideas and the information, leaving Caine to run the gang. He asked the odd favour, but it was worth it. The Cockroad gang was now the Caine gang again, and it wasn't just feared, it was respected.

'Listen up!' Caine shouted, pausing until he was sure of everyone's attention. 'We need to get some good out of Hunt's death. The Irish will be restless, stirred up by their Father Brennan. They'll expect us to stay low and soften, but if we back off now they'll take it for weakness. So we'll do the opposite. Come down even harder on those that don't pay, and tell them the charges are going up. And we'll deal with that bloody priest, tonight. We'll show them who runs Avon Street.'

Chapter 7

'If you've done wrong, Richard, you know I will not judge you,' James Daunton said. 'You know you can speak freely to me.' He sank into the armchair facing his friend, waiting for some response.

Richard continued to stare into the fire, the lines in his forehead etched deep and unmoving; his eyes almost lifeless, as though his mind were somewhere else, somewhere far less comfortable. 'Give me some time.' His voice was unusually quiet. 'I was at the Coroner's Court this morning.'

James looked around the room searching for distraction, his eyes drifting from one item of furniture to the next, drawn to their imperfections. The ottoman under the window was scuffed at the base, the keyhole of the writing desk at its side was badly scratched, and the sofa had a tear which had been repaired poorly. He needed no reminding that the furniture was old and ill-matched; at odds with the newly decorated room, with its fine purple flock wallpaper, but he could never dispose of them, not with the memories they held. He knew the origin of every scratch and mark to every piece and remembered where each had stood in his family's home in Ireland, when he was boy.

James stared up at the mantelpiece, bare except for the Louis XIV clock and the pair of ornate Georgian silver candlesticks, bequeathed to him by his father, their lustre now dulled and darkened by the gas mantles. The letter was there behind the clock, where he had put it on Richard's arrival. He tried to put it from his mind and looked back towards Richard.

'My apologies,' Richard said, as though he had sensed the glance. 'I needed some time to settle and control my temper.'

'I can see you are troubled,' James said. 'Can I help in any way?'

Richard sat back a little further in the chair, propping his cane at its side. James watched him, waiting for him to answer and saying nothing. When he eventually spoke again his words were slow and deliberate. 'I have to rid my mind, somehow of these feelings. I could not return home, not with this melancholy.'

'You can talk for as long as you need,' James said. 'I would hate Charlotte or Charity to see you like this. Was it the accident you told me of, to that man and his daughter?'

'It was no accident,' Richard said. 'Thomas Hunt killed himself and murdered his daughter.'

'But why?' James asked.

'The police said he had been drinking all evening and returned home with a jug of beer. His family had a room in some filthy lodging house off Avon Street.' Richard's speech was growing faster, harsh and less controlled, and James remained silent when he paused. 'When he got home, he found his wife of twenty years had been arrested for shoplifting. The others in the house – God knows how many there were, living there…they told the police that he flew into a terrible rage and sent his four older children to bed. His neighbours said he grew calmer then, for a while, and sat in the kitchen singing quietly, with his three-year-old daughter upon his knee.'

Richard paused again, as though the scene he was describing was somehow drawing him in. His voice became softer, slower, more questioning. 'She was his favourite, they said. The neighbours left him then, thinking him more settled, but when they went to their beds, he must have walked down to the quay with his little girl and straight into the river.'

James waited for a moment in the silence, before replying. 'It is tragic, Richard,' he said, 'but such things happen, particularly in the Avon Street shambles. You need to put it out of your mind. There is nothing you can do to change what has happened.'

'Yet I feel I need to understand,' Richard said, his voice softer still. 'If you had seen the little girl's face; it still haunts me. I try to forget, but I cannot dismiss the memory of her face from my mind. How could he have killed his own daughter?'

'It is beyond understanding,' James said. 'Perhaps it was madness, or the drink. Something must have pushed him to do what he did.'

'But they are not reasons,' Richard said. 'Surely a man does not suddenly go mad, without cause. How could he have done it? If it was the drink, then the thought was there to start with.'

'Since we do not know what drove him to it, perhaps it would be better to err towards pity,' James said. 'I have an old friend who might know something about the deaths. I can try to find out more.' He could see Richard was absorbed again in his own thoughts and doubted he had even heard what he had said. 'But you cannot undo what is already done, and I do understand your feelings, believe me.' He hesitated, waiting for a reaction, but Richard said nothing. The silence seemed endless and needed breaking. 'Perhaps though there is something that I can do,' James said. 'I will go to the police and put myself forward to represent the mother in the Magistrate's Court. At least we can try to re-unite the surviving children.'

'I would be pleased if you could do that,' Richard said, smiling for the first time.

'In a more just world your work in Avon Street would enhance your reputation,' James said. 'Yet I fear you should take care that it does not become too widely known. Your more lucrative clients do not expect to see their physician working with the poor.'

'Someone has to do something. A quarter of the city lives in squalor and disease in Avon Street and the other three quarters pretend they do not exist.' Richard paused. 'At the same time I cannot neglect my living. I need to progress and to do that my name must be known.'

'You have a kind heart, but you take the weight of the world on your shoulders,' James replied. 'This melancholy must in part be due to overwork. I've told you so, many times. You have your practice, your work in the Mineral Hospital and then you take on more in Avon Street. It is too much, I have warned you.'

'There are too many doctors in Bath and too few paying patients. I have been here seven years and I seem still to be struggling for business.'

'You underestimate yourself,' James said. 'Your skills are highly thought of in the city and to be frank, you never seem that short of patients or money. I wonder at times whether it is you who wish to progress further, or Charlotte who wishes it so. She has, perhaps, too much of a liking for fine things.' When he turned back to his companion, he saw the reaction on his face and regretted his words.

He remembered when the two of them had first met Charlotte, almost five years ago. She was one of the most beautiful women he had ever seen. He had wanted her for himself, but from the start Charlotte seemed to have calculated which of them represented the better prospect as a husband and provider; or perhaps it was simply whom she could better control. Richard had courted and married her within a year.

'That's unfair James.' The rebuke in his friend's voice was clear. 'You cannot know how happy Charlotte has made me.'

'I beg pardon,' James said. 'I have no right to make such remarks. I know how much you love her.' He looked up. Richard was staring at him now as though looking for some deeper meaning in his words.

'You have changed, James,' he said, 'ever since you took up with Frank Harcourt and his cronies. You rarely come to dinner. You ignore your work. You gamble heavily, drink to excess and indulge in God knows what else.'

'Don't hold back in your criticism.' James tried to laugh, but only managed a thin smile. 'At least Frank knows how to enjoy himself and find some excitement and pleasure in this monotonous city. You may not have noticed, but I have grown ever so slightly tired of Bath, with its constant tedious dinner parties, and concerts, and recitals, and the unending polite conversation, and obsession with conventions and manners. I have spent so much of my life trying to live up to the expectations of others. Can I not now be free, to live life as I want?'

'So you find our dinner parties tedious?' Richard asked.

James had no problem in laughing this time. 'I meant no insult to you Richard, or to Charlotte. You are wonderful hosts, but I have a life outside your dining room. Besides, you are very much alone in your opinion of Frank. He has been a loyal friend to me, and is almost universally admired, and welcomed, in the highest levels of Bath society. He has introduced me to important people and they have welcomed me into their circle.'

Richard smiled and rose from his chair. 'I do not expect you to be any less loyal to Harcourt than you have been to me. I know he is popular and well received, yet there is something in his manner that I do not trust.' He paused. 'You should be aware, James, that I have heard talk lately, regarding your debts. There are rumours that you are rapidly approaching insolvency. It worries me.'

'I suppose I would be the last to hear such things,' James said, trying to look unconcerned. He wondered just how far the word had spread and found himself calculating what he owed and to whom; eighty pounds due to be paid shortly on the lease of the house; his debts to Frank had now reached at least sixty pounds and he owed fifty to Richard, with more again owing to tradesmen and merchants. He tried to put it behind him, preferring to remember the two hundred pounds he had safely hidden in the house. Provided all of his debts were not called in at once, he should have enough stake money for the card game and still be able to satisfy some of his creditors.

'You know that if the rumours grow stronger you will be finished in society and in your profession,' Richard said. 'Where will you borrow then? The banks will not lend to you and there is a limit to how much I can help.'

'I hope that it will never come to that,' James replied, 'though it is true that I have some temporary difficulties. My brother's estate in Ireland has been hard hit for some time, and as a consequence he has delayed sending my annuity this year.' James stood, wanting now to put the conversation behind him. He took the tin whistle from the writing desk and handed it to Richard. 'Will you give this to Charity from her Uncle James,' he said.

Richard took it with a smile. 'She will love it, and will probably send her mother mad, with the playing of it.'

James returned the smile. 'I know you mean only good by what you say and I take it so. Let us both have some tea.' He pulled on the long knotted silk cord by the drawing room door, before walking over to the window. Moving aside the slightly grubby lace curtain, his knees resting on the ottoman, he looked out over South Parade. The winter sun looked tired as it broke through the clouds, sending intermittent shafts of white light onto the hills, like transparent pillars, holding up the grey sky above the city. A slight scattering of snow from an earlier shower had left the street and wide pavement outside the house white, broken only by a few footprints here and there.

James watched the hansom cab come to a halt outside Richard's house and the coachman jump down and assist two young women to disembark. The ladies were giggling nervously and making a great show of the inconvenience of the cold and wind. A sudden gust lifted the bottoms of their long coats and sent flurries of snow, blown from the rooftops, flying down the street. A nut seller stood on the corner of the street, under the bare-bone branches of an elm tree, his tray as full as it had been when he had first stood there some hours ago, his breath steaming small clouds of exhausted air into the bitter cold. 'There are two young ladies visiting your house,' James said.

'Perhaps it is as well then that I am staying a little longer,' Richard replied. 'If Charlotte is entertaining her friends I should not disrupt the gathering. Charlotte's friends do not find me sufficiently entertaining and make little secret of the fact. I am apparently too serious in my demeanour.'

James laughed and was about to reply when there was a loud knock on the drawing room door. The sound preceded only by the briefest of moments the door being flung open. James smiled as Mrs Hawker bustled in with a tray. 'I've brought you some tea and Oliver biscuits,' she said. 'Sure, I knew you wanted something and I wasn't about to climb two mountainous sets of stairs, just to go down them again to fetch something up.' He noticed she was out of breath and the crockery rattled as she placed the tray down on the occasional table.

Reluctantly James recognised, not for the first time, that Mrs Hawker was growing frailer with age; she must be almost sixty now. She still kept her hair long, but always tied up in a bun, out of sight at the back of her head. It was as white as snow. He wanted to sit her down and tell her to rest, but he knew she would have dismissed his concern in the same way as she tried to dismiss her age. 'You've read our minds as usual, Mrs Hawker,' he said.

'It wouldn't do you no harm to tend to this fire I made you either, Master James,' she said, vigorously poking the embers and sending a golden eruption of sparks up the soot-blackened chimney and not a few onto the hearthrug. 'You could do with some good exercise. Why not go out for a brisk walk?'

He took some logs from the basket and piled them on the fire. Their bark was still damp and smelt of wet leaves and dark forests, reminding him of the peat fires at home. He watched as the flames licked the air and the dampness of the wood spat its defiance at the flames. Mrs Hawker returned his smile and nodded to Richard. 'It's always a pleasure to provide for Master Richard,' she said. 'I only wish as how I could say the same for all Master James' friends. There's one or two who wouldn't get offered an Oliver biscuit in this house, but might get something else with their tea, if I was to have my way.'

'Go and rest, Mrs Hawker,' James said, smiling. 'I'm sure you poured yourself a cup of tea before you brought the pot to us. It will be getting cold.' She seemed oblivious to his comment, but he noticed her smile as she left.

'I hope you will pardon me for pointing it out,' Richard said, grinning, when Mrs Hawker had shut the door behind her, 'but your relationship with Mrs Hawker is hardly that of master and servant. Surely at her age she finds it difficult to cope with running the house. What has become of the maid who used to attend you?'

'The cook left, and then the maid, for no apparent reason,' James said. 'But I do little entertaining and the house suits me as it is. Besides, as you well know, I do not think of Mrs Hawker as a servant,' he said.

'My sincere apologies,' Richard said, 'I know she means a great deal to you. Once again I have delivered a sermon rather than showing the understanding that should be expected from a friend.'

'You have no need to apologise,' James said. 'You have always been a true friend and I take no offence from what you say. Now Mrs Hawker has no staff to order around, she has turned her wrath on me, but it is from love. She means more to me than any living soul, and I would never see her hurt. If I could persuade her that she should not act as a servant then I would do so, but she is a formidable lady and knows her mind too well.'

Richard took the walking cane that had been propped at the side of his chair and holding it at its base passed it handle first towards James. 'I would like you to accept this,' he said. 'You must live your life as you wish, but Thomas Hunt's death has made me more aware of the desperation in Avon Street, if I needed any reminding. I know you go there with Harcourt and the others and I urge you to carry this when you do so.'

James smiled as he took the stick by its handle. 'It is very fine, but I cannot accept. I rarely carry a cane and I know you are particularly fond of this one.'

'You must accept it,' Richard said. 'It was of reassurance to me when I began visiting Avon Street, particularly at night.' He pointed to the handle of the cane. 'Feel for the row of pearl buttons at the base of the grip.'

James stood and gripping the cane, felt for the buttons with the thumb of his right hand. One of them, he could sense, was raised slightly higher than its companions and he pressed it, almost automatically. The hilt of the stick slid effortlessly to the ground, revealing the first few inches of gleaming silver blade that it had housed, before the tip of the cane came to a halt on the burgundy carpet. 'You spend more time in Avon Street than I ever do. Surely you have greater need of a sword-stick?'

'Not any longer,' Richard replied. 'I am well acquainted with the parts that are safe and those that are not. Besides the people know me now; they would not harm me.'

Discarding the scabbard, James instinctively adopted a fencing pose, cutting the air with thrusts and parries and slicing swipes. For a moment he was a boy again; remembering his father's fencing lessons; sparring with his elder brother, Michael, who seemed always to let him win, despite the fact that he was by far the better swordsman.

'Do not be misled by the thinness of the blade,' Richard said. 'It is Spanish craftsmanship at its finest. It was my father's gift to me and now it is my gift to you.'

'I truly cannot accept it,' James said, 'it must mean a great deal to you.'

'It means more to me to know that you carry it with you. I kept it by me when I needed it, but it is you who may have a real need for its company now.'

Chapter 8

James was dressing when he heard the distant knock on the front door below. He had gone to bed early, as he had resolved, slept well, and woken reasonably refreshed, and with a new-found optimism. Pulling the curtains slightly apart, he felt their momentary resistance where a pool of water had frozen, holding the bottom of the fabric to the windowsill. Small silver slivers of ice fell to the ground and shattered noiselessly.

He looked out at the misty morning and shivered, before moving to the wash-stand and pouring water from the jug into the bowl. After splashing icy handfuls onto his face, he rubbed the back of his neck with numbed fingers. The chilled water drove the last of the sleep from his mind. He was buttoning the collar of his shirt when he heard the knock on the bedroom door. 'What is it, Mrs Hawker?'

'Father Brennan's here to see you.' The concern in her voice was clear. 'He's in a terrible state, and he has news from your brother Michael in Ireland. There's something wrong. You must come down, now.'

James felt apprehensive; his stomach knotted. 'Tell Sean I will be down directly.'

'I've put him in the study,' Mrs Hawker replied, 'and given him some tea. I'm sorry, but I've not yet set the fire in the drawing room.'

James sat on the bed to put on his shoes. 'Don't fuss so, Mrs Hawker,' he said. The study will be fine, and I'm sure Sean will not care.' He realised now, all too well, how much he had been dreading the visit. The letter from his brother had been explicit; *'Do not reply until you have spoken to Sean'*. Now he was here and James was in no hurry to begin their conversation, though he already knew in his heart the direction it would take. He took his neatly folded jacket from the linen press and walked downstairs.

James was taken aback at the feeling of apprehension that struck him as he reached for the doorknob of the study and not only because of the matters they were about to discuss. He had allowed his friendship with Sean to fade, yet they had been so close, as boys. He had even moved to Bath in part because it was now Sean's home, yet he had seen him less and less as time had gone on. James tried to calculate how long it was since they had last met and decided it must be at least a year. It seemed almost as though he were about to meet a stranger.

James threw open the study door. 'How are you, you mad Oirishman?' he said, and then froze as he took in the appearance of the priest. His freckled face was cut and grazed, one eye blacked and swollen, his red hair pulled forward in an attempt to conceal the bruising on his forehead. It was some moments before James regained his composure. 'What's happened to you?'

'It's fine it is to see you too, James,' Sean answered, shaking his hand.

'What's brought you to this state? You're a priest. I thought you had set aside violence from your life?' The unaccustomed sense of moral superiority felt good for a moment.

Sean laughed. The laughter must have caused him pain and it showed briefly in his expression. 'Save your pity for my opponents. Sure it's them who are after having grazed knuckles and bruised toes this morning.'

'Who did this?' James asked.

Sean's tone changed, as though he had left behind all memory of himself as the smiling Irish priest. 'I was set on by a gang last night down in Avon Street.'

'But why?' James asked. 'Did they not know that you are a man of the cloth? Or was that reason enough, because you are a Catholic priest?'

'So many questions, James; let me catch my breath,' Sean sat, looking blankly around the room, his eyes halting only for a moment on the pile of papers on the desk. Then, slowly, the anger began to assert itself in his features. 'This was not the work of your anti-Catholics. It was done on the orders of a man by the name of Caine. A man rightly called after his biblical namesake.'

'But what has he against you?' James asked.

'He controls a gang of thieves in Avon Street. Caine lends money and when people can't pay, he has them beaten, until they do pay, and pay, and pay again. He's driven all the other money lenders out.' His anger had grown now, and was all too clear in his voice.

'But what has this Caine to do with you? Have you been borrowing money?' James asked.

'No, but my parishioners borrow from him. The street sellers borrow to buy their stock, the homeless borrow for a night's lodgings and the hungry borrow to survive. He traps them in a snare of debt and no matter how much they repay, they always end owing more.' He hesitated for a moment, his face showing a growing sadness. 'One of my parishioners, a man called Thomas Hunt, owed Caine money and he couldn't pay. His wife tried to steal from a shop; I suppose to pay the debt. But she was caught. On Sunday last he drowned himself, and his young daughter with him.'

'I know of this. In fact I had intended to ask you if you knew what drove him to it, though surely now he is beyond the concern of the Catholic Church. He has committed two mortal sins, in taking his own life, and murdering his daughter. Is he not therefore excommunicated and destined for hell in the eyes of your church?'

'I cannot forgive these terrible sins, but I trust my God has greater understanding and mercy than his church. Besides I knew Thomas Hunt and though his crimes were terrible, yet he was not a bad man at heart. He'd had no regular work for almost a year and taken up the drinking when he had a spare penny or two. "Only once in a while, faither," he would say to me, but I knew that when he drank, he drank fit to drown his soul.'

'How did he survive?' James asked.

'He took what work he could find, as did his wife, and they scavenged and bought and sold, until they had sold all they had, and then they borrowed, and I suppose they stole. He came to me days before his death, asking to borrow four pounds to pay off his debts. I said I had no money, but I could have found it somewhere. In truth I thought he would drink it away. I had judged him already. I could have helped him, and instead I did nothing.'

'You were not to know what was in his mind,' James said.

'I had neither faith, nor charity and I took away his hope,' Sean replied, 'and for that I deserve no forgiveness.'

James smiled, hoping to give reassurance, to show understanding. 'My friend Dr Wetherby gave evidence at the Coroner's Court. I promised him that I would seek out Hunt's wife and represent her. He was very upset by the deaths. I believe that with the right magistrates I could free her from prison. In fact I trust that with a little persuasion the shop she stole from might be persuaded not to proceed with the case.'

'You've good intentions, James,' Sean said, 'but Imelda Hunt isn't in prison. She's been committed to the mental asylum for women. When she was taken to identify the bodies, it destroyed her mind. She's lost her tongue, doesn't speak any more; sits all day with a blanket bundled up in her arms, as though it were her child, rocking it to and fro. If the blanket is taken away from her, she picks at her arms, with her fingernails, until she draws blood. Then they have to tie her to her bed. I visit her, but as yet she doesn't recognise me, or even acknowledge my presence.'

'It is beyond imagining,' James said, 'I hope you can help her.' He paused watching the emotion on his friend's face, knowing that the priest understood the woman's pain all too well and even shared it with her. 'But why did Caine attack you?'

'For months I've been preaching to my congregation not to borrow from Caine. I've actually named the man in my sermons. I said I would set up a Friendly Society, help them to pay off their debts. It would be somewhere they could save when times were better and borrow in bad times. No one seemed to listen until now, until they saw what Tom Hunt was driven to. But now they are asking me to set up the Society and it is a promise I do not know how to keep. The people have no money to put in and I have none to start it, but for all Caine knows it already exists.' Sean looked at him, his eyes imploring.

'How can you be sure it was this man, Caine?' James asked, trying to ignore the request implicit in the priest's words and eyes.

'I recognised his men. Word had obviously reached Caine of what I proposed, so he did this to warn me, but it will not stop me. I will not let him win. I owe it to Tom Hunt and his daughter. My only concern is that the people will take the law into their own hands. I have put about the word that I was robbed and recognised no one. You know what would happen if they ever took to the streets of Bath?'

'Of course,' James replied. 'The troops would be called in, at the first sign of unrest. The authorities would like nothing better than to find an excuse to drive the Irish from Bath, now they are no longer needed for the railway. But aren't you afraid for yourself?'

'I'd be a fool if I wasn't,' Sean said, 'but you more than anyone know what I think of bullies,'

'That I do, and I helped you once when the odds were against you,' James said. 'Is there anything I can do now?'

Sean's expression suddenly changed and James saw the distant judging face of a priest again. 'Your brother Michael asked me to visit you and explain what's happening on the estate. It is so long since you've been in Ireland. It's as though you are ashamed of where you come from. You've read Michael's letter, I take it?'

James bristled, felt the condemnation building for the coming sermon. 'I've read the letter and read it again, and I still cannot truly accept its contents. I knew the famine in Ireland was bad, but Michael had always written that the estate was not as badly affected as others. He said that my father's investments were still producing income sufficient for my annuity and to see them through the worst of times.'

'You're neither stupid nor uncaring, James. You never return to Ireland, but you knew what was happening. In the last four years, the country has lost a quarter of its population. A million people have migrated with only the clothes they wore, to whatever country will have them. Another million have died of starvation and disease. These are not just numbers, they are men, and women, and children with souls. They are not even strangers. Sure, you even knew some of those who've died, and yet you choose to think it was someone else's problem! Why do you think there are so many Irish now in Bath and Bristol?'

'But the newspapers each month said that the next year would see a recovery and that thousands of pounds were being raised through charity and the Poor Laws to help those who needed it. I've even contributed myself. Michael kept writing that he was replanting and investing and helping the tenants, and that I should not be too concerned.' In his heart he knew he had believed what he wanted to believe, hiding from the truth, hunting out every diversion that life offered.

'And each year you received your annuity and thought, if I am fine, then the rest of the world must be fine.' Sean stood and began pacing around the room gesticulating as he spoke. 'I've seen glimpses of hell on earth in Ireland, stood on hilltops and felt sick from the stench of potatoes rotting in the fields, in every direction. I've mouthed prayers over open famine pits, as they threw in the bodies, one on top of another; men and women and children together, with no names on their graves. If the tenants farm as little as half an acre of land, then they get no assistance from your Poor Laws – so they leave their farms so that their children will be fed in the Poor House and then the landlords rip the roofs from the houses, so that they can never return.'

James read Sean's feelings in his face; saw the scenes he painted in his mind. He knew that he had chosen to ignore what was happening. 'But Michael would not do such a thing,' he said.

'No, Michael could not do that to people he has known since he was a child, but soon he will have no choice. Few of the tenants have paid rent these last four years.'

'Why didn't Michael tell me this earlier? Why did he not ask for help?'

Sean sat again, a little more composed. 'And did you ask him if he needed help? Isn't he the eldest, the inheritor and doesn't he feel that responsibility like a boulder tied around his neck?'

'When he wrote, Michael said that my annuity would be delayed this year. I will return part of it to him when it is paid.'

'That's not the whole truth,' Sean said, hesitating. 'That's why he asked me to call on you, before you replied. Michael is distraught. There is no more capital. Your father's investments have long gone, swallowed by debts and your brother's compassion for others. All that is left is the house and the land. If you want your annuity this year, then land will have to be sold and more will follow until the estate is gone and the tenants with it. The choice is yours.'

A thousand thoughts spun through James' mind. The investments were supposed to remain in place to provide for him, and now they were gone. Yet he had half suspected as much, when he had received the letter. Outwardly he fought to keep control, to show not the slightest muscle twitch of emotion, to reveal nothing of his feelings, yet his mind was in turmoil.

'You must understand that Michael had no choice,' Sean said.

'Then tell him to keep the annuity and the land.'

Sean glared, seeming now to direct all his anger at him. 'Don't you dare to be resentful, when Michael needs your understanding. Go to Ireland and help him!'

'Tell him he has my understanding. He is my brother and I forgive him. In fact I should have done exactly the same. But as to help, I do not have the ability to help him now,' James said. 'I have things to do here in Bath, and besides the estate is his responsibility.'

'You've turned your back on your God, your country, and now your brother, and what have you put in their place, other than your self?'

'What can I do to help?' James asked.

'If you won't go to him, then send money. With all that you earn and what you've received each year in the past, surely you have put money aside? Michael desperately needs your help to survive the year and plant again for the next season.'

'Would that I could; I may be a solicitor, but I am hardly successful in the sense of business.' The guilt was swallowing him again. He knew what money he had saved in the past, he had spent, or gambled away, over the last year or so. All he had now was the two hundred he had put aside and that he needed if he was to stand a chance of making good.

'The year's rent on this house falls due next month,' he said, 'and I have barely enough to cover the eighty pounds needed for that. I have little put aside.' He thought again of the card game, it was his last chance to come through this and make amends. 'But I have money coming to me in the near future and I will help as much as I am able then. I willingly forego the annuity, but I can do nothing else for now. I will serve Michael better by staying here in Bath.'

'Then so be it. Will you at the very least write to Michael?'

'I will write,' James said, but the words felt hollow; what could he write? Money was all that would make any sort of difference. He thought of Michael having to sell the land and tasted the sense of loss that he would feel. They had, between them, betrayed their father; all that he had worked for throughout his life, lost in so few years after his death. He thought of the tenants – generations of the same families – now without a living, without food for their children, without a future. It was as though Sean had held a priestly mirror in front of him and forced him to see his sins.

'I'll be going now, James,' Sean said, as he made for the door. 'I've some work to do and then I have a message to return to Mr Caine. The people of Avon Street have suffered enough and I'll not stand by and see them bullied out of what little hope they have left.'

'You should not go alone,' James said, 'I will accompany you, if you're willing to wait a little.' He needed to do something, to bury his feelings in an act of contrition.

'This is not your fight, James,' Sean said, but his expression said more and James could tell that his offer had already been accepted. Perhaps a delay might even allow Sean's rash temper to settle a little.

'If it's your fight then it's mine,' James replied. 'Give me a chance to put things right between us. Let it be as it was . . . You may see from my desk that I have a great deal of work outstanding and there are some papers that I must complete this morning. But call for me after lunch and we will deliver the message to Mr Caine together. I am not who you think I have become.'

Chapter 9

As Belle entered the room, Jenny looked up momentarily from her seat by the worktable and then turned away, trying to hide her face, but Belle had already seen that she had been crying. Her first thought was that something had happened to Molly, but she was asleep in the middle of the bed and looked fine. 'What's happened?' she whispered softly, as she walked over and placed a hand gently on Jenny's shoulder.

'The debt collectors came,' Jenny said. 'Most of the money I had left from selling the bonnets is gone ... If only you had been here.'

'But you had more than enough to pay them.' Belle hugged her close for a few moments, and then sat her back down before fetching another chair and sitting opposite her. She leant forward and took Jenny's hands in her own. 'Calm yourself now and tell me what happened.'

'It wasn't Tommy and his brother,' Jenny replied. 'It was the man he warned me of, Jeb, and he was worse than Tommy described, a filthy pig of a man. He came in without knocking, and grabbed hold of Molly.'

'My God,' Belle exclaimed. 'He didn't hurt her did he?'

'He sat on the bed and made her sit on his lap,' Jenny said. 'I could tell she was afraid, but I didn't want her to see that I was, too. I told her to come to me, but he wouldn't let her go. He kept stroking her hair with his filthy hands and saying what a pretty girl she was, but it was the way he said it.' She hesitated for a moment, lost in her thoughts. 'I told him that I had money, enough for the payment and more and he let her go and lay back on the bed, with his stinking clothes and muddy boots. Molly ran to me crying.'

'At least he didn't harm her,' Belle said.

'No, but the look in his eyes . . . ' Jenny said. 'I asked him how much he wanted. He didn't answer at first. Then he told me not to worry about the money. He gave me this look and said, "We can come to an arrangement over payment, if you were to treat me nice. No one needs know." Then he grinned and held his arms out to me.'

'I'd have stuck the scissors in him,' Belle interrupted.

'I thought of it,' Jenny replied, 'but I wouldn't have stood a chance against him, and besides Molly was watching all this . . . Then he said I could always work for him, said I could earn more in a couple of hours on my back than sewing all day.'

'The pig!' Belle said. 'The filthy pig.'

'I just wanted him to go,' Jenny sobbed. 'However much it was. I said I'd pay him. I knew what payment was due and offered it to him, but he told me that he was a day late collecting, and that he'd have to charge me for that, and that the rates had gone up. In the end I gave him what he asked for though it was much more than was due.'

'What did he do?' Belle asked.

'He took the money and left, said he'd be back next week and that I should think about his offer. I comforted Molly as best I could and eventually she fell asleep.' Jenny looked Belle in the eyes. 'There was more than enough there to cover the payment, he just pocketed the rest.'

'This has to stop,' Belle said. 'Have we enough for the rent?'

'Yes, it's already paid, but I don't know what we'll do next week.'

'I'll sell my mother's brooch and I want no arguing from you. Don't worry,' Belle said. 'It should keep us going for a little while.'

'In future I shall go to Caine's house and pay on the day before it's due. I will not have that man coming here again.'

'But won't that be dangerous?' Belle asked.

'No more dangerous than that man coming here,' Jenny said.

Sean set a rapid pace which James found difficult to match in the newly fallen snow, even with his cane to help his balance. 'I knew you wouldn't let me down.' Sean said. 'Do you remember all those years ago in school when those three lads had me cornered? It was yourself who came to my rescue then. I stood there wetting myself while you tore into them, howling like a banshee.'

James remembered what had happened as though it had been yesterday, the three lads backing Sean into a corner. On another day he might have ignored them, he thought, but his instincts had taken over. It was the look of terror on the young Sean's face; the lack of mercy on the faces of his tormentors. 'How could I forget it,' he said. 'But as I recall you gave a decent enough account of yourself once you got started.' He smiled at Sean, feeling their friendship alive again, as though the intervening years had never happened.

'It was you gave me the courage,' Sean replied, 'and I learnt a lesson that day. I'll not stand by now and see anyone else suffer as I did then, nor let them stand alone. And I'll never forget what you did.'

'You think too highly of me,' James replied. 'It was simply chance that put me there when you needed help.'

'Chance or destiny or fate or God,' Sean said. 'Call it what you will. Something links our lives for some purpose. I prefer to think it is God. I only regret I did not hear his voice when Tom Hunt asked for help.' He paused. 'Perhaps I did; but perhaps I didn't listen well enough.'

James found himself thinking of his father, a man who seemed to take courage, and honour and loyalty, for granted, as though they were characteristics given to everyone from birth, along with the responsibility to take care of those who needed help. At times it had made him seem cold and arrogant, driven by a certainty and moral code that left little room for weakness, but James now remembered him in a different light; remembered the look in his eyes when he gazed at the portrait of his dead wife, and his smile when he watched them playing as boys, believing he was un-noticed.

His thoughts were interrupted as Sean stopped for no apparent reason on the corner of Southgate Street and turned around. 'I wonder if he ever came to Bath,' he said.

'My father?' James asked, bemused, as though Sean had been reading his thoughts.

'No, not your da,' Sean replied. 'Why would I be wondering about your da? Good man though he was. I meant, Jesus Christ.' He made the sign of the cross, to James' embarrassment and to the obvious aggravation of several passers-by. 'Have you not heard the legend that the Christ's uncle, Joseph of Arimathea, owned lead mines in the Mendips and that he brought him there when the Christ was a young boy. They even say that after the crucifixion, Joseph took the Holy Grail to Glastonbury with the blood of Christ in it.'

'I've never heard that,' James said. 'Do you believe it?'

'I like to think it's true,' Sean said. 'There's a thorn tree in the ruins of Glastonbury Abbey, and doesn't it still flower every year at Christmas. They say it grew from a staff that Joseph planted in the ground when he arrived. And the farmers up in the Mendips have a saying, "As sure as Jesus went to Priddy Fair." I wonder what he thinks when he watches his people now.'

Then, without waiting for an answer and still apparently deep in thought, Sean pointed to the window of a lodging house, before setting off again. James looked at the sign that hung there, "No Irish, No Blacks". He'd never noticed it before. He was going to say so to Sean, but he was already too far ahead, and James had to run to catch him up, leaving the broad streets behind them.

Sean's route now took them through grimy alleyways and lanes and courts. He seemed oblivious to the filth, as James picked his way carefully through the open sewers and piles of rotting waste. Eventually Sean stopped in front of a house. It was a large building with many of the windows bricked up, to avoid the window tax. It looked almost derelict. At the side of the front door was a pigsty with two emaciated pigs rooting through scraps of rotting vegetables and mouldy bread. Sean pushed his way through the door, half hanging from its hinges, and James followed him down the unlit stairs, to the cellar.

As they entered the kitchen, the stench was overpowering. The source of the foulness was quickly apparent; pools of water stood stagnant, here and there, on the bare earth floor, their odour leaving little doubt that they were the leaking effluent from some cesspit. The stove in the corner belched out acrid grey smoke, which hung suspended from the ceiling, cloaking the stench of raw sewage, but adding to the foulness of the air. James struggled for breath, as if the air had been sucked from his lungs, and replaced by some noxious, acidic gas.

A man stood as they entered, and snatched up a poker from beside the kitchen range. 'No one invited you in here, you papist bastard, or your fancy friend.' The hatred in his face would have sent James backing towards the door, but Sean strode towards him and did not stop until they stood face to face.

'Put the poker down or I'll bend it around your ugly head,' Sean said, 'and you know well that I can.' The two stood immobile for what seemed like minutes, locked together in a contest of wills.

The man was shorter than Sean, but powerfully built. His bald head was like a cannon ball, balanced on his shoulders, with no neck between the two. His eyes were small and set deep, beneath heavy brows. James found his fingers playing almost automatically with the row of pearl buttons at the top of his cane.

'You're not welcome here,' the bald-headed man said, gripping the poker so tight that his knuckles whitened. 'But we're always happy to take a penny or two from your flock of Irish sheep.' He backed off, still holding the poker, and leered at Sean, as if the two shared a guilty secret. 'Your bog-trotters are always glad to stay here,' he said. 'Three pence a night, and only two pence if they shares a bed, and you'd marvel at the numbers that seems overjoyed to share a bed for the night. They knows there's no papist rules here and they love it. They can meet a new wife or new husband every night, as young or as old as the one they lies next to, and they can change them the next night.'

'Look at this,' Sean said, walking over to a dark patches on the wall, barely discernible against the dirt and grease. He ran the edge of his hand across the patch and a cloud of insects peeled away. Some cascaded to the ground and scuttled around while others flew off in different directions. James scratched his scalp. 'These are the better class of vermin you'll find here,' Sean said. 'Cockroaches just live off filth as God intended, but men like our friend here create the filth, and draw others into their depravity, lower than the lice and tics that infest the beds.' Sean approached the man again, his arms flat against his side.

'It's your Catholic lice that like what we give 'em, Father,' the man said, sneering. Yet he backed away and his speech was cut short when Sean punched him full in the face. The punch was fast and as unexpected by James as it had been by the man. He reeled, but did not fall. The poker fell from his hand, and as he reached down he grasped the handle of the knife that protruded from his boot, and drew it. 'I'll do for you, you bastard, if you ever set foot in here again. This is Nat Caine's house and if you cross him you're a dead man. This won't be the end of it, he'll do for you.'

Sean stood stock still, unmoving as the man pointed the knife towards him, but James thought he could detect a quavering in his voice when he spoke. 'Gobshite. Tell Caine that Sean Brennan will not be put off by a beating, and I'll not rest until he is out of this city.'

James held his cane out in front of him, pointing at the man. 'You can tell Mr Caine I look forward to seeing him in court.'

'And who are you?' the man spat back, between clenched teeth.

Sean reached for his arm as though to restrain him. 'His prosecutor will be Mr James Daunton,' he said, as he felt Sean tugging him back towards the door.

Returning home, James and Sean went into the study. They had hardly spoken on their way back. 'You should not have told him your name, James,' Sean said.

'I have no fear of them. They may hold sway in Avon Street, but they have no power elsewhere in the city. It's you who must exercise caution, Sean. That man would have killed you without a second thought.'

'He'd not have killed me without Caine ordering it first. But I don't underestimate them, and neither must you. That was the house where Thomas Hunt and his daughter spent their last few weeks on earth with thirty other souls.' Sean hesitated. 'People ask me how God could allow Avon Street to exist without intervening.'

'How do you answer?'

'It's Man who created Avon Street, and God that gave us the conscience and ability to put things right.'

'I understand now why you hate Caine,' James said. 'I was proud to stand next to you today.'

'No one else will do it,' Sean replied. 'The local peelers are on his payroll, and the authorities would rather pretend that Avon Street does not exist. But I try not to hate Caine, and I should not have used violence. It was not what I wanted. There are other ways of beating him.'

'If I could find money, Sean, what would you do with it?' James asked.

'So much,' Sean replied. 'I could lend to those who borrow from Caine, help them to pay off their debts and loosen the hold he has on Avon Street. The more they borrow from him, the more they need to pay him back and the less they have to live on.' The tempo of Sean's speech grew faster as if his thoughts had been held back for too long, waiting for a sympathetic ear. Now the dam had burst, and the words flooded out. 'I also have a mind to start a co-operative market, such as they set up in Rochdale. I can buy a sack of potatoes for half of what I would pay if I bought it pound by pound, and the same holds true for milk and butter and coal and many other things. Most of the parish buy in pennyworths and get charged double the price.'

Sean looked him straight in the eye, as if willing him to share his vision. 'There is a cellar in the church where we could store food and sell it to parishioners in pennyworths, but at the same price as it costs to buy by the sack full. There's no reason why we can't provide some basic schooling for the children and perhaps a work area for the mothers, where they can work together, but not have to pay some sweatshop for the privilege. It's not plans I'm short of, it's only money.'

'Wait a while,' James said, 'I will return directly.'

He went up to the drawing room and opened his writing desk. Taking out one of the array of drawers, he reached to the back of its compartment and pushed the small, recessed lever. The mechanism released a narrow concealed drawer behind the pen rack and James withdrew its contents. In all there were twenty ten-pound notes. James replaced thirteen of the notes in the drawer and took the other seven with him back to Sean.

'I may have exaggerated my financial condition earlier, Sean,' James said. 'I have seventy pounds here, get fifty to my brother and use the other twenty as you will.' Sean leapt to his feet and, grasping the notes, threw his arms around James. Despite his injuries, the strength of his hold almost drove the air from James' body.

'One of the men is travelling to Ireland tomorrow to see his family. He's trustworthy and if I give him a shilling, he'll deliver the money to your brother quickly and safely.'

'No one who saw us today would believe you were once the bullied one,' James said. 'It was good fortune that brought us together that day in school.'

'God guides us into each other's lives for some reason and he does so more often than we suspect. What happens then he leaves to us.'

He looked at Sean. The sense of peace in his expression was so powerful that he felt uncomfortable, caught in his stare. James looked away and laughed. 'Stop your religious ramblings. You're my friend, not my priest, and besides I could have walked away that day.'

'But you didn't,' Sean said, his expression now brimming with mischief.

'I have a favour to ask,' James said, anxious to change the subject.

'Ask it.'

'Richard was upset at the drowning and the death of the little girl. See if you can find some way of getting Hunt's children out of the workhouse and find them a home. I think it might help set his mind at rest.'

'That won't be easy,' Sean answered, 'not without splitting them up. There's no one I know of who could afford to take on all four children. Most struggle to feed their own. I'll see if they have relatives in Ireland, for they have none here, but even if they have family it would be a terrible burden to impose on them.'

'What if I was to help with money?' James asked.

Sean laughed. 'And don't you have enough money troubles already? Why do you suddenly wish to become a philanthropist?'

'Perhaps a guilty conscience; perhaps if I help others, my own luck will change; if you cannot do anything now, at least look into the matter for me.'

'God doesn't strike bargains, if that's what you're thinking, James,' Sean said. 'If you do good, it must be its own reward.'

'We'll see,' James replied. 'Perhaps God will help me raise more money.'

'That's not his way and you know it,' Sean said. 'You are a good man, James, you know deep within that you have a purpose in life. You keep denying it, but it won't be denied.'

'I deny nothing,' James replied. 'We each control our own lives.'

'So we think, and perhaps we do,' Sean said, 'but I know each of us comes to this life with lessons to learn, something our souls need to understand. There are patterns to our lives; a purpose and a plan, which puts obstacles in our path, time and again, until we have understood and learnt the lesson they teach us. Recognise the lessons you need to learn, James, face your demons with the same courage as you faced Caine's man today.'

Chapter 10

Belle sat in a corner of The Garrick's Head, a loose bundle of papers on the table in front of her. Her earlier anger had by now settled into frustrated annoyance. Still she shuffled the papers again and again, careful despite her feelings, to keep them dry and clean for their return at the end of the play. She willed herself to take in the scribbled words, but her mind kept returning to that afternoon.

She had learnt her lines days ago for the new production. Then when she had arrived at the theatre earlier that day, Cauldfield had changed her part. Her role now was to be played by Daisy, his lover, while Belle was to play a lesser role. Daisy had laughed out loud, her enormous breasts, invariably on show, visibly shaking. 'Don't worry for me, dear,' she had said. 'I learnt your part a while ago and you'll soon learn mine, there ain't many lines.'

Belle's new role had been scrawled on the sheets that now lay in front of her, the cues often longer than the lines themselves. Only the leading man had the whole text of the play, though it was wasted on Cauldfield. He was only ever concerned with his own part. Arrogant and lazy, he would not even allow proper rehearsals because, he said, they 'dulled the performance'. Just once she would have liked to work with a copy of the full text, but books were expensive and it was so much cheaper to give each actor a scribbled version of their own lines.

The Garrick's Head was one of several places in Bath where the worlds of polite society and the underworld crossed paths and mingled. It had been relatively quiet when she came in, but the tavern was now a sea of noise, though it was still comparatively early in the evening. Clouds of pipe and cigar smoke hung over the mass of jostling bodies and in her annoyance she was all too easily distracted.

The theatre tavern had only one qualification for admittance, as far as Belle knew, and that was a requirement that the men dress and deport themselves like gentlemen. Whether or not they were was a different matter. It was to be expected, she supposed, in an establishment which was once the home of Beau Nash, the man who had introduced the wealthy to Bath; and Bath to the pleasures of the rich. The bar room had once been Nash's parlour, where he had entertained his guests with gambling and other pleasures. It was in this room that a man was run through with a sword for being caught with another man's wife. It was behind a door on the floor above that the woman was later found hanging. They said she still haunted the house, a lady dressed all in grey.

Belle picked out his voice at once amongst the others, booming loud above the noise of conversation. She wondered if he had already seen her, wondered if his loudness was for her benefit. For a while she resisted the urge to search him out. Then, looking up, she saw him; tall, thin, well dressed and still wearing that smile, standing in the centre of an adoring crowd – it was Frank Harcourt.

She could not pretend otherwise – he was handsome and charming. The men around him seemed to hang on his every word. She watched him using his smile, as he always had, yet she had never noticed before how little his eyes smiled. They seemed empty and soulless and as she watched and remembered, his good looks seemed to fade. How could she ever have loved him, she wondered, when the sight of his grinning face now turned her stomach?

Harcourt had his left arm around a girl with flame red hair, whom Belle had seen often around the theatre foyer. She was a prostitute of some standing. His right arm encircled another younger girl, who had only recently been seen around and who, Belle assumed, was new to the profession. His face showed little recognition of the girls' presence, though his hands seemed busy enough.

Belle followed his gaze as he looked towards the doorway. It was clear from his expression that he knew the man who had just entered. He smiled in his direction, his grin even broader, though his eyes were as empty as before. This man was also handsome, though he had a more Mediterranean look about him, his skin darker than was fashionable, and his hair a little wild. He had a Roman nose, which might have detracted from his looks, but in fact lent character to his face, and, unlike Harcourt, his eyes seemed very much alive when he smiled.

Belle looked back towards Harcourt. He was staring at her now and she sensed that he had been doing so for some time. She turned away, but continued watching from the corner of her eye, trying to feign a lack of interest. As his friend approached, Harcourt released both girls from his arms. They stood looking, unsure of what to do next, the redhead draping herself over his shoulder. His right hand took his friend's offered hand while his left hand seized the man's forearm, then he looked back towards her. He was smiling again, leering, as if he knew that she was still watching him.

Belle understood all too well that Harcourt was staging a performance for her benefit, yet she felt compelled to watch as he took hold of the red-haired girl again. She thought he was talking to the younger girl, though he looked at neither of them. It was her that his eyes were fixed upon. She tried to look away, but somehow his empty eyes kept drawing her back. The girl was walking over now, walking in her direction.

Belle picked up the papers from the table and pretended she was reading them, but the girl came nearer until she stood beside her. She was very young. 'That man over there,' she stuttered, pointing towards Harcourt, 'he sent me to fetch you.' There were tears in her eyes. 'I'm only doing what he said. He told me I was not pretty enough for his friend, and that I should fetch you.'

She looked at the girl, who couldn't have been much older than thirteen or fourteen. Belle rose and told her to dry her tears, guiding her to the seat she had vacated, making time to think, arranging her papers purposefully on the table, knowing that Harcourt was watching her. Perhaps he expected her to pretend nothing had happened, or to be embarrassed, or to cry, or to run away. They were all thoughts that had run through her mind, but she would not give him the satisfaction of behaving as he expected. As she walked towards him, she saw his grin fading.

'My friend is in need of companionship,' Harcourt said.

'Go to hell,' she said. 'I know the truth of who you are, and I'm not afraid to tell others if you push me further.' He looked suddenly less sure of himself, and, just for a moment, she regretted the threat. She turned to walk away, but Harcourt reached out and grabbed her shoulder, pulling her back towards him. His grip was strong and all the pain of betrayal came back in that moment.

Belle wheeled around and in one instinctive continuous movement slapped him with all her strength. His eyes seemed to come alive with the slap; sharp and small and cold, like a rabid dog. He stepped back, the shock as clear in his expression as the vivid red marks left by her fingers on his cheek. The bar room rang with laughter for a moment, and then equally as quickly fell silent.

Harcourt stood frozen for a second, all eyes on him. 'You'll tell none of your lies,' he said, letting loose the girl in his right arm and drawing back his hand. At first Belle thought he was going to rub his cheek, then she realised he was going to punch her; his face was twisted and ugly with hatred. She flinched, taken aback by the sudden hate on his face.

Time stood still as she waited for the blow. Then she was aware of the other man stepping forward, putting himself between them and taking Harcourt by the shoulders. She heard the sound of her rescuer's laughter. He looked back at her, momentarily, over his shoulder, careful to keep his body between her and Harcourt and he smiled. 'Let's have a round of applause please gentlemen for the next bare-knuckle female boxing champion of all England.'

Belle could feel the hesitation in the crowd as they watched and waited for Harcourt's reaction. Then Harcourt too smiled and began to clap, slowly. His response seemed to break the tension and soon others began laughing and clapping. Belle stared for a moment at her defender, her face burning with fear, and anger, and so many other emotions.

Her defender turned towards her. 'James Daunton,' he said. 'I apologise for my friend.'

Belle turned and walked away. By the time she had got back to her table Harcourt was already ushering the others towards the door. The one who had called himself James Daunton smiled uncertainly over to her, as if seeking reassurance, but she looked away.

James breathed the cold night air deep into his lungs. It felt good after the smoke and heat of the room, and the awkwardness of the situation. With each inhalation he pictured the woman again, striding through the crowded room. She had brushed aside over-familiar bodies and hands, as though they were the thin branches of trees straddling her path. He pictured her face and remembered as she had drawn nearer the scattering of fine freckles around her nose, which the powder could not hide. Her long auburn hair had been loosely tied back in a bun, but wisps hung down here and there, framing her face. Most of all he remembered her eyes. Her eyebrows were not fashionably shaped, but dark and rounded, accentuating the deep blue-grey of her eyes.

It was as though those eyes were still looking at him now. If only she had smiled, he thought.

His thoughts were shattered by the hand that gripped his arm. Harcourt looked intently at him, half smiling, and yet there was something in his expression that James had never seen before. 'You have saved me from my own temper,' he said, 'and I thank you. But never apologise on my behalf again.'

The vehemence of Frank's reaction to the slap had taken James by surprise. He had always marvelled in the past at Frank's quiet assurance and even temper; his ability to charm almost everyone he met, no matter what their standing in society. 'Did you know that woman?' he asked.

'I believe I met her once,' Frank replied. 'She's an actress by the name of Belle Bennett, as far as I remember.'

'I was a little taken aback at your reaction,' James said tentatively; willing Frank, somehow, to put his mind at rest. 'What was it she said about knowing the truth of who you are?'

'Ramblings and rantings,' Frank replied, 'nothing more. Put it from your mind. I lost control for a moment. As I said, I am indebted to you. Now let's speak no further of it.'

'The other night, in the ale house in Southgate Street, did I do or say anything untoward?' James asked, realising that a change of subject was called for.

Frank laughed. 'Not at all,' he said. 'Do you not recall? You were enjoying yourself and in a generous mood. You insisted on reimbursing me for the dinner, and kept buying drink after drink, for all the company. I tried to dissuade you, but you would have none of it. My friends all said how amusing they found you.'

James tried to smile, if only to conceal the embarrassment he felt. 'I believe I drank too much.'

'Perhaps I should not have introduced you to the special ale there, it can be very strong. I usually avoid it myself,' Frank grinned. 'You kept insisting we play cards.'

'I take it I lost?' James interrupted.

Frank laughed. 'I'm afraid so. I hope that you at least remember that I lent you ten pounds. That's seventy in all that you owe me.'

'Of course I remember,' James lied.

'I'm sure you will fare better at our next card game,' Frank said.

James hesitated, misgivings flooding his mind. 'I think it might be the sensible thing for me to bow out of the game. My gambling has cost me a great deal of late, and there is little indication of my fortunes changing.'

'All the more reason to think that you are due a change in luck,' Frank said. James sensed the anger, barely concealed by Frank's smile, heard it in his tone when he spoke again. 'I have gone to a great deal of trouble in setting up this game. It was on my insistence that you were included, and now you calmly inform me that you intend to bow out.' Frank's voice was raised and the others were looking at them. 'It would be dishonourable to withdraw now!' he said. 'It would make me look a fool in the eyes of the others and as for you, well . . . ' He hesitated. 'It will not take long for word to spread that you are probably without money, and I need not explain what that would mean for your reputation and your career.' He turned his back and joined the others.

Frank's outburst had taken him by surprise, though looking back James could remember other occasions when someone had fallen out of favour. He found himself thinking of when he had first met Frank. It seemed an age ago, but it could not have been more than eighteen months, he calculated. It was at a game of cards, but a very polite game with small stakes, in the Assembly Rooms. He never played for more than pennies then. Frank had talked his way into the game as though he had known everyone there all his life, though in truth he knew none of them, yet his clothes and manners were those of someone who was comfortable in a sophisticated society.

Frank had explained that he was newly arrived in the city and James had befriended him at first, almost out of a duty of politeness, but their acquaintance had quickly grown to friendship. He had introduced him to a select group of his more boisterous friends. Frank seemed to have endless energy and an unquenchable thirst for pleasure, always able to seek out knew experiences and gain access for chosen friends to places they hardly suspected existed. Gradually he had supplanted him at the centre of the circle and the group had swelled considerably and grown more boisterous. Only Richard had resisted his friendship.

He watched Frank now, organising the party, as though he were marshalling a band of willing volunteers. He had been a good friend and it would be wrong to embarrass him, even though his behaviour tonight had been unacceptable. James walked over to join the others, but most were already leaving. He shook a few hands and Frank turned to him as the last of them departed. 'Have you thought more?'

'I will play,' James said, 'but it will be the last time.'

Frank smiled, more himself now. 'So be it. I knew you would not disappoint me.' He stroked his angular chin and turned away, as though to depart. 'I hear you flew to the rescue of another friend earlier today, a Catholic priest I believe? I did not realise you were a Catholic?'

The question stung like an accusation. 'I used to be,' James said. 'Sean Brennan is an old friend, but how did you know . . . ?'

'News travels quickly in Bath,' Frank interrupted. 'Your friend the priest is involving himself in things he does not understand. I know the reputation of those he has made enemies of, and they are not to be crossed. Ask your friend Dr Wetherby, he's always nosing around Avon Street.'

'I was simply helping an old friend,' James said, 'as I would help you, if you were threatened.'

'So be it, James, but I must ask another favour.'

'Ask it.'

'The money you owe me, I need it to be repaid.'

'I do not have that amount about me at present,' James replied, taken aback at the request. He would have to repay the loan at once now, he knew it. It was a debt of honour. But that would leave him with only sixty pounds – forty pounds short of the stake he needed for the game.

'I did not expect payment now, James,' Frank said. 'Perhaps you could bring the money to me in the Pump Rooms, tomorrow? Shall we meet at noon?' He hesitated. 'I would not ask, but I find I need the money more urgently than I had thought and I must have cash for our card game. Our opponents will not accept markers.'

'But are we not going on somewhere now?'

'No, I will see you tomorrow in the Pump Rooms. I have another engagement this evening.'

As Belle stood at the back of the large stage waiting for her next cue, it felt like an eternity since she had delivered her last line. The part was undemanding, a serving maid whose major function was to be murdered at the beginning of the first act and to reappear as a shrouded ghost in the last.

Daisy was stuttering through her part with a broad grin, as though it was a comedy. At times the audience laughed when the line was not meant to be humorous, but they remained for the most part polite. The play, poor though it was, seemed to hold their attention well enough, and the house was three-quarters full.

Belle had loved the Theatre Royal since she was a child and her parents had performed there. The dressing rooms, and scenery stores, and costume rooms had been like an enchanted kingdom then, and she still felt much of their magic now. At times she almost sensed the presence of her mother and father in the wings, as though they were waiting for their cue; waiting to walk back into her life. Sometimes, at least for a while, she could even convince herself that they were still there, ready to make their entrance.

She looked out at the brightly lit theatre. Three tiers of boxes lined the sides of the auditorium, the highest rising far above the stage, reaching almost to the lofty ceiling. It was the boxes that brought in the most money, each with its own ante-room for entertaining. Almost half of them, she noticed with satisfaction, were occupied.

The uproar from the stage box to her right, as its door opened, took her by surprise. The noise from the ante-room drew even the audience's attention. From the volume of sound a sizeable crowd might have been expected to emerge, but there were only two men and two women.

Belle studied the people who had entered. The box was so close as to be almost part of the stage. There was no doubt. It was Harcourt and he smiled at her and affected an elaborate bow. Then the two men turned to the audience and bowed. The redhead and her friend curtseyed and blew kisses, displaying their ample cleavages, and received a round of applause and whistles from the young bucks in the audience.

They took their seats as noisily as they entered and it was some time before the audience took any interest in what was happening on the stage, by which time Daisy had lost her place and Cauldfield was speaking the same line for the third time. By the time Daisy spoke, the audience was laughing again and the mood was broken.

When Belle's cue came, she looked, as if he had compelled her, up to the stage box. As she began speaking, Harcourt smiled and stood, whistling loudly. The others in the box began laughing and soon the audience joined in. As Belle stumbled over her words her voice was drowned by the tumult; then, as if satisfied with the uproar he had created, Harcourt and his party bowed to the crowd and left.

Chapter 11

The following morning James went to the Catholic Church in Orchard Street. The day was warmer than he had expected, the air suffused with a fine drizzle. The church was unlocked and deserted, heady with the sweet scent of incense and candles. James made his way down the aisle between rows of oak pews, shaking the water from his coat. The droplets caught the light like tiny jewels as the sun pierced through the early morning mist and shone through the windows.

There was little to show that the church had formerly been a theatre, though James could make out the outline of a stage box in the plaster to the left of the altar; to the right, where its companion box should have been, stood an organ. The former Catholic Church in Bath had been burnt down by a rioting mob in 1780 with little opposition from the authorities, or so Sean had told him. Dr Brewer, the Catholic leader, was apparently hounded through the streets, refused sanctuary in the Guildhall by the town council, and turned away from every other church. It was the management of The White Hart Hotel who in the end gave him refuge and saved his life. Perhaps that was why, James thought, that though few of them could now afford to eat or drink there, let alone stay, 'The Hart' was still viewed with almost religious reverence by the Irish community.

James looked up at the altar with the crucifix at its centre, flanked by eight sombre stone pillars. He felt compelled to make the sign of the cross. It was an instinct of upbringing rather than faith, yet still he couldn't stop himself. He made his way behind the altar to the small chapel beyond, but there was no sign of Sean. Turning to leave, he instead sat in the front pew, staring up at the three niches built into the wall behind the altar, one each for Christ and two of his disciples or apostles or saints. He wondered vacantly who they were and then remembered his father's funeral. It was the last time he had been in a church.

He had been sitting there for some time, lost in thought, when Sean emerged from the chapel behind the altar and genuflected before approaching him. 'Where did you come from?' James asked. 'I went into the chapel and you were not there.'

'The monks of Downside were a canny crew, James. When they converted the old theatre they built a tunnel from the church to the priest's house. The riots were still fresh in their memory, so they were. I confess that I use it occasionally, but only to stay out of the rain.'

'It's very grand in here,' James said.

'Too grand,' Sean replied, 'particularly when most of the parish live in destitution; still it is as it is.'

'Have you already sent the fifty pounds to my brother?' James asked, aware of the abruptness of the question. He could see the surprise on Sean's face.

'The man who was taking it left at dawn,' he replied.

'What of the other twenty pounds?' James asked, almost forcing the words through his dry throat.

'I still have it.'

'I am very sorry, Sean, but I need the money back,' James said, avoiding the priest's eyes. 'In a few days I will give you double the amount. It is as much for Michael as it is for me.' He heard the tremble in his own voice and watched helpless as Sean stood looking at him, his expression slowly moving through anger and disappointment, to pity, or was he just imagining it. Either way, each expression seemed to hurt more than the last.

'I'll fetch it now,' Sean said.

When he returned Sean pushed the money into his hand and James took it, almost running from the church. He called over his shoulder, 'I'll more than double it when I bring it back,' but the words did nothing to assuage his guilt.

As James walked into the Pump Rooms his conversation with Sean was still echoing in his mind. This was the centre of Bath's social universe, a world that James knew well and one in which at most times he felt comfortable, but not at that moment. The room was full of people and noisy voices, as it always was at midday, but the sound could not drown the conversation in his head.

He looked around at the elegantly dressed, vying for each other's attentions whilst assessing the degree of style of their neighbours. The comings and goings, arrivals and departures, of the people who mattered, were posted daily on a notice-board to keep the other people who mattered informed about who they could, or could not, hope to see, or hope to be seen with. Thomas Hunt's departure would not be listed, he thought, final though it was, nor the comings and goings of his wife and children.

The ritual here was well established and James knew it as well as any of those gathered. The social elite would meet daily in the Pump Rooms, between seven and ten in the morning, as a string quartet or Hanoverian band tried to compete with their conversations. They would talk of the weather and politics, the theatre and the royal household, but mostly they would talk of each other. From there they would emerge into the town to take the air in Henrietta Gardens, or the Royal Victoria Park, or Sydney Gardens, where stewards ensured that the commoner classes, or anything which might cause offence, were excluded.

And if the weather was poor, the shops in Milsom Street offered a welcome alternative. It boasted of being the finest shopping street in England for hats and shoes, gowns and suits, furniture and ornaments, all displayed in the most luxurious surroundings, with staff who were attentive and always at pains to demonstrate due deference. Ladies and gentlemen were free to shop at leisure without the danger of coming across the milliners and cobblers, dressmakers and tailors, carpenters and potters, and all the various artisans who worked for a pittance in the filthy sweatshops, back-rooms and factories to provide for their every need.

After their morning's excursion the gentlemen and ladies would return to the Pump Rooms for a glass of spa water to help with their digestion before lunch and to agree arrangements for the afternoon or evening. The warmth of so many bodies in the building made the large log fire almost superfluous. James knew he was accepted here by virtue of his profession and manners and clothing, and the illusion that he still had money. If rumours grew stronger about his debts, then this was the place where it would happen; where the word would spread and he would be excluded from society.

James paid for his spa water at the fountain, set in its own room-sized alcove beside the sculpted fireplace. He stared at the well waters, steaming behind the marble balustrade and surrounded by stained-glass windows; an altar to the God of perpetual youth, its busy attendants serving mass and distributing communion. The whole room gave the impression of a temple transported through time, with its lofty Doric pillars supporting a high, sculpted ceiling and triangular stone pediments above each doorway. He had often read the Greek inscription above the entrance to the rooms, 'Water is Best', as though all life's ills could be cured through a glass of the ill-tasting liquid.

The water, as usual, was served up in one of a host of much used and battered pewter beakers, and as always it tasted to him as though it had been run through a mixture of sulphur and iron filings. He told himself, as everyone did, that it was good for his health, and took up his customary position beneath the oak, long-case clock, which in its turn stood beneath the statue of Beau Nash mounted high on the wall above.

James began viewing the comings and goings around him, like all the others, with a polite smile to one and a nod of the head to another. He looked up. The large chandelier in the centre of the ceiling was playing games with the rainbow light it caught from the tall windows. Its mirrored reflections flitted from one face to another, like small butterflies of light.

James picked out Frank Harcourt at almost the same moment that Frank saw him. Frank adopted a smile of acknowledgement and walked towards him through the swelling throng. As he reached out his hand in greeting James discreetly passed him the small bundle of bank notes. 'Seventy pounds,' he said.

Harcourt unobtrusively pocketed them, uncounted, and smiled. 'Thank you, James. I thought it would be better to settle up before tomorrow night's game. I trust you are not inconvenienced by the matter.'

'Not at all,' James replied.

'You understand that no one can be admitted to tomorrow's game without stake money of a hundred pounds. This is not a game for tradesmen and artisans.'

'I understand fully and I have money already set aside,' James said, calculating the shortfall he needed to make up. Even with the twenty he had got back from Sean, after repaying Frank, he had only eighty pounds. He still needed a further twenty pounds.

'Do you have plans for this evening? Frank asked.

'Yes I fear so. There is someone I need to visit.'

'It is as well, for I also have someone I need to see this evening,' Frank said, smiling.

When James reached the home of his friends, Richard and Charlotte, he knocked loudly three times on the front door and fixed a smile to his face. He had watched the house from his window for some time, to ascertain that they had no visitors. When the maid answered the door he shot past her.

'No need to announce me, Dorothy,' he shouted, handing her his hat and cane and flying up the stairs. 'Your master invited me earlier.'

'They are in the drawing room,' Dorothy said.

James stopped at the top of the stairs and flipped a silver thruppenny piece towards her, watching it arc through the air spinning over and over. At the bottom of the staircase, Dorothy caught it and stooped in a mock curtsey. 'Thank you, sir,' she said, smiling.

'A small token of my gratitude, Dorothy.' He bowed and paused for breath at the drawing room door. Then he knocked, and, without waiting for a response, burst into the room. Richard and Charlotte leapt to their feet in surprise.

'Richard,' he said. 'Thank you for your invitation; I have come to visit you and to see your lovely wife, Charlotte, again.' He strode across the room and, taking Charlotte's hand, he bowed and kissed it, before stepping back.

'I take it you would like a whisky?' Richard said, walking over to decanters and glasses, which stood on the mirror-backed mahogany sideboard.

'A whisky would be excellent,' James replied.

Charlotte turned to Richard, who smiled uneasily. 'Richard should not have invited you, James, without discussing it with me first. We are expecting guests for supper and I have not had a place set for you.'

'I must have forgotten I invited James to visit,' Richard said. 'Perhaps we could set another place?'

'The dining table is already laid,' Charlotte said. 'I do not believe you know our guests, James, but you are welcome to stay. There would of course be an odd number around the table,' she added. 'Would you like me to have the table reset, James?'

James could imagine the uproar it would cause, the maid rushing around resetting the table; Charlotte fussing with the decorations and writing out a new name card in her impeccable copper–plate writing, with its exaggerated loops and flourishes and at the end of it all, his presence would still upset her carefully arranged and ordered world. 'It would be too much trouble,' he said, taking the tumbler of whisky from Richard, 'and besides I had planned only a short visit.' Only Charlotte could make an invitation sound so firm a rejection while maintaining such a welcoming smile, he mused.

'I understand, James,' she said, her face relaxing. 'You seem a little agitated, has your day been so exhilarating? You must find us very dull by comparison?' Charlotte's soft hazel eyes and glossy blonde hair lifted her pretty face into the realms of striking beauty. The tightly curled ringlets bunched at either side of her head framed the perfect symmetry of her face and her flawless alabaster complexion. Her tiny, perfectly formed lips opened in a smile, displaying teeth as white as milk. As James looked at Charlotte, he found it difficult to imagine anything in her life being anything other than perfect.

'My elation began when I entered your home and not before,' James said, with a slight tremble in his voice, entering into the spirit of Charlotte's game. She accepted the compliment without comment. He wondered what she was thinking. Then she smiled at her reflection in the over-mantle mirror above the roaring log fire and turned towards him. 'Do call again, James,' Charlotte said. 'You know you are always welcome.'

James finished the whisky. 'I will not inconvenience you longer,' he said. 'Perhaps you could see me out, Richard?'

As the two men walked down the stairs Richard stopped and turned to James. 'I don't recall inviting you this evening?'

'I am afraid it was a subterfuge, Richard. I need to borrow twenty pounds.'

'I take it you are gambling again?' Richard said.

'I simply need twenty pounds. Do you have it, and will you lend it to me?'

'I will lend it to you on one condition. This will be the last time. Twenty pounds is a great deal of money. You may have the money, but if you take it, you give me your word, win or lose, that this is the last time you will gamble. If you go on you will be ruined and I refuse to be a part of it.'

'I had resolved as much myself,' James said as Richard led him into the surgery. Richard unlocked the bureau and opened one of the drawers. There was a substantial amount of money within and James watched as Richard extracted four five-pound notes. 'This will be the last time I gamble,' James said, as he took the money.

'Then stop now.' Richard said as he relocked the bureau. 'Some of the people you mix with are dangerous. I take it that this gambling venture also involves Harcourt?'

'Frank will be involved, as will several others.'

'I will warn you again, to be wary of the man,' Richard said. 'I should not tell you this, but again, perhaps I should have told you before.' He hesitated and his voice grew quieter. 'I have a patient, a lady. She was until lately of very good health and one of the greatest beauties in town. Now she rarely smiles and is dependent on laudanum for her sleep. She was involved with Frank Harcourt in a far more intimate sense than she should have been and wrote several letters to the gentleman before she saw sense and broke off the relationship.'

'Some ladies find it difficult to resist Frank.' James smiled, hoping to break the mood.

'This lady certainly rues the day she met him,' Richard said. 'She has paid Harcourt a considerable amount of money to get those letters back and as yet he still holds them all and is still threatening to take them to her husband.'

'I will speak to him,' James interrupted. 'I am sure I can appeal to his better side.'

'You will do nothing of the sort,' Richard snapped back. 'The man has no better side and if he discovered she has told anyone of his blackmail, there's no telling where it would end. Just take care and don't mention our conversation under any circumstances to anyone, and particularly not Harcourt, merely tell him that he is not welcome in this house.'

'Let me at least give you some good news before departing,' James said, as Richard led him to the front door. 'I spoke to the manager of Jolly's in Milsom Street today. It is the shop in which the wife of the suicide victim was caught shoplifting. They have agreed not to proceed against her.'

Chapter 12

The cold gloom of Avon Street was full of shadow-shapes and blackness, strange scuttlings and half-imagined whisperings. The fear which gnawed at James' insides was as cold and empty as the alleyway in which he now found himself. Part of him felt too drunk and despairing to care what was happening, but his need to find sanctuary was strong. He struggled to piece together his memories of the evening, to restore some sort of order to his mind.

He had set off for The Pig and Whistle tavern, at the edge of Avon Street, with every penny he owned about his person, hoping, before the night was out, to be a much richer man. In the upper rooms of the tavern some of the richest men in the city were meeting to play cards and he knew he had more than enough skill to match any of them, except perhaps for Frank Harcourt.

In the beginning he had played well, even better than Frank, and been successful. But he realised now that he had stayed too long, and drunk too much, and gradually begun to believe in his own infallibility. Eventually the cards had turned against him and by the end of the evening, pushing for one more win, he had lost everything. He stayed after most of the company had left and continued drinking with Frank, who had won a great deal. Eventually they had stumbled out of the hostelry together, and he had followed Frank deeper into the Avon Street maze. Then, somehow, they had become separated and James gradually realised that he had lost his bearings.

His stomach fought desperately against the foul stench from the filth-filled gutter that meandered uninterestedly down the middle of the lane, its path dammed at intervals by rotting vegetation and faeces, forming stagnant pools that fed its onward course. When the next downpour came it would undoubtedly carry the effluent into the cellars of the hovels around, on its way to the River Avon. James tried to keep as close as possible to the edge, but the lane was narrow and his body ricocheted periodically in the soot-black darkness, from wall to wall, as he stumbled on.

His overcoat had been lost in the game, along with his gold pocket watch and silver card case. His long, black frock coat was now stained and scuffed at the shoulders and arms, and the right sleeve was torn at the elbow. His hat lay in a pigsty, some yards away, where the wind had taken it. The bottoms of his impeccably tailored trousers were drenched from unwanted excursions through the gutter and its foul contents had seeped through the stitching in his shoes and soaked his feet.

He had little idea of where he was or the direction in which he was heading, but gradually his fear was becoming his servant, rather than his master. Panic was slowly clearing the fog from his brain and restoring some semblance of co-ordination to his body and a greater degree of control to his legs. He leant against the wall of one of the tenements that lined the alleyway. The damp, oily film that met his touch repulsed him and he felt the surface crumble beneath his hand, as though it was fashioned from barely dried river mud.

James remembered some of the places he had passed, signs scratched on walls and daubed on rough boards – Lockyer's Court, Back Street, Bull Paunch Alley, Lambs Yard, each of them more squalid than the last – all part of the Avon Street rookery, a labyrinth of back-to-back slums, boarding houses, paupers' hovels, stables and pigsties. In his entire journey through the rookery he had seen no one, but for some time he had been conscious of footsteps echoing his own. Now, as he paused for breath, he knew he was not alone.

At the lower end of the lane he could make out the black silhouettes of three or possibly four men. They were, he estimated, about forty yards away. As he focussed on the shapes, one of the men produced a cutlass from beneath his coat and began passing it between his hands, with slow, mesmerising deliberation. James turned to look back the way he had come. The footsteps he had vaguely heard behind him had now stopped at the entrance to the alleyway. In the dull yellow candlelight that shone from a grimy, almost opaque, ground-floor window, he could see the outline of three men. Each man held a wooden stave or club.

In his mind he was already facing the prospect of receiving a bad beating and even of his life being brought to a premature end. He felt for the small raised pearl button on his sword cane with the thumb of his right hand. He pressed it and the oak wood casing slid smoothly to the ground. In its place two feet of well-polished steel blade caught what little light there was in the alleyway. He leant forward with slow deliberation and grasped the sword's casing in his left hand.

He knew that the doors of every house in the lane would be barred against him; he had no business being here, a foreigner in a hostile land. The windows of the houses were mostly cracked or broken, the holes stuffed with filthy rags and oilskin. The doors were makeshift covers of loose boards, driftwood and packing cases, roughly nailed and tied together. It would be easy to force his way into a house, but where then? He would be trapped like a rat, waiting for the terriers.

James pressed his back lightly against one of the doors as he looked from group to group. The two bands were equidistant and neither as yet was moving. If he did nothing then both groups would advance with only one possible outcome. If he chose one group and attacked, he knew the result would probably be the same, but there would at least be an interval before the other men joined the encounter – a small chance of escape.

Moments before, his only thought had been that this was a filthy place to die. Now his own logic took him by surprise. The involuntary tremble in his hands and legs was steadying. The hollow feeling in his body had begun to recede. The inevitability of his death had brought a certain calm and resolution that he had not felt before. He saw in his mind a picture of a continuing world of everyday things in Bath, unchanged except for his eternal absence and smiled at the stupidity of it all. Had it been another night, there might have been some reason for this well contrived ambush. On another night he would have had something worth stealing and he would gladly have given it to them. They might have been satisfied with a purse of gold and the sight of his sword may then have held them at bay.

He briefly contemplated calling to them, explaining that he had nothing of value; but quickly dismissed the idea. Why should they believe that a gentleman would have nothing worth stealing? Why would they give him opportunity to explain? By the time they discovered the truth he would be dead, or they would kill him anyway, in their frustration, and steal his clothes. The thought of being found naked and dead in this place seemed pathetically worse than simply being found dead.

He resolved quite suddenly, but with great clarity of will, to attack the group at the top of the alleyway. He reached for the money pouch in his coat pocket. It contained only pennies and farthings, but it could still cause enough of a distraction, he thought. He threw the purse and money in the direction of the lower group, reasoning that by the time they had located the purse, they would have been delayed if only for a few seconds. As he prepared to run, he heard a soft voice at the top of the alley. It was too quiet to hear what words were spoken yet he knew it was not the voice of any of the footpads. They had each turned away to look at the speaker and James could hear them laughing.

The moment's distraction was more than he could have asked for and at the sound of the laughter James began running, his eyes fixed on the group and his voice roaring some innate primeval battle cry. As he approached them, one of the men raised his fist, ready to strike at the unseen person. The next moment the man lay inert on the ground, though James had heard no shot fired. Within seconds he was nearing the two remaining men who seemed frozen by this surprise attack from both sides. He held out the sword in front of him, half hoping, half expecting that they would clear a path, but neither man moved. He felt the sword penetrate the taller man's front, not knowing if it were in the chest or stomach or groin. As the sword made contact James felt the momentary resistance as it pierced the skin and flesh, then the blade made contact with bone and jarred his arm. The man toppled backwards and the sword came clear of his body.

The third man stood unmoving, unnerved, as James' shoulder sent him crashing into the wall. The other man punched him as he fell. By then he could hear the footsteps running towards them and rapidly making ground. Now James too froze, shocked at the success of his onslaught, uncertain as to what had happened, and equally uncertain as to what to do. He wanted to bend down, to see how bad the man was that he had caught with his sword. Instead his rescuer grabbed his sleeve, pulling him and shouting, 'Run now, if you want to live!'

James sensed his companion's pace slowing and the two of them stopped running almost in unison. They had reached Southgate Street, he realised. The footsteps of their pursuers had grown fainter in the last few minutes, finally fading into the darkness of the night. James stood stock-still, listening, the upper half of his body leaning forward, his hands supporting its weight on his knees, his lungs fighting for air. He raised his head just far enough to look towards his companion – who was breathing normally without the slightest sign of distress. He was dressed in plain calico trousers and a rough smock, a cap pulled down over much of his face. A cord crossed his chest diagonally, securing a canvas bag firmly to his back.

James sheathed the sword in its cane, dreading the thought of seeing it, loathing the feel of it in his hand. He held out his right hand to the man. 'I am James Daunton,' he said, 'and might I have your name?'

'John Doyle,' the man said. He had seemed taller as they raced through the streets, but James could see now that he was about the same height as himself. He could make out little of the man's face beneath the peaked cap, but it was apparent that he had a snub nose, almost as small as a child's, although his expressionless face was broad and showed none of the innocence of a child's face.

John looked uncertainly at his proffered hand and then grasped it firmly. His hands were much bigger than his own, and calloused. As John looked up from beneath the brim of his cap James found himself staring at the large brown eyes and youthful face, which still betrayed little sign of emotion. He tried to put an estimate of age on the man but found it impossible.

'I owe you a great debt, John,' James said. 'How can I repay you?'

'I don't want payment; I didn't do it for reward. Let's just keep walking,' he said.

'I'm truly grateful,' James said. 'But I must repay you. You saved my life.'

'You could give me the price of a bed for the night and a meal for the morning. That'd be payment enough.'

James reached towards his pocket and then remembered throwing his last few coins at his attackers. He withdrew a handkerchief and mopping his brow said, 'I can do better than that. You will return with me now to my home and Mrs Hawker will give you more than enough to fill your belly.'

'I'd be glad of food now, or in the morning, wherever it comes from,' John replied, 'but we have to get away from here.'

'I think we have left them far behind by now,' James replied. He could hear the nervousness in his own voice.

'It's a bad mistake to underestimate your enemies,' John said. 'We oughta go now, and quickly.'

'Come along then, it's a pleasant evening, we'll walk through town,' James said, feeling the weakness in his legs and regretting that he didn't have the money for a cab. John was silent, as though still listening for footsteps as the two of them made their way through town. The sense of relief that James felt at his escape was growing, but he could not drive out his unease. His hands kept reliving the sensation of blade on bone; trembling as the fear returned in waves. He realised again what he had done, how close he had come to death and his fear, now, was even more real than it had been in the alleyway.

They stopped at the end of Bath Street, by the fountain with the carved figures of the four seasons at its base, dwarfed by the huge gothic arches rising above the stone pool. The fountain ran with spa water, hot from the underground water course, steaming white in the cold dark air.

'I'll take a drink,' John said.

James too drank, peering into the ground-floor windows of The White Hart Hotel. They were still dimly lit, as the night porters, cleaners and boot boys went about their duties. The silhouette of a woman was plain against the curtains of an upper room as she walked back and fro trying to pacify a baby whose cries could be heard in the stillness of the early morning air. Then the two set off at a faster pace towards South Parade.

Belle half expected Harcourt to be there again that night, but when she had looked up at the stage box, it was empty. Had it been occupied by someone else it would have set her mind at rest, but the fact that the seats remained unoccupied troubled her all through the performance, as though her tormentor might arrive at any time. The part was undemanding and yet she still found it difficult to concentrate, or to put anything greater than the minimum effort into her performance. It was a relief when the evening was over and she made her getaway from the theatre. She left before anyone had noticed her leaving, almost running to the sanctuary of the room in Bridewell Lane.

From the moment she opened the door Belle could tell there was something wrong. The room was like an oven and Jenny was sitting on the bed supporting Molly's head with one hand while holding a bowl in front of her, into which Molly was being violently sick. Jenny looked up, 'Thank God you're here.'

'What's wrong with Molly?' Belle asked, ripping off her coat and gloves and throwing them on the floor.

'It's the croup,' Jenny replied.

Belle froze for a moment, fearing instantly for Molly's life but not wanting to show her panic to Jenny. 'Why did you not send for me?'

'And cause you to lose your employment?' Jenny replied. 'There was nothing you could do.'

'I would have come.'

'I know you would, but Molly could not move from the bed anyway. I sought out a doctor at about midday and he told me to put Molly into a hot bath up to her neck. I did it, and she seemed a little better for a while, but then the coughing started again.'

'Has he done nothing else?'

'Yes he called early this evening and she has had two leeches on her neck to suck out the poison, and he put a blister paper there.'

Belle reached forward and stroked Molly's forehead. She was hot and dripping with sweat. 'Did he give her no medicine?'

'Yes, he sent a boy two hours ago with some powdered Ipecac. I mixed it with a little wine and she took it, like the brave girl she is. It's worked well. She's already been sick three or four times. I'm sure the poisons must be coming out.'

'She's so hot though,' Belle said, stroking Molly's forehead again.

'The doctor said to keep her warm and keep the windows closed lest the bad airs enter and she develops a chill. Can you help me with the blister paper?'

Belle took Jenny's place on the bed, cushioning Molly's head in the crook of her arm, and began unwinding the bandage from around her neck until the blister paper was exposed. When Jenny returned with the scissors, Belle gently prised the paper from Molly's neck and dabbed away the residue of caustic chemicals from around the large blister on her neck.

'Will you do it? I can't bring myself to,' Jenny said, holding the scissors out to Belle.

She took them and tentatively burst the blister, trying to catch the clear fluid with the end of the bandage as it rolled down Molly's neck. 'It looks too clean to be poisonous,' Belle said, handing the scissors back. Jenny handed her a damp flannel and she cleaned the dampness away. 'You sit with Molly and I'll empty the sick bowl and wash the flannel,' she said, but before she could move Molly began retching again. Her body seemed drained and too tired to struggle for life.

Chapter 13

Nathaniel Caine sat up and looked around him. Slowly he began to piece together what had just happened. The headbutt had taken him by surprise and knocked him unconscious. Tommy Wood lay next to him in the alleyway, moaning with pain. Caine reached an arm behind Tommy's head and pulled him into a sitting position. 'What happened to you?' he asked.

'The bastard stabbed me in the stomach,' Tommy replied, trying to smile. 'It hurts terrible. Do you think I'm going to die?'

'No, lad,' Caine replied, but the boy looked bad.

His brother was worried too, as he stood over them not knowing what to do next. 'Come on, Tommy, get up,' he said, offering a hand. Caine watched as Harry took the boy's hand and pulled him slowly to his feet. Tommy was holding his free arm to his stomach and couldn't straighten at first against the pain.

Another of the men helped Caine to his feet. He felt unsteady and the ache in his head was growing worse. Caine massaged his bruised forehead and stood for a while waiting for his balance to return. Revenge would come quickly, he vowed to himself, and it would be a hard justice. He would make sure of it. 'Where are the others?' he asked, but no sooner had he asked the question, than the other two gang members appeared around the corner of the next street.

'They got away,' one of the men shouted.

'This is a bloody sorry business.' Caine spat a gob of phlegm into the oil-streaked surface of the puddle where, until recently, he had been lying. 'Let's get home,' he said. The six men walked in silence, Harry Wood and Caine helping Tommy between them.

The ignominy of defeat hung heavy on Caine. He had had beatings before, more than he cared to remember, but mostly at his father's hands when he was too young to defend himself. He found himself remembering the last time he had come off worst in a real fight. It had been twenty years ago, when he was seventeen. The scar on his cheek was a constant reminder of the humiliation he had suffered that day, if he needed any reminder. The Cockroad gang had been led by someone else then. He struggled to remember his name . . . It was Silcox; George Silcox. Caine traced the curve of the scar with the tip of his index finger; the scar that Silcox had given him.

Caine could picture himself as he had been then, a scrawny thing, but tall, with a good reach and fast fists. Silcox had been leader of the Cockroad gang, though everyone knew it was a Caine that should rightfully lead the gang. Silcox had known it too, that's why he had drawn him into the fight, knowing he was a potential challenger. Silcox had fought him and won, and left him with that scar to remind him of who was boss.

It was almost a year before he had got the chance to get even with him. He'd made sure that he was stronger by then, made sure he was ready. He had beaten Silcox in a fair fight. Then he had waited for Silcox to come to, before smashing his right knee with a spade. George Silcox walked with a crutch after that, and to his dying day. A Caine was once again, back in control of the Cockroad gang, as it had been for generations before, as it should have been. He'd got his revenge then and he would get it this time too.

The front door of the house in Hucklebridge's Court was heavy and secured by a large lock. As Caine unlocked the door, he could hear the bolts being pulled back on the other side and as they entered, the large man who had unbolted the door stood there to meet them.

'Ow did it go?' he asked.

'Bloody awful, now get back to your post, Lem,' Caine roared, sending the gatekeeper backing into the small room he had just vacated. 'Give your brother some brandy, Harry,' he said as they walked down the stairs to the kitchen, 'and be sure to pour some on his wound before he drinks it all; that young 'un's always got a terrible thirst on him.'

Jeb and two others were sitting at the table in the kitchen drinking. They all rose as they watched Tommy being helped into the room. Harry Wood grabbed the bottle from the table and helped his brother to a seat by the fire. Caine watched as he pulled up his brother's shirt to expose the wound and poured some of the brandy into the cut. Tommy winced at the pain, before grabbing at the bottle and putting it to his lips.

'Take his coat and shirt off,' Caine bellowed. He could tell that Tommy fully intended to drink himself senseless and knew that he would soon achieve his ambition. He walked over to him and placed a hand on his shoulder, pushing him backwards to examine the wound. 'One of you lads fetch me a good sheet from my room,' he said, turning to the men, 'and do it now.' He looked at the small cut in the boy's skin, it seemed nothing, little more than a scratch and yet it bled in a stream and the skin around it was already raised and red. He tried to stem the flow with his grubby palm, but still it wouldn't stop.

When the sheet came he wiped his hand and ripped it into strips, wrapping the cloth around the boy, binding the wound, watching it soak up the blood. 'Best let him rest now,' he said, patting the lad on the head and turning away.

'Ta, Nat,' the lad said smiling. 'That feels more comfortable now.' Caine looked back over his shoulder watching Tommy take another long swig of the brandy before putting the bottle on the floor, wincing as he reached forward.

Caine said nothing as he watched Tommy becoming more lethargic. The boy didn't look right, not for such a small wound, but he'd seen wounds as small as that kill a man before now. He walked over to the lad and placed his hand on his forehead. He felt hot and sweaty, but then he was lying close to the fire and the kitchen was very warm after the cold of the night. The boy reached forward for the bottle again and swigged on the brandy.

'That's it, you drown out the pain, lad,' Caine said.

'I told you it was a mistake, us trying to set up in Bath,' Harry Wood said.

'Don't cross me, Harry,' Caine spat back. 'We were getting nowhere in Cockroad, generation after generation risking execution for the sake of a chicken here or a few pieces of gold there. There's rich pickings in Bath and we're picking more than anyone else. People look up to us. We're men of substance. If you think you can do better than I, let's settle it now.' Caine produced the wide-bladed knife from his belt. The room fell quiet and its occupants froze in whatever they were doing.

Harry raised himself to his full height and stared back. Caine could tell he was thinking of drawing his own knife. He could see the bone handle shining where it protruded from under his jacket. 'The lad's ill,' Caine said, 'you'd best tend to him.'

'Don't fight, Harry,' Tommy said.

'Don't worry, Tommy, I'm not fighting,' Harry replied. 'I'm not crossing you, Nat. You can put the knife away, I just think we'd be better in Cockroad, where people know us, and know not to cross us.'

'Cockroad's the devil's armpit, in the middle of nowhere,' Caine replied. 'It was fine when there was money to be had on the highways, but all the rich pickings travels on the trains now. Cockroad's sent three generations of my family to the gallows, or to the colonies, and your family's no different, and what did they have to show for it? There's no money to be had robbing farmers and collecting fear-money from those who has nothing to lose.'

'You're right,' Harry said. 'All I've got is Tommy here and me ma and a cousin in Gloucester jail. I know you're trying to set us up good, but we could have set up in Bristol where we know people, instead of Bath?'

'The Bath peelers can be bought a damn site cheaper than in Bristol. We're not just feared here, we're respected. Ain't that worth something to you?'

'I'll take money over respect anytime, but you're the boss. I'll follow you whatever you decide. I have to, I ain't got your brains.' He laughed and held out his hand and Caine cautiously resheathed his knife and shook it. 'Sit down, Nat,' he said. 'Tommy looks like he's drunk his self to sleep now. It's been a long night and we're all tired.'

'Aye, you're right,' Caine said, sitting in an armchair by the fire.

'Why did we go after him tonight?' Harry asked. 'We're not footpads. We don't rob toffs; you said they cause too much fuss.'

'It were meant to be a warning to the priest,' Caine replied. 'The man we were after is a friend of his.'

'Word will get out,' Jeb said. 'Six of us beaten by two men.'

'He was supposed to be alone and drugged and incapable,' Caine replied. 'I didn't know he had a sword, or where that other bastard came from.' He could feel his temper rising.

'People will be laughing at us,' Jeb said.

'Then we'll have to be sure we wipe the smiles from their faces,' Caine replied. 'We'll come down even harder on them for the next few days. All of you, do you hear that?' he shouted. The men grunted their agreement.

'What about the two men?' Harry Wood asked.

'Don't worry about them, we'll see to them in good time, and it won't be just a beating.'

'But who are they?' Harry asked.

'The one we were after goes by the name of James Daunton and I know what he looks like, and where he lives.'

'I'll have the bastard, for what he's done,' Harry said.

'We'll see to him, don't you worry,' Caine replied. 'We've got to sort that priest out too and before he gets the Irish organised against us . . . Now, how about a hand of cards before I go to my bed.' Caine moved over to the table. He knew it would not be that simple. The Irish were on a razor's edge and the priest was the razor. He looked over to Tommy Wood, still stretched out immobile on the chaise-longue, his brother kneeling beside him and feeling his forehead. Harry fetched a pitcher from the table. Caine watched as he dipped some cloth in the water, and bathed his brother's forehead.

'How are you doing, me babs?' Harry asked.

'I climbed higher than you,' his brother said. 'I got right to the top of her. You said I couldn't do it, but I showed you, didn't I? And when I got to the top I carved me initials so everyone would know I was the first to climb her.'

'What are you talking about?' Harry asked.

'You said you'd already climbed the oak but you hadn't, had you?'

'No,' Harry replied. 'You was the first and only one to climb the oak.'

'Don't worry about the cuts and scrapes, they'll soon mend, they always do. I'll tell ma I fell over running.'

Caine stood and walked over to the two. 'Nat!' Harry shouted. 'Tommy's not making any sense; he thinks we're young kids again. He's talking about climbing that big oak tree in Cockroad.'

'Leave him be, he's probably drunk, he's had half of that brandy and he's lost a lot of blood for such a small cut,' Caine said. 'He's probably playing the fool again; you know what he's like.'

'Look at him, Nat. He's too poorly to play the fool. He's like he's on fire, but he's shaking with cold.'

The crash was loud as the bottle fell from Tommy Wood's grasp and smashed on the flagstone floor. Nat leant closer and felt Tommy's forehead. 'You're right,' he said 'the young 'un is bad. He was burning up a minute ago and now he feels ice cold.' Turning to the card players, he said, 'One of you fetch some blankets and someone bank up the fire.'

'He needs a doctor,' Harry said.

'Aye, get our friend, the one that doesn't ask questions. Tommy's lost a lot of blood already and I can't see how bleeding him of more is going to help, but a bit of laudanum will take the pain away and give him a good sleep. Fetch him now. Tommy's a special lad and I'll not see him go without. Tell him Nathaniel Caine has asked for him personally and give him two sovereigns.'

James turned the key in the lock of the large front door and straightaway scraping and scratching noises could be heard from the other side. John Doyle seemed startled at the sounds and looked to James as though he was poised for flight. As the door swung open, a small brown and white terrier looked up at them and barked just once, quietly. James bent down to stroke the dog's head.

'I've no liking for dogs,' John said as the terrier began energetically sniffing the bottoms of his trouser legs.

'John, this is Admiral Nelson,' James said, 'my housekeeper's dog. He is better known to his friends as Horatio. As you can see he has a patch around his eye, and all the qualities one expects of a guard dog. If his fearful bark fails to deter the housebreaker, he will simply lick the miscreant to death. Won't you, Horatio?' He bent over and stroked the dog's ears but could see that John was still not at ease as he led him through the echoing hallway and into the study.

The room was hot after the cold of the night and the guttering flames of the two gas lamps, which had been turned down low, added to the warm glow from the embers in the fireplace. James threw his jacket onto the chaise-longue under the window and then poked the fire and added a few small logs, creating a fountain of gold and red sparks, and sending wisps of wood smoke curling around the lip of the mantelpiece and into the room. The logs quickly crackled into life, and the small flames flicked over the bark and sent shadows dancing onto the walls.

'You say very little, but I am still curious as to why you came to my assistance?' James asked.

'God only knows; maybe just because I was there, or maybe I didn't like the odds. Does it matter?'

'True,' James said. 'You at least helped, and I suppose it does not matter why.' It did matter to him though. Part of him needed to know why Doyle had intervened, but it was obvious that the man would not be drawn further. 'There is a hint of some accent in your voice,' James said. 'Where are you from?'

'I'm from Boston,' John said, 'but that was a long time ago. I've done a lot of travelling since and I ain't been back in years.'

'Ah, a Lincolnshire man,' James said.

'No,' John replied, 'Boston, Massachusetts.'

'Oh, an American,' James said, as he took off his shoes and stockings, leaving them in a sodden mass where they fell, before sitting in an armchair at one side of the fire and warming his feet. He gestured for John to sit in its partner on the opposite side of the hearth, but he stood immobile and uneasy, staring at the closed study door as though he was waiting for something. Seconds later the door swung open, framing the formidable shape of Mrs Hawker, in nightdress and dressing gown, a walking stick raised above her head.

'I keep telling you, Mrs Hawker, you're supposed to knock on the door before entering,' James said.

'And I keep telling you that you should return home at a decent time and not at this ungodly hour. When you have the manners to listen to me, I will have the manners to knock. And who's your man here, come to burgle us, and do God knows what other foul business?'

'I'm John Doyle and I don't steal from good folks, or conduct any other foul business,' he said.

'Well, you're a sparky one and no mistake,' Mrs Hawker responded. 'We'll give you the benefit of the doubt for now, and leave the rest to time. Sit yourself down and stop standing there menacing us all. I suppose you both want to eat?'

James smiled. 'Yes, we are hungry, but we will fend for ourselves.'

'Away with you,' she said. 'What do you want to eat?'

'A chunk of cheddar and some bread will do us fine,' James said, 'unless there's some of your pie left and perhaps a little ham and some pickles. I promised John here that we would feed him.' His demands were as much to set Mrs Hawker's mind at rest as they were about hunger.

He saw her examining his discarded jacket with its various stains and rips. It looked worse than he had imagined. 'What on earth have you been doing?' she asked, attempting to remove some of the dirt from a sleeve. He told her he had been involved in a scuffle and that John Doyle had given him assistance. She was obviously concerned, and he said nothing about the nearness of his escape, or the fact that he had stabbed a man. Mrs Hawker frowned as she gingerly picked up the shoes and stockings with the tips of her fingers.

They ate well and when they had finished James showed John up to his room. When he returned to the study, Mrs Hawker was clearing away the plates. 'You know nothing of that man and yet you bring him into your home and let him stay for the night. I shall keep my door locked and you should do the same,' she said.

'I know he saved my life, Mrs Hawker, and that I had no other way of rewarding him.'

'That's as may be,' she replied, 'but he has the run of the house and he looks a rough sort.'

'Then lock your door, Mrs Hawker, and if it makes you easier I shall lock mine. Leave the dishes and get to your bed. I will go up when I know you are safe behind your door.'

When Mrs Hawker left, James felt the weariness creep slowly into every part of his body, but he knew that his thoughts would not allow him to sleep. He had almost forfeited his life, stabbed a man, lost all his money, and could no more help his brother now than he could help himself. Neither could he dismiss the image of Sean's face when he had taken the money from him and Richard's words when he had borrowed from him. He would keep his promises to them though, and more. He vowed to himself to change the way he lived. He would work, as never before, to pay off all that he owed, and he would help his brother and Sean.

Tommy Wood showed no sign of pain now. The doctor may have done little else, but at least he had taken away his suffering. 'Well, doctor?' Caine barked. 'Can you save him?' The man's hands were shaking and as he turned the sweat on his face said all that needed to be said.

'There's nothing I can do. Nothing any doctor could do.'

Caine studied Harry Wood's face, as he cradled his brother's head in his arms. 'Get out, doctor, while you still can, and don't let Harry see you again.' He tossed a coin in the man's direction, but the doctor made no effort to retrieve it in his haste to leave. The coin fell to the ground and Caine picked it up again.

He walked over and put a hand on Harry's shoulder. He looked at Tommy's face, drained of any colour, the eyes sunk deep and dark. 'Best say your goodbyes, lad. I fear he's dying.' Harry turned and looked up at him. There were tears in his eyes, but he was holding them back. He looked for a moment as though he was going to speak, but he said nothing.

Tommy's breathing got louder for a while and then became very quiet, as though he had stopped breathing altogether. Shortly afterwards the rattle started, as though each breath was pained and stuck fast in his throat. Caine had heard it before. It stopped for a while and Harry held him closer. Just for a moment Tommy opened his eyes. 'Come on, me babs,' Harry said. But everyone in the room knew he was going. Then Tommy breathed his last breath.

It took five men to subdue Harry and hold him down until his rage had passed. Then they left him alone with his brother.

Chapter 14

When John awoke he realised it was almost mid-morning, long after the time he had intended to be up and gone, but he did not stir. Instead he lay awake for almost an hour, listening to the lone birdsong through the bedroom window, allowing his mind to drift aimlessly with its territorial melody, enjoying the stillness of the house and letting his memory meander.

Last night had not gone the way he had planned it. He knew well enough what he should have done, what he had spent weeks planning to do, but when the moment had come, he'd lost his nerve. Yet the emptiness it had left inside him was almost welcome, there was nothing left to lose now, even his money was gone. Most of it had been spent in London with the old friends he had sought out.

Each meeting had been relatively enjoyable at the start, exchanging reminiscences and half-remembered, much embellished, anecdotes, making him forget for a while what he had lost. Then the silences had intervened and the unwelcoming looks from wives and families for the stranger who was a reminder of other days. To them he was a threat, an underminer of relationships, a caller-back to a former life at sea, and long partings and uncertain futures. They could not see how he envied them.

There were no loved ones to resent his presence in the lives of other old comrades he had sought out. Yet somehow they made him even more conscious of his irrelevance. As long as he was with them, he was welcome to join in drinking sprees and any other entertainment that offered itself up, particularly when he had money in his pocket. But he knew that when he left he would not be unduly missed, and that once he had gone he would be remembered only now and then, as the subject of some half-forgotten story. They'd all known what he should do, confirmed to him what was already in his mind. Some of them even offered to help, but what he had to do, he had to do alone, or at least that's how he had felt then.

For a man of his build, John prided himself that he could still move quietly, when he chose to. He had waited until the house was completely silent; waited until he could hear no movement from below. Only then did he leave the bedroom and make his way downstairs. The door of the drawing room opened silently and closed without the slightest resistance. The room was deserted.

He made his way to the ground floor and the front door, trying to remember each creaking board on the stairs and landing from the night before. He descended with barely a sound. Yet at the bottom of the stairs, he had taken only a couple of paces towards the front door when the dog came running towards him carrying an old worn slipper, which he dropped at his feet and nuzzled towards him with a quizzical look. Then he barked, a single gruff murmur, deep in his throat.

John froze. He thought of picking up the shoe and throwing it for the dog to chase. He could be past it and through the door before the dog knew what was happening. But now James Daunton was calling through the half-open study door. 'Is that you, Mr Doyle?'

'Yes, I'm just going,' he shouted back, making his way to the door. 'Thank Mrs Hawker for the food last night, it was the best I've had in weeks.'

'Won't you come in and have a cup of tea, Mr Doyle?' James said, opening the door of the study.

'I wanted to be on the road before the morning was over,' John replied.

'But I promised you breakfast. Please stay for something to eat and drink before you go.'

'I'd be glad of some food, but I'll take it in the kitchen. I don't wanna fuss made.'

John knocked on the door of the kitchen and waited for an invitation to enter. There was nothing other than the thought of food that might have made him stay; he had no money and no idea of when he would next eat.

'Come in,' Mrs Hawker shouted.

John shivered as he entered the warmth of the kitchen from the cold of the hall and the steep, narrow, lower staircase that led down to the cellar rooms. He could feel the damp in the air from the clothes drying on the clothes-horse suspended from the ceiling, but the kitchen was lit by a deep golden glow from the fire in the black-leaded kitchen range and the soft morning light from the low basement window.

This was obviously her kingdom he thought. The pine table at the centre of the room was worn and bleached white from constant scrubbing and she was busy at it now, her hands covered in flour. John felt strangely at home, the air seemed full of half-remembered childhood smells of cinnamon and cloves; honey and molasses; and the lingering scents of baked pies and spit-roast joints.

'I've called in to say goodbye,' he said, 'before I set off on my travels, and Mr Daunton said I could have something to eat before leaving. Don't go to any trouble though. I can see you're busy. If you can spare a hunk of bread and a slice of cheese I'll take 'em with me.'

'You'll do nothing of the sort. You'll sit at that table so, and you'll not move until you can eat no more. You look in need of a good meal and for that matter a bit of care.' She wiped the flour from a corner of the table, sending a white cloud drifting down to the floor like a fall of fine snow. 'I suppose you want something as well, Patch,' she said, looking past him.

John started. He was unused to being taken by surprise by anyone, yet, turning, he saw no one, until he looked down and saw the dog looking up expectantly, the slipper still gripped in his jaw. When he sat by the space Mrs Hawker had cleared at the table, the dog dropped the slipper in the fallen flour at his feet. When he did not respond the dog picked up the slipper and dropped it again in front of him, looking up into his eyes, nosing it towards him several times, each time looking up into his face for some sort of response.

'Master James calls him Horatio,' she said, 'but I prefer to call him Patch. If he gets confused at times, he never seems to show it.'

'Does he want me to throw it for him?' John asked.

'He wants you to pick up the slipper,' Mrs Hawker replied.

John picked up the slipper, 'What should I do now?'

'Just sit with it in your lap for a while and then put it back on the floor,' Mrs Hawker said. 'He followed me home from the market a few years ago and when he wouldn't leave I threw a slipper at him.

He just brought it back, and I let him stay. Now if he likes someone he gives them his slipper. He must like you.' Her face had softened as though the dog's approval counted for something in her mind.

John unslung the bag from his shoulder and threw it down in the corner. It landed with the heavy thud of metal on stone. He looked up at Mrs Hawker as she studied the bag, a large china rolling pin in her hand. He smiled. 'You've nothing to fear from me, you know,' he said. 'That's my baccy tin and a couple of other things lying at the bottom of the bag, not the silver candlesticks from the drawing room.' She looked at him quizzically. 'Oh, the thought crossed my mind,' he said, 'after all I've no money and silver fetches a good price, but I've stole nothing. I'm not a thief and besides Mr Daunton may have some funny ways, but he trusted me and it's a while since anyone's done that. I'd not steal from him even if I was a thief. You can go up and see for yourself if it'd set your mind at rest.'

Mrs Hawker smiled. 'It won't be necessary. I can tell you're a good man. It's in your eyes.' She hesitated. 'So you like Master James?' she asked.

'He seems fair,' John replied. 'But he shouldn't go in the places he does.'

'You seem a man of the world,' Mrs Hawker said. 'Where will you go after you've eaten?'

'I'm heading for Bristol and then to sea,' he lied.

'Whatever would you do that for?' she asked.

'See the world agin and taste what it has to offer. Besides that's my trade and I need money to live,' John said.

'You're free to do as you please of course and if you want to run away that's up to you, but I sense you might want to stay,' Mrs Hawker said, her tone almost questioning. 'You've an unhappiness inside you that you may be able to hide from others, but not from me.'

'You're a wise woman,' John replied.

'Wise enough to know that you don't find what you're searching for by wandering the world. Sometimes you see more by staying put for a while, not that I've seen much of foreign places.'

'I do have unfinished business in Bath,' John found himself saying. The words seemed to tumble from his mouth, and he wondered how this old woman had managed to coax the admission out of him, with so little effort.

He felt her studying him as though the need to make some decision about him was rattling around in her brain. 'This would be a good billet for someone who needs time to find themselves,' she eventually said. 'And I've a feeling that's what you are looking to do.' He could almost see her mind working now and it was not the mind of a feeble old woman, but more like a she-wolf protecting her cub. He was sure that anyone who underestimated Mrs Hawker did so at their own risk. 'Besides, Master James might need someone like you, someone who he can trust, and knows how to look after themselves,' she said.

'How's that then?' he asked.

'He got himself into trouble last night. It worries me that he goes to places that he shouldn't, and gets into such scrapes.'

'They weren't just out to rob him. They could have done that easy, as soon as he parted from his friend,' John said. 'I'd watched them in the tavern. Why would they attack someone who had lost, rather than the winner?'

'Master James has some friends that make me uneasy, and I really fear for him sometimes. You are needed here and there aren't many I would say that to. Besides I'll sleep better with another man in the house,' Mrs Hawker said.

The feeling that this was somehow where he was meant to be had already begun to take root. 'But what would I do if I stayed?' John asked.

'I can speak to Master James and get him to offer you a position. I'll explain to him that I need help about the place, which in truth I could do with. It'd raise his standing too, to have a manservant about the place, not that he cares much for such things. But of course it's Master James that must make the decision.'

He studied her smile. Her words said she was only the housekeeper, but her expression told another story. 'Can you truly see me playing the manservant?'

'No, but I can see you as a friend who knows his way about. It may be a while before Master James can pay you proper wages, but you'll eat well and have a comfortable roof over your head. And it would give you time to find your bearings.'

He found the idea suiting him: not the job, but the fact that he could afford to stay in Bath and finish what he had started. 'You'd make a good recruiter for the navy Mrs Hawker and there's no doubting that this would be a good berth.'

Mrs Hawker looked him straight in the eyes, as if readying herself for the final act of persuasion. 'I had to persuade the housekeeper and the maid to leave, because I knew money was short. But I'm not as young as I was, and I find it difficult coping with the heavier work on my own.' She smiled, a warm and persuasive smile, which John felt sure she was capable of producing at the drop of a hat.

'I could maybe stay a while, but not too long or I'll grow fat on your food,' John replied.

'Good, it's settled then. I'll make up a plate of herrings and heat some vegetable mash. You butter some bread and then I'll speak to master James while you eat.' She waited for a while before adding, almost as an afterthought, 'I have a footman's uniform about the place, from the early days, when we were better set up, and Master James ran a proper household. He was much the same build as yourself, as I recall. I can alter his old uniform to fit you this very afternoon.'

'Hold your horses,' John interrupted. 'I said I didn't mind the thought of helping with chores and such, but I didn't agree to no flunkey's rig.'

'Don't you worry,' Mrs Hawker said. 'Master James doesn't entertain very often, but it would raise his standing to have a manservant about the place, and it may put off some of these tradesmen that keep hounding him for money.' She looked him up and down, as though already measuring him for the uniform. 'And besides, you'd look very smart. I'll have a word with him while you finish your food. Then I'll put some water to boil, and you can drag the bath into your room and fill it up.'

'But I'm not wearing some servant's outfit,' he spluttered.

'Tidy yourself, and at least allow me the pleasure of doing the alterations. Let me think that we're a fine house again, with a footman. Then it'll be ready, just in case you change your mind. You'll probably never need to wear it – at least not often. It's up to you of course.'

John hardly believed it when he found himself smiling and nodding his agreement.

Mrs Hawker brought a tray of food to James in the drawing room and smiled at him as she placed it on the occasional table. Her expression was almost girlish and James found himself suddenly remembering the stories she had told him as a boy. He smiled at her. 'Do you remember the stories you told me about my mother and yourself, when you were young girls? How you would play together in the nursery when your work was done and you'd both make believe that my mother was the maid and you were the lady of the house.'

'She was a rare lady, your mother,' Mrs Hawker replied, smiling. 'I loved her as though she was my sister.'

'I used to make believe that it was my mother who had told me the stories.'

'And so she would have, had she lived,' Mrs Hawker replied. 'I have a favour to ask.'

When Mrs Hawker asked him to take John on as a manservant, he demurred at first, knowing he had no money to pay him. But for once she seemed insistent, and he understood all too well, even without her arguments, that the household duties were too much for her to cope with. He had tried to persuade her in the past that they should replace the maid who had left so suddenly, but she would have none of it. Yet now she seemed positively eager to take on John. The notion of having another man about the house seemed somehow to be important to her peace of mind, though she seemed reluctant to be specific as to why.

Eventually he gave in and agreed to employ John, at least for a little while. He decided that he would sell the silver candlesticks and a few other items of value he had around the house, though the thought pained him. But at least it would tide them over until he began earning more. Perhaps Richard might also help if he could convince him that he had changed his ways.

When she had gone, he picked at the food for a while before laying it aside half eaten. It was a welcome relief when Father Brennan arrived a little while later, though it was clear to James that he too was agitated when he met him at the front door. Sean seized James' arm and led him back into the study as though he were the man of the house and James the visitor.

'Sit down, James,' he said, closing the door behind them. 'I have some bad news. A few of the men of the parish came to me in the late morning with rumours that they heard around Avon Street. There was a fight last night and a man died. He was a member of Caine's gang, and they say Caine is looking for the man responsible.' Sean hesitated. 'The name they heard was yours, James.'

James felt waves of nausea sweeping through his body. 'He's dead . . . the man's dead,' he said. He found himself reliving the sword thrust over and over again, feeling the impact of the blade, seeing the man fall. He knew he had to say something. He struggled for the right words as though if he chose well they might anchor him in reality. 'Yes, I was involved in a fight, but it was more of a skirmish,' James said. 'I didn't know he would die. It was self-defence.'

'It's all my fault,' Sean said. 'When we went to the boarding house Nat Caine obviously got word that you were my friend. He attacked you, I think, to warn me off.'

'We cannot know that,' James said. 'They may have just been trying to rob me . . . But how could he die? It was only a thin blade. I've never as much as hit anyone since I was a boy. How can I have killed him? Who was he?'

'He was a lad of about seventeen years by the name of Tommy Wood. From what I hear he was very popular, given the fact that he was a member of the Cockroad gang. He leaves a mother and a brother.' Father Brennan paused. 'Would you like me to hear your confession?'

'But I never meant to kill someone.'

'We cannot change the past. If you are truly sorry you will be forgiven.'

'I'm sorry he died, but if I was in that position again I cannot say that I would not do the same again. I was fighting for my life. I didn't know he would die. I wasn't thinking clearly. I should have aimed for his leg, but I didn't aim at all. I just ran.'

'We have to live with the results of our actions,' Sean said. 'The man I punched at that lodging house could have fallen and hit his head on the ground and died and I too would have been a murderer. You chose to take up the sword and now you may find it difficult to put down again. All of our actions have consequences.'

'I will have to live with what I have done,' James said.

'And I,' Sean said. 'If I had turned the other cheek to Caine, none of this would have happened. We cannot always predict the consequences of our actions, nor even be aware of them all. Throw a stone in a pool and the ripples reach out. I bear guilt for this with you.'

'I must make amends,' James said. 'I must answer to the law.'

'There is no making amends with Caine's gang and the law will not be involved. Tommy Wood's body has already been smuggled out of the city and will be buried in Cockroad. These men are their own law and will seek their own retribution. You are in danger, James. I think you should leave Bath and send Mrs Hawker away, for if they cannot hurt you they will hurt those closest to you.'

'Should I go to the police?' James asked.

'And say what; that you have murdered someone? The peelers would arrest you and Caine's gang would either get to you in prison or wait for your release; besides, some of the peelers are already in the pay of the gang. These men control Avon Street. Their reputation isn't lightly earned.'

'Are you saying I should simply run away? How can I stay in hiding when my life is here? I couldn't hide forever.'

'You cannot fight these men, James,' Sean said. 'Run while you can. You'll be safe in Ireland with your brother.'

'We have the same enemy now, Sean. If you will not run, then why should I?'

'Think about it carefully, James. Don't make any rash decisions.'

'You're right, I need time to think,' James said. 'Perhaps I should go to Ireland . . . but it seems wrong.'

'You could help your brother, if you went to Ireland,' Sean interrupted, 'and you would be safe there.'

'My brother has problems enough without having to care for a coward. Whatever comes I have to face it,' James said. 'You above anyone should understand. Thank you Sean for coming and telling me this, but could you go now. I must think. I don't fully understand yet what to do. You must keep this news to yourself.'

When Sean left, James went up to his room and retrieved the sword-stick from under his bed. He drew the sword from its cane scabbard and plunged it into the water-jug, watching the patches of brown residue that clung to the blade melt into scarlet clouds, swirling and eddying in the water, growing ever paler and indistinct. He ran his fingers over the blade, removing every trace of blood and then washed his hands, over and over again.

When he was finished he took the jug into the hallway and poured its contents out of the back window. Then he returned the sword to its scabbard and sat on the corner of the bed. He felt suddenly very old, like an empty shell, uncertain of who he was, and who he had ever been. There was no way of undoing what he had done, no making amends, no way of wiping it from his memory. Sean had asked him to confess, to ask for forgiveness, but he knew there could be no forgiveness.

When he felt the first sob take root and grow, shaking his body from deep within, he did nothing to suppress it. But when he felt the howl of pain begin forming in his throat, he buried his face in his hands and held the sound within, until it became part of him.

Chapter 15

Caine watched as Harry Wood took another long drink from the bottle of brandy, before picking up the pistol and taking aim. 'Leave off drinking,' Caine said. 'You'll need all your wits about you.'

'I could drink the whole bottle and not feel it,' Harry replied. 'When you've got this much hate burning inside, there's no liquor that can touch you.'

'Do you understand everything?' Caine asked. 'Do you want me to go through it again?' Harry's mood scared him; it was as though he no longer cared if he was caught. All that seemed to matter to him now was killing Daunton.

Harry fingered the trigger of the gun and smiled. 'No, I know it well enough. But it still seems too quick. I'd have liked Daunton to die slow, like Tommy did, and I'd have watched him squirm and feel the pain.'

'Dead's dead,' Caine spat back. 'If you do it like we said, you'll see his face and he'll know he's going to die. That's an end to it. You don't want to feel the rope around your neck, do you?'

'The rope doesn't scare me,' Harry said. 'He's took Tommy. That's all that matters.'

'No,' Caine said. 'What matters is that Daunton dies, and no one comes after you. That's what Tommy would have wanted.'

Molly was drowsing now, so tired that even her repeated bouts of dry coughing did not disturb her. Belle had agreed with Jenny that they take it in turns that night sleeping, so that one of them would always be awake should Molly need anything. But despite her agreement Jenny kept pacing around the room, rushing back to the bedside at Molly's slightest cough. Belle sensed all too clearly that Jenny was ready to drop with nervous exhaustion.

'Bring your chair next to mine, Jenny, and rest,' she said. 'This pacing is only tiring you out.' Jenny must have been too tired to argue and did as she was told as though part of her welcomed the permission to rest. She brought the chair around the bed and sat as Belle took her hands in hers. 'Did the doctor say how Molly got the croup?'

'I didn't like to say, but when I told him she had lately been running around in the park, he told me that might be the cause.'

Belle was startled. 'How could good fresh air and exercise cause the croup?'

'He said that little girls are more delicate than boys, and should avoid too much sporting exercise.'

'I'm sorry,' Belle said, 'I'm not used to children and she was enjoying herself so much. You said how well she looked when she came back from the park. I'll never forgive myself if this is my fault.'

'I know you would do nothing to hurt Molly,' Jenny replied.

'How did you pay for the doctor and the medicines?' Belle asked. 'I will give you all that I have.'

'It took all that I had,' Jenny said, 'but the doctor would not come out until he was paid. I will have to borrow a little more . . . and please don't scold me, needs must where the devil drives. I will go to Caine's house as soon as I am able.'

'I'm sorry,' Belle said, 'but you could hardly cope with what they were demanding before. How will we manage if you borrow more?' One look at Jenny's face was enough to show Belle that she had neither the will nor the energy to argue. 'Put your head down on the bed for a while,' she said. 'I'll watch Molly.'

'Promise to wake me if I fall asleep,' Jenny said.

Within minutes Jenny was asleep, and Belle did not wake her. Instead she picked up her coat from the floor and draped it over Jenny's shoulders and then went to the other side of the bed to lie next to Molly. Though she dozed fitfully she never slept so deeply that Molly's slightest cough did not wake her. But then Molly began vomiting again, and Jenny woke, and thereafter they took it in turns to care for her.

When morning came, Molly took a drink of water though Belle could not tell if the little girl was awake, or asleep, or somewhere between. 'Shall I mix some more ipecac?' she asked.

'She should have some more,' Jenny said, taking hold of the girl's hand, 'yet she's so weak. I can't believe that there is any more infection left in her body to vomit out.'

'Go down to the kitchen now, Jenny,' Belle said, 'and have something to eat. I will care for Molly.

'I cannot leave her,' she replied.

'Then you will grow weak and unable to care for her properly. At least go for a walk. When you return you'll be more refreshed.'

'What of you?' Jenny asked.

'When you return I'll eat and wash and take some air. Now do as I say and leave Molly to me for a while. We'll leave off the medicine for a while.'

Belle took Molly in her arms. She felt so small and vulnerable and Belle felt powerless to help her. She found herself yearning for her father's strength, so practical and calm when times were bad. He had been trained by his father as a carpenter, and when he could not find acting work, he took up the trade again to put food on the table. He might have done better as a carpenter than an actor, she thought, smiling to herself.

She pictured him standing over her when she was Molly's age, shaking his clothing; felt for a moment the sawdust and wood-shavings falling like dry, fragrant snow onto her head. She swept her hair back with her free hand and listened as if to hear her mother pretending to scold him, listening to the laughter in her words. They had both understood how much he loved the stage and how he hated every moment he was parted from it, yet he never complained; took whatever life threw at him with a broad back.

Belle had been bathing Molly's forehead for only a few seconds when Jenny returned. 'I found this pushed under the front door,' she said, passing the note to Belle and taking Molly from her arms. 'It has your name on it.'

Belle recognised the handwriting immediately. She broke the seal and read the letter. 'Go and eat now, Jenny,' she said, refolding the note. 'I have to go out later.'

When James came down to the drawing room that morning his mind was still haunted. He had slept badly, and each succeeding nightmare had been filled with death, and fruitless flights of escape ending inevitably in capture. The house was still, but he knew Mrs Hawker would have been busy about her work for some time by now. He felt scared, as though his dreams had crept into the day, yet he was clearer in his thinking now, strengthened by an understanding of what needed to be done. There were others to think about now.

James listened when the kitchen door slammed and prepared himself as he heard the familiar sound of crockery rattling on a tray as Mrs Hawker made her way up the bottom stairs. She must not see his feelings. He waited as she stopped in the hallway, put the tray on the hall table and then knocked before opening the door of the study. She gave him a note and then returned to the hallway for the tray. As he opened it, Frank Harcourt's visiting card fell onto his lap. 'When did the message arrive?'

'About an hour ago,' Mrs Hawker said. 'The messenger said no reply was expected, so I left you sleeping.'

He read the note. "Have booked a table for lunch. Will call for you at eleven. Regards, Frank."

Mrs Hawker placed the tray with a plate of bacon, eggs, toast and a pot of tea on the table beside his armchair. Then she threw the curtains wide. 'Mrs Hawker,' James said, rubbing the life back into his face, 'I've been thinking a great deal and you have to trust the conclusions I have reached. You must do what I ask, just for this one time and without question. I want you to pack a bag immediately and go this morning to stay at Richard's house, overnight.' He paused for a moment, watching her reaction, but resumed before she had a chance to speak. 'We may be going back to Ireland for a visit, though I am not yet decided when. In the meantime you must not return to this house until I have said so.'

'I'd love to go back, but what's amiss? Why must I go to Master Richard's house?' she asked.

'For once you must obey me in this. Now do as I say and before you pack, please send John Doyle in to see me.' He knew his tone was brusque and saw the hurt and confusion in her face.

'Very well, but I'm not happy with this and I might as well tell you,' she said.

No sooner had Mrs Hawker gone than John Doyle appeared at the door. 'Did you want me?'

'I wanted to thank you and to give you this,' James said, passing John the handful of coins that he had gathered together from around the house.

'Is this my first wages?'

'No, I regret that after all I will not be able to offer you a job. In fact it would be better if you were to set off immediately for Bristol and the ship you were seeking. The money is to thank you. I only wish I could have given you more, but I hope it will help you on your way.'

'Is this on account of what happened the other night?'

'The man died,' James snapped back. 'They will be after us, and they know who I am.' He scribbled a note on one of his calling cards and handed it to him. 'I realise that I have little right to do so, but I have two favours to ask of you before you go.'

'Ask them,' John said.

'Take this card to Dr Richard Wetherby at number ten, down the street and bring him back here. Then when I tell you, escort him and Mrs Hawker and Horatio back to his home. After that you are free to do as you please, but get away from here as quickly as you can.' James looked at John. There was no trace of fear in John's eyes and he wondered if the man was capable of that emotion. 'It's best you leave here. I am certain that they do not know who you are, or what you look like. It was dark and your cap was pulled across your face. Go now while you can.'

'What about you?'

'I have been advised to go to my brother in Ireland, but have decided against it. I will not run. If they want revenge then I must take my punishment, but no one else must suffer for what I have done. It's better to take a beating and let the thing be over.'

'Are you sure a beating will satisfy them?' John asked.

'No, I wish I was. But you must go now,' James replied.

When John had gone, James went in search of Mrs Hawker, who as he suspected was busy cleaning the kitchen before departing. Against her wishes he made her leave the room as it was and sent her again to pack her bag. She picked up the footman's uniform that lay over the back of a kitchen chair and left, muttering under her breath.

John brought Richard to the study. James tried to keep his anxiety from his face. He smiled and then turned to John. 'Make ready to leave as quickly as you can.'

'I've packed already though Mrs Hawker was trying to stuff more into my bag when I last saw it,' John replied. 'I'll go and keep her busy until we're ready to go.'

James waited until John had closed the door behind him and then turned to Richard. 'I must ask for your understanding and patience,' he said. 'I have no time for explanations now, but I beg that you accommodate Mrs Hawker and Horatio this evening and make arrangements for her to travel to Ireland as soon as possible.'

'I will do as you ask,' Richard said, 'but some explanation, please?'

'Very well, I stabbed a man two days ago,' James said, 'and he has died of his wounds.'

'My God!' Richard exclaimed. 'How did it happen?'

'A gang set on me somewhere in Avon Street. I do not know where exactly. I managed to get away but I stabbed one of them in my escape.'

'He was one of Nat Caine's men, was he not?'

The question took James by surprise. 'How did you know?'

'Everyone in Avon Street knows Caine's name. I work sometimes with a doctor down there. Well, he calls himself a doctor, but I doubt he holds any medical qualification. He calls on me to patch up his mistakes. I saw him yesterday. He told me he had been called to one of Caine's men, but the man had died.'

'Do you think he has told the police?'

'I very much doubt it. He was in fear for his own life for failing to save the man. He told me he was leaving Bath and asked if I would call on one or two of those he was treating.' Richard rubbed his forehead, still lined with concern and disbelief. 'I never thought for a moment the man was killed by anyone outside Avon Street, let alone by you, James. What were you doing there?'

'Enough! Please no more questions,' James replied. 'Please take care of Mrs Hawker. I will call on you again when there is more time and I will answer all your questions.'

'One last question and then I will go and do as you ask,' Richard said. 'Who is that man you sent to fetch me?'

'An American by the name of John Doyle, he is the one who saved me. I had intended taking him on as a manservant, though now I have asked him to leave.'

'How did you know he was not involved in the attack himself?' Richard asked.

James ignored the question. 'He will carry Mrs Hawker's luggage to your house and then he will be gone. Thank you for your help, but the sooner everyone has left, the better I will feel.'

James called to John and Mrs Hawker as he looked out from the study window. There were one or two passers-by, but no one lingered and no one seemed to be paying the house undue attention. James led Richard out of the study and opened the front door and bid them goodbye as they made their way down South Parade towards Richard's house.

As he closed the front door he felt the trembling in his legs again and grabbed for the edge of the hall table to steady himself. He willed himself to look at his reflection in the mirror above the table, but his eyes remained fixed on the floor below. Then slowly he straightened, letting go of the table, and stared at his reflection. His face was red and sweating, but gradually the trembling dissipated and he felt his mind stilling. He was ready now, he told himself.

It was almost an hour after Mrs Hawker and John Doyle had left that James heard the loud knocking at the front door. He had by then shaved and changed, and was wearing his overcoat, ready to depart. He noticed that John Doyle had not returned for his bag and he thought at first that it might be him, but it was Frank Harcourt, punctual as always. James held the door firmly at an angle and pushed the bag with his foot, out of Frank's field of vision.

'What, no servant to answer the door?' Frank asked, smiling, attempting to peer over James' shoulder to the empty hallway beyond. 'Times must be hard when a man has to answer his own front door.' James held the door more firmly, barring entry. The deep, sonorous ticking of the long-case clock seemed to fill the space behind him as though its sound, echoing through the hall and stairwell, was betraying the emptiness of the house.

'What became of you the other night?' Frank asked. 'I turned around and you were gone. I searched everywhere for you.'

'I was set upon by a gang of footpads.' Part of him wanted to say more, to tell him all that had happened, to ask for his help, or at least for his advice. Yet something held him back. Let time tell, he thought.

'My God! You were not harmed were you?' Frank said.

'No, I escaped, with the help of a friend.'

'Who was he, this friend?'

'I do not know his name, but he went on his way straight afterwards, with a suitable reward in his pocket.' The unease was still there, deep within him. He did not know why the lie came so effortlessly to his lips, almost without thinking. But the lie remained and when he looked at Frank he wondered if he knew.

'But I thought you had lost everything at cards?' Frank said.

'You underestimate my resourcefulness. Let's be on our way. Where are we to eat?'

'I have booked a table at the Bath and County Club, but first I have to meet someone for a few minutes at a house in Queen Square.'

'I really do not understand why you have come all this way to collect me when you live practically on the doorstep of the County Club,' James retorted. 'Why did you not simply send a message for me to meet you there?'

'Because I enjoy your company, James. There is no call for us to hurry and my meeting will need but a few minutes at most. You shall wait for me outside the doors of the club, and we shall enter together.'

As they emerged from the doorway James noticed a man leaning against the railings on the other side of the street, looking towards the house. The man looked in their direction before setting off ahead of them. James watched him as he hurried away and wondered if it was in his imagination that he seemed to keep looking back towards them. He pointed him out to Frank, but he dismissed his concerns, and the man had soon disappeared from view.

Despite Frank's assertion that he enjoyed his company he spoke very little, yet James was glad not to be alone. If there was to be an attack, Frank had always proved resourceful as an ally. As they reached the corner of Queen Square, Frank stopped to blow his nose. 'You cut across to the gardens now, James,' he said. 'The house I am visiting is a little further along the road. I will see you in front of the County Club, wait for me there.'

James crossed the road over to the gardens which lay at the heart of the square. As he closed the ornate, black, iron gate behind him, he looked up to see which house Frank was visiting, but he was nowhere to be seen. The County Club was on the opposite side of the square, a matter of two minutes walk, but James held back. He walked only as far as the obelisk at the centre of the gardens and stopped, still curious to see which house Frank would emerge from. For a moment he thought he had caught a glimpse of John Doyle on the opposite corner, then he decided that his imagination was playing tricks again.

James had been standing by the stone monument for almost five minutes, scanning the row of houses facing him, when he heard the voice some distance behind him, calling his name. As he turned, he was aware only of the sudden wave of intense pain which engulfed his body. He could not differentiate the sound of the shot from the shockwaves in his brain, and by the time that his body hit the ground, he could no longer hear, or see, or feel anything.

Chapter 16

As John returned from escorting Mrs Hawker to the doctor's house, he had seen James walking down the street with the tall stranger, the one who had been with him that night at the card game. His instincts had taken over and he followed them all the way to Queen Square. It was instinct too that had driven him to conceal himself in a doorway in Wood Street, just off the square. Then, as he watched, James and his companion parted company.

James had walked on. It seemed unlikely that he had seen his companion hurriedly retracing his steps away from the square, yet he seemed to be waiting for someone. When John looked out again from his hiding place, James was staring in his direction so he pulled back into the doorway.

The sound of the shot had followed soon after and put all else from his mind as its thunder echoed around the buildings of Queen Square. When he emerged from his hiding place John could see James' body lying inert in the centre of the gardens. He sprinted across the road and towards the obelisk, vaulting the railings.

By the time he reached the centre of the gardens, a young woman was already kneeling, holding James' head in her lap, pressing the hem of her skirt against the growing circle of blood soaking through the shoulder of his coat.

'Is he dead?' John shouted.

The woman looked up, her auburn hair falling across her face. 'I'm not sure,' she said. 'I don't think he's breathing, and his face is cold.'

'I'll get a cab and take him home,' John said. 'Stay with him.' By now a crowd was building and he knew they had to be quickly away from there.

'I don't intend to leave him until I know how he is,' she said.

John ran to the road and quickly secured a closed four-seat brougham cab and told the driver to bring it to the gate at the bottom end of the park. Running back, he struggled to pick James up and raise his body over his shoulder. Once done, he was relatively easy to carry the short distance to the cab.

'I want to come with you. I need to know how he is,' the woman said, following John.

John turned, 'I don't know you. For all I know it was you who shot him.'

The woman pushed past him. 'We can argue here, while a larger crowd gathers, and we wait for the peelers to arrive, or we can get away now. I did not shoot him, and I'm sure if I were to show any violence to him in the future, you would be more than capable of subduing me.'

She mounted the carriage and held out her arms to help convey James' body to the seat, resting his head again in her lap. She took off her scarf and held it underneath his coat against the wound in his shoulder.

'What's wrong with him?' the cab driver called.

'Nothing,' John replied. 'Take us to South Parade.'

'There seemed to be a lot of interest in your friend, for nothing,' the cab driver called.

'He was drunk if you must know,' John shouted. 'He shot at a pigeon and then fell over and banged his head on the ground.'

'They're a bloody nuisance.' the cabman said, 'I don't know as why folk feed they vermin. I don't blame him, but I expects you want to be away from here. I dare say there'll be a little extra in it for me if we get away fast?'

'Go now. You'll be paid well,' John said.

The cabby whipped up the horse in reply and the cab sped through the city. As they passed the Institute Building, John called out, 'Take us into South Parade, then take the first turning and stop around the corner.' The cabbie did as he was told. As soon as they stopped, John leapt down and paid him with a generous amount in excess of the fare, aware for a moment that he had used most of the money James had given him that morning. 'Wait here,' John said, before running around the corner and up to the door of Dr Richard Wetherby's house and surgery. The maid answered the door. 'Is your master in?'

'He is,' she replied. 'But he doesn't see anyone without an appointment.' He could read the disapproval in her face as she looked him up and down.

'Fetch him now and then be about your business,' he said. As he had hoped, his expression and tone were enough to send the maid scuttling off up the stairs. She returned in a matter of moments with Richard Wetherby. He greeted John, but John said nothing, staring at the maid hovering in the background.

'That will be all thank you, Dorothy,' Richard said, smiling at the young girl.

She curtseyed and went down the stairs towards the kitchen. 'It would be best if we were unwatched,' John whispered. 'James is badly injured.'

Richard called downstairs to the maid. 'You may take the afternoon off, Dorothy, and cook also, but don't come upstairs again. Don't worry about tea, we will fend for ourselves, but either go out, or remain downstairs until this evening. We are not to be disturbed.'

'Thank you, sir,' she called back. 'I'm sure cook will enjoy a trip to the shops, or a walk, sir.'

Richard closed the door to the lower staircase and turned to John. 'How bad is he?'

'I think he's still breathing, but he's in a bad way.'

'Do you need help to carry him round?'

'No, we must attract as little attention as possible. Prepare what you need to treat a gun shot injury and make sure the curtains are closed.'

John went outside and checked the road again. The pavement outside James' house was deserted and the house as far as he could tell was unwatched. He walked slowly to the corner of the street, looking behind him with every couple of paces. It was all taking too long, minutes that he knew James could not afford, but it had to be done properly, there were lives at stake and not only James' life. He waited just long enough at the corner to see the maid and cook emerge from the basement stairwell of the doctor's house and then he ran to the cab.

James was muttering incoherently. When John tried to take hold of him he lashed out with his fists for a moment before passing out. John battled to pull him over his shoulder, with the woman's help. As he struggled back to the doctor's house under the weight of James' now lifeless body, he heard the woman behind him, calling to the driver, 'Drive on now. Forget you have seen us.'

John carried James into the house and moments later heard the woman slam the door behind them.

'Put him on the table,' Richard said, as he opened the surgery door, 'and help me to get his coat and jacket off.' The two of them wrestled with James' clothes as he began again to thrash out with arms and legs. John noticed that Richard's clean white apron was already bloodied.

'You should not be here,' Richard said, glancing at the woman as he cut away James' shirt. 'Who are you?'

'My name is Belle Bennett and I am acquainted with this gentleman. I would like to help and I have no intention of leaving until I know how he is.'

'His pulse is racing, yet his breathing is very shallow. He has lost a great deal of blood from the look of your dress and scarf,' Richard said.

John looked up and noticed for the first time that the front of Belle's dress was covered with blood. She seemed to pay it little attention, but instead busied herself collecting up the bloodied tatters of James' shirt. She put them in a bucket under the table, along with her scarf. 'Will he live?' she asked. She looked, John thought, as though her distress was genuine.

'I don't know,' Richard said, but his expression made his anxiety all too clear. 'Who shot him?'

'I didn't see who did it,' John replied. He looked at Richard and saw the suspicion in his eyes. 'Why would I have brought him to you if I had shot him?'

'A man on horseback fired from the road outside the Queen Square gardens, some distance away from him,' Belle interrupted. 'He called out his name and then shot him with a pistol.'

'Let us hope then that the lead ball is not too deep,' Richard said. 'His coat and jacket were thick and should have protected him a little, and the distance of the shot is in his favour.'

John turned to Belle. 'It seems somewhat of a coincidence that you were nearby at the time?'

She bristled, her annoyance clear. 'Why should I not be there, my home is only a short distance away.'

John thought she seemed uneasy and wondered if she was telling the truth. 'Did you recognise the one who shot him?' he asked.

'He had a scarf pulled up across his mouth and I couldn't see who it was.'

'Now is not the time for investigation,' Richard interrupted, obviously uneasy. 'I need your help Mr . . . ?'

'My name is John.'

'Hold him down for me, John. Will you hold the tray of instruments for me, Miss Bennett? Take a clean towel from the pile and mop the blood from the wound whenever it begins to build. John, you keep hold of him.'

John watched, mesmerised, as Richard took a long-bladed scalpel and opened the wound a fraction. At first James fought to get free and then he passed out. Richard began probing inside the wound with a finger. John could tell from his face when he had finally located the lead ball. Once found, it took Richard only seconds to extract it with a pair of tweezers, but then the blood began flowing freer. James came to for a moment and moaned incoherently for a few seconds, the pain contorting his face, before he passed out again.

John had seen plenty of blood at sea. There were times when he had even been called on to assist the ship's surgeon. Richard's voice dragged him back from his memories. 'John, while he is unconscious turn up the gas mantles and light that lamp and bring it over here. I need more light. You need to hold the lamp with its beam pointing into the wound, but be careful, it is very hot.' John held the lamp, staring into the bloody mess of the wound.

'The main blood vessels seem to be intact and the blood loss is slowing,' Richard said. 'I think his clavicle, his shoulder bone, is fractured but it has prevented a deeper wound and the open tissue appears relatively clean.' He looked up, obviously annoyed. 'Hold the lamp nearer, John. I cannot see what I am doing. And hold it steady.'

John tried to steady the lamp, transfixed, as he watched Richard picking out the fragments of clothing with long surgical tweezers from the gash that his knife had left, before cleaning inside the wound.

'Thread that needle with silk, Miss Bennett, while I clean the surface of my cut,' Richard said. 'Then hold the two edges of the wound together.'

He sewed the skin closed with the curved needle that looked like a fishing hook and then took hold of James' wrist. 'His heart is still racing; we should let him rest now. I'll check there is no one in the kitchen. If it is safe I will fetch you and you can wash yourselves while I watch James.'

John looked up as Richard opened the surgery door. Outside he saw one of the most beautiful women he had ever seen. 'Charlotte!' he heard Richard exclaim, as he tried to close the door behind him. 'You should not go in.' The woman pushed past him and entered the surgery before slamming the door closed behind her.

'What has happened to James and who is that woman?' she asked. 'Why is a woman like that in my house?'

John looked at Belle. If the insult had hurt her, she did not let it show in her expression.

'She is an acquaintance of James,' Richard replied. 'She helped me to treat his wound. James is badly injured.'

'I ask again, what happened to him? Was it this woman?'

'He has been shot, but not as far as I know by Miss Bennett.'

'Why must he bring his lowlife into our home?' Charlotte said. 'He mixes in God knows what sort of circles and now he has brought these people into our lives.' She broke off, sobbing, and wiped her eyes with a delicate white lace handkerchief. 'I'm sorry,' she said, talking to her husband as though they were alone in the room. 'I know James is your friend and I do care what happens to him, but I don't care for the life he leads and I worry that he will draw you in. What if your daughter had seen this? If he has put her in danger I will not forgive him. That woman is part of a world she should know nothing about.'

John watched Belle again and still she showed no emotion, as though she were oblivious to Charlotte's insults.

'Miss Bennett is very distressed and her frock is covered with blood, would you have me send her away?' Richard asked.

'What if one of your clients should see her here, with her face made up, and those clothes?' Charlotte said. 'What sort of doctor would they think you were? She is dressed for the evening in the middle of the day!'

'I'm sorry; I have been a little too pre-occupied with keeping James alive to pay much attention to Miss Bennett's appearance,' Richard said.

His answer seemed only to inflame Charlotte's anger more. 'I doubt you saw much beyond her neckline.'

'That is enough,' Belle said. 'I understand I am not your invited guest, but I will not be spoken of in this way. I do not need to apologise to you for how I choose to dress, or deport myself, and nor will I.'

'I will not continue this conversation while James' life is in danger, Charlotte,' Richard said. 'And you have been unfair to Miss Bennett.'

'I'm sorry,' Charlotte sobbed. She dabbed at the corners of her eyes with her lace handkerchief. 'You must of course tend to James, but it is disturbing to see my home transformed to a battlefield-hospital.' She gestured to Belle. 'Come with me, Miss Bennett.'

John watched as Charlotte stepped into the hallway. He noticed her looking into the mirror for a moment, dabbing away the last of her tears before tidying her perfectly coiffured blonde hair. Belle joined her and the two women stood still for long staring seconds, as though each was rehearsing what to say, each wondering who should speak first. Then Charlotte smiled, as if suddenly conscious that everyone was watching her. She reached out as though to take Belle's hand and shuddered. 'You have blood on your hands!' Turning away, she beckoned for Belle to follow. 'Come with me, my dear, and we'll put your dress to soak and you shall choose one of mine to wear home. You can wash as well, and tidy your hair.'

'But I should stay,' Belle said.

'You will be more help to James when you are changed and refreshed. Richard will call us if his condition changes. Come to my room and pick a dress. You can return it at your convenience and I will have it cleaned.' Charlotte smiled seemingly at no one in particular and closed the surgery door behind her.

John stood by the window and pulled the curtains slightly back, to look out on the street. The road was growing dark and the street-lights had not yet been lit, but he was still able to see the two men under the tree opposite James' house. He closed the curtain with a jerk of his right hand. 'I feared as much,' he said. 'They've tracked us down.'

James mumbled something incoherently as if he had half-heard what was being said, but it was obvious that he was still unconscious. Richard put his hand to James' forehead. 'Are they watching this house?'

'No,' John said. 'I don't think so. There's no reason as yet for them to connect us with you, but they might start putting two and two together unless I can persuade them otherwise. Is there a way of getting into his house without them seeing me?'

'Go into the garden at the back,' Richard said. 'There are several walls between the two houses, but it is dark enough for you not to be noticed if you stay to the bottoms of the gardens. I'll get James' back door key from Mrs Hawker upstairs, and let her know what has happened.'

When Richard returned John took the key from him and Richard led him into the back garden. The walls were easy climbing and John got to the back door of James' house with little difficulty, and, as far as he could tell, unseen. He went downstairs and lit the gas mantle in the kitchen on a low flame; checked the door was securely locked and pulled across the heavy bolt. Then he went to the drawing room, pulling the curtains closed in the darkness, but making sure he left a sufficient gap for any light to show through before he lit two candles.

In James' room, as he was drawing the curtains, one of the men outside looked up and pointed. John drew back behind the wall. When he looked again, he could see only one man outside. He lit the longest candles he could find and began searching the room. There was a holdall in the cupboard and he packed it with as many clothes as he could fit in, grabbing from the linen press the first things that came to hand until the bag was bulging. He recovered his own canvas bag from the hallway, which seemed heavier than he recalled it being. Then he locked the garden door behind him.

The journey back to the doctor's house took much longer as he had to manoeuvre the baggage without making a noise and alerting the owners of the gardens he was passing through. Staying as far as possible to the bottoms of the gardens, he moved stealthily, but methodically, and breathed a sigh of relief as he entered through the back door of Richard's house. There was no apparent sign of his trespass having raised the alarm in any of the households he had crossed.

Richard greeted him with a weak smile when he returned. 'What have you done?'

John threw the bags down in the hall. 'Suffice it to say that our watchers will believe that James is in his own house, at least for a while . . . How is he?'

'He is recovering. His fever has gone, his breathing is strengthening, there is very little bleeding from the wound and the colour is returning to his face.'

'That's good news.' John said. 'I heard your wife earlier, saying she did not want your daughter put at risk and she is right to be concerned. There's no immediate danger now they believe him to be at home, and either dead or dying. There's no reason for them to be searching elsewhere, but we only have a little time to consider our next move.'

'What will you do?'

'We can't stay here, it is too dangerous,' John said, all too aware of the truth of his words.

'Where will you go?'

'That I don't know . . . Do you have any ideas? You know the city better than me.'

'Give me time to think,' Richard answered.

Chapter 17

Frank Harcourt knocked on the front door of the house in Hucklebridge's Court and found himself admitted by a scowling Jeb. He could see the hatred in the man's normally lifeless eyes. Frank knew Jeb despised him for his manners and intelligence, resented his closeness to Caine. He tried to retain a smile, but found Jeb's expression eating away at his confidence and as he felt his own smile receding he watched the sneer grow stronger on Jeb's face. He knew he had made a devoted enemy and not one to be taken lightly.

Frank said nothing as he made his way down to the kitchen, knowing that he would need to watch his back in future. Perhaps it was time, he thought, to try and make life a little less secure for Jeb.

He could sense the jocularity in the room below, immediately he entered. Harry Wood walked over to him and shook his hand. Frank smiled, 'I told Daunton to wait outside the County Club. Did you get a good shot at him?'

'He didn't budge from the centre of the gardens,' Harry replied. 'But I guessed he wasn't going to move and I had a clear shot, so I dropped him where he stood. Is he dead?'

'I don't know,' Frank replied. 'I delivered him as we agreed, but I had no intention of getting caught up in his murder.' Harry's smile disappeared. He was looking at him as if to say – you haven't the guts to do the job properly.

'You should have stayed, that's what we agreed,' Caine said. 'It's just like last time. You only did half the job.'

'What do you mean by that?' Frank asked. 'I played my part last time.'

'You were supposed to deliver Daunton incapable and alone,' Caine spat, 'and you told us nothing about him carrying a sword stick.'

'He was drugged,' Frank said, 'I doctored his drink half-way through the game and I knew nothing of the swordstick, or the other man.'

'Well what's done is done,' Caine replied. 'We got him this time and we'll soon know where he is, if he's still alive. I've sent two men to watch his house and another two around the hospitals.'

'He has a friend,' Frank said. 'A doctor called Wetherby who lives down the road in number ten. I should have told you. He may have been taken there.'

'Fool!' Caine snapped. 'We should have been watching his place.'

'Did anyone recognise you, Harry?' Frank asked, hoping to deflect them.

'Not as far as I know,' he replied, smiling again. 'I had a gentleman's coat and I was sat on a gentleman's horse. I pulled up my scarf before I shot and I was away before anyone took notice of me. Then I set the horse free by Crescent fields and changed into the clothes I stashed away this morning. As far as the world knows, Daunton was shot by a gentleman, and there are plenty of gentlemen that Daunton owes money to, from what you said. There's nothing to bring the peelers to this house.'

'Let's hope he's dead,' Caine said. 'And perhaps it'll stop the priest from meddling when he realises we'll make others suffer for his interference.'

'I've been true to my word, Nat,' Frank said. 'I've delivered him to you twice now.'

'Fair enough,' Caine said. 'But if he'd taken his beating like a man the first time we wouldn't have been put to this. He killed Tommy, and no one kills one of my lads without paying for it. Tommy was a good lad.'

Frank smiled. This was how it should be. Caine was in his debt again. Things had worked out for the best, he thought. Daunton had been useful in the beginning. He'd introduced him to the right people, given him a place in society. His naivety had been helpful then, but he had become tedious, and besides, without his money he was becoming a liability. Everyone knew he was in debt and no one wants to know a debtor.

'The way's clear now then, Nat,' Frank said, 'once we've stifled the priest we can get on with business.'

'He can't start his lending now,' Caine said. 'He's no money and he'll soon understand that it was him that caused Daunton's death. We'll hear nothing more from him.'

'Now there are no distractions,' Frank said, 'perhaps it's time for one or two selective burglaries. I've some houses in mind that would pay well.'

'We'll be ready whenever you tip us the nod,' Caine replied.

Frank took Caine to one side as the rest of the men devoted themselves to more serious drinking. 'I thought you might have dispensed with Jeb by now. He's a dangerous man, and not to be trusted.'

'It suits me to have him about for now,' Caine said. 'I want him earning his way back into my favour and I don't want the path too clear for Harry, especially now he's got the taste of blood. Jeb worries people and that suits me fine, as long as I know that I worry him.'

'You know I'm with you, Nat.' Frank smiled. 'They both know I'd never help anyone but you.'

'Don't get any ideas,' Caine said. 'I run this gang. I value your help and I pay you well for it, but don't think you're more important than you are. The lads would never follow you, if you was to try and take over. If I left it to Jeb you'd already be dead meat. He reckons you know too much. If you ever cross me . . . ' Caine paused as the door flew open. 'What news, Lem?' he asked.

'It started to get dark and we saw candles being lit in Daunton's house and the curtains being drawn,' Lem said. 'He's in there all right, but whether he's dead or not, I don't know.'

'Did anyone else go in?' Frank asked.

'Not as I saw,' the man replied.

'Well get back up there,' Caine said, 'and watch for anyone going in or leaving. And keep an eye on the doctor's down the road . . . '

'He's called Wetherby,' Frank interrupted, 'Doctor Richard Wetherby.'

Lem nodded in reply and reached for the bottle on the table. 'Put it down,' Caine said, 'and do as you're told when I tell you.' He laughed as Lem slammed the bottle back on the table and ran from the room.

'While we're about it, Nat,' Frank said, 'there's someone else who's begun meddling in my affairs and would benefit from a small lesson in doing what they are told.'

'Who's that?' Caine asked.

James was still lying on the table in the surgery when he came to. He looked around the room. Richard and John were talking, but approached as soon as they saw him stir. Richard tried to restrain him at first but he would not be restrained. He could not rest now.

They helped him down from the table and supported him as he made his way to the couch under the window. He knew they were speaking to him, but he could get no sense at first from their words, as though they were talking in a foreign language. His mind would not focus as he struggled to piece together where he was and how he had got there. Richard held out a spoon of something, he was saying it was for the pain.

'This will help,' he said, 'but it will make you drowsy.'

James swallowed it. 'This feels unreal.' His awareness was slowly increasing as he wiped the sweat from his forehead with his left hand. 'I keep telling myself to wake up. No one's ever wished me dead afore.' The pain was intense. It picked at his consciousness, heightening his awareness.

'Rest now,' Richard said, 'you are still not recovered.'

'Why are you still here, John?' James asked, his mind full of questions. 'Do you know who shot me?'

'I'm sorry, Mr Daunton,' John replied, 'I didn't see whoever it was, but we believe it was someone on horseback, waiting for you in the square.'

'You were there, John. I saw you. Why did you follow me?'

'I was concerned,' John said, 'and I was proved right.'

'There's no end to this,' James said. 'It must be Caine behind it. When they find out that I'm still alive they'll try again to kill me, and eventually they'll succeed, unless I do something.' His only hope, he knew, was to escape to Ireland, but something held him back. Deep within, the thought kept revisiting him; he wanted to hit back, to fight them. 'I don't know how to fight the likes of these,' he mumbled to himself, as though still dreaming.

'Don't think you're alone,' John replied. 'You're not. You have friends. I'm willing to help.' He seemed sincere, James thought, but how could he trust him? Why was he so keen to risk his life for a comparative stranger?

'Whatever I do, I have to get away from here,' James said, his mind slowly recovering, his thoughts becoming clearer. 'Charlotte and Charity must not be put at risk by my presence. I need somewhere to recover and to think.'

'Where can you go?' Richard asked. 'You're not well enough to travel far. Would Sean Brennan take you in?'

'I'm sure he would, but Caine's men already watch him and I could not allow him to put his own life at risk,' James said. In his mind, James went through a list of names; realising that the number he could call friends had diminished in recent years, just as the number of acquaintances had grown. When he thought of those who would help and whom he could trust, the list seemed pathetically short. He could not stay with Richard or Sean without endangering them, and as for hotels he knew he would soon be tracked down. 'There is of course Frank,' he said. Even as he spoke, the words felt hollow, triggered a deep unease within him. Thoughts flitted through his mind that he preferred to dismiss.

'Are you mad?' Richard exclaimed. 'Please do not seek Harcourt's help. He is not to be trusted. When will you come to your senses and heed my warnings?'

Richard's response was to be expected, James thought, and yet this time the sincerity of the outburst struck home, though he still could not believe that Frank would betray him; they were too close to even consider it. 'Well then, there is Charlie Maggs,' James said.

'The man is a thief and for all you know is linked with this Caine gang. Go to Ireland, James, as soon as you are well enough. You'll be safe there . . . or go to the Constabulary.'

'I cannot go to the Constabulary and if I go to Ireland I will only add to my brother's problems,' James said. 'No, I will not run, and you misjudge Charlie. He is at heart a good man, and besides a former thief might make a good ally now. He knows all there is to know about hiding, and he owes me money. He may well be willing to give me refuge in payment of his debt; he was certainly grateful when I defended him. No one would think of looking for me at his house.'

'But surely the Constabulary keep a watch on Mr Maggs, and may he not be in league with this Caine?'

'Charlie was one of the best safecrackers and burglars in England, but he hasn't committed a crime in years. He was innocent when I defended him, though all the evidence pointed to his guilt. He could not burgle a house at his age, with rheumatics of the joints and the gout. Charlie has a house in The Paragon and I am certain that he would hide me, and know how to keep me hidden. I think he can be trusted.'

'I would be wary of Mr Maggs,' Richard said, 'and yet I would rather you trusted him than Frank Harcourt.'

'I understand your concern, but I need somewhere now.' James hesitated. His enemies seemed to be all around him, and in truth he no longer knew whom it was safe to trust. A wounded animal would look for somewhere safe to hide and recover, but where was there? It would have to be Charlie, but would he take him in, and for how long could he trust him? James beckoned Richard closer, and whispered to him, 'Can I ask yet another favour?'

'Ask it,' Richard replied, his voice also hushed.

'I cannot pay you now, but I promise that I will.'

'I don't look for repayment,' Richard said. 'If I can help in any way, you know that I will.'

'Find me a house and rent it for a month or so; somewhere on the edge of the city, a place where the coming and going of strangers will not be noticed. I may not be able to prevail on Charlie's hospitality for too long and besides, we may need a bolthole.'

Richard looked relieved, but could make no reply as their conversation was interrupted when Charlotte and her companion came into the surgery. 'I am glad to see you recovering, Mr Daunton,' the woman said.

James recognised her immediately. She was even more beautiful than he remembered, and he was lost for words in his growing confusion.

'I think it right and proper that you dress more appropriately now that you are recovering,' Charlotte said, passing a shirt to her husband.

Richard and John helped him to put on the shirt. 'I have only a vague impression of your presence Miss . . . ?' James said, struggling against the pain to remember her name.

'Miss Belle Bennett,' she replied, 'I was in Queen Square when you were shot.'

'You were the actress in The Garrick's Head,' he said, wondering with some disquiet at the coincidence of her being there at the time of his attack.

'You remember me,' Belle said. 'Yes I was and still am an actress.'

'I thought you were well known to James?' Charlotte said.

'Merely an acquaintance,' Belle replied.

James wanted to speak but instead only winced from the sudden pain as he tried to move. He looked down at the bandages around his wound. There was a dark patch of red, but the bleeding seemed to be slowing and the fabric was relatively dry to his touch. The pain was still intense whenever he moved, though.

'Wear this,' Richard said. He had fashioned a sling to support his arm and take its weight away from his wounded shoulder. He helped him with the shirt and James threaded his arm painfully into the bandage and sighed as he felt it take the weight.

James looked again at Belle, 'I'm sorry we meet again under such circumstances.'

'It was Miss Bennett who stopped you from bleeding to death,' Richard interrupted. 'She is an excellent physician.'

'I did what anyone would have done,' Belle replied.

'I think not Miss Bennett,' James replied.

'I simply helped you, as you helped me in The Garrick's Head that night.'

James had thought her striking that night; her pride and anger accentuating her beauty. Yet now, as a more compassionate and gentler side of her nature softened her every feature, she seemed even more beautiful. He was conscious that he was staring at her, and she at him. 'Frank apologised to me afterwards,' he said. 'Though perhaps it would have been better if he had apologised to you?' Her expression changed and he read plainly the obvious distaste on her face at the mention of Frank's name.

James looked away, his glance taking in the others. 'I have put you all in danger,' he said. 'For that I apologise . . . I must get away from here quickly and put you at no further risk. Charlotte can you get some of the blood off my jacket and coat, I will trust in the darkness to hide the worst of their appearance. And perhaps I can borrow one of your hats, Richard, to make me less recognisable.'

His mind flooded with questions. He daren't ask if anyone had seen Frank Harcourt. He was too terrified of the answer, too alarmed at the reaction that the mention of his name seemed to provoke. He needed to trust people now more than he had ever needed in the past, and yet he was unsure of whom he could trust. John Doyle had helped him, but why had he followed him? But he had already told John his plan. Perhaps that had been a mistake, none the less it would be better to take him with them now, than set him loose. He found himself wondering at the coincidence of Belle being in the square at the very time he was shot, but tried to dismiss the thought.

Richard smiled at him. He could at least trust Richard, but he had a family and no matter how willing he might be, they could never be put at risk. John Doyle interrupted his thoughts. 'Let's not be hasty, Mr Daunton. There is still a man in the street outside and he is watching your house, he will be on the lookout for anything out of place. You won't get far in your current condition and he is bound to notice anyone staggering down the street with injuries. We need to think this through.'

'If I were to leave with James, I mean Mr Daunton,' Belle said, 'it would be less obvious. We would simply look like a couple leaving a social event, where the man has had a little too much to drink. Arm in arm, I could help him walk.' She looked around the room as though waiting to hear some better idea, but none came. 'I also have a favour to ask of you, doctor,' she said, drawing Richard to one side. James struggled to hear what was said, but to no avail.

After a while Richard broke off his conversation with Belle. 'I will have a cab waiting around the corner,' he said to James, 'and you could go to Maggs' house, but what about Mrs Hawker? She will not remain here without you.'

'I will go and explain to Mrs Hawker,' John said.

'No,' James replied. 'I will speak to her if you fetch her to me and then we will all leave together as though we were leaving a party.'

'I thought you wanted Mrs Hawker to go to Ireland?' Richard said.

'I know her too well to even hope that she will go without me now,' James said. 'Perhaps you can get the luggage to us later, Richard, and take care of Horatio for a while? He's a good dog.'

James took some time to explain to Mrs Hawker all that had happened that day and to set her mind at rest concerning his condition. Eventually, they all assembled in the hallway. Belle and Mrs Hawker wore bonnets which covered much of their faces and James wore one of Richard's larger hats. Richard was already wearing his coat and James was surprised to see him carrying his doctor's bag. 'Are you coming with us, Richard?' he asked.

'No; I have another patient,' Richard said.

As they prepared to leave, Belle said, 'Five people cannot leave the house inconspicuously. The more we try not to be noticed, the more we will draw attention to ourselves, so we should do the opposite. You must all be actors. We have been to a party which we have enjoyed, so we must laugh and chatter and make noise as though we hadn't a care in the world.'

When they emerged onto the street, James felt his own lack of acting skills was mirrored on the part of the other three, but was more than compensated for by Belle Bennett's, who laughed and giggled as though she hadn't a care in the world. Eventually they all found their voices and in a mist of noise they went down the street and around the corner to the waiting cab. James put his good arm around Belle's shoulder and Belle's arm was around his waist, and they walked down the street like lovers. For a moment at least, he was conscious only of the nearness of Belle.

'Don't look, but I'm sure there were two men watching your house,' John said. There is only one now.'

The cab was waiting around the corner in Duke Street as Richard had arranged. James boarded quickly, helped on by John and Mrs Hawker, and after the strained laughter of their exit from Richard's house the group fell into an exhausted silence. The weight of pretence had been lifted and they could find nothing to put in its place. James looked out of the coach window as Belle and Richard walked down the street together.

Chapter 18

Molly had been steadily growing weaker when Belle had left the house that afternoon and she feared the worst on her return. As she led Richard into the room in Bridewell Lane, Belle saw at once the surprise and poorly concealed anger on Jenny's face. But as soon as Jenny saw Richard she composed herself, her hand flying almost instinctively to her hair which had gone without brushing for days. 'I thought you had deserted us,' she said, obviously straining against her pain and anger. 'You said you would only be gone for a little while.'

'I'm sorry I was so long, Jenny,' Belle said. 'How is Molly?'

'Worse,' Jenny said. 'At least I think she's worse. I don't know what to think. I'm at my wits' end.'

Belle ran to Molly on the far side of the bed and Richard followed. 'This gentleman is Dr Richard Wetherby,' Belle said. 'He has come to see Molly and he is a very fine physician.'

'I'm sure what Belle says is true,' Jenny said, curtseying to Richard, 'but I have no money to pay you, not now, doctor.'

Richard smiled in response. 'You look so tired, Jenny,' he said. 'You must take some rest if you are to help Molly.' His words had not made her any less concerned with Molly, and yet Belle thought she saw a certain lightness in her expression that she had not seen for days. 'Miss Bennett has helped a friend of mine and if I can help her friend in return, then no payment will be necessary,' Richard said.

He took off his coat and handed it to Jenny. She took it awkwardly, as though she had never taken a man's coat before. Richard sat on the bed and stroked Molly's forehead before looking around the room. 'It is very hot and airless in here,' he said.

'The other doctor told me to keep her warm,' Jenny said.

'I take it you have given Molly a hot bath and Ipecac and I see that she has been blistered on the neck?' he said.

'Yes we've done all that we were told,' Jenny replied. 'Do you have any other medicines?'

'I regret not,' Richard said. 'Molly is very weak and fevered. But let us not give up hope. The human body has great powers of recovery. There is a speculation that I have heard in connection with the croup. Some believe that cool night air can reduce the inflammation and release the phlegm. Wrap Molly warmly in a blanket and sit with her by the window.' He took Jenny's hand. 'Do not lose faith,' he said. 'I will do all that I am able. Sometimes loving care achieves more than medicine.'

'Should we give her more Ipecac?' Belle asked.

'I think she is too weak and wasted to vomit more,' Richard replied. 'The Ipecac should have done its work by now. We must rely on the body healing itself. Give her no more medicine but plenty of water to drink, with a little sugar or honey dissolved in it.'

Belle followed Richard's glance towards Jenny who was beginning to cry. She rushed to her side and put an arm around her shoulders. 'Come now, Jenny,' she said, steering her towards the window.

Richard opened the window slightly and placed a chair beside it, motioning for Jenny to sit. 'I have opened it at the bottom a little, so that she breathes in the cool air, but not so wide that her body is cold. Keep it so and bathe her face with a cool moist flannel from time to time.' Belle picked Molly up, wrapping a blanket around her, before placing her in Jenny's arms.

Richard made his way to the door. 'Call on me if she shows signs of growing weaker,' he said.

Belle helped him with his coat, and whispered, 'Will she live?'

He turned to her, his voice also quiet, 'Only time will tell. She is very weak, we can only trust that her spirit is stronger, but give her no more medicine. If she were my daughter I would give her no more. I will visit again tomorrow.'

'You know we cannot pay you?' Belle said.

'I want no payment. Now look after Molly and be sure that Jenny takes some rest.'

Belle saw Richard out. When she returned Jenny was still crying. 'Don't worry,' Belle said, 'Molly will recover.' She wished that she believed it.

The journey to The Paragon was relatively short. James pointed out the house to the others as soon as they drew near, and called to the driver, 'Only a little further now, cabbie!' He waited until they had gone some distance past the house and then shouted loudly, 'Stop here!' Having stepped down from the carriage, as if by some unspoken agreement they waited, like statues, as it turned and made its way back down the road. Then when it was out of sight, they began walking back to Charlie Maggs' house.

It was some time before James' knocking was answered. They listened to the sounds of two locks being turned, and then two heavy bolts being drawn back, before the front door of the house in The Paragon was opened. Charlie Maggs peered out into the dull evening light over a pair of spectacles perched precariously on the end of a nose which looked as though it had been squashed in an accident with a door, or some less accidental encounter with a fist. Holding the door open just wide enough for him to see his visitors, and just narrow enough for them to be unable to see but the slightest view of his hallway, it was obvious that he recognised no one.

It was also apparent from his manner that Charlie Maggs was not accustomed to receiving callers at this, or any other time of the evening. His leathery face was as creased and lined as an old pair of gloves and each change of expression set the lines in animated movement. James stepped forward into the light and said 'Good evening, Mr Maggs.' Before he could utter another word Charlie had thrown the door wide.

'I recognise that voice,' Charlie said as he extended his right hand. 'James Daunton, the solicitor.' In answer James opened his coat with his left hand, revealing his arm in a sling. Charlie withdrew his hand with a look of sympathy. He was a great bear of a man, and his powerful if rotund frame was exaggerated by the shortness of his legs. All the lines in his face re-arranged themselves and where before they had made his frown forbidding, they now amplified the warmth of his smile.

'May we come in?' James asked. 'As you can see, I'm not in the best of health.'

'Of course, of course, and bring your friends with thee.' Charlie led them towards the wide staircase leading to the first floor but Mrs Hawker broke off from the party and instead turned the handle of a door on the ground floor. 'I take it this leads to the lower stairs for the kitchen?' she said as a bemused Charlie Maggs looked on.

'Aye it does that, but what would you be a wanting with the kitchen.'

'No offence intended,' Mrs Hawker replied, 'but seeing as how you answers your own door and noticing that your hallway hasn't seen a duster or a broom for a while, I'm guessing that there's no Mrs Maggs, and no one else who does for you. So I'm going to make us all a nice pot of tea whilst you entertain your guests.'

'You're right in everything you say, missus, but you're a guest. Would you be so kind as to tell me your name?'

'My name is Mrs Hawker,' she replied, 'and I go by no other. But I make very good tea, so you get on with your entertaining and I'll get on with the tea making.'

'She's a spirited woman, that one,' Charlie said, when she was out of sight and earshot. 'I've seen her afore at your house, but we've never been introduced. What would her first name be?'

'My mother called her Angela,' James said, as they climbed the stairs, 'but it's been a long time since anyone has addressed her as anything other than Mrs Hawker.'

'I wouldn't presume to call her anything else, without her agreeing to it,' Charlie said. 'But I can see why she's called after the angels,' he added. 'Now come into the drawing room and rest.'

James, like John, stopped and looked in awe around a drawing room crammed with furniture and ornaments and paintings and clocks, to an extent that little vacant space remained on floors or walls. Pieces of bronze and pottery and glass fought for space on tables and plinths, mantelpiece and hearth. With so much in the room it was almost an achievement for so few items to actually match each other, James reflected. Furniture when it was of the same period was in different styles, or un-matched woods, or from different countries of origin. Pseudo-Egyptian figurines stood on ornamental Greek plinths, whilst on the mantlepiece china dogs snapped at the heels of brass sphinxes and bronze elephants and everything was covered by a film of dust, broken only by occasional smudges of soot from the fireplace.

'What do you think of my abode?' Charlie asked.

'It's very tasteful, and yet manly,' James said. John nodded in agreement and looked around as though in admiration.

When Mrs Hawker kicked the drawing room door, Charlie Maggs duly opened it. She bustled in, brushing past Charlie with a tea tray. 'I understand we may be staying here a while, so I bolted the front door.'

James shuffled nervously. 'That depends on Mr Maggs' hospitality and I have not asked him yet.' He hesitated, looking deep into Charlie's eyes, suddenly aware of how little he knew the man. 'Before I ask you, Charlie, you need to know what has brought us here and the dangers involved and Mrs Hawker deserves a fuller explanation of what has happened.'

James told them how he had lost all his money in a night's gambling, how he had been set upon when he was drunk and acknowledged John Doyle's bravery in coming to his assistance. He explained how he had stabbed one of his attackers and that the man had later died. His eyes were busy throughout, studying the reactions of Mrs Hawker and Charlie. With Mrs Hawker all he saw was sadness and pain. Charlie seemed almost suspicious, with a growing unease in his expression. His eyes seemed somehow more callous and scheming; perhaps he was already preparing his excuses, or worse still, rehearsing his betrayal. Were the eyes really windows on the soul, or only mirrors, reflecting his insecurity, James wondered.

When he spoke about Nathaniel Caine and the Cockroad gang he saw Charlie's expression change again, as though all the warmth had drained from his body. His eyes became sharper and James noticed his still-powerful hands clenching and unclenching, pulling the skin white-tight on his knuckles. He paused, waiting for the man to say something, but Charlie put no words to whatever he was thinking. As James told him what he had pieced together of the attempt on his life and built towards asking for sanctuary, Charlie interrupted.

'I need no asking,' he said. 'You are welcome to stay and this gentleman too, if he wishes,' he said, nodding towards John Doyle, 'and of course Mrs Hawker.'

'I don't know if John should stay,' James said, his mind in a quandary, welcoming a potential ally, but fearing another betrayer, and one who already knew their hiding place. 'It might be better if you were to leave Bath, John,' he said. 'Though you are of course free to do as you please.'

'I have no need to be elsewhere,' John said, 'and I will not run.'

Charlie looked John up and down as though he were trying to read his character. 'Brave words, if I might say so.' John gave him a cold look, but said nothing.

'Then we will stay,' James said, trying to ease the tension between the two men. Telling the story had brought the pieces together in James' mind. The losses at cards, the attack by the Cockroad gang, and the attempt on his life, were all, he finally admitted to himself, linked with Frank Harcourt. It was Frank who had won at cards, he who had guided him drunk into Avon Street and then left him. Frank had arranged to meet him by the County Club and it was there that the assassin had been waiting. Yet still he found it difficult to accept that he had been betrayed by someone who he had thought of as a close friend. He buried his face in his good hand and the weariness swept over him, washing away what little strength remained in his body.

Mrs Hawker rose to her feet and said; 'I think we've had enough talking for one night. Perhaps you can give the gentlemen a brandy, Mr Maggs.'

'There's whisky in the decanter there, gentlemen, and you can help yourself, but I generally abstains from the stuff.'

Then you can show me the rooms and where you keep your spare bedding,' Mrs Hawker said, 'and I'll make up the beds for everyone. You'll pardon me for saying so, but your home lacks a woman's touch, Mr Maggs, and that's what I intend to give it tomorrow. But for now we all need our rest.'

'I'll give you a hand, Missus,' Charlie said.

Chapter 19

When she woke, Belle had little comprehension of when she had drifted into sleep, nor for how long she had slept. She sat up in bed and looked immediately towards Jenny and Molly. 'You should have woken me,' she said.

'You were exhausted,' Jenny replied.

'And so must you be . . . How is Molly?'

'Little changed, but at least she seems no worse.'

'Let me take her for a while,' Belle said, getting off the bed and walking towards them.

'I would be grateful.' Jenny kissed Molly's forehead before passing her to Belle. She rubbed the arm in which she had been holding her daughter and then her shoulder. 'I think I have caught a chill in my bones from the open window.'

'Do you think the cool night air has helped Molly?'

'I can't say. But she has slept well. Whenever she's started coughing I've woken her and given her a few sips of water.'

'I think she is breathing a little easier,' Belle lied. The girl sounded much the same, but Jenny smiled in response. 'Lay down for a while, and I will tell you all that happened today.' It was obvious that Jenny needed little persuasion and as Belle began the story, she collapsed onto the bed. Belle spoke quietly, describing first her walk to Queen Square in immense and slow detail. When she looked up she could see that it had had the desired effect, Jenny was already asleep. Belle stopped talking and waited awhile for a response, but none came.

She bent close to Molly then and continued her story, whispering softly. 'I helped a gentleman today, who came to my rescue once, when no one else would help. He is more handsome than I remembered him.'

She paused, smiling for a moment at Molly, checking that she was still fast asleep. 'He was very much afraid today, although he tried not to show it, and in his fear he was still concerned for the others around him.' She smiled to herself, gently caressing Molly's cheek and forehead. 'I know he would care very much if he were to see you like this, Molly. I would like to help him, as I would like to help you, but yet I feel powerless to help either of you.'

Molly coughed, but did not stir. Belle looked over towards Jenny, but she was still sleeping soundly. She manoeuvred Molly gently into the crook of the opposite arm and kissed her forehead.

James woke early that morning, uncertain whether it was the pain or some bad dream that had awoken him. As he struggled to dress himself, the reality of his situation swept through his mind in ice-cold waves. Piece by piece, he understood his circumstances in all their starkness. He had ended the life of another human being. He now had powerful, ruthless enemies who wished him dead, and who had already tried twice to kill him. They had driven him from his home, from his friends, from his possessions, from his livelihood, and from his place in society. He was now running for his life, unsure of where was safe, whom he could trust, and who might betray him. His debtors too were pursuing him but he had no money, and without his employment, he had no means of making any. The estates in Ireland were failing, and his brother was desperate for help which he was unable to provide.

With each thought, everything he had once accepted as real seemed to crumble around him. There were only two courses of action open to him now. He could give in, or he could fight, but to give in, to despair, he knew would achieve nothing. It was far better now to take responsibility for his life and fight, no matter how uneven the odds; besides there were others to think of: Mrs Hawker, and his brother, and Sean, and now John and Charlie. In truth there could be only one choice. He would try to make amends for what he had done, and for letting down those that were closest to him, and he would somehow take on Nathaniel Caine, no matter how the odds were stacked against him. After all, he had nothing more now to lose, except his life.

When he went out into the hallway, the house in The Paragon was full of the smell of polish and black lead. Mrs Hawker had been true to her word. It was obvious to James that she had risen early that morning and begun her assault on the drawing room. He found himself suddenly smiling when he saw the three places set at the long, polished oak table in the dining room.

A few minutes later Mrs Hawker came in with John and Charlie, both carrying trays. 'You'll have to make do with ham, eggs and toast. There's very little in the kitchen, and I will need some money if I am to go shopping,' she said.

'I have no money,' James replied. 'And it might be better if you stayed in the house. You might be recognised and followed and we cannot afford to be discovered so soon.'

'But none of these scoundrels knows me.'

'Don't you go worrying yourself, Mrs Hawker,' Charlie said, as he put his tray in the centre of the table. 'You tell me what you need, and I'll go and fetch it all after breakfast.'

'I'll make some sense of that kitchen then,' Mrs Hawker replied. 'I'll need some more cleaning things as well as food.' She turned to James as she was leaving. 'Just ask John if you need some help cutting your food up.'

James smiled, and waited for her to close the door before turning to the others. 'I've been thinking, gentlemen, and I'll be frank with you. My first inclination was to get far away from Bath, but I know that Caine will not let this rest. If he cannot kill me, he will hurt those close to me. If I run, I would always be afraid that some day he would track me down. I am determined not to let my fear rule me, and since I will not run, and I cannot hide for ever, so I must fight him. I may not be able to defeat Caine, but perhaps I can make his life troublesome for a while and hopefully distract him from more vulnerable targets.'

'That's the second fine speech I've heard in as many days,' Charlie interrupted. 'But I know Nathaniel Caine and the Cockroad gang. He will do things to achieve his ends as even I wouldn't contemplate doing, let alone a fine gentleman like yourself.'

James grinned. 'Don't defeat me before I begin. I know all too well that Caine is strong, and that I am not, but I would rather not accept defeat quite so readily, as though I stand no chance.'

'You said I, not we,' Charlie replied. 'Why do you assume as you're on your own? You've helped me in the past, so it seems only fair that I try to help you now. Why do you think I took you in?'

'You've helped enough already, Charlie,' James replied.

'I'll be the judge of that, young 'un,' Charlie barked back.

James was lost for words and the room fell silent for a moment. Then John cleared his throat noisily, as though needing to fill the silence, and spoke. 'We do have something in our favour. While we remain hidden, we have power. We know who our enemy is, and where they are. They've no idea, for the moment, where we are, or even whether you're still alive, James. They'll find it difficult fighting an enemy they can't see.'

'I thought you would be leaving,' James said. 'I will not see either of you risking yourselves for me.'

John laughed. 'What and miss a good fight? No, I'm staying. I think you probably need a couple of friends right now. I know my way about, and Charlie obviously has skills that can be put to use. If we lack strength in numbers, that's how it is. There are always those who'll fight for the right price.'

'You don't know how Caine fights,' Charlie said, 'and those who sell their fists will like as not change sides for a better price. You can't trust them.'

'I know more than you think,' John replied. 'And I know very well that we are outnumbered.'

James' mind spun in a frenzy as if a new sense of purpose had begun to displace the fear that he had been battling. 'I still have some friends and perhaps connections that I can call upon. There may be a way we can address the imbalance of power, but we would need money and I have none.'

'I don't have very much,' Charlie replied, stroking his chin. 'But as you know, I has certain skills that can make us money. Seeing you with your arm bound up puts me in mind of something we can try, but it'll need some preparing.'

'I know that I cannot take the Cockroad gang on alone, James said. 'But I cannot ask you to risk your lives.' He hesitated, trying to work out the implications, and when he spoke again it was almost as though he was talking to himself. 'We would need to trust each other, as we have never trusted before'

'You are not alone. There are three of us,' Charlie said. Then he smiled, 'And we have Mrs Hawker on our side. Just rest now and build your strength for what's coming.'

James looked at the other two. At least for a while he was not alone. How long they would help him, how far he could trust them, he could not tell, but it did not seem to matter now. They had already given him more than he had any right to expect, and he felt stronger for it. Patience and strategy were what mattered.

'If we confronted him now,' James said, 'Caine would wipe us out without giving it a thought, but if we dictate the terms of engagement, we can give him a contest. We have to play the long game; take no risks. We can't meet him head on; so we light a fire over here to distract him, and while he tends to that, we go around the other way and catch him unawares. We'll play him like a game of chess, Charlie, always planning at least one move ahead.'

Chapter 20

Belle watched as Jenny stirred and then woke. It was mid-morning. Jenny immediately rose from the bed and rushed over to the window where Belle was sitting with Molly in her arms. 'How is she now?' she asked.

Belle stood slowly, aware of an ache deep in her back, and offered Molly to her mother. Jenny took her into her arms but Molly showed no signs of stirring. 'Her face feels so cold,' Jenny said, the anxiety all too plain in her voice as she sat by the still-open window.

Belle leant forward and felt Molly's forehead. 'She does feel cold,' she said, 'but it's only to be expected and there's no perspiration.' She moved her hand slowly under Molly's nose, fearing the worst for a moment and then smiled. 'Her breathing is stronger,' she said. This time it was not a lie. Molly's breathing *was* stronger.

Belle stretched, shrugging off her exhaustion, and looked around the room. Jenny's faceless drawings, pinned about the wall, danced in and out of the corners of her gaze, as though they had come to life. Belle tried to focus weary eyes and looked down at the two of them sitting by the window, watching in delight as Molly opened her eyes and freed a hand from the blanket, then reached out and touched Jenny's nose with her fingers. 'Molly cold,' she said. 'Drink please.'

Jenny laughed and covered Molly's face with kisses. 'I'll fetch a drink now,' she said, standing and handing her back to Belle. The girl was still pale and her body felt weak, yet Belle could see there was a change in Molly. She hugged the little girl to her and spun around in celebration. 'Slowly now, Belle,' Jenny said, fussing around them with a broad grin on her face, 'you don't want to make her sick again.'

'I feel suddenly hungry,' Belle said.

'Shall I make us some breakfast?' Jenny asked.

'No, I'll do it, and I'll fetch a drink first for Molly,' Belle said, knowing that it was what Jenny had wanted her to say. 'You spend some time with Molly. She is still very weak.' Belle felt her own strength draining away. In the course of two days she had seen two people close to the point of death. Most of the night she had been preparing herself for Molly's passing, rehearsing how she would console Jenny, practising being strong for the two of them. But she knew she wasn't that strong, and now all she wanted to do was to cry with happiness and let the pain out.

In the kitchen she let her tears flow, great sobs wracking her body, but when she could cry no more she was conscious of a new strength. The happiness of the moment washed over her like a warm summer shower. She felt strong; stronger than any of those who might wish to crush her spirit.

'What do I do, now that I am a prisoner?' James asked. 'There's a limit to the time I can spend resting. How do I occupy my mind?'

Charlie looked up from across the room, his face confused. 'Should we have a game of chess?' he asked. 'I have newspapers, a copy of the Bible, somewhere, young'un, but no other books as I remember.'

'I have something in mind,' James said. 'I cannot just sit reading newspapers and playing chess. I have a favour to ask you, Charlie.'

'Ask it.'

'Do you think you can turn me into a housebreaker?'

Charlie laughed at first, and then his face grew serious. 'No,' he said, 'and why should you want to learn. You need to build your strength again.' He sat in silence, obdurate, signalling by his expression that the subject should not be raised again. Then he turned to James. 'Tell me about Mrs Hawker.'

James smiled. 'My mother and Mrs Hawker grew up near here; in the village of Midsomer Norton. Mrs Hawker was twelve years old when my mother's family took her on to be mother's maid. Mother was only a year younger.' He paused for a moment, ordering the memories in his mind. 'When she married, she took Mrs Hawker with her to the house in Ireland as her lady's maid. My mother was nineteen then, and ten years later she was dead. After that, Mrs Hawker took care of me. Years later, when my father died and my elder brother Michael inherited the estate, I came to Bath and Mrs Hawker came with me as my housekeeper.'

'How old was you when your mother died?' Charlie asked.

'Two,' James replied. 'My mother was so fond of Mrs Hawker that her dying wish was that I be placed in her care.'

'You must be very attached to Mrs Hawker then?'

'She is all I have of my mother, and the closest to a mother I have known for most of my life.'

James watched as the smile spread across Charlie's face. He found himself enjoying the old man's sudden look of contentment, but still the question nagged at him. 'Charlie,' he said. The old man looked at him. 'I really need to learn to think like Caine, and to have some of the skills he has, if I'm to survive. Please teach me.'

'Not that again,' Charlie replied. 'I had an apprentice once; only once. It were the son of a good friend and I took him on as a favour to his father.'

'Well why not train me?' James asked.

'Because it ended badly.'

'But this is different,' James said. 'If it ends badly, then it ends badly, but I need your help. I already owe you so much, I realise that, but you must know that I would never betray you.'

'I owe you as well, young 'un, and I recognise it. You defended me when the peelers had already decided I was guilty. You were the only one who trusted it weren't me, and you never looked down your nose at me.' His expression grew graver. 'Somebody set me up for that job knowing the peelers would like to see me do time for things I've done in the past. I think that were Caine.'

'I knew you weren't guilty,' James said.

Charlie smiled. 'I can teach you some of my skills if you're willing to learn. If you're fighting rough, I suppose you need some rough skills. Much as I appreciated your skills at the law, you won't get far arguing your legal precedents with Nathaniel Caine.' He laughed, appreciating his own joke. 'But don't expect too much, and don't blame me if it ends bad.' James smiled and nodded his agreement. 'Then come with me now,' Charlie said. 'But it will be hard work and I'll not treat you like a gentleman, but as an apprentice.'

'That's only right,' James said. 'You will be the teacher, and I the student.'

James followed as Charlie led him to a small bedroom on the top floor. The walls of the room were panelled; the room itself sparsely furnished; the floor had only a small rug and the bleached wood floorboards creaked beneath their weight. There was a child's bed, but no other evidence that a child had ever been in the room. Against one wall stood the only other pieces of furniture in the room, a stout pine table, scratched from heavy use, but scrubbed clean, and a single chair.

On one wall hung a heavy tapestry, which, in the absence of any other decoration and ornamentation, appeared out of place. Charlie Maggs bent down in front of the wall-hanging and began rolling it upwards. When it was fully folded, he secured the whole of the tapestry to the brass hooks from which it was suspended. Bending down, he removed a small floorboard and reached inside. A narrow panel swung open in the wall, revealing another small, dark, windowless room. Inside, all manner of tools were mounted on the wall and stacked on various shelves; sheets of metal and glass stood on the floor with rows of locks mounted on boards and three complete safes. Cobweb curtains lay draped over all that was within and dust lay thick on every surface.

'As you can see,' Charlie said, 'I took my profession very serious and this were where I polished my skills, where I taught my apprentice.' The pride was clear in his expression, as was his generosity of spirit. James knew he was giving him a gift, the most valuable possession he had to give; he was sharing the profession he held as highly as any degree from a university. 'I ain't used the room for some time now since I retired, but you'll find a broom and some rags in the corner and that'll be your first job as my apprentice. Clean everything and get to know the tools and what you might do with them. When I return you can tell me what you have learnt.'

'Don't expect too much of me,' James smiled.

'Nor will I,' Charlie said, 'but I see now that you were right to ask. The skills you might learn would be as good for getting you out of a place where you don't want to be as they are for getting you in some place where folk would prefer you weren't.'

'I'll see what I can do,' James said.

'Aye, and it'll come all the easier when you have the use of two arms,' Charlie replied. 'See that row of locks on the plank with a big number one chalked at the top, well that is the easiest. The picking tools are all in that belt hanging by the tool bag. See if you can open one lock before I get back; after you've cleaned up of course.'

Charlie left the outer bedroom, closing the door behind him. James heard the key turn in the lock and then he was alone with his thoughts. There was little space to move in the hidden room and James found each task doubly difficult with his right arm in the sling. Nevertheless, he removed the worst of the cobwebs with the broom and began sweeping, stopping occasionally to move the sheets of glass and metal. The resulting pile of dust he had no means of picking up, so he swept it into the bedroom and under the rug.

He moved the tools one by one, and took them to the bedroom table and began cleaning them with a rag. Each had been lovingly cleaned before they were put away and although they were now dusty there was no sign of rust on any of them. There were drills and drill bits, files and saws of different sizes, screwdrivers and chisels, a jemmy with sundry attachments, an adjustable wrench, a sheath knife, an oil can, a tin of gunpowder, a jack and various implements that James could only guess as to their purpose. He returned them all to the room, duly cleaned, before he placed the belt of lock-picking tools and the row of locks mounted on the plank marked number one on the table.

Unrolling the belt of tools, he found a number of keys. Some were ordinary keys that had been filed down and their edges softened; others he guessed were skeleton keys. There were several picks which resembled surgical instruments, their thin polished shafts holding hooks and probes of differing sizes and shapes. At the end of the roll was the thinnest pair of pliers that he had ever seen.

There were four locks mounted on the plank and he started on the first, which logic told him would be the easiest. He began with the filed keys which seemed to be the simplest to use, but got nowhere. Then he tried the skeleton keys, but still the lock prevailed. He used the picks and although gradually he began to form some idea of how they should be used he still could not open any lock. His systematic approach was gradually abandoned as he shifted between different methods to no avail. He cursed the uselessness of his right arm as the sweat built on his forehead and he began studying the tools and locks in earnest.

When Charlie returned, James was still bent over his work. Charlie looked at him with a slightly bemused grin as though he was surprised to find him still working. 'So how many locks did you manage to open then?' he asked.

'One,' James replied, 'the bedroom door that you locked before you left.'

'You've learnt a valuable lesson then, but let's see if you've learnt the most important lesson. How did you open the bedroom door?'

'There's a wide gap at the bottom of the door. I pushed a sheet of the newspaper that you left on the table, under the door, then pushed the key out until it fell on the newspaper. Then I pulled the newspaper, complete with key, back under the door and opened the lock.'

James waited for Charlie's congratulations but watched instead as he rocked with laughter. 'Every little guttersnipe knows that trick. So you learnt very little then? You should have used the outsiders.' Charlie retrieved a pair of thin pliers from the room. He opened the door and put the key back in the lock on the other side, then stepping inside, grabbed the bottom end of the key through the lock with the point of the pliers and turned it in the lock.'

Charlie must have seen his crestfallen look because he smiled. 'I'm only joking with you, young 'un. I expected to come home and find you asleep on the bed. I thought you might be too high and mighty to do the cleaning, and too used to having everything set on a plate before you to persevere with the locks. You'll make an apprentice, but you must work at it.'

'But why should I have used the outsiders instead of the paper?' James asked.

'Because the key might make a noise falling on the paper or drop awkward and bounce clear, leaving you on the wrong side of the door, and what if there was no gap under the door? The paper's a good enough trick if you have no outsiders, but no good to a professional.'

Sitting in the drawing room with Charlie, when his lessons were completed, James heard a knock on the front door and a little while later John appeared with Father Brennan. 'I brought him like you asked,' John said.

James looked at Charlie. His whole demeanour had changed. His face was red and his body stiff. He sat glowering at Sean as though they were old enemies. 'I've made you all welcome and you come and go as you please,' Charlie said. 'But I'll not have a Catholic priest in my house, sat at my table.' He almost spat the words and looked ready to assault Sean.

As Charlie was about to stand, James rose and stood directly in front of him. 'If you cannot accept Sean, then we will all leave,' he said, staring into Charlie's eyes. He could hear the man's breath, coming faster; almost feel the heat from his body.

'That won't be necessary, James,' Sean interrupted, 'I'll go now.'

'Then we will all go with you,' James said. Days of stored frustration gripped him now, ruling his emotions. 'Know this, Charlie, you claim to welcome anyone who is an enemy to Caine, yet you reject the only man that Caine fears.' The silence was a dark oppressive cloud between them, as James stared at Charlie.

'Stay and let the priest stay,' Charlie said after a long wait. He looked like a man who had just been bluffed into discarding a winning hand and resented losing.

James turned and looked him in the eyes. 'Only if you are sure?' he asked.

'I'm sure,' Charlie said. He was still frowning, but he held his hand out to Sean. The priest walked over and shook it. The brevity of the handshake was obvious, but James was relieved, knowing that in truth, at least for the moment, they had nowhere else to go.

'It's good to see you're still breathing, James,' Sean said, 'the talk was that you were dead and the Cockroad gang were claiming credit.'

'As you can see I am still alive,' James replied. 'But I need your help. I intend to take on Caine, but even with the assistance of Charlie and John I have little faith that we can defeat him.'

'So you're not going to Ireland?' Sean asked.

'No, I'll not run, nor add to my brother's problems.'

Sean looked towards John, 'You, I take it, are the man who is becoming the hero of Avon Street for flooring Nathaniel Caine. No one knows your name so they're inventing a past for you; they say you're a gypsy, and a bare-knuckle boxer.'

'I'm neither,' John said. 'It was a lucky blow; I took him by surprise.'

'What help can I give you?' Sean asked, turning to James.

'We need to recruit some assistance, some good Oirish lads who can use their brains as well as their brawn. We would pay them, as soon as we have money.'

'You are asking me to give my blessing to a war, that will have casualties,' Sean replied. 'I'm not sure I could do that. The Cockroad gang are hated in Avon Street and there are plenty who would fight them and who need money. But you would be asking men to risk their lives.'

'But you told me that you were worried that they might take to the streets in their hatred of Caine,' James said.

'That's true,' Sean said. 'But how would this be any better?'

'There would be a plan and discipline to our fight,' James replied. 'I have no wish to add further deaths to my conscience. We need to out-think Caine, but to do that we need to gather intelligence; discover their weaknesses. I cannot leave the house, Charlie is too well known in their circles, and John cannot do it alone.'

'There are men who would help and who would make good allies, but they would need paying well, particularly those with families,' Sean said.

'Four men would be enough for now,' Charlie interrupted. 'We need probably three around Avon Street and one in Hanham.'

'Why Hanham?' James asked.

'The gang's home is still in Cockroad, in Kingswood forest. That village is so tight around the gang that no stranger could hope to pass unnoticed. There's not a house that's not in some way dependent on the gang, but there's an ale house in Hanham, The Blue Bowl, where they go. A stranger could get in there and that's the only way to find out what's happening.'

'I'll see what I can do,' Sean said, 'but what about money?'

'Leave that to me,' Charlie interrupted.

The moment Belle left the Theatre Royal that night she was aware of the man who was following her. She wasn't sure why she had particularly noticed him, or why she felt his presence so strongly. He had been standing in the alleyway by the side of the theatre. She could barely make out his shape, but he was smoking a pipe and she saw the red glow from the tobacco embers as the man drew on it. As she set off across Saw Close, she heard him tapping out his pipe. Then he began walking, and his footsteps echoed hers.

Her instinct was to move faster, but she fought it and instead walked more slowly, to hide the apprehension she felt growing within. As she slowed, so did the following footsteps. The man seemed to be taking his lead from her. She turned around. He was not far behind, but following him was a second man. She felt a little easier. The second man, from his top-hatted silhouette, was a gentleman. He was roughly as far behind the other man as she was in front of him, and as she moved on their footsteps merged. She quickened her pace and heard theirs growing quicker.

As Belle turned into the darkness of Bridewell Lane, she began running. The footfalls behind her increased their pace, but this time it was only one set of shoes that she heard on the cobbles. As she reached the boarded-up door of the derelict house at the top of the lane she noticed for a moment that the boards had been ripped away. Then, as she drew level with the opening, a man stepped out, barring her path. He smiled and she felt a momentary confusion; then he grabbed her arms and threw her into the building. She fell to the ground, feeling the rubble cutting through her coat, biting into her face and legs.

When she looked up, there were two of them in the doorway. She struggled to her feet. One of the men moved as if to let her past, but the other punched her in the face. She fell to the ground again, and the man began kicking at her body and legs. She pulled herself into a ball, feeling the blood trickling down her face, trying to protect her head. 'What are you doing?' she heard a voice say, as though in a dream, or a nightmare. 'You'll kill her. We was only meant to scare her.'

'Bugger off if you don't like it,' the other man responded.

The blows stopped for a moment and she looked up, through fingers clasped over her face. The other man had gone but her assailant was standing over her, untying the belt around his trousers. She summoned the last of her strength and let out a scream. The man froze and then turned to look behind him. She could see the outline of a tall man with a top hat.

'Leave her, you animal,' he said. She recognised the voice immediately. It was Frank Harcourt. Belle lay in the rubble watching, powerless, as her attacker turned away. Then he retied his belt and spat. 'You have her then,' he said, pushing past Harcourt.

'It wasn't meant to be like this,' Harcourt said, as he walked nearer, his shoes crunching in the rubble. She felt the scream building inside her again. 'But you have a loose tongue and my past is no one's business but mine.' Her fingers tightened around the stone she felt under her hand. 'I trust you enjoyed the entertainment I arranged for you in Queen Square? Perhaps now you will understand the consequences of crossing me. You know how far I am willing to go, so keep your mouth shut!'

Belle drew her arm back and launched the stone, watching it sail over his shoulder. Frank turned his back and walked away.

Chapter 21

When Nat Caine walked into the small room, he could already see the fear in Jeb's eyes; smell it in the sweat of the man. 'You've let me down again, Jeb?' Caine said. He felt a momentary thrill of anticipation as he watched Jeb trying to avoid his stare, his eyes like a trapped rat's, searching nervously for an escape.

'I just do what you tell me, Nat,' Jeb said.

'But that's not true, is it?' Caine grinned. 'You don't do what I tell you. I asked you to do a favour for Harcourt. I told you to give the actress a scaring. I didn't say to beat her half to death, or to violate her.'

'Harcourt could have stopped me sooner, if he'd wanted,' Jeb sneered. 'He did nothing, just stood there watching and waiting till she screamed. I was going to have her before he got the chance. What's it matter what I did? She's only some whore of an actress.' Jeb paused as though for a moment he had half-sensed some way out. Caine let him hang onto the thought, just for a few seconds. 'What's she know about him anyway?' Jeb asked, looking less worried. 'What's he so scared of?'

'That don't matter to you,' Caine said. 'You can't control yourself and you put us all at risk.' Caine walked up to him, watching as Jeb backed away, his eyes darting from one corner of the room to the next, looking for a path to the door, but Caine cut the angles with every step.

'I've been thinking all morning what to do with you,' Caine said, taking the knife from his belt. He watched as Jeb backed further into a corner, one hand hovering towards his boot. Caine put his knife on the table. 'I've decided not to kill you so you can put your knife there, next to mine, and take your beating like a man. This is just between us. There's no one else to watch. I'm giving you the chance you've been looking for.' He stared into Jeb's eyes, knowing he was going to make his move. 'Put your knife on the table, Jeb!'

Jeb reached down and pulled the knife from his boot with two fingers as though he was going to comply, but Caine knew him too well. Jeb took one step forward, swivelled the knife in his hand and lunged at him.

Caine was ready and turned to one side, dodging the blade, grabbing Jeb's knife arm, bringing his knee up at the same time into the man's stomach. Jeb doubled over and Caine grabbed a hank of his lank, greasy hair with his left hand, pulling his head forward, bringing his knee up again to meet Jeb's face. Jeb stumbled forwards and Caine twisted his arm back, forcing him to loose the knife, kicking it spiralling into the corner of the room.

'You're a stupid fool,' Caine said. 'It was between you and Harry as to who I'd hand the gang over to, but it ain't anymore.' Caine kicked Jeb's prone body over and over again, feeling the tightness in his stomach loosening with each kick. 'I ought to kill you,' he said. 'As from now, you just sit in here, out of my sight and watch the door. As for pay, you take what I give you.' He leant over, grabbing Jeb's shirt, pulling his head free of the ground. 'Do you understand?'

Jeb said nothing, his face bloodied and swollen. 'I asked if you understand?' Jeb nodded his head and Caine punched him one last time. As he turned away, Jeb slumped, unconscious, to the ground, a trickle of blood seeping from his nose, into the dust of the floor.

Caine felt suddenly calm. It was done for now and, who knows, Jeb might still be useful for the right job. He could use him to do for the priest when the time was right, and then let the Irish have him, but he would have to watch him even more closely now.

Each breath felt to Belle like she was being stabbed. She opened her eyes and saw Jenny sitting at the bedside. 'How did I get here?' she asked, struggling to sit up in the bed.

'Don't you remember?' Jenny asked.

Gradually the pictures formed in her mind, but the pieces were jumbled and confused; memories mixing with imaginings. The last thing she remembered was screaming and throwing the stone. How long she had lain there after that, she could only guess. She recalled the effort of climbing the stairs and then opening the door of the room, with little memory of how she got there, and remembered the relief of its sanctuary as she collapsed on the bed and let the darkness take her. It was the same sense of warmth now, easing her mind gradually from the pain of remembering. She smiled at Jenny and then began crying. At first she felt as though she could stop at will, but the sobbing gradually took control until her whole body shook with emotion.

Jenny helped her to sit, placing the pillow in the small of her back. 'I'm not as strong as you think,' Belle blurted out.

'What happened?' Jenny asked. 'Were you robbed?'

'No, just beaten, but I don't want to talk about it, not yet.'

'What you've been through would make anyone cry,' Jenny whispered to her.

'It's not just what happened last night,' Belle sobbed, 'I feel as though I've been so close to tears, so many times, these last few months. I'm at my wits' end. If it wasn't for you and Molly ... ' She could get out no more words and was about to give way to tears when she saw Molly sitting at the table, her face full of concern and confusion.

'You're stronger than you credit,' Jenny said. 'You got yourself here and collapsed on the bed and then there was no waking you. I undressed you and saw the cuts and bruises. It took me an hour picking out the pieces of grit and small stones from your cuts, and bathing your wounds, and you didn't stir once.'

Molly ran from the table and stood at the bedside, uncertain what to do. Then she ran to the dressing table and fetched Belle's brush and began brushing her hair. Belle wiped her tears in the sheet and smiled.

'Pass me the mirror, Molly,' Belle said. She gently probed the abrasions and bruises on her face while examining her reflection. One eye was swollen and bluish, but Jenny had done a good job on the various other cuts and scrapes. Good face powder would cover the worst, but not for a couple of days, not until the wounds had begun healing.

'Jenny you must take a note round for me to the theatre,' Belle said. 'I cannot work like this.'

'I'll get you the writing things, I'm sure they will understand. They know you never miss work.'

Belle did not share Jenny's confidence. This was just the opportunity Cauldfield had been waiting for; the chance to have her dismissed from the company.

The household in The Paragon had slipped into a reasonably comfortable life over the last few days, James thought. Almost as though the odd assemblage had recently arrived in the city and were setting up home together. Mrs Hawker flitted as nimbly as her age and weight would allow around the various rooms, dusting every one of Charlie's excessive number of ornaments, pictures and pieces of furniture.

Charlie appeared the most animated and the happiest with the new household arrangements. The smell of Mrs Hawker's cooking seemed a constant source of delight to him and his already large frame had begun further expansion around the stomach area within days of her taking up residence. He no longer ate out, as had apparently been his habit, but had instead taken to eating his meals in the kitchen with Mrs Hawker, despite her feeble protests. The closer Charlie grew to her, the easier James found it to trust him.

James had grown used to eating with John Doyle in the dining room and already felt their relationship was changing from master and servant to a more equitable friendship. John was easy company and at times, when he dropped his guard, he was also very entertaining. He seemed to have seen most of the world, at least once, in his travels. But try as he might, the more James sought to get to know John, the less he seemed to learn. There were still too many secrets between them to feel any sort of understanding of what lay behind the façade.

Each time John left the house, James found himself wondering if he would return; worrying that when he did return, he might bring others with him. All he was sure of was that the longer John spent cooped up in the house, the more restless he was becoming. He wondered how he could ever be sure that he would not betray him when he knew so little about him. Someone would have to take the letters, but should it be John? Yet he could not keep him confined. He would have to trust him. He needed to trust him.

When he heard the rap on the door that day, James ran to the drawing room window and pulled the curtain open, just far enough to look out. He could not see who was at the door, but a few minutes later Charlie appeared at the drawing room door with Richard Wetherby.

'It's good to see you, Richard,' James said. 'Are Charlotte and Charity well?'

'They're both well, James,' Richard said.

'Have you introduced yourself, Charlie?' James asked.

'I have,' Charlie smiled.

'I've come to re-dress your wound,' Richard said, returning Charlie's smile. His expression seemed contrived and short-lasting and James could tell that Richard was uneasy. 'You'd better sit down,' Richard resumed. 'I'm afraid I bear bad news.'

'What is it?' James asked.

'I have been treating the daughter of Miss Bennett's friend who was very poorly, but is now recovering well.'

'But that is good news,' James interrupted.

'When I called to ascertain Molly's progress this morning I found Miss Bennett beaten and bruised from an attack yesterday.'

The shock of the news and the strength of his feelings took James by surprise. He wanted to go to her, to do something. He made to rise from the chair, but Richard put a hand on his shoulder. 'Is she badly hurt?' he asked.

'I have examined and treated her, and she is well enough now,' Richard said. 'But she is still bruised and will not be at her work for a few days.'

'I should go to her,' James said.

'You should do no such thing,' Charlie said, discarding the newspaper which until that moment had seemed to absorb his full attention. 'Who is the woman and can she be trusted?'

'She is an actress at the Theatre Royal,' Richard said.

'And I would trust her with my life,' James exclaimed. The words took even him by surprise, and yet he recognised their truth at the instant that he voiced them.

Charlie's expression changed from concern to interest, his face distracted and thoughtful. 'So she might be relied upon?'

'Relied upon for what?' James asked.

'Nothing,' Charlie replied, 'an idea occurred to me, that's all.' He picked up the newspaper again and disappeared behind it as though he had no further interest in the conversation.

'Is there anything I can do to help her?' James asked. 'How did it happen?'

'She would not say how it happened,' Richard said. 'At first she even tried to tell me she had had a fall. When I pressed her, she admitted she had been attacked, but refused to be drawn further.'

'How is she now?' James asked.

'She is obviously still shaken, but she has recovered well and by sheer fortune has no permanent injuries,' Richard replied. 'I called at the theatre and told them she will not be fit for work for at least a week. I thought a doctor's visit might help safeguard her employment.' He hesitated. 'But I fear there is more.'

'Oh God, what more has happened?' James said.

'I visited your house last night; the kitchen door was off its hinges. The house is in a terrible state, the remainder of your clothes are gone and the French clock and candlesticks too. In fact everything of value has been taken.'

'What about the portrait of my mother?' James asked.

'That's safe and unmarked. I got a carpenter in this morning to rehang the kitchen door. I've paid three months rent rather than let the landlord see what happened. He seemed satisfied, though he had been expecting you to pay for the year.' Richard paused. 'Dorothy, our housemaid, came with me to help tidy the house and when she saw the damage she burst into tears. She said someone had approached her on the previous day and given her money to tell if I had treated your wounds.'

'What did she tell them?' James asked.

'She says she told them nothing,' Richard replied. 'She said that she hadn't seen you for a while and didn't know that you were injured.'

'Do you trust her?' James asked.

'She told me that they had bribed her, but that she liked you and would not betray you or my family,' Richard said. 'She could have said nothing if she had chosen to do so and I would have been none the wiser. I would like to believe her.'

'Are you sure no one followed you here?' Charlie asked, from behind his newspaper.

'There was no one watching James' house or mine when I left and no one followed me,' Richard said. 'I don't believe we are in any danger but Charlotte is going away with Charity this evening to stay with her parents for a few days, and they have taken the dog with them. Charity has become very fond of Patch. But enough talk, I must examine your wound.'

James took advantage of his offer to help in removing the sling and his shirt. 'I'm sorry, Richard,' he said. 'I'm not concerned at the loss of a few possessions; objects can be replaced, but lives are precious.' As Richard leant closer, he pressed something into James' hand.

It was a key. James pushed it into the waistband of his trousers, cold against his skin.

'The house is Number 12 Walcot Parade.' Richard whispered. 'I've rented it for three months, should you need it.' He drew back, watching for any sign of movement in Charlie's newspaper and then began to unwind the bandage and remove the dressing. 'It's healing well,' Richard said. 'How's the pain?'

'It's bearable,' James replied, 'and getting easier. I owe you so much, Richard, and I don't know how I will repay you.'

'I have done nothing I would not do again,' Richard said. 'Now say nothing more of it. I can give you something to help you sleep, but I would prefer not to.'

'I understand. I need to keep a clear head. I want no medicines.'

'I wish everyone felt the same,' Richard said, 'half the city takes "Collis Browne's Chlorodyne" or some other concoction of opium and cannabis to help them feel better.' He smiled. 'They feel better because half the time they are walking around in a dream.'

'I prefer not to dream,' James said, 'but I have had a great deal of time to think these last few days.'

'I see a change in you,' Richard said. 'So much has happened, yet despite it all you seem somehow stronger, James.'

'Perhaps I've come to realise the value of so much I took for granted; true friendship, people like you and Mrs Hawker and my brother and my new friends. He smiled at Richard and then grinned in Charlie's direction, hidden behind his newspaper, but listening he knew. 'Perhaps I also now understand that I have to be responsible for my own actions.'

Richard smiled and fastened his bag. 'I will leave you now. Rest as much as you are able.'

'Take good care of Miss Bennett,' James called as Richard opened the drawing room door. 'Give her my best wishes. I very much wish I could call on her.'

'I'll see you out, doctor,' Charlie said, as if deciding to act the concerned host after appearing largely to have ignored Richard's presence during his visit. 'I'd like a private word with you, if I might.'

James put the key, unseen, under the cushion of the chair. He would take it to his room later. At least now they had a bolthole should they need it, but it was best to say nothing to the others, at least for the moment.

It was some time before Charlie returned and James was pleased to see that John was with him. 'I have some favours to ask,' James said. The two men drew up chairs opposite him, like a council of war.

'Go on then,' John said.

'Caine will suspect by now that I am still alive, but will not know where I am, or how bad are my wounds. It would be safer for all concerned if he were to believe that I am somewhere other than Bath.'

'Agreed,' Charlie said.

'This evening I intend to write letters to some of my more loquacious acquaintances, together with some of the tradesmen to whom I owe money. I will say that I am indisposed and have gone to London for medical treatment and to recuperate. With the smallest amount of good fortune, I hope word will eventually get back to Caine. It may throw him off my scent, at least for a while.'

'It sounds a good notion,' John said.

'But obviously the letters must be posted from London,' James replied.

'I'll take them up tomorrow, if Charlie can lend me the fare?' John said.

'I have enough for that,' Charlie said, 'provided you don't go first class.' John shook his head and laughed. 'But we need to raise more money soon,' Charlie resumed. 'I can't keep paying. I said I had an idea before and I'm sure of it now. I'll need to visit Bristol over the next few days, if we're to make it work. If it does, we'll have plenty.'

James looked at Charlie, expecting some explanation of his plan in Bristol, but none came. He turned his gaze to John. 'I have another favour to ask of you when you return from London.'

'What is it?' John asked.

'I saw you that night with Caine's gang. I want you to teach me how to fight, even if I am one handed until my shoulder heals.'

'Good thinking, young 'un,' Charlie said. You can learn from John in the day and I can teach you in the evenings and set you some tasks to learn. It's best to keep busy.'

John nodded, 'I'll teach you, but you won't enjoy it.'

Chapter 22

'I shall return to the theatre today,' Belle said. Jenny looked puzzled and concerned, but said nothing.

Then as Belle put on her coat she spoke. 'It's been only four days since you were assaulted, and Dr Wetherby said most strongly that you should rest for at least a week.'

'That may be so,' Belle replied. 'But you know our circumstances as well as I. You have not made a penny since Molly was ill, and I have not earned anything since I was assaulted.' Jenny looked for a moment as though she was going to interrupt, but Belle silenced her with a motion of her hand. 'My savings, such as they were, are now gone, and you are worse in debt after paying for a doctor and medicine. The longer I leave it, the more likely it is that I will lose my job. And that doesn't bear thinking of.'

Jenny did not reply, but her expression said it all. Belle smiled at her hoping that she could convey in a look that she did not blame her in any way; that what was done, was done. She bent over the bed and kissed Molly before leaving.

When Belle arrived at the theatre, the first people she met were Cauldfield and Daisy, his ever constant companion. It was as though they had sensed her intention and were waiting for her to appear; two grinning hyenas mocking their prey.

Cauldfield dipped in a mocking bow to Belle and said, 'Oh, my dear, you look so poorly.' Then he paused, smiling with satisfaction at Daisy. Belle said nothing, staring into Cauldfield's eyes in a battle of wills.

He turned away, looking to Daisy again. 'I wonder if she's been fighting for her honour with a gentleman friend.' Then with every last sign of mock concern expunged from his face, he laughed.

Daisy giggled in response. 'I can't see you going on stage like that, dear, unless you're to play a prize-fighter.'

Cauldfield took Daisy's hand. 'I almost forgot to tell you, Miss Bennett, that Mrs Macready gave strict instructions that you were to report to her office as soon as you returned to duties. I should go there directly my dear, Mrs Macready seemed very perturbed by your absence, when I last spoke to her.'

Already worried, Belle now felt on the edge of panic. She fought not to show it, but her mind was racing. To lose her position in the middle of the season, with no savings to fall back on would be disastrous. She could find a company that would take her on. She knew enough people around the country to do that; but it would mean moving. Even then, to find a new position within a few days would be next to impossible.

John Doyle's punch caught James squarely in the space between the bottom of his rib cage and the top of his stomach. He gasped for air, fighting to stay upright and backing towards the corner of the room, but John came after him, his feet seeming to almost skate across the floor without leaving the ground. James braced himself for another punch, but instead John ducked down and kicked out, sweeping his legs from under him. As James collapsed breathless to the ground, John drew back his right leg and launched a kick, which stopped inches from James' prone body.

John laughed. 'Get up then, you coward. Defend yourself.'

James struggled to his feet and lashed out with his injured right arm. John ducked to the side and danced away from him, laughing again. 'Use your anger.'

James lashed out again, this time with his left fist. John sprang out of his reach, laughing again. 'Use your anger, but be its master. Keep control.'

James launched a kick and nearly caught him. 'That's better,' John said, 'but keep your balance when you kick. If I pushed you now you'd be over.' He brought his arms down to his side. 'Rest now for a while. Get your breath back.'

James sat in the corner of the room, his back to the wall. 'Do you think me a coward then?' he asked.

'Nah,' John replied. 'I just wanted you to get your dander up, to put a bit of a bite in your soul. I know you're no coward, but I want you to learn, and quick. Goading is just part of the lesson . . . Is your arm playing up?'

'It's fine,' James said, trying to ignore the pain.

'If you can defend yourself with a bad arm, think how much stronger you will be when you're better.'

James smiled. 'Give me a few minutes to catch my breath . . . Tell me a little about your life.'

John laughed. 'You mean how I learnt to fight?'

'No,' James said. 'Tell me about your life. What made you go to sea?' He expected him to evade as usual, but instead John smiled and began to speak as though it was the beginning of a story.

'Ever since I was little kid, I'd go down to the harbour in Boston, every chance I got. In the packet season you'd see over a hundred ships down there, sloops and barques, and brigs and schooners, bound for Baltimore and Washington, New York and Philadelphia. Sometimes you could barely get down Commercial Street for all the carts and barrows and wagons loaded with grain.' He paused for a moment and James could see the young boy that he once had been, alive again in his smile. 'They say Venice is beautiful, and I can vouch that it is, but those canals are no more beautiful than the channels that run betwixt the wharves in Boston, with all the piers of Long Wharf, and City, and Mercantile. And there's no finer site than a whole fleet of ships beating it into the harbour under full sail, between T Wharf and Commercial, and not letting go a halyard until they're berthed and ready to tie up.'

John paused and smiled again, almost as though he was alone in the room, talking to himself. 'It's strange though, when I left home, I didn't make for the harbour. I just kept walkin' like I had no idea where I was heading, like I wasn't ready, as though I still had thinking to do. I walked about forty miles till I found myself in Gloucester. Got work on the fishing boats. It was only when I'd been there a while that I got the notion to travel further. So I found a merchantman, and then another and just kept travellin', sometimes on American ships, sometimes British, but I've told you that. You know I've seen a fair bit of the world, and had my ups and downs.'

'Why did you leave Boston?' James asked.

John hesitated, his face more serious. 'My parents had planned a life for me that they didn't see fit to consult me on. Their plans didn't agree with mine, so I left when I was sixteen.'

'You were brave to leave when you were so young,' James said.

'Not so brave,' John replied. 'It would have been brave to stay and persuade them to let me lead my own life. Instead, I've hurt my parents and left my younger brother and sisters to fend for themselves. For years I never even wrote to them and I carry the guilt of that now. For the last couple of years I've written from time to time, but I've never been back and it's been too long now.'

'You should go back whilst you still can,' James said, 'I wish I could see my parents again, but now it's too late.'

John smiled. 'Maybe you're right. Rest now, James, you're all tuckered out. You've done enough for today. Tomorrow afternoon we'll practise again.'

James held out his good arm and John helped him to his feet. It was true. James was exhausted; glad that his physical exertions were over for the day; pleased that he felt he knew John at least a little better. 'I'll go back to my locks then,' he said.

So it had been for the last few days. James' life had been subject to a rigorous routine of training, either under John or Charlie. Each evening Charlie showed him some new technique for picking locks, teaching him how to recognise the appropriate pick or skeleton key for each particular lock. He taught him how to take locks apart and put them back together, until he understood their various strengths and weaknesses. James learnt how to pull bars out of a window frame, or how to jack them apart if they were too firmly fixed. He grew accustomed to the feel of the tools and learnt how to use them with precision and speed and, though still in awe of Charlie's expertise and frustrated at his own lack of progress, with each achievement and skill mastered, James felt his confidence grow.

What Charlie was up to still remained a mystery. Every other morning over the course of the last five days he had put on his best trousers and frock coat and gone out, saying he was off to Bristol. Each evening he had returned to inspect the tasks that he had set for James and to give him further instruction. Whilst James worked under his supervision, Charlie wrote in his notebook and would not be drawn on what he was planning.

The door of Mrs Macready's office was already ajar and swung open as Belle knocked. Sarah Macready was a woman whom Belle respected a great deal, though they had rarely spoken since her appointment, and then only polite small talk and passing greetings. She did not concern herself, day by day, with individual actors. Instead she communicated with the company, as was customary, through the leading man, Cauldfield. Yet it was obvious that she cared deeply about her theatre, and not only as a business. Belle had often seen her sitting in a vacant box, or standing in the wings, seeming to will the best from her actors and actresses and drinking in the reactions of the audience.

'Come in,' Mrs Macready said. She was intent on the papers laid out before her as Belle entered and stood in front of the desk. Mrs Macready seemed almost oblivious to her presence and Belle felt like a child again, waiting to be scolded, dreading the punishment. Her mother's punishments had never involved more than a few harsh words and were always followed by a hug. She could not imagine Mrs Macready hugging her.

'Sit, my dear,' Mrs Macready said, her eyes still locked on the work in front of her. As Belle sat, Mrs Macready returned the pen to its holder and looked up. Belle felt her eyes surveying the various cuts and scrapes on her face. The woman's stare, like a hawk's, was unblinking. 'Please tell me that the injuries apparent on your face are not due to some drunken escapade.'

'They are not, ma'am,' Belle replied. 'They are not due to anything I did wrong.'

'Do you wish to tell me about it?' she asked.

'I will if necessary,' Belle said. 'I do not wish to lose my employment. But I would prefer not to.'

The woman's eyes seemed to soften a little. 'A Dr Wetherby called on me and explained that you were unwell. He spoke very highly of you and begged me not to press you on the events that led to this. I will, therefore, respect his and your requests.'

'Thank you,' Belle replied. 'He is a very honourable man.' She wondered if Mrs Macready suspected there was something between them.

'I do not doubt it,' Mrs Macready said. 'And you, my dear, are very talented, but I suppose you already know as much.' Belle blushed. She could usually accept compliments with grace, sometimes believing, sometimes not, but Mrs Macready was different. This was a woman who had been in the theatre all of her life and was so widely respected. She had come from the successful theatre in Bristol and single-handedly saved the Theatre Royal in Bath after years of falling audiences and loss-making productions. 'You don't remember me do you?' Mrs Macready asked, smiling.

Belle was confused by the question. 'You saw me at my appointment.'

'Of course, my dear, but you don't remember me from before.' She looked Belle full in the face and smiled again, raising one quizzical eyebrow. 'Your features are still the same, though you are a little older of course,' she went on. 'You see, I knew you when you were a little girl. Your parents were in my company in Bristol for a season, before they moved to Bath and then to York.'

'You knew my parents?' Belle asked.

'Knew them and respected them, as hard working actors,' Mrs Macready said. 'They would have been proud of you, my dear.'

'Then you are not going to dismiss me?' Belle asked.

'No; I am well aware of how you might have earned Mr Cauldfield's spite. The man is an arrogant bully who has squandered the undoubted talent he once had. His name has carried him for years. Your place is safe and you may leave Mr Cauldfield to me.'

'Thank you, Ma'am,' Belle said.

'You may call me Sarah – when we are alone. Now get off with you, Belle, and if you truly are well enough, make sure your face powder covers those bruises. We have audiences to please.'

Chapter 23

When Belle opened the door to Charlie she felt as though she was greeting an old friend, though she had met him for the first time only a couple of days ago. She would, she thought, probably have been reluctant even to let him in that first time, if Dr Wetherby had not warned her of his intended visit.

Charlie's first visit had been to ask a favour and by the time he asked it, there had of course been no denying him. His smile spoke volumes. He was a rogue without doubt, but he was a charming rogue, and someone who would probably be a good friend if given half a chance, she thought.

'Come in, Charlie,' Belle said. 'You must meet Jenny and Molly for they missed your last visit.' She turned just in time to see Molly disappear behind Jenny's skirt.

'Hello, Jenny,' he said, then he hesitated, looking around the room. 'And Molly, wherever you are hiding.' He paused again, waiting for Molly's answer, but she remained in hiding. He edged forward, speaking softly. 'I'm Charlie, a friend of Belle's, and I have gifts for you.' He walked over to Jenny and got down on the floor beside her with a noisy cracking of knee joints. Then he produced a parcel from under his coat. As Molly peered out from behind Jenny's skirt, Charlie began opening the parcel. 'I've heard you've been poorly, young Molly,' he said, a smile in every crease of his lined face. 'So here's a friend to help you get better.' With an exaggerated flourish he produced from the wrappings a doll in a brightly coloured dress, its wooden face painted with bright red cupid lips and brilliant blue eyes. Molly took the doll, hugging it to her, and then leant forward and kissed Charlie on the nose.

It took him a while to get to his feet again. When he did, Charlie reached into his pocket and presented Jenny with a silver thimble and Belle with a length of scarlet silk ribbon. 'Small tokens,' he said.

'You are too generous,' Jenny said.

Charlie grinned. 'Don't be worried at taking gifts from an old man. They really didn't cost me much, I 'as a few friends who can lay their hands on things quite reasonable.' He played with Molly for a while, as though she were a grandchild he had met for the first time. Only gradually did he bring the conversation around to the reason for his visit, though Belle knew it could never have been far from his mind.

'Did you manage to get them items what we talked about?' he asked.

Belle nodded, 'Yes, I have them.'

'Then we'd better be off, if you'll excuse us, ladies,' he said, bowing in turn to Jenny and Molly.

Belle saw James walking down the staircase towards them, as Charlie ushered her into his house in The Paragon. Instead of his normal gentleman's apparel he was dressed in a workingman's calico trousers and a loose-fitting shirt. The transformation in his appearance was striking and she must have shown her surprise. James seemed embarrassed, quickly trying to tuck his shirt into the belt of his trousers. 'You look much better than I expected . . . I mean to say, you look very pretty, as though you are fully recovered, Miss Bennett.' He blushed. 'I'm sorry I'm blathering like an eejit.'

Belle smiled, enjoying his confusion as he stumbled to find his words, and to find some right order to place them in. 'I am much better, thank you, Mr Daunton, and you also seem well. Though I see you have altered your taste in clothing or has the fashion for gentleman's apparel changed without my noticing it?'

'I have been working,' he said, as though this was sufficient explanation. His face was still flushed. 'I'll go and change. I really wasn't expecting visitors. It's been some time . . . '

'You will indeed,' Charlie interrupted. 'Miss Bennett has brought you some new clothes in this parcel and you will need to wear them when we depart for Bristol.' Charlie handed the parcel to James. 'Go and put them on. We'll wait for you in the drawing room.'

When James returned to the drawing room he was wearing the full army officer's dress uniform that Belle had *borrowed* from the costume store. It suited him she thought.

'Excellent,' Charlie said. 'You'm every inch an officer.'

'The trousers are a little loose around the waist,' James said, appearing lost in his embarrassment and confusion.

'Don't be impolite,' Charlie said, 'Miss Bennett has gone to some trouble and not a little risk to get these things for you.'

'I'm sorry, Miss Bennett,' James said, holding the waist of the trousers in both hands. 'The whole thing's a little confusing. I did not mean to be ungracious, but I feel I'm the only one who doesn't know what's happening.'

'That's easily remedied,' Charlie said. 'I'll fetch you some braces while Miss Bennett completes your disguise. Mrs Hawker can put in a couple of stitches at the back.'

Belle resisted the urge to laugh and instead smiled, as demurely as she could manage. 'Sit in the chair by the occasional table, Mr Daunton, and close your eyes. Even the redoubtable Mrs Hawker will not recognise you when I've finished my work.' She set to work with tweezers on James' eyebrows. 'This may hurt a little. You have very distinctive eyebrows, Mr Daunton, but perhaps a little too distinctive.'

'This is not an experience I am accustomed to. Are you sure it's necessary?'

Belle could feel his breath at times on her cheek. She half expected him to resist her, but instead he moved his head in compliance with the slightest touch of her fingers and maintained a lazy smile on his face throughout. When she had finished her work on his face she said, 'Now let us see what we can do with this hair.' She ran her fingers through his hair and his smile seemed to deepen. When she had finished cutting, she stroked the sides of his head to ensure that the hair fell right and was even on both sides. He opened his eyes, staring into hers, and she felt drawn for a moment into the exchange.

Then she smiled and put a hand over his eyes. 'Now close your eyes. I don't want to get this powder in them.' She felt herself smiling, wanting to giggle. He closed his eyes and sat still while she finished the work of greying his temples. 'You can open them now, but close your mouth tight.' Belle applied some resin to James' upper lip and, unfolding a piece of tissue paper, took out a false moustache and applied it to his face.

Charlie had come back into the room with the braces. 'What about a scar?' he said. 'Such as he might have got from a sabre.'

'Patience, Mr Maggs,' Belle said. She took out a small pencil and drew a thin line on James' left cheek and then worked at its edges with rouge and other cosmetics before blending in the clear resin she had used to apply the moustache. 'That should hold well', she said, stepping back to admire her work. 'Just pray that it doesn't rain.'

She watched, admiring her work as James got up and looked in the mirror above the mantelpiece. His long black hair was now shorter and greying. His thick black eyebrows were thinner and no longer met at the bridge of his nose. The scar on his cheek looked as though it had been there for years and he had a fine thick moustache. The disguise was complete.

Belle wondered for a moment if James was looking at his own reflection in the mirror or hers, but he turned as John Doyle came into the room dressed in full footman's livery. Belle saw the surprise on James' face, his confusion all too clear.

'How do I look?' John asked, grinning at James. 'Mrs Hawker stuffed this outfit in my bag before we left, thinking I could sell it, but as it turns out she's had her real wish and I'm wearing it.'

'Why are we dressed like this?' James asked. 'It seems as though everyone but I am fully aware of what is going on. Could someone perhaps enlighten me?'

'Sit down and I'll tell you what we are going to do,' Charlie replied.

'I must go soon,' Belle said, feeling not at all guilty at her enjoyment of James' discomfort. 'Please get the uniform back to me this evening, before it is missed, Charlie.' He nodded his agreement and smiled. 'You look very handsome, Mr Daunton,' she said, enjoying her advantage. He looked taken aback by the compliment and as bemused as before.

'Do you truly think me handsome?' James asked.

'But of course,' she said. 'You are more fetching than . . . ' she hesitated and walked over to him. Leaning close she whispered in his ear . . . 'than the most handsome peacock in Bristol Zoo.'

'You are mocking me,' James said, putting on a hurt expression.

'Handsome is as handsome does,' Belle replied, 'and I'm sure you will do very well. Won't he, gentlemen?'

During the coach journey to the station, James tried to take it all in, as Charlie went through his plan. When they reached their destination

Charlie handed over seven shillings and sixpence for three first class tickets to Bristol. They had a carriage to themselves, and during the journey Charlie tested them on the plan, time and again. It was obvious that it had been researched meticulously, but James was still nervous. Charlie gave him and John three slips of paper, each outlining the information needed for the three addresses they were to visit.

'Why have you left it so late to tell us the plan?' James asked. He resented, slightly, his lack of involvement, though in fairness he could not think of how he might have improved on the scheme.

'Because if I'd told you sooner, you would have got nervous and started putting obstacles where none exist,' Charlie replied. 'You need to be fresh to carry this off, and you need to have your wits about you. If you'd prepared too long, you wouldn't sound proper. It's best this way.'

At Temple Meads Station they took a landau up to Clifton where they alighted a hundred yards from the first address they were to visit. Charlie quickly ran through the plan one last time, reminding them of the names. They agreed their meeting point before James and John made their way to the first shop. James straightened his uniform and checked that the moustache was stuck firmly, before adjusting his aching right arm in the sling.

The sign above the heavily barred window said 'R. Smythe – Silversmith', just as Charlie had said it would. A small brass bell mounted on a spring above the door tinkled in greeting as they entered. 'Good morning, sir,' the effusive shop owner said. 'Please take a seat.' James sat and John stood dutifully at his side.

'Mr Smythe,' James said, 'I am newly returned from India, where as you may observe I sustained some injuries. My wife and I intend now to settle in Bristol, and to celebrate our new beginnings we are giving a rather select dinner party for twelve guests.' James mentioned the name of the venue. Charlie had done his research well, the tavern was well known in Bristol for hosting a better class of dinner party in its upper room. 'Naturally we will require the finest silver plate for our guests as they are accustomed to nothing less, and I would like to hire that silverware from your establishment.'

Mr Smythe showed him a wide variety of centre-pieces, cutlery, carvers, serving dishes, tureens and decanters of an obviously high quality of workmanship, in the very finest silver. It was not until they began discussing dates and times and delivery arrangements that James said, as though in passing, 'I chose your shop, Mr Smythe, not only because of the obvious quality of your wares and the fact that you come highly recommended.' He dropped the names of some acquaintances he had in Bristol, whom he knew would impress the man. The man smiled effusively, drinking in the compliments. 'But I had another reason for choosing you,' he went on, 'and you may find it rather amusing.'

'I'm sure I will,' the shopkeeper replied, with an even more exaggerated smile.

'It is quite an extraordinary thing,' James said with a broad grin which he felt pulling at the corners of his newly acquired moustache, 'but we have the same name.'

'You mean, you also are called Smythe?'

'Not just Smythe, but R. Smythe. My name is Richard Smythe.'

'We differ in a small way then,' the silversmith said, 'for I am Roger Smythe. I hesitate to suggest it, but I wonder if we are related in some way.'

'Possibly, distantly,' James replied. 'My people are the Dorset Smythes. Perhaps you know my aunt, Lady Mildred?'

As Charlie had predicted, the silversmith's face took on an expression of awe. It had assumed that very same expression earlier in the week when by Charlie's account he had entered the shop to buy a new snuff box. Charlie had suggested that he had heard the name Smythe in connection with someone of prominence in society. Mr Smythe had been only too keen to explain his very distant relationship to the Dorset Smythes.

'Sadly, I have never met Lady Mildred,' the silversmith said.

'Well we must see what we can arrange,' James said, 'now that I am to live almost as your neighbour.'

Mr Smythe almost fainted on the spot and whereas before his service had been attentive, he now began positively fawning. But when he began totalling the final account for the hire of the silver James noticed that the price had crept up slightly from what they had been discussing earlier. When Mr Smythe had completed his reckonings he presented the account to James, explaining that it included an element of refundable deposit.

'One hundred and twenty-five pounds; that appears perfectly reasonable,' James said, reaching towards his pocket with his left hand.

'Damn,' he exclaimed. 'I have forgotten my pocketbook; it's so damnably awkward dressing with one arm.'

'I can still take your order,' Mr Smythe said, 'and you can return later with the money.'

'No, that simply will not do,' James fired back, 'the arrangements must be finalised today. I will send my man home with a note,' James said looking in John's direction. 'My wife can send the money here in a matter of minutes. Do you have pen and paper? You will have to write for me for I have still not mastered the art of writing with my left hand.'

Mr Smythe produced a sheet of headed writing paper and James began dictating.

'Just open with, "My dear," then write, "Urgently need one hundred and fifty pounds. Give money to bearer. Will explain this evening." Then just sign it "R. Smythe" and be so good as to give the note to my footman.'

John took the note and left the shop. The two men discussed the weather for a while and the attractions of Bristol. As time passed, James remembered to appear more and more agitated. Still there was no sign of John's return. The conversation grew increasingly uncomfortable, until after about twenty minutes James said, 'This delay is unacceptable and I begin to fear there is something amiss. I will return home and see if I cannot find my man. If he comes here after I have gone, take the money from him, otherwise I will return later.'

James left the shop and made his way straight to the designated meeting point. John was already there and had collected one hundred and fifty pounds from a confused Mrs Smythe. Charlie, as they had planned, had taken John to the same address to which he had followed Mr Smythe two days earlier.

Several hours later, and James had assumed the names of Mr J. Kennet and a Mr G. Waldergrave, who were both silversmiths in the Clifton area. John had collected, with Charlie's guidance, a further two hundred and eighty pounds from the homes of Mrs Kennet and Mrs Waldergrave, who had been as surprised as Mrs Smythe, but did not hesitate in complying with their husbands' written requests. James comforted himself with the thought that when the deception was discovered, the various wives would at least have the notes written and signed by their respective husbands as proof that they had simply been following instructions.

The three hailed a cab and were soon on a train returning to Bath.

Chapter 24

The moment Charlie entered the room Molly ran over to him and
threw her arms around his legs. 'This parcel's not for you, Molly,' he
said, handing the package to Belle. If Molly was disappointed she
tried not to show it.

Charlie turned to Belle. 'Did I not return it in good time? Am I
not a man who's good to his word?'

'With over half an hour to spare,' Belle replied, trying to hide her
relief in a smile.

'Mrs Hawker's run a hot iron over it,' Charlie said, with an obvious
satisfaction for a job well done. Molly was still holding onto his legs
and now carefully placed her tiny feet on top of his. He took hold of
her hands and walked around the room taking her weight with each
step on his feet. The room rang with her giggling until Charlie sat her
at the table and produced a small bag of candied fruits from his pocket.

'Did it go well, Charlie?' Belle asked, as Molly began devouring
the unaccustomed treat.

'Better than I had hoped,' he replied, 'but we couldn't have done
it without your help. We know you took a risk getting hold of the
uniform.'

'It was nothing,' Belle lied, the words coming automatically to her
lips. 'Did Mr Daunton carry it off well?'

'Like a man who had spent years in the army,' Charlie replied.

'You should have seen him, Jenny,' Belle said. 'He was so handsome
in the uniform.'

'This is for you,' Charlie said, handing her a small purse.

Belle opened it and found four five pound notes and twenty
sovereigns. Jenny ran to Belle's side, as excited at the sound of the

money as Molly had been at the sight of the candied fruits. 'I've never seen so much money,' Jenny exclaimed. 'Can I hold it?' Belle handed her the money, and watched as she threw the notes in the air and trickled the coins through her fingers, before picking them up again and smelling the money in her hands, as though it was some exotic spice she had never encountered before.

'This isn't my money, Jenny, it's ours,' Belle said. 'It means you can pay off your debts and buy some materials and we'll still have some left for the future.'

When Charlie had gone, Belle finally let out the sigh of relief that she'd been holding back since his arrival. She put the parcelled-up officer's costume by the door, lest she should forget it, not that she could.

'You look relieved,' Jenny said, the concern clear in the lines of her forehead.

'Nothing for you to worry yourself with,' Belle replied. 'I was afraid that Charlie would not get the costume back to me in time for this evening.'

'That money is yours, Belle,' Jenny said. 'There's no call to share it with us. We've done nothing to help you.'

'That's not true, Jenny,' Belle replied, 'I owe you so much. The two of you have done more for me than you will ever know, and I don't mean repairing my clothes. You are my family now, and a family shares its good fortune.'

'You are very kind and I will not refuse your help.'

'My fortunes have changed, Jenny, and not just in terms of the money. I had more good news yesterday that I haven't told you. That's the reason for worrying over the costume. I can't afford for anything to go wrong in the theatre now.' She felt the excitement building, it was too wonderful to contain, and she ran to Jenny and threw her arms around her. It was like a signal to Molly who ran across the room, laughing, and wrapped her arms around Belle's legs. Belle turned and picked Molly up, dancing around the room with the girl in her arms.

'What's happened that's made you so happy?' Jenny asked.

Belle sat Molly on a chair and pulled another two chairs across the room in a small circle. 'Sit and I will tell you,' she said, excitedly.

'Sarah Macready called me to her office again yesterday. She swore me to secrecy and said that Cauldfield had been a disappointment to her and would not be invited back for the next season.'

'Well, that is good news,' Jenny said, a broad smile lighting her face.

'There is even better news,' Belle said, unable to contain her excitement. 'Later in the season Mr Macready is coming to Bath to appear in a production of *Macbeth*. As the star, he will naturally take control of that production. Sarah Macready has written to him already, suggesting that I play Lady Macbeth. She received his reply yesterday, and he said that he will accept her recommendation. I am to act with Mr Macready.'

'Why does she not live with her husband?' Jenny asked.

'No,' Belle replied, laughing. 'Mr Macready is not Mrs Macready's husband. They just have the same name. Mr Macready is one of the best actors in the country. You must have heard of him? Just think: I am to be his leading lady. They say when Fanny Kemble acted opposite him as Lady Macbeth, she was black and blue from the passion of their scenes, and he even broke her finger.'

'Well you have quite enough bruises already,' Jenny said.

'He's not a violent man – well perhaps he is – but not intentionally, he's just very committed to his art. They say he insists on rehearsals for every production and he doesn't just mouth his words, he lives them.'

'I'm sorry,' Jenny said, 'but he sounds an odd character.'

'If he is odd then I wish more actors were odd,' Belle replied. 'I am so looking forward to acting with him.'

Belle took the money and opened her trunk. She laid it carefully under some clothes. 'We must plan carefully how to use the money, and in the meantime it should be safe in here.'

James heard steps on the stairs and opened the door of the dining room just as Charlie reached it. 'Don't worry; he's here,' Charlie blustered as he pushed his way past James. 'I fetched him after I'd taken the costume back to Belle.' It was obvious to James that he was not in the best of moods. Charlie went to sit at the dining table where John was sorting through the money they had brought back from Bristol.

When Sean appeared at the top of the stairs James took him to one side. 'How was he with you?' he asked quietly. 'He was very reluctant when I asked if he could call for you.'

'Your man Charlie walks quickly, given the length of his legs,' Sean replied. 'He was after staying a few paces ahead of me all the way. I'd guess it was on the chance that someone might see him in the company of a priest. But he knows what he's doing. If anyone had followed us, Charlie would have smelt them out.'

James showed Sean to a seat at the table as the other two looked up. 'I take it I shall be a man more at peace with my conscience if I don't ask where this fortune came from,' Sean said.

'I'll pay it back when this is over,' James said, 'and we hurt no one, other than in their pockets.'

'Don't be stupid,' Charlie said. 'We worked hard for that money and we took only from them as could afford it. There'll be no paying back by me.'

John smiled. 'There's three hundred and ninety pounds after Belle's share, which divides up nicely into one hundred and thirty pounds each for the three of us. I ain't ever seen so much money, let alone earned it, and we've cleared it in a day.'

'I take it this isn't honest money,' Sean said. Charlie muttered something under his breath, scowling at the priest. John also looked at Sean, his expression distrustful. James could feel the tension between the men. John and Charlie sat at the table, pulling their share of the money towards them, mirroring each other's actions and making it clear that no one would part them from their spoils.

'Sean, I know you might not approve of where the money comes from, but I want you to get fifty pounds of my share to my brother to help with the estate, and I would like you to accept fifty pounds for your schemes. The other thirty should go to fund our campaign.'

'What schemes are these?' John asked.

'There are so many,' Sean said, 'though most are still in my mind at present. I want to set up a Friendly Society where the poor of Avon Street can save and borrow. It's cheaper for them to pay rent by the week, but most struggle to pay even a night's lodgings. They survive by selling things, but few make enough in a day to buy their stock for the following day, so they borrow and then pay back a third or more on top at the end of the day, for what they have borrowed. So the following day they have to borrow again and so it goes on.'

'We know all this, priest,' Charlie interrupted.

James looked around the table as Sean paused. Both John and Charlie were counting their money again, seemingly oblivious to

Sean's words. 'It would be like a bank for them,' Sean went on. 'Then they wouldn't need to borrow from Caine.'

His words seemed at last to have had an impact. Charlie looked interested for the first time. James seized the opportunity. 'This could be our first strike against Caine,' he said. 'We can't confront him head on yet, but we can begin sapping his strength. Caine depends on his money lending. Take it away from him and he's a deal weaker, and he won't like it.' He could see the thought taking hold in Charlie's mind.

'And what does your Pope think of you using Church funds to give back to the people?' Charlie asked.

'To be sure, they'll not miss a few pounds from Bath in the Vatican, when our needs are so much greater than theirs. Besides I try to fund my non-Church schemes through benefactors like James rather than the collection plate.'

'And how many benefactors do you have?' John asked.

'So far it's only James,' Sean said, the laughter lines around his eyes deep etched and a broad grin on his face. 'But I'm very hopeful that God will help us.'

'Well you can add me to your list,' John said. 'I did little enough to make this money, so I will match James' thirty pounds for the fighting fund and give ten pounds for your Friendly Society. At least I will know then that you will be less likely to try and save my soul.'

John and James turned to look at Charlie, who was busy re-counting his share. 'You are part of our enterprise too, Charlie,' James said 'but of course we cannot ask you to contribute.'

'And neither will I,' Charlie said, 'I'm no Robin Hood.'

'No one would ever think it,' John said, 'but I can think of at least one lady of our acquaintance who admires a man who gives to the poor, and helps his friends.'

'You mean Mrs Hawker,' James said with a broad grin. 'You are correct. Mrs Hawker has always admired generosity in a man, and of course if the fight goes well there may be more booty to come.'

'I'll not be forced into giving,' Charlie said, 'but if there are those whose needs are greater than mine, I suppose we must pull together. I'll put thirty in the fighting fund, providing I gets a share of any booty to come, and providing I can take out what it's cost me in train fares and food and all the rest.'

'Come on, Charlie,' James said, 'the least you can do is to match John's contribution.'

Charlie scowled and stared at Sean. 'Very well, the priest can have ten pounds, but it's agin my principles helping Catholics.'

'We note your principles, Charlie, but now we have money we can begin the campaign,' James said.

'What is this "fighting fund"?' Sean asked.

'We need to hire some men to even up the odds. Have you considered what I proposed?' Sean looked concerned, but James pressed on. 'I need good men, bright, and young, and handy in a fight, but we don't want loose cannons.'

'It still concerns me,' Sean said.

'You have my word that I'll not put their lives at risk,' James said. 'And we would be hitting back at Caine. Please trust me,' he said. 'You help choose them. Make sure they're sensible. Take thirty pounds with you for paying them and we will keep the rest here. When you need more money ask Charlie, he will be our quartermaster.'

'Very well,' Sean said.

James grabbed his hand and shook it vigorously before turning to John. 'Perhaps you can check over the men when Sean has chosen them and tell them what they need to do.'

'I'd be glad to be doing something,' John said. 'But what will we do?'

James did not want to admit that he had no real plan as yet. 'Go down to Avon Street for a few days and get the lie of the land first, John. Gather information and then we'll plan the next step.'

John grinned, as though he savoured the idea, relished the thought of action. 'I'll pack some things now and get down there, do some scouting around. I'll lodge there a few days. Perhaps you can meet me in The Pig and Whistle tomorrow, Charlie, at noon? Then I'll come and see you, Sean, and meet the new recruits.'

James momentarily felt a loss of control. Charlie and John were both going their own ways, taking the initiative. It was not a bad thing in itself but he knew the fight against Caine was a war, not a battle. It needed to be planned and controlled. They were outnumbered and if they were divided they would be beaten. Someone had to be in control, and since it was his fight he must take responsibility.

'Sean!' James said. The priest turned to him and the others stopped talking. The strength of his exclamation took even him by surprise. 'When Caine sends his men out collecting debts, how many are there?'

'If it's to a business, there may be three, or four, or even more of them. If they're collecting small debts it's generally one, or maybe two.'

'Then that is where we begin the campaign,' James replied. 'When you have the men, organise them, John, and take back what Caine's men have collected. Take no risks. Pick out the ones who are most vulnerable and never tackle them unless you outnumber them.' He hesitated. 'You must ensure that none of you are ever recognised, and there must be no killing.'

'You should be able to do that easy enough,' Charlie said. 'They spread themselves thin sometimes, but Caine will soon be wise to it. He'll soon be on guard and send out more men.'

'That's precisely the effect we want,' James said. 'Our actions will make him uneasy. The moment he responds, we stop the attacks, but by then he will be wondering if he has opposition in Avon Street, and he'll be distracted from other things. All it needs is a couple of days, a couple of attacks.'

'You need to get them at the end of the day when they've plenty of money with them,' Charlie said.

'No!' James exclaimed. 'That's when they'll be on guard. Take them when they least suspect. It is not the money we are interested in, it's the disruption.' John and Charlie nodded their understanding. James looked around the room, at each of the men individually, knowing that they were about to embark on a course of action where the only certainty was risk. 'Good luck, gentleman.' He smiled, hoping that it would convey a sense of optimism. 'I sincerely thank you for your friendship and trust and support. Now I need to get back to my locks and Charlie needs to tell Mrs Hawker about his generosity.'

The humour was forced. The gratitude was genuine, and matched only in intensity by the guilt he felt at hiding from his pursuers while others took risks on his behalf.

When John and Charlie left, Sean showed no sign of moving. It was plain that he had something on his mind. 'I have some news regarding Thomas Hunt's family. I have found two families willing to take on his children, and now I have the money to pay for their upkeep. They will still be separated, but they will at least be out of the workhouse.'

'That's good news indeed,' James said, 'but what of his wife?'

'Imelda is stronger and she at least recognises me now, but it will be some time before she is well enough to care for her own children.

She asks how they are, but she still doesn't want to see them. I've also learnt that she has family in Ireland.'

'Could the children not go to her family?' James asked.

'Oh, if only it were that simple. They are farmers, but they were evicted from their tenancy. I have people trying to track them down, but they might have emigrated or died, for all that's known of them.' Sean hesitated. 'You could still go to Ireland.'

'It's gone too far now,' James replied. 'I have a responsibility to provide some ending to what I have started. Caine has put himself above the law and above justice. He must be opposed. Besides there are people in my life now that I care a great deal about.'

'Then sure it must be God's will,' Sean said. 'He has brought those people into your life, the people you need to guide and help you.'

'So you believe this is my destiny?' James asked dismissively.

'Destiny implies you have no free will,' Sean replied. 'I only mean that when you need help, sometimes it comes in unexpected ways.' He paused. 'Do you think all this has happened by chance?'

'Charlie owed me money and John happened to be there, the night I was attacked,' James replied. 'Yes, I believe it was chance. No more lectures, Sean, please.'

'Sometimes the meaning in our lives is lost in what happens from day to day,' Sean said, ignoring the plea. 'Perhaps we're only meant to understand it at the end, or perhaps when something shakes us from our complacency? I've enough trouble understanding the mind of man, let alone the mind of God.'

'Is it wrong to fight Caine?' James asked.

Sean remained silent for a while. 'He is hurting a great many people and needs to be stopped. But whether you can take him on without becoming like him and putting your own soul in peril I do not know.'

'I've had a great deal of time to think in the last few days,' James replied.

'And I see its effect already,' Sean said. 'I see signs of the old James Daunton again.'

'You mean the James Daunton who is terrified for his life and doesn't know what to do.'

'You seem to know what to do,' Sean said, 'and I believe that you're not just fighting for your own life.'

'You're determined to see the best in me, Sean.'

'You are what binds us,' Sean replied. 'Who knows what we might achieve together.'

John packed the canvas bag with a few clothes and set off. It was
easy to lose himself in the crowds once he reached Walcot Street. He
felt almost as he did on the day he left his parents' house in Boston.
At last he had only himself to worry about again; he was free and
the noise and bustle around him were like music after the confining
stillness of the house.

Walcot Street was where all the London traffic came and went;
the busy main entrance to Bath. The street was vibrant with life;
taverns, inns and ale houses, stables and shops, and so much traffic.
But as John crossed the road it felt almost as though he was entering
another world, a world where death and not life, was the master. The
sound of the traffic seemed suddenly drowned in the bellowing of
cattle and the bleating of sheep. The stockyards, slaughterhouses and
Beast Market stood cheek to jowl here, building after building, each
backing onto the steep slope down to the river, each full of the stink
of death.

As he drew closer, he saw the ragged children in the alleyways
between the buildings, picking at unattended carcasses and the piles
of bones, in search of a meal. He found himself imagining the streams
of blood and offal running down to the River Avon beyond. Out of
sight, below, by the river, he knew that other children, the 'mud larks',
would be scouring the riverbanks in search of what could be used or
sold, up to their waists in the oozing rich-red river mud, their nostrils
full of the stench of sewer outflows. So it had been, in every port he'd
visited and every stretch of navigable river in every city he had seen.

It was a relief when he reached the High Street. Here the stalls
of the butter market spilt over to meet those of the fish market. The
costermongers' barrows littered the street and they shouted their
prices and extolled the quality of their merchandise, as customers
haggled and criticised the quality of their offerings. Seagulls wheeled
overhead, shrieking noisily, darting white wings in the winter sun,
swooping down to fight over some occasional discarded fish guts,
or an unattended barrow. Their violent shrieks reminded him of the
sea and of freedom, but he knew he had work to do before he could
leave. He began to plan his next few days as he made his way across
the city, and into the Avon Street shambles.

Charlie had briefed him well. Avon Street had once been home
to scores of taverns, but the increasing presence of the police and
licensing magistrates had reduced their number to three. John went
first to The Smith's Arms and then to The Odd Fellow's Arms,

but learnt little in either. They were both much as he expected, poorly furnished and dirty; but warm and well lit. Needless to say, pickpockets, thieves and prostitutes seemed well represented in both establishments, but John felt instinctively that the likelihood of a customer being robbed or receiving a beating was greater in The Odd Fellow's Arms than The Smith's Arms.

The Fountains Inn was the last on his itinerary for the day. The place was packed and noisy when he entered, busier than the others had been. John fought his way to the bar and claimed his space. The empty-eyed barman studiously refused to acknowledge his existence, preferring instead to lazily distribute a pool of beer over the bar top with a cloth that had once been white. John was conscious though that the young barmaid had been watching him from the moment he entered. As he looked in her direction, she rewarded him with a broad smile. 'What's your pleasure?' she asked.

'I'll have a navy rum and take a drink for yourself,' John said, passing a couple of copper coins to her over the shoulder of a man standing alone, both elbows on the bar as if he were about to dive into the quart tankard in front of him.

'A navy fellow, eh?' the man said, turning to look at John. 'Just back or just leaving?'

'Landed in Bristol two days ago off *The Tempest* back from the China Seas,' John said.

The man made more room for John and he put his glass on a relatively dry part of the bar. 'We was destined to meet,' the man said, his worn face straining into what seemed an unnatural smile, showing teeth stained brown with tobacco. 'Here's me going through a bad patch and there's you newly paid and looking for a chance to make a bit more. I were just on me way to the pawn shop with me missus' gold wedding ring and I bump into you. Would you be interested in buying it for a fair price?' he asked. 'I'll not get its true worth at the pawnshop.'

'It would depend,' John said.

'Depend on what?'

'Depend on whether it's real gold or not, and how much you want for it.'

The other locals showed little interest in their conversation. John could tell from their expressions that they'd seen it all before, as had he. He noticed that the landlord took himself off to the other end of the bar.

'Let's see it then,' John said, as the man eagerly reached inside his waistcoat pocket. He produced the ring and dropped it on the bar where it rang with the true ring of gold. John picked it up from where it lay and dropped it – again the ring rang true.

'I'll give you five shillings for it,' John said.

'Done,' the man replied. 'Just let me kiss it once for good luck,' he said, reaching towards the ring on the bar.

John seized the man's hand. 'You didn't listen,' he said. 'I'll buy this ring, not the brass one you have in your hand. Let's take a look.' He prised the man's fingers painfully apart to reveal a brass ring identical to the one on the bar, including a stamped crown mark.

The man struggled to free his hand. The ale house had grown quiet and John was aware of the watching, expectant eyes all around him. People on either side began backing away, making space for the fight to come. John studied the man's eyes. He was angry, but he was nervous, and John thought he could beat him, but it would draw attention and he was not sure if that would be a good or bad thing. If the man had friends there, he knew it was him who would get a beating. He tried to measure the feeling in the room. No one was backing the man up, or trying to intervene.

John watched as the man's left hand reached down to his boot, and out of the corner of his eye he saw the bone handle of a knife protruding from the leather. He kicked him in the ankle, and grabbed the man's wrist as he reached down for the knife. Then he turned him, pulling his right arm up behind his back and using his own left arm to put him into a choke-hold. 'You can leave with your arm still working, mister, or you can leave with it broken,' John said. 'It don't matter to me either way.'

'Do as he says. Get out!' The words came from behind him, and John could not tell if they were addressed to him or the man he was holding. He turned to look over his shoulder. The man who had spoken was standing just behind him. He had an ugly, pockmarked face, and John noticed he had a scar under one ear, where his earlobe hung unnaturally loose, like an extended fleshy earring.

'Get out, Fletcher,' the man said, 'and don't come back. We've had enough of your tricks in here.'

John let go of the man, who grabbed at the rings from the bar. Before he could get them, the man with the ragged ear reached across and snatched them from him. 'I'll have those,' he said. 'Now get out and don't let me see you in here again.'

The ring man didn't even argue. He spat on the floor and left to howls of derision from the crowd.

John turned to his newfound ally. 'Thanks for your help, stranger. I'm John.'

'Jeb,' the man muttered.

'I got caught with the same trick in Shanghai a few months ago, and I wasn't going to get caught again,' John said, grinning. Jeb's expression remained fixed in a scowl. 'A drink for my friend here,' John shouted, winking at the barmaid.

'Same again, Jeb?' she called with a giggle in her voice, 'and a navy rum for you, sir?'

'Well I were never one to turn away a free drink,' Jeb said.

'And have one for yourself,' John called to the barmaid whilst holding his hand out to the man and smiling. Jeb returned his own version of a smile and shook the hand that John offered. His grip was hard, and greasy with sweat.

By lunchtime the following day John Doyle was nursing a hangover, but was already well acquainted with the strength and disposition of the Cockroad gang from Jeb's drunken ramblings. He was surprised how easy it had been to befriend the man, and yet how uncomfortable his friendship felt. Perhaps it had been too easy; was it really he who had led Jeb on, or was it Jeb who all the time had been testing and reeling him in?

When he walked into The Pig and Whistle, Charlie Maggs was already sitting at a table tucking into a plate piled high with chops, potatoes, swedes and turnips covered in thick brown gravy. 'Sit down,' he said. 'I took the gamble that you would still be alive, and ordered the same for you with a pint of beer.'

No sooner had John taken the seat opposite him, than a steaming plate, at least the equal of Charlie's platter, was placed in front of him. 'Don't worry,' Charlie said. 'I was so confident in you that I've already paid for it.'

'Have you seen Caine's den?' John asked.

'Yeah, I took a walk down there this morning. The place is like a bloody castle; big strong front door with a man on watch outside, and another inside I dare say.' Charlie seemed to hesitate, watching him as he prepared to speak. 'If it were just you and me, John, I reckon we could beat them and there's a lot worth taking in that house, but I'm not sure if James isn't too much of a gentleman.'

John stared Charlie in the eyes. 'He's got a stronger spirit than you might think. That was a good idea of his, going for Caine's collectors.'

'I don't much care for giving the money to the priest though,' Charlie said, the disgust clear on his face.

'Without the priest we'd get no help, and the three of us can't take Caine on.' There was a moment of distrust in Charlie's eyes, John thought, as though they were playing a game of cat and mouse. 'Is it just the money with you then?' he asked.

'Nat Caine and I go back a ways and I hate the man more than you can know, but the money's worth having and would make the hurting of Caine a good deal tastier,' Charlie replied. 'But why have you got involved?'

'I've got my reasons and it's not all to do with money. That's all you need to know.' John studied his expression, waiting for a response, but none came. 'The priest's not like any other man of the cloth I've come across. Priest or not, he's a real fighter.'

'I've never liked Catholics and especially Irish Catholics, but you take your allies wherever they come from I suppose,' Charlie replied.

'We need help,' John said. 'And James and the priest can get that help. Be straight now, Charlie, are you with us, or do you want to go your own way.'

Charlie grinned and held his hand out and John shook it. 'We both know where we stand now. I just needed to know we both think the same. Your reasons don't matter to me. But I need to know as you can be trusted, and I'm sure on that now.'

John grinned at the old fox. 'I've done some digging. There's no shortage of people willing to talk about Caine and the Cockroad gang. I met this one called Jeb, with a ragged ear, who seemed to know his way around.'

'I know Jeb,' Charlie said, 'he's a nasty piece of the devil's work.'

'He's got a runaway tongue though, and no love for Caine.'

'Scum!' Charlie said. 'He's no love for anyone but his self.'

'He told me there's a couple of escape routes in the house, just in case the peelers come visiting,' John said.

Charlie nodded. 'I saw the one, the walkway bridged from the second floor to the house down the road, but Caine has no real fear of the peelers. All the local ones are in his pay.'

John studied his face. It was as though Charlie knew everything about Caine and his den already. 'Jeb told me there's another one, a tunnel out of the cellar leading to the house next door.'

'That's worth knowing,' Charlie replied. 'The good thing about escape routes is that they also gives you a way in.'

'Jeb reckons the place is as strong as any jail,' John said. 'But the good news is I think he can be bought. He may have been drunk, but it was as if he were drawing me on, looking for an ally against Caine. He's a lonely man and it's obvious why.'

'It would be good to have someone on the inside, but I'd rather it weren't Jeb,' Charlie said. 'He'd sell out his own mother for a shilling.' He paused, deep in thought, and then said, 'At the back of the house there's a small tumbledown-looking outhouse. That's another way in, but there's allers two on guard there, because they do a lot of business at the back. It needs some thinking about and I…'

Charlie stopped talking as did most of the others in the crowded room. John was aware that for a moment the only sound in the room came from his own knife and fork. 'What's wrong?' he asked.

'Shut up,' Charlie whispered. 'Nat Caine's just come in with three of his men.'

'Is Jeb with him?' John asked.

'I can't see him,' Charlie replied.

John turned and watched as Caine, smiling, made his way to the bar. He pushed his long, oily black hair back with the palm of his right hand as he walked, his small unblinking eyes surveying the room. A human corridor seemed to form through the crowd as though he was Moses parting the Red Sea, until a drunk, barely able to stand, backed into him.

Caine stopped and grabbed the man, his huge hand almost encircling his neck. 'Take him outside and learn him to be respectful lads,' Caine said, smiling. Two of the gang members took the man and led him, unresisting, out of the door. John hoped the alcohol would numb the drunk's pain. No one moved to the man's defence, nor spoke a word of resistance.

'I hope you and the lads will take a drink on the house,' the landlord said.

'Fetch us a bottle of gin – the good stuff.' The landlord poured four glasses. Caine grabbed the bottle before he could take it away and slammed it down on the counter. 'Let's hear some noise. This place is as quiet as a church.'

Gradually conversations resumed in an uneasy hum. John looked up. 'Ignore them,' Charlie said.

'I want to be sure Jeb isn't with them,' John replied. 'He'd recognise me.'

'I'll say if I see him,' Charlie muttered under his breath.

John continued eating until he became aware of the shape looming beside him. 'Who have we here then?' Nat Caine said. 'If it ain't my old mate, Charlie Maggs.'

Charlie craned his neck to look up at Caine. 'Hello, Nat,' he said, 'it's been a long time.'

'I 'erd as 'ow you was retired, Charlie? Then I heard the peelers had you for a job.'

'That's right, I am retired. Someone tried to get me some time in jail for that job. You know damn well it weren't down to me.'

'I wonder who'd do a thing like that,' Caine said, smirking. 'If you were ever to think of coming out of retirement, Charlie, I hope you know the new rules for stolen goods? Anything what gets taken in Bath gets offered first to Nat Caine, and if I don't want to buy it, you pays me a commission anyways, that's if you can find another fence in Bath. It's quite simple, even for an old 'un like you. And who's this?' he asked, pulling the shoulder fabric of John Doyle's shirt. 'Ain't I seen you afore?'

John stared into Caine's eyes. In his mind he relived the moment when he had rescued James. He fought the compulsion to stand and head-butt Caine again, as he had done that night. But instead he sat motionless, hoping that Caine had not seen him clearly enough then to recognise him now.

'That's my nephew, John,' Charlie said, giving John no time to speak. 'He's arrived today to visit his old uncle.'

'And does you steal things, John?'

'Only the odd kiss,' John replied in an affected tone that cloaked his anger and disguised the gruffness in his voice.

'Don't turn your backs on this one, lads,' Nat shouted at the room in general.

Charlie slammed his fist down on the table. 'Leave us in peace, Nat; we're no trouble to you.'

'I don't suppose so, old man,' Caine replied, 'but keep your nose clean, Charlie, and out of my business.' With that, Caine finished his drink and walked back to the bar.

John saw the cutlery trembling in Charlie's hands. 'I ain't afraid, if that's what you're thinking,' Charlie said. 'I hate Caine. He took the only apprentice I ever trained on a job one night; only a young lad he were.' He paused for a moment, lost in his memories. 'The job went wrong and they got caught by the owner. Instead of running Caine stood his ground and there was a fight. The lad got knocked out and then Caine knifed the man. He killed him stone dead, and then he left the lad with the knife in his hand. The boy was hung before his nineteenth birthday, and his father's never spoken to me again. I've not trained anyone since, not till James.'

'I've no appetite,' John said, pushing his plate aside. He looked up in time to see Caine and his cronies leave the inn. The sense of relief in the room was almost palpable. 'I could do with a rum or a brandy. How about you,' John asked, 'what's your tipple?'

'I don't take spirits!' Charlie snapped.

John was taken aback at the strength of his response. 'How's that then?' he asked.

'Because they affect me bad,' Charlie spat. 'I've done some wrong things in the past and it's usually when I've been drinking. I'll have a beer sometimes, but nothing stronger. Anyways, you'd best go and see the priest now, and help him decide on the men we need. You can't trust a priest to choose the sort of men we're looking for.'

'I think you're wrong, Charlie. I'm glad he's on our side, priest or not. It's time we started making life uncomfortable for Mr Caine.'

'I'll be off,' Charlie said.

'Tell James I'll see him in three days time,' John called to him as he made for the door. He watched him through the window as he disappeared into the crowd. Then he saw the man emerge from the doorway opposite the tavern and set off in the same direction. He looked as though he might be following Charlie. John made for the door, but by the time he had pushed his way through the crowded tavern and got out into the street, both men were out of sight. He set off following the path that Charlie might have taken, but neither man was anywhere to be seen.

Chapter 25

While she was walking to the house, Belle tried to rehearse their meeting in her mind, what she would say, how he might respond. It left her feeling awkward and she resolved to keep their meeting short and businesslike. She tried to convince herself that she was visiting James to thank him for the money, and to see how he was recovering from his injuries, but she knew there was more to it than that. She liked him and she knew she had to warn him, before it was too late.

Mrs Hawker smiled when she opened the door, 'Miss Bennett, please come in.' Belle thought she seemed somehow different, more at ease, perhaps it was Charlie's influence. The old rogue was obviously smitten by her. He'd spoken about little else as he had accompanied her on her last visit to the house.

As Mrs Hawker took her hat and coat Belle fought the urge to grin and turned it into a smile. 'Is Mr Daunton at home?' she asked.

'I'll call him now,' Mrs Hawker said. But Belle was already conscious that he was watching them, tentatively peering around the wall at the top of the stairs, like a schoolboy spying on his elders. When he saw that she had seen him he smiled and ran down the flight of stairs taking the steps in twos, until he stood in front of her, looking slightly flustered.

'Miss Bennett,' he said. 'How wonderful to see you.' She smiled in response. He seemed to be staring at her mouth. She ran her tongue self-consciously over her teeth and took out her lace handkerchief and dabbed at the corners of her lips as delicately as possible, lest there were some smudge or mark on her face.

'Mr Daunton,' she said. 'You are staring at me. Is there something amiss?'

'My apologies,' he stuttered. 'I simply had not noticed the whiteness of your teeth before.'

'Thank you.' Belle laughed. 'I will take that as a compliment, although no one has ever complimented me on my teeth before. I feel a little like a horse.' She put the handkerchief away with a sense of relief. 'I thought I would call, and see if you were recovered and if you needed anything.'

He looked flustered. 'You are very kind. As you can see, my arm is now free of the sling and troubles me less. As for needing anything, I need only to be free of these walls, but in the absence of freedom your company is very welcome.'

'I am glad that you value my visit so highly,' she said, unable to resist the urge to grin. 'I'm sure there are prisons far less comfortable than this.'

He looked embarrassed. 'I'm sorry,' he said. 'I put that badly, I should of course be more gracious and grateful for what I have. But you too were recovering from injuries, as I recall, when we last met?'

There was a question in his voice that she instinctively avoided. 'I am quite recovered now,' she said.

He showed her into the morning room. 'I am so glad of your company. Please take a seat and let us talk.'

She smiled again as she sat. 'I think you are glad of anyone's company, whether it is mine or someone else's would make little difference, Mr Daunton.'

'You are wrong; it is your particular company I am glad of. But I think by now you should call me James. We may never have been formally introduced, yet you have seen me without my shirt and I have lain in your lap, conscious or not. But I feel I know so little of you.'

Belle began to feel embarrassed and hoped that it didn't show in her complexion. 'You know I am an actress, what more can I tell you?' she asked.

'What of your people?' James asked. 'Where are they from?'

'My people, as you call them, were both actors who travelled around the country where the work took them. Both my mother and father died within a few months of each other, some years ago. I miss them very much.' She felt the emotion rising, sharper than she had expected. She looked down at her hands, and then up again towards his face. He seemed more vulnerable, less sure of himself, or was she seeing what she wanted to see.

'I'm sorry,' James replied. 'It is obvious that you still feel their loss keenly.' He looked into her eyes for a moment and then turned away. 'My parents too are dead. My mother died when I was too young to remember her and my father several years ago. I lived in Ireland then.'

His words made her want to lower her guard a little and his expression made her want to understand him better. 'It must be a great sadness to you to have lost your mother when you were so young,' she said. 'My own mother died when I was sixteen, little more than a year after my father. Their love gave me so much strength, but I wish I could hear them now, telling me that they are proud of what I have achieved, and what I am trying to do with my life. I would give anything to have them still here.' The sudden strength of her feelings almost made her cry and she tried to compose herself.

He smiled, and it felt warm, and open, and understanding. 'It must have been very difficult for you, and to have to bear the loss, and to go on alone, and at such a young age. Perhaps it is easier to bear the loss of someone hardly remembered, though for me, growing up, it never felt so.' He hesitated. 'As to my father, I sometimes feel I have let him down in not living up to his expectations.'

'Perhaps they are your own expectations,' Belle replied. 'I'm sure that your father wanted only for you to be happy.'

'Perhaps so,' James replied. 'And I am fortunate I suppose, in that I still have a brother, and I have good friends.'

'Like Harcourt,' she blurted. The words were out of her mouth before she had had time to think.

He looked taken aback. 'Him and others,' he said. 'But please do not judge me by the hurt that he has obviously caused you.'

She tried to go back. To pretend she had never mentioned Harcourt. 'I have no brothers or sisters, and though I have many acquaintances, I count few as friends, other than Jenny and Molly.' She found herself telling him about them; about Molly's illness and Jenny's courage in bringing her up alone, and her struggles and ambitions and all the small things in their lives. He listened, nodding here and there, and smiling, or mirroring her concern. If he was uninterested then he did not show it, but when she stopped speaking, he said nothing, as though lost for words. Belle felt self-conscious again in the silence; awkward and compelled to fill the quiet. 'I have had some good news of late,' she said. 'I am to play Lady Macbeth opposite Mr Macready.' She had blurted it out so inappropriately. He must think her a selfish, empty-headed fool, but his smile seemed responsive and genuine.

'He should be honoured to act opposite you,' he said, taking her hand and kissing it. 'But I hope he will not take you from Bath.'

Instinctively she went to pull away her hand, but left it still and he took it lightly between long fingers. His touch felt warm, his hands gentle. She wanted to look down, to see her hand in his, but feared he might let go. 'Don't make assumptions about me, because I am an actress, Mr Daunton,' she said. The words came out too roughly, too dismissive, she thought.

'I make none,' he said, keeping hold of her hand, 'whether about you as an actress, or as a woman.' His smile was warm and reassuring.

'If events had not brought us together you would barely have noticed my existence, Mr Daunton.'

'That's not true,' he replied. For a moment his words seemed to drain away, as if other thoughts had intervened. 'I remember our first meeting in The Garrick's Head as though it were yesterday. I am still uncertain whether it was your spirit or your beauty that dazzled me greater.'

Belle felt herself blushing and looked away. 'A woman can achieve a great deal with powder and paint,' she said.

'And yet, unless I am mistaken, you wear neither today, and are even lovelier.' He paused. 'But I see that I embarrass you. Tell me, why did you become an actress?'

She felt pressured for a moment, unsure of herself. 'Acting is all I've ever known and all I want to know, as far as occupation.'

'I could never be an actor,' James replied. 'Playing all those parts, I should forget who I really was.'

'I could never be content to be only who I am, or who the world tells me I should be,' Belle replied. She felt she needed to understand him more; to find out why he was so close to Harcourt. 'But who then is James Daunton?' she asked. 'For we all play parts, do we not?'

He looked taken aback as though he had never needed to question who he was. 'I am a gentleman and a solicitor; reasonably well educated and now in better health again, though a little in fear of my life,' he replied.

She hesitated; he looked a little embarrassed, she thought, yet she could not hold back. 'I think there is truth in what Shakespeare said, that "All the world's a stage, and all the men and women merely players." It is the parts we choose to play from day to day that make us who we are.'

'I agree,' he said, 'but sometimes we are not free to choose.'

'How can you say that when you have enjoyed every advantage in life,' she interrupted. 'You did not have to choose Harcourt as a friend and take your pleasures, like him, from those who have none of your advantages.'

'That is unfair,' James spluttered. 'I believe I am basically a good man and loyal to my friends. I do not wish harm to anyone and neither do I seek to exploit others.'

'Then why did that man try to kill you?' Belle asked. 'Who was he?'

For a while James was silent, avoiding her eyes. Then he began to speak and the story seeped from him, his tone sombre and confessional. At times he looked at her as though seeking some sign of understanding, at others he looked away as if fearing her judgement. When he told her that the man later died, she saw no triumph in his expression, but only a deep regret and sorrow. She let the silence linger for a while when he stopped speaking. She wanted to say that she understood and forgave, but it was not forgiveness that he was seeking, for it was clear that no one could forgive him, but himself. Eventually she said the first words that came to her, 'Harcourt changes everyone around him.'

'I thought he was a good friend,' James replied. 'But now I see him differently.'

Belle considered her response carefully. 'After I slapped him that night when we were in The Garrick's Head, he took to coming to the theatre with the sole purpose of unnerving me. He was very successful in achieving that purpose, but it appears that it was not enough to satisfy his spite. When I was beaten, he was also there, watching. I believe it was he who arranged the beating, as a punishment and a warning, for embarrassing him in front of his friends.' She saw the shock on his face. She wanted to tell him everything, but held back, still unsure.

'Are you certain it was him?' he asked.

She felt the tears coming to her eyes, but held them back, as she removed her hand from his. 'Look at this,' she said, passing the well creased piece of paper to him. 'Open it.'

'This is in Frank's handwriting,' he replied.

'Read it.'

James read the note aloud, his face uncertain and questioning. 'Be in Queen Square at 11:00 this morning. Watch and learn.'

'He left that note for me the morning you were shot. Do you think it a coincidence?' she asked. 'He has turned me into someone afraid of shadows and he has led you nearly to your own death.' She wanted to explain more, but her sense of shame strangled her words and she held back.

He too sat wordless for a while, as though taking in what she had said. When he did speak, his words were cold and considered. 'I will make sure that he suffers for what he has done.'

'I believe you,' Belle replied. She could see the hurt of betrayal in his eyes. 'But you must not put your life at risk, he is a dangerous man.' She felt guilty, as though she had now pushed him towards actions that might endanger him, and yet she knew she had to make him aware.

'I thought Harcourt was a friend,' James said, standing and walking over to the fireplace. 'I'd seen him use others, seen the coldness in him at times, but I believed we had a true friendship.' He paused and for a while Belle thought he had almost forgotten that she was in the room. 'I can see now that Harcourt tried to drive away any true friends I had, but what did he want from me?' he asked. 'Richard told me that he was a blackmailer, that he held letters from a woman and was extorting money from her. I passed it off, as though it were nothing, refusing to think him capable of such a thing. Now I understand how much hurt Harcourt must have caused that woman, while I did nothing.'

Belle wanted to tell him all that she knew about Harcourt, but again her shame kept her silent. The sadness was clear in his face when he sat down again. She wanted to comfort him, to take him in her arms, to explain how Harcourt had used her too, but she didn't trust herself to speak. She could not let Harcourt's ghost destroy the feelings that she had for James. In time perhaps, he might accept it better, but not now, not yet. 'I must go,' she said. She passed him the card. 'Dr Wetherby and Charlie know where I live, but I have written the address down for you, should you need to contact me. Send for me if I can help,' she said, putting on her bonnet and gloves.

The echoes of their conversation still haunted the morning room after Belle had left. The room now felt cold and empty; the house even more like a prison. He longed to open the front door, to walk beside her and enjoy the crisp winter's day. Instead he wandered between lifeless rooms, breathing listless air, and inventing meaningless duties to occupy himself, all the time brooding over what she had told him.

Back in the morning room he could still catch a hint of her perfume in the air. He stared at the card she had given him, as though he could know her better simply by reading it over and over again. She had been little more than an acquaintance, yet she had helped and encouraged him; even put her own life in danger for all he knew. He wondered what lay between her and Harcourt; how close had they been and what had come between them? He refused to let the idea of Belle and Harcourt together take root in his mind.

As he rejected the thought he felt himself smiling, remembering his foolishness. He had actually complimented her on her teeth, as though she was a horse, and said nothing to contradict the impression. All he had been thinking of was the delicious curve of her mouth as she smiled, the soft pinkness of her lips, but he couldn't have told her that. He sat down, trying to remember the things she had said and searching for different meanings in the words she had used. There was so much he had wanted to say, so much he wished he had said differently.

It had been so difficult to confess to her what he had done, and yet the truth had spilled out in a torrent of words, like flood-waters he had been unable to hold back. She had seemed to understand and her face had shown nothing but compassion, yet he knew she must think less of him – how could she not? Yet more than anyone he needed her to understand that he was not who she might think he was, that his actions had been so much against his nature.

And each time he pictured Belle now, he saw Frank beside her. He imagined her lying beaten on the ground and Frank mocking her. He thought of the note and how Frank had lured him into the ambush. It was obvious that he had set him up to be killed. He saw pictures in his mind of Frank's grinning face, but the smile was a sneer. Richard had warned him time and again about the man, and he had ignored all the warnings. His mood grew darker as his mind filled with thoughts of revenge. Yet he knew if he was too hasty, he would put everyone at risk.

When Belle returned to their room in Bridewell Lane there was no sign of Jenny and Molly. Almost without thinking, she crossed to the trunk to check that the money Charlie had given them was still safe. Some of it disappeared a couple of days ago, and now, lifting the clothes she had hidden it beneath, she saw that more was gone. She was about to count what remained when the door flew open and Jenny and Molly came into the room. Jenny's arms were full of parcels. Belle replaced the clothes quickly and slammed the lid of the trunk down.

'You've seen I took the money then?' Jenny asked. Molly ran and hid behind the curtains.

'I told you it was ours to share,' Belle said. 'I don't care that you took it.' She tried to hide her disappointment. 'It's just that I was looking forward to us planning how to spend it and perhaps going shopping together.'

'I'm sorry,' Jenny said. 'I wanted to pay my debts off as soon as I could and now it's done. No more debt collectors. My slate is clean and I shall keep it so!'

'I am pleased,' Belle said. 'That's the best use for the money, but I didn't realise you were so much in debt.'

Jenny smiled though it seemed to hold a hint of sadness. 'We wanted to buy something else, didn't we, Molly?' she said, as she laid the parcels on the bed and took another from under it. Molly ran from her hiding place and jumped onto the bed. Jenny pointed, and Molly picked up one of the parcels and took it to Belle.

'It's a pretty dress,' Molly said, handing it to Belle.

'And it's for you,' Jenny said.

Belle unwrapped the parcel. 'It's so beautiful,' she said, holding the skirt to her waist and whirling around the room. 'And such a lovely shade of blue.'

'I ordered the material days ago,' Jenny said, 'it was exactly the colour I had in mind for you. I had my friend make the skirt while I worked on the bodice. We had to work in her room so you wouldn't suspect anything. And Molly was a good girl and kept our secret, didn't you, Molly?' she said.

Molly grabbed another parcel and began jumping on the bed, giggling.

'Can I see the bodice?' Belle asked.

'Not yet,' Jenny said. 'It needs some finishing touches; some beadwork and ribbon or lace around the cuffs and neckline, I haven't decided yet, and I think I could improve the skirt a little. We will be busy while you are at work, won't we, Molly?' Jenny walked around the room, taking down a sketch here and there and laying them out on the table. 'Which look do you prefer?' she asked.

Belle looked at them all and pointed. 'This one,' she said. 'It's so elegant, but not too fussy.'

'Then that one it shall be,' Jenny said. 'I've some things in my bottom drawer and I must confess I've bought a little bit of lace and some turquoise and jet beads that will be perfect.'

Belle put the skirt over the back of the chair and hugged Jenny. 'I don't deserve a friend as true as you,' she said, and then added, 'so we shall see no more of that awful Jeb.'

The sadness seemed to return to Jenny's face. 'I found Harry Wood at Caine's house. He told me exactly what I owed, and I paid him the full amount. Harry said he would make sure that Jeb never called again, said his brother would have wanted it so.'

'Was his brother not with him?' Belle asked, dreading what the answer would be. She felt suddenly cold, remembering what James had said.

Jenny looked for a moment as though she was about to cry. 'He told me his brother had died, but would say no more.'

'I know you liked Tommy,' Belle said. The truth screamed out to be told, yet she held back. She had never lied to Jenny, rarely held back the truth, yet she could not bear to tell her what she knew – not yet.

'I did like him,' Jenny said. She produced a handkerchief and dabbed at her eyes. 'Perhaps I had not realised how much, until now . . . I shall miss him.'

'You need some time alone,' Belle said. 'I'll take Molly for a walk and we will talk later. Nothing must ever come between us!'

'Don't be silly,' Jenny replied, 'as if anything could.'

'I thought Charlie might have been followed when he left me, but I wasn't sure,' John said, the moment he entered the morning room. 'I got Sean to send word to you to be careful.'

'You were right,' James replied, 'but Charlie's not a man to be underestimated. He knew they would try to find where he lived. He told me that he led his follower around town for a while and then lost him in Milsom Street.'

'So we're safe?' John asked.

'Not as safe as I would like,' James replied. 'It would be easy enough for Caine to track Charlie down if he needed to. He's too well known and Caine knows the same people. We must hope that his mind is on other things for the moment. He has no reason to suspect that Charlie and I have any bond, as far as I know.'

John placed the parcel he had been holding onto the floor in front of him with a resounding thud. 'Before I open this,' he said, 'I need to tell you what I have been doing for the last few days. I met up with Father Sean, in Orchard Street.'

'Did he find men willing to help us?' James asked.

'He could probably have found sixty at the pay he is going to give them, but he was very selective. He approached only those who he knew would be willing and who he felt could be trusted. In the end we were left with five.'

'Are they good recruits?' James asked, his mood shifting, his confidence increasing.

'Well, four of them are big lads, handy with their fists and pretty smart too. We did what you said. Over the last three days we've robbed three of Caine's men. Was that enough?'

'It's good; three is enough. It will leave Caine looking over his shoulder, wondering who is opposing him. Was anyone hurt?'

'Caine's men got a few bruises, but nothing they won't recover from.'

'And no one was seen?' James asked.

'No one,' John replied. 'We didn't take much from them though'

'It's not money we are seeking,' James replied.

'I've told the lads to lay low for a while now,' John said. 'Brendan and Patrick are staying in Bath, so they can keep an eye on Caine. Diarmuid is going to take lodgings in The Blue Bowl in Hanham and see if he can't find out something about the Cockroad gang nearer to their home.'

'What about the others you recruited?'

'Well there's Billy,' John said with a grin. 'He can out-talk any Irishman I've ever met, which is saying a lot for a man born in England. He claims Ireland is where he should rightfully have been born, seeing as he loves the place so much and since he's married to a Kerry woman; says all he wants is enough money to live there. He's the smallest of the lot, but he's a terrier, just won't back down for anyone, and he knows his way around.'

'What does Sean think of him?' James asked.

'He was reluctant to take him at first. He thought he was a little impulsive and unpredictable, but Billy talked his way in. He could convince the Pope that he was Episcopalian, that one.'

'You're obviously very taken with him,' James said.

'He's a good lad and so is Tom, though he's the exact opposite of Billy. He's as quiet as a church mouse, but everyone says he has a way with horses that's uncanny, and he can drive anything on wheels whether it's pulled by a single horse or a team of six. It's a skill we thought was worth having.'

'Will five men be enough?' James asked.

'Probably not,' John replied, 'but it's better for now to have a few we can trust than a whole posse, that we're not sure of. We could have chosen more, but we don't want loose cannons. I put Brendan in charge, he's sensible enough and the others respect him.'

'How many men does Caine have?' James asked.

'It's difficult to say. There are twenty or so gang members in Bath and they say maybe another half a dozen in Cockroad. But my guess is that he can call on another dozen or so when he needs them; but they're just hirelings, mercenaries, if you like. They have no loyalty as such to the gang.'

'So we are pretty much outnumbered, should it ever come to a fight?'

'Make no mistake, James, at some point it will come to a fight, which is why I took these off Caine's men,' John said, unfastening the brown paper parcel.

James looked down at the two pistols nestling in their brown paper wrapping. 'I never wanted this. I don't want to kill again.'

'And do you think I want to kill? Do you think I am so different to you? I've seen more than enough killing in my life; most of it justified by some government or other.' John paused. 'I told you I worked for five years on ships trading with China.'

'I remember,' James replied, 'but what relevance has it to this?'

'You British have a great fondness for tea and silk and porcelain, but you hadn't enough gold to pay the Chinese for them, and no goods that they wanted in return, so you traded them opium from India, until the Chinese emperor saw what it was doing to his people and outlawed it. He even wrote to your queen asking her to stop the trade in misery, but it did no good. So the Chinese seized and destroyed 20,000 chests of opium that the British had in warehouses in Canton.'

'I recall reading in the newspapers of the Opium Wars,' James said. 'We concluded a treaty with the Chinese seven years ago. It must have been in 1842 or was it 1843?'

'Your great victory was in 1842,' John replied. 'I was there when your army demonstrated the power of British cannons loaded with grapeshot being fired into narrow Canton streets, filled with civilians. I saw the blood and bodies. And afterwards you made the Chinese pay six million dollars for the opium they had destroyed, and give you Hong Kong.'

'Why does it concern you so much?' James asked.

'It didn't at first,' John replied. 'To me opium was like any other goods you trade. I've even smoked some myself, mixed with a little baccy, and it made me feel good. But the Chinese refine it and smoke it on its own and in great quantities. I saw what it was doing to the country, but it didn't matter. How they lived their lives was up to them and they didn't mix with Europeans very well. Made it clear what they thought of us foreign devils. Then a few years ago I met someone who made me question, and think about things, and I began to see things differently.'

John stood and strode around the room. After a few seconds of silence he spoke again, his tone more measured and controlled. 'Sean reminds me of her sometimes in the way he thinks and what he says. I've spent a good deal of time in his company these last few days and we talked mainly of the famine in Ireland. Do you know what struck me?' he asked, turning to James and then turning away. 'It's the simple fact that most people are repelled by the thought of taking a gun and holding it to someone's head and pulling the trigger. Yet they are perfectly happy to do nothing while a million people starve to death. Sean called it a sin of omission. Not something you've done wrong, but things you haven't done, times when you should've spoke up, but didn't, times when you should have done something, but held back.'

'I'm sorry, John,' James said. 'The sight of the guns shocked me; perhaps made me more aware of what we are up against and what we might have to do.'

'You think you know me because you know I can fight, and because I don't wear my heart on my sleeve,' John said. 'But that don't mean I find the idea of killing any less terrible than you.'

'I understand, John, and I'm not one of those who think their background and upbringing makes them somehow superior. I admire your strength, but I also admire what I know lies beneath.' James stood and held his hand out to John. 'Friends,' he said, half questioning.

John took his hand in a firm grip and shook it. 'Friends.'

Chapter 26

To be betrayed by a friend is bitter medicine and the thought of striking back kept needling at James. Now he saw Frank for who he was, understood for the first time the hurt he had done, not just to him, but to Belle and to others; and slowly the impulse to seek justice and revenge turned into a colder, more pragmatic way of thinking. Though he was still nursing an injury and was a virtual prisoner in Charlie's house, yet James felt stronger than he had for years. There was a discipline now to his day in learning new skills from John and Charlie. They had opened his mind and challenged him in ways that tested his own understanding of who he was. Yet he felt frustrated that others were fighting his battles for him. His restlessness had been growing for days. He needed now to become an active participant in the war he had started, and his first battle, he resolved, would be against Frank Harcourt.

It was this resolve that sent him running down the stairs to the kitchen that morning. 'It's time I did something,' he said, as he flung open the kitchen door. The scene before him took his voice away for a moment. Charlie had an arm around Mrs Hawker's shoulder, whispering into her ear, as she sat at the table. She instantly leapt to her feet, blushing, knocking her head against Charlie's head in the process. 'Good lord, Master James,' she shouted. 'You almost did for me, bursting in like that, shouting like a mad thing. Now sit yourself down and I'll make you a nice cup of tea.'

'I would love a cup of tea,' James said, realising that his embarrassment was nothing compared to hers. He wondered if he should say something about what he had seen, but felt too awkward. Politeness and diversion seemed the best course of action, for the moment.

What he was about to propose could not be done lightly. 'I'm sorry to interrupt you with my entrance, but I have resolved to put the skills Charlie has taught me into action. Do you think I am ready, Charlie?'

'Well young 'un,' Charlie answered, still red faced. 'You'm as ready as you'll ever be in terms of picking locks and shifting catches, but it depends what you has in mind.'

'I'm going to rob Harcourt, to hit him where it will most hurt – in his pocket.'

'Well I don't like the idea of you stealing,' Mrs Hawker interrupted, now recovered from her embarrassment. 'That's not how you were brought up.'

'I'm not taking it up as a profession, Mrs Hawker,' James replied. 'But I know now that Harcourt was behind the attacks on me, and on Miss Bennett, and I intend to extract some justice.' He looked at Mrs Hawker, who seemed unconvinced by what he said.

'We could just give him a beating,' Charlie said.

Mrs Hawker gave him a disdainful look. 'Two wrongs don't make a right. What would your father have thought?'

'I think my father would approve. Not of a beating, but of justice. There is an element of honour in what I intend. Harcourt holds letters with which he is blackmailing a lady. I intend to take them and return them to her. If I happen to find other valuables in the process, then I believe there would be some justice in relieving him of them and putting them to better use.'

'Where's Harcourt's house?' Charlie asked.

'In The Circus.'

Charlie frowned. 'That's bad news. There's always peelers round there.'

'I was thinking of eliciting Miss Bennett's assistance,' James replied. 'I remember well what you taught me; that the easiest way into a house is through the front door. That's providing Miss Bennett is willing to help, but we need to make preparations today. I need you, Charlie, to visit Miss Bennett and ask her to call urgently and tell Tom to come. It must be him that drives Belle. It must be someone we trust.'

Charlie nodded his agreement and James turned to Mrs Hawker. 'I need you, Mrs Hawker, to sew some strong deep pockets into the lining of my overcoat, the one with the shoulder cloak. I do not want to draw attention to myself carrying a bag. Most of the tools I'm likely to need should fit into pockets providing they are sturdy.'

'I'll do it if your mind's made up,' Mrs Hawker replied, 'but please don't go taking risks. I don't want to see you injured again or worse.'

Most of that morning James spent ensconced in the drawing room with Charlie and John. Under Charlie's guidance he drew plans of Harcourt's house. Though he knew the layout of several of the rooms, he had to guess at others, but even then Charlie insisted that his guesses be based on whatever objective information he could draw upon. They were all in agreement though that their success or otherwise would largely depend on Belle.

Tom joined them after lunch and explained with a toothless grin where he could *borrow* a hackney cab.

'No,' James said, 'you must hire a cab for the evening. I don't want to attract any police attention and Miss Bennett must not be put in danger.'

'It'll cost you,' Tom said.

'Charlie will give you the money,' James replied. 'We will look on it as an investment. Do you know where you can get a cab for a few hours?'

'I can get one,' Tom said.

In the late afternoon, Belle arrived wearing a dress of pale blue. James wanted to compliment her, to say that it made her eyes even more dazzling, but he felt awkward in the presence of the others. He wanted to say that the dress made her look so young, such a free-spirit, but all he said was, 'Such a pretty dress, Miss Bennett. Is it new?'

She took the compliment with a smile. 'Yes, quite new. My friend Jenny made it for me.'

'It's perfect for tonight,' Charlie said. 'You look a proper lady.'

'Miss Bennett is always a lady,' James found himself saying, before he could hold back the words. She smiled and nodded to him, but he found himself avoiding her eyes. 'I intend to rob Harcourt's house tonight and take whatever he treasures most.'

James looked up to gauge Belle's reaction. He had expected an element of pleasure on her face, but he saw none.

'Not for me,' she said. 'You are not doing this for me?'

'For you, and for me, and for everyone else he has hurt,' James said. 'I understand if you do not want to be involved, but I will proceed by other means if you are unwilling. You will not dissuade me.'

'Then tell me what I can do to help,' Belle said. 'My only proviso is that I must be in the theatre by half after seven.'

'Tom will get you there. Won't you, Tom, and you'll look after Miss Bennett?'

'To be sure I will,' Tom said.

Belle felt uneasy that evening waiting in the hackney cab on the corner of Brock Street, by The Circus. The longer they waited, the more her discomfort grew. In part it was nervousness, she knew, but there was more to it than that. She kept thinking of how she had deceived James, not in what she had said, but in what had been left unsaid.

When James had told her that he was going to steal all that Harcourt valued, she had wanted to blurt it out, 'He has a safe in his bedroom on the second floor.' But she couldn't bring herself to tell him, not in front of the others. She had tried again, when he had seen her to the door, but the words still wouldn't come. If she had said it, she knew what conclusions James would draw, and he would have been correct, and she would not have known how to explain. He must know though, about Harcourt and her, yet he had never pressed her. She wondered what Harcourt had told him about her? She wanted to tell James everything, to make things open between them, but she couldn't, not yet.

The sound of the peep-hole in the roof of the cab being slid back shook her from her thoughts. Tom was leaning over from his seat, peering into the cab, giving her a wide smile, seemingly unashamed of his largely toothless mouth. 'We're all depending on you, Miss, and that we are.'

'Thank you, Tom,' she said, returning his smile. 'Your words make me feel so much better.'

Tom laughed. 'If you don't mind me saying, Miss,' he said. 'You're as pretty tonight as any girl in Ireland.'

'You're very kind, Tom,' Belle replied. 'And they all say you're such a quiet man, who wouldn't say boo to a goose?'

'Ah, what do those eejits know? And besides, why would I be wasting my blarney on a bunch of ugly men? I've always had a greater liking for talking to the ladies.'

'I can see that,' Belle said.

'In truth I've always had a bit of a gift for it, so I have, but I haven't always been missing my front teeth. It's just that some of the women I enjoyed talking wid had husbands or sweethearts and the more I enjoyed the talking, the more teeth I ended up losing.'

'You're a handsome man, teeth or no teeth,' Belle said.

'You're very kind to say so, miss.' Tom paused for a while, as though reflecting on what he was about to say. 'And I may not always give out much, but I take a powerful lot in. Only this afternoon I got the idea into my head that you already have eyes for someone. Not that I thought I stood a chance for a moment.'

Belle laughed. 'Get away with you, Tom, and keep your eyes where they should be.'

Tom leaned back and his face disappeared from view, though she could hear him chuckling to himself and then whistling some cheery tune. It was almost quarter to seven and they had been waiting for over three quarters of an hour, occasionally completing a circuit of the green, but always returning to the same place to wait, as Tom whistled away to himself.

The Circus was one of her favourite places in Bath; at least it had been until Harcourt. The circular street was built in the shape of an amphitheatre, the tall houses with their pillars and pediments forming a continuous perimeter wall, broken only by its three entrance roads. The ring of houses like a lofty coliseum overlooked the green at their centre, as though it were the arena of an amphitheatre. The homes were well-lit, reflecting the status of their residents. The upper floors looked almost like boxes in a theatre, looking down on the drama that was about to unfold.

Billy was breathless and sweating when James answered the door to him. 'Harcourt's gone out, Mr Daunton,' he said. 'John sent me to fetch you and I've run all the way.'

'We'd better go quickly then, Billy,' James said. 'But no running, I don't want to attract any attention with these tools in my pockets. Besides I doubt I could run with the weight of this coat.' James was conscious that he too was sweating. He pulled the scarf up over his face. It was a cold night outside, and the scarf would not look out place, but would keep his face hidden.

James had gone some distance when he realised that Billy was no longer at his side. He also noticed that the two men approaching him were laughing, one of them gesturing to him to turn around. When he looked over his shoulder he saw Billy, at first standing stock still, then taking giant steps that extended his legs to their furthest reach, like a circus clown. 'Come here, Billy,' he said, 'and walk properly.' The two men walked past, laughing.

'I said that I didn't want to attract attention,' James said.

'And that's why I was doing it,' Billy said. 'While they were busy looking at me, they couldn't pay any attention to you.'

'Thank you, Billy,' James said. 'But walk with me now and let's not draw attention to either of us.'

'What will we talk about?' Billy asked. 'Will I tell you a tale or two?'

'Let us talk of Ireland,' James said. 'I hear you love my native land.'

'I do,' Billy said. 'I love every part of her, with her rolling green hills and soulful mountains and wicked seas.' He stopped talking for a few moments as if picturing the scenes he described.

'What is your favourite part?' James asked.

'Kerry,' Billy said. 'I love those great mountains looking down at shining lakes and sea.'

'When were you last there?'

'That's the sad part,' Billy said. 'I've never been to Kerry or any other part of Ireland, but I know I love it just the same. I love the people and their way of speaking and their way of thinking and everything about them. My wife's from Kerry you know and she paints a picture of the place with her words, better than any of your painters could make. One day I'll go there.'

'I hope so, Billy,' James said. 'I'm sure you won't be disappointed.

When Belle saw James enter The Circus from Bennet Street, there was someone with him. She guessed it must be Billy, another of the Irish lads. She looked away from them and towards John Doyle, waiting under the trees at the centre of the green, watching out as they had arranged, in case Harcourt should return.

As James stepped for a moment through a pool of direct light from the street lamp she saw him pull down his scarf a little and light a cigar. Then as soon as he had lit it, he dropped it to the ground and stubbed it out with his foot. Billy picked up the cigar and walked away. Belle looked instantly towards John Doyle as he also took out a cigar, lit it and blew out a plume of smoke, a sign to them all that Harcourt had not returned, and that it was safe to enter the house.

As James began walking slowly around the perimeter of The Circus towards Harcourt's house, John turned to face the landau and raised his hand to his head. It was the signal Belle was waiting for. She rapped on the roof of the cab, but Tom had already set the horse walking slowly into The Circus road, beginning its three quarters circuit toward Frank Harcourt's house.

They had completed half their circuit when Belle first saw the peeler. She wanted to warn James, but there was nothing she could do. Their paths seemed somehow destined to collide. Willing James to look up, she watched helplessly, and then she rapped urgently on the cab roof and shouted, 'Slow down, Tom.'

By the time the peeler stopped him, seizing both his arms, the cab had drawn quite close. Belle felt the horses slowing almost to a stop and resisted the urge to call out to him. She willed him to break free; he could make a run for the cab and Tom would whip up the horses and be away from there. She looked towards them again. The constable was laughing now. Tom must also have seen it, for she felt the horses moving to a gentle trot again, as the constable walked away.

When they reached Harcourt's house Tom slid back the roof partition and looked in. 'Are you ready?'

'I'm ready,' she said. Tom climbed down and knocked on the front door of Harcourt's house. Belle looked back and saw James crossing the top of Gay Street now, walking slowly, though she knew that his every instinct must have been to run. She turned to look for the constable. John Doyle was chatting to him in an animated fashion, making sure that he stood with his back to Harcourt's house, so that he saw nothing of what was about to happen.

Belle heard Tom knocking again on the front door as she turned to watch James' progress. She turned back as the door opened. James was kneeling now, near the house but in the shadows, to all appearances fastening his shoe. He smiled momentarily in her direction. She wanted to smile back, to reassure him, but she could not risk it.

As the maid opened the front door Belle looked past her into the well-lit hallway. She remembered the hallway well, standing in Harcourt's arms that night, before he had taken her upstairs. She had believed then it was the start of a new life. He had been so tender and loving, and she had believed it was a new beginning. Yet that night was the last time he had spoken to her, until they met at The Garrick's Head and she slapped him; from love to hate with so few words between.

Now all his discretion made sense. She had thought he was protecting her reputation, yet all the time he had been protecting his own. She smiled to herself, thinking that if he hadn't been so discrete, tonight's venture would have been impossible. The maid might have recognised her now, but he had made sure that even the servants didn't see her that night. He thought himself so clever.

Belle put on the stern look that she felt appropriate to a lady addressing a member of staff. The young housemaid who had answered the door was reluctant to leave her post. Tom was gesturing to her, pointing to the cab. 'Bring the girl down here, cabman,' Belle called, as the maid stood, flustered, dithering in the open doorway, a good twenty feet away. 'I do not intend for the whole of Bath to be informed of my business.'

Tom was urging the girl to step over to the cab, but she would not be moved. 'What's your name, girl?' Belle called in her finest cut glass accent, her tone controlled and just loud enough to be heard. 'I will not shout in the manner of a fishwife to domestic staff.'

'My name's Emily, miss,' the pretty girl replied with a shy, half apologetic curtsy.

'Well, Emily,' Belle said in a soft but authoritative voice, 'if you are a polite and helpful girl, I will reward you with a shilling.' Emily smiled and practically ran to the cab, holding her skirt in her hands. The second that the girl had passed James, Belle looked from the corner of her eye. James was already up the flagstone pathway and through the front door and running down the corridor beyond.

Belle asked the girl if this was the home of Mr Ben Johnson. Emily said she had heard the name, but had no idea where he lived. Belle nevertheless gave her four silver thruppenny pieces, counting them slowly into the girl's hand, one at a time. 'Thank you for your help, young lady,' she said, before rapping on the cab roof and instructing Tom to drive on.

As James reached the top of the stairs, he felt his heart pounding. He concealed himself as best he could to watch the hallway below and regain his breath, peering around the edge of the stairs. It was then he saw the trail of footmarks that he had left on the newly polished hallway floor. The maid closed the front door and turned. Taking the bottom of her apron in her hand, she began busily polishing the coins Belle had given her. She had reached the door to the lower staircase into the basement before she finally slid the coins into her apron pocket.

James took a handkerchief from his pocket and wiped the bottoms of his shoes before carefully descending the stairs again and wiping the marks from the marble floor. The door to the lower staircase was closed and he could hear the muffled chatter and laughter from below stairs.

He had only opened the study door a few inches when the hinges began screeching their resistance. He froze, listening for the answering silence from the kitchen in the basement below his feet, but their chatter was still audible and uninterrupted. Reaching inside his coat, he found the leather pouch and took out the small oil-can wrapped in cloth. He smoothed the grease into the hinges with his finger and then wiped them clean with his handkerchief. The pungent smell of the oil filled the air, and he prayed that it would soon be lost in the scent of candle wax in the hallway.

Inside the study the gas mantles had been turned down, but the roaring fire added to their dim ochre light. James surveyed the room, the curtains were open and he knew he could be seen from the street were anyone to look into the house. He dropped to all fours and crawled over to the writing desk.

The central drawer and the top drawer of the right-hand pedestal were locked. He reached for the ring of small brass keys in his coat pocket and opened both drawers. Their contents were disappointing – account books, invoices and receipts. Despite Harcourt's attitude to spending he was obviously meticulous in running the household. James relocked the drawers and made his way back up the stairs.

The drawing room was lit by the tentative glow of a dying fire with no flames to penetrate the darkness. He left the door open far enough to allow in the light from the candelabra in the hallway and made his way to the secretary table. It was locked; a good sign he thought. Harcourt was bound to keep any confidential papers or valuables in a secure place. He could even remember Frank unlocking the secretary table on one occasion when he was searching for papers.

James took the small stub of candle from his pocket, lit it and placed it on top of the secretary table. He noticed his hands were shaking and he wiped the perspiration from his forehead and willed them to steady. None of the small brass keys would budge the lock of the central hinged panel.

He took out the belt of skeleton keys and lock-picks and carefully rolled it out on the carpet. His first choice of picks was correct and he felt the lock give way to his probing. Pulling down the cover, he was disappointed at the contents. Inside were a few banknotes, a small column of gold sovereigns, a snuff box and a selection of tie pins, but nothing that warranted the risk James was taking. He left them undisturbed.

As James was about to close the desk he noticed the thin scratch marks in the veneer of the desk top, caught in the spluttering light of the candle. Above the scratches, where there might have been a drawer or compartment, there was instead a blank wooden panel. He prised at the panel gently with an ivory-handled letter opener, but it would not budge. He knew there must be a catch or lever somewhere that released it, but where? Nothing was going as he had planned it. Charlie had been right. Picking locks was one thing, but burgling a house was different, the fear clouded your mind, pushed you into panic.

In the distance, he thought he could hear footsteps on the lower staircase. He strained to listen, blowing out the candle on top of the desk. There was no doubt now, he could hear a door opening on the ground floor. James closed the front panel of the desk and walked over to the doorway. Out in the hallway, he stood in the bend of the staircase. The voices were coming from the study below.

'I'll see to the fire and curtains in here, Emily, and you go up and bank up the fire in the drawing room and turn down the bed in the master's room.'

'Can't you turn down the bed?' the other voice replied. 'I hates going in his room.'

'You're the under-maid and you do as you're told,' the first woman said. 'You'll soon learn. There's money to be made in that room, between them nice silk sheets.'

James wondered for a moment if the maid would use the servant's staircase, but knew instinctively that in her master's absence she would not. He made quickly for the stairs and the second landing, stopping only to snuff out two of the candles of the candelabra in the hallway, listening to their feeble spitting, hoping the girl would stop and relight them and give him more time. He was on the second landing before he remembered the candle he had left standing on top of the secretary table. It was too late to retrieve it now.

He heard the girl stopping to relight the candles, as he had hoped, before going into the drawing room. The second-floor landing was in darkness and there were two bedroom doors before him. James opened the first and looked in but could see little in the darkness.

The other door was locked, with the key still in the lock. He reasoned that it must lead to an unused bedroom. Turning the key, he went into the room, closing the door behind him. He could hear the girl now, walking up the stairs to the second floor. His heart was racing and he willed himself to take in slow, quiet breaths in readiness to push past her and run.

She stopped for a while in the hallway as though she had heard him, but then went into the other bedroom. James felt his heart pounding faster and tried to steady his breathing, fighting the urge to run. After a while he heard the bedroom door close and her footsteps retreat down the stairs. He felt his heartbeat slowing again and as his eyes gradually grew accustomed to the darkness he fumbled around the perimeter of the bed, searching for a bedside table and candlestick.

When he found what he was looking for James lit the candle and breathed a sigh of relief, as the smell of sulphur and molten wax filled the air. He crossed to the window and looked out. Below he could see the gas lamps along The Gravel Walk, the popular promenade around the parkland, leading to the Crescent Fields. A high wall encircled the long garden stretching down from the house. At the side of the window was a gutter-pipe reaching down from the roof. James blew out the candle and sat on the bed, wondering what to do next.

Returning to the hallway, the light took him by surprise. The maid had lit a candle which now stood on the hall table, and fluttered in the breeze of cold air as he closed the bedroom door. Taking the candle, he went into Harcourt's room and found what he was looking for. There in the corner of the room was a large and solid safe. He knelt beside it and studied the lock. It was going to take a lot of work. He unrolled the belt of tools and found what he was looking for.

James carefully unwrapped the blank key with its wax covering from the lint cloth and gently inserted it into the lock, turning it slowly and feeling it engage with the wards of the lock, discovering through touch and sound a little more about the mechanism. When he withdrew it, etched into the wax was a perfect impression of the lock.

He smiled, studying the imprint, selecting in his mind the lock-picks he would use.

The sudden noise was like thunder, driving all thoughts from James' brain. Someone was rapping loudly with the head of a cane on the front door. Within seconds, he heard the answering sound of feet running and the door being opened. 'You have left the front door unbolted again,' a man's voice muttered. The voice was indistinct, but James knew it was Harcourt. 'How many times must I tell you, always bolt it when I'm out?' he shouted.

'It's hard to reach up there, sir,' the woman's voice replied, 'and the bolt's stiff.'

'I'll get someone to attend to it,' Harcourt snapped.

'Yes, sir,' the woman replied.

James fought against the panic, ordering his mind to compose itself. He wrapped the waxed key back in the lint cloth and rerolled the tool belt as he heard the front door slam closed. He must try to act as Charlie would; no mistakes, no panic. He heard the bolt being slammed shut on the front door with some force and then a key being turned in its lock. Then he heard the footsteps on the stairs. James peered over the edge of the stairwell and saw Harcourt.

Belle tore into the room in Bridewell Lane. 'Help me get this dress off, Jenny. I don't have very long and I must change before I go to the theatre.'

'Don't you like the dress?' Jenny asked.

'Of course I like it,' Belle said, tugging at the fastenings on the skirt. 'It's the most beautiful dress I've ever owned and I love you for making it, but I cannot wear it to the theatre.'

Jenny remained seated at the table by the window, continuing with her sewing as though uninterested in Belle's plight. Belle left off her exertions with the skirt fastenings and walked over to her. 'I haven't hurt you, have I? It's simply that I want to keep it for best. You know it is the prettiest dress I own.'

'No,' Jenny replied, her face serious, 'you have not hurt me.' She laid down her sewing. 'But you are hurting yourself.'

'How so?' Belle asked.

'You think the dress will set you apart from the others. It will confirm their opinion of you; that you think too highly of yourself. Is that not what you think?'

'Perhaps so,' Belle replied, knowing that what Jenny said was true. 'Why should I confirm their opinion of me?'

'Why should you not?' Jenny asked, not waiting for a reply. 'If you went dressed in rags, would they think any better of you? Cauldfield has already poisoned their minds, but if you show that you are above his nastiness then it may give the others cause to think. Perhaps it will confirm their opinion, perhaps not, but what will you lose by it? I know who you are and so do you. You are gentle and caring, not cold and vain, so wear the dress with pride, just for today.'

Belle drew up a chair and sat beside her. 'If I had a sister, Jenny, I could not love her more than you. I will wear the dress and to hell with their opinion.'

James suddenly remembered the candle stub he had left on the secretary table. Downstairs, he heard Harcourt muttering to himself as he opened the drawing room door. James listened intently but could not make sense from Harcourt's mumblings. Then he heard him slam the door, his footsteps going back down the stairs to the hallway. He was running. James waited for him to say something, or raise an alarm, but there was nothing.

Then he heard Harcourt open the door to the basement stairs. 'Make up the fire in the drawing room,' he bellowed. 'But first bring a bottle of wine up to the study, Emily.'

James edged noiselessly down the stairs to the first-floor landing and crept into the drawing room. He laid the tool belt out quickly, selecting the same pick he had used before. The wards resisted for a moment, but he managed to half close the lock of the desk before retrieving the candle stub. There must be no sign that anyone had been here.

He was half-way up the stairs when he heard the footsteps on the staircase again, but this time it was a woman's tread. He walked slowly, keeping his body flat against the wall where he couldn't be seen. At the top of the stairs he looked down and saw the girl struggling with a bucket of coal. He went into the unused bedroom again. Sitting on the bed, James reviewed his situation with all the calmness he could muster.

There seemed only one option now. He climbed out onto the window ledge and sat looking for a moment at the light from the kitchen window, far below. As he struggled to his feet he was conscious of the weight of his coat with all the tools in its various pockets. It felt like a lead coffin hanging from his shoulders, threatening to tip his balance.

He closed the window behind him and, taking out his knife, shaved a piece of wood off the frame and inserted it between the two sash windows to ensure that the top window stayed in place and did not come crashing down and alert the house to his presence. He reached out and grabbed the gutter-pipe with his right hand, keeping his body flat against the window.

The pipe felt sound and he edged over towards it, first with his right leg and then with his other arm. As he let it take his weight, his coat felt heavier than ever and his right arm began aching as though he was tearing through the newly healed muscles and tendons.

Chapter 27

James sank into a chair, ignoring their questions. 'Could I have a drink, Charlie?' he said. 'Whisky or brandy, anything as long it's strong. You'd all better have a drink.'

'I'll get them,' John said.

'Not for me,' Charlie interrupted. 'Best not. I can see from your face that there's nothing to celebrate.'

'The only part that went well was Belle getting me in there,' James said. 'Harcourt came home before I could take anything. There's a safe in his . . .'

James' words were cut short. 'I bloody well knew it,' Charlie shouted. 'We should have had a lookout and some way of warning you. I always took a lookout along with me, but you kept saying he'd be out for the night once he left.'

'It wouldn't have done any good. What could I have done even if I'd had a warning?'

'Did he catch you?' John asked.

'No,' James replied. 'I got out of a bedroom window and climbed down a gutter-pipe into the back garden.'

'So we've achieved nothing,' Charlie said, 'but at least you weren't caught and you didn't break your neck. I'd never of heard the end of it from Angela . . . I mean Mrs Hawker.'

James smiled and out of the corner of his eye caught sight of John grinning. 'You're wrong, Charlie. We have achieved something. I found his safe and I have this.' He stood and took off his coat, fishing in a pocket for the belt of tools. Walking over to the table, he unfurled the belt and extracted the small carefully wrapped lint parcel. He placed the wax-covered blank key gently on the table.

'What's that?' Charlie asked.

'The safe in Harcourt's room is a Chubb,' James replied. 'I can tell you enough about it for you to work out its type. And this, gentlemen,' he said, picking up the key, 'is a pretty fair impression of the lock.'

Charlie took the key from him and examined it, turning it in his hand as though meeting the imagined resistance of a lock in his mind, assessing each angle and edge of the wax impression, registering the shape of each line and mentally constructing each microscopic turn. Then he smiled and put it back on the table. 'I tell you, young 'un, I couldn't have done better me self,' he laughed. 'I can make a key from this without a doubt.'

'It's one thing to have a key,' John interrupted, 'but how are you going to get in? We can't pull the same trick again.'

'We could bribe one of the servants,' Charlie said, 'but we would need to do some fishing first and it would take time.'

'Never!' James exclaimed. 'Can you imagine what Harcourt would do to those girls if he even suspected they were complicit in robbing him? How long do you think it would take him to get out of them that they were involved? Besides they're probably already too scared of him to take a bribe, and we don't have the time for elaborate plans. We'll have to break-in this time.'

'That'll take some organising,' Charlie said.

James grinned at him. 'I know how it can be achieved and when. There's a ball next Saturday and nothing is more certain than that Harcourt will be in attendance. I saw the invitation on his dressing table. I may not know Harcourt as well as I believed, but I do know he will be there.'

He paused, thinking through the plan he had put together on the walk back to the house. 'The ball starts at six o'clock and the orchestra will play two hours of formal dances, which will hold little interest for him. Between eight and nine the assemblage retires to the Tea Room for drinks and buffet. It's then that Harcourt and his friends will make their appearance, but he'll have been drinking for most of the night before that, readying himself for the more lively quadrilles and country dances.'

'How do we get in?' Charlie asked.

'The garden at the back of Harcourt's house slopes down to the parklands and backs onto The Gravel Walk, the path that goes round the park. The basement of the house is below ground at the front, but level with the ground at the back.' He hesitated, picturing the terrifying view he had had, sitting on the window ledge. It seemed well worthwhile now. James could already see the interest on Charlie's face; see his mind working. 'There are bars on the back windows on the ground and first floor, and they could be forced, but it's too near the kitchen to risk the noise, but the gutter-pipe leading up to the roof passes right by a bedroom window on the third floor and that window has no bars. That's how I got out.'

'Then we have a place of entry,' Charlie said.

'Better still,' James replied, 'I have already greased the window frame so that it moves freely. When I got onto the ledge I shaved off some wood from the window frame and jammed it between the two windows so they stayed in place. Pull the wood out and the window will slide open easily, provided he does not notice the catch is undone. The only problem is that the bedroom door is kept locked from the other side, but the key is left in place, at least it was tonight.'

'I've taught you well,' Charlie replied with more than a little pride evident in his broad grin. 'You're a better apprentice than I would ever have thought.'

'There is one other problem,' James interrupted. 'And perhaps it is the worst of all. It was one thing sliding down the gutter-pipe, taking my time, but even then I felt the weakness in my arm. It aches like the devil now and I may not have strength enough to climb the pipe.' The room fell into a momentary silence.

'Then I'll do it,' John said. 'I'm used to climbing.'

'That makes sense,' Charlie said. 'You've prepared the way well. All John needs do is climb in. There's no need for any fancy stuff. He can open the bedroom door with an outsider if it's locked.'

'What's an outsider?' John asked.

'James knows what I mean,' Charlie replied. 'Leave it for now, I can soon teach you how to use one.'

'Is it decided then?' John asked. 'Shall I do the job?'

'We could wait until I am recovered,' James said. 'But the opportunity is so perfect and the job needs climbing skills, not an amateur cracksman, with a weak arm. Besides, in truth you would probably do a better job than me, if my luck tonight is anything to go by.'

John smiled, 'I know you want to do it, to get even with Harcourt, but you've made the right decision.'

'If John is to go unchallenged he will need to be attired as a gentleman,' James said. 'I am sure Mrs Hawker can alter a jacket and trousers of mine to near enough fit you. The best of it is, John, you don't need to carry heavy tools when you're climbing. All you need is the outsider, and the key that Charlie will make and a candle stub for light. All of them will fit into your jacket pockets.'

'You've learnt well, young 'un,' Charlie said.

As Charlie refilled the two whisky glasses for John and James, Mrs Hawker bundled through the door, struggling with a tray of steaming serving dishes heaped to overflowing with chops and potatoes and vegetables. She placed it on the end of the dining table and the air filled with the scent of rosemary. James felt the whisky beginning its work on his mood and appetite.

'What happened when you bumped into that peeler?' John asked.

James laughed. 'I was trying to keep my head down and watch Belle's cab out of the corner of my eye. Tom seemed to be going too fast. The next I knew, I found myself walking into the constable's arms.'

'What did he say?' Charlie asked.

James cleared his throat and endeavoured to lower the pitch of his voice with several trial coughs. 'He said, "Watch where you're going now sir, it's a dark night to be in such a hurry," and he gave me this quizzical look.'

'What did you say?' Charlie asked, the laughter lines spreading from his eyes.

'I said, "My apologies, constable, I am a little poorly and keen to get home to my bed." I feigned a bout of coughing to convince him of my poor health. Then I just wrapped the scarf tighter around my face. He warned me to be careful of the frost and touched the edge of his hat with the tips of his fingers. I was relieved though when I saw you talking to him,' James said, turning in John's direction.

John grinned. 'I asked him the way to Pulteney Bridge and gave him a life story in the process, but it was easy talking nonsense, having spent so much time in Billy's company.'

'That was a messenger at the door,' Belle said to Jenny, as she ripped the note open and began to read. 'James is safe, thank God. I hardly slept last night for worrying.' She scanned the few lines of the letter, conscious of Jenny's questioning expression. The sense of relief was at first intense, but as she read on, her anxiety grew.

'What is it?' Jenny asked.

'The note says so very little,' Belle replied, 'save that "the venture was in part a success" and that "our mutual acquaintance is unaware that we had called on him." He says they plan to "visit him again", but that I should not make contact until I hear further.'

'Then all is well,' Jenny said. 'From what you said last night, you put yourself at some risk. I am glad this is an end to your involvement. Let them get on with their plans and you keep well away.'

'I am worried for them though,' Belle said. 'I have no idea of what they intend to do, but I am sure that there is danger in it. I wish James would forget Harcourt. If he is caught, or any of the others, I know Frank would kill them without conscience.'

'Then you are well out of it,' Jenny said.

'But how long must I wait to hear?' Belle said. She knew he was trying to protect her, yet a part of her felt shut out and excluded from his life. 'If I was involved,' she said, not sure if she was talking to Jenny or herself, 'at least I would know what was happening and what danger he was in.'

The following Saturday night, John set off with James and Billy towards Harcourt's house. It was just after five o'clock in the evening. The Assembly Rooms where the ball was to be held were only a five-minute stroll from Frank's home in The Circus and the ball was due to commence at six.

The city streets were already busy and John sensed the expectant buzz of activity as the ranks of the fashionable prepared to impress their peers. He drew comfort from the fact that their presence in the centre of The Circus was almost invisible in all the comings and goings and preparations; as friends met friends, servants were dispatched on last minute errands, and the upper orders made their way to the ball. The air reverberated with the sounds of hooves and wheels on cobbled stones, from the traffic of landaus, hackney cabs, gigs and carriages.

'Keep that scarf tight around your face, James,' John said. James smiled momentarily before pulling the scarf up to cover the bottom half of his face.

'I could do with a scarf,' Billy said, 'to keep my neck warm.'

'After tonight you'll be able to buy yourself one and an overcoat,' John replied. Billy was always the keenest of the Irish lads to volunteer for any activity that brought him closer to the centre of the action, his enthusiasm always accompanied by grinning good humour. His chatter as usual was endless and John and James had little need to speak in carrying out the pretence of conversation. Billy even managed to make them laugh at one of his stories. It was a relief to John, whose nerves were frayed, though James appeared, at least to him, totally at ease.

'I will get myself a scarf,' Billy said, 'and a nice new waistcoat, so I can show off the watch you bought me.'

John smiled. Billy kept taking out the watch, polishing and admiring it, telling them the time at regular intervals. 'I see you bought yourself a silver chain to put it on,' John said. 'You did buy it, not get it by some other means?'

'Do you think I'd put a stolen chain on a watch like this?' Billy said. 'I wouldn't insult you by putting it on a stolen chain.' He dangled the watch in the air, with obvious pride.

'It's a fine chain,' John said.

'And it's a fine watch,' Billy said.

'Best see that no one takes a fancy to it,' John said.

Billy stuffed it back out of sight. 'They'd better not, or they'll have me to answer to.'

At a quarter after six they saw Harcourt leave the house. As James had predicted, he did not walk towards the Assembly Rooms, but instead set off down Gay Street towards one of his preferred watering holes in town. 'I'll follow him,' Billy said, 'and if there's any sign of him returning I'll run ahead of him and give the front door a pounding to warn you.' He laughed. 'It's like being a kid again. Do you want me to try to slow him down if he's on his way back? I could trip him, or pick his pocket, or something.'

'No,' John said. 'Keep an eye on where he is for an hour and then get home and don't let him see you. None of your tricks now, Billy, just be safe. And no drinking.'

'I'll be a Will-o'-the-wisp, and not a drop will cross my lips,' Billy said. Then he gave them a broad grin, before setting off after Harcourt.

John laughed. 'Let's give him five minutes James and then get round to the back of the house.'

The path they called The Gravel Walk was kept reasonably well lit, but it was quiet by night. 'That's the house,' James whispered, and began fishing in his pocket. 'When you have cleared out the safe, place this on top of it, where it will be seen.' John took the calling card that James handed to him.

John looked at the card. 'What if he fetches the peelers in?'

'He won't,' James said. 'And if he did they would have to find me, and then explain how I was able to climb the gutter-pipe and break into a house and safe; a man of my background. Besides we were friends, I have left any number of my cards at his home in the past.'

John took the card and laughed. 'I'll do it,' he said as he looked up and down the path before entering the bushes which fronted the wall of Harcourt's back garden. The houses in The Circus looked even more immense from the back as the ground fell away to the park, but now that he was actually doing something John felt his nervousness recede.

The wall presented little challenge. He climbed onto the outhouse roof and tested the down-pipe. It creaked a little but felt sound enough. When he started climbing he was in his element again. As he climbed, he listened for signs of movement, watching for lights being lit or moved, but no one stirred. Gradually he inched his way up the pipe towards the window.

He felt the small flecks of mortar and dust falling on his head and hands long before he heard any noise. John clung on motionless for a while trying to see above him, holding his body close to the wall. Just above his head and level with the middle of the window was a bracket clamping the pipe to the wall. He could see now that one of the bolts which held it in place had worked its way loose from bearing his weight.

It seemed almost funny, John thought, that he had climbed masts and rigging in the middle of ocean storms and survived and now he was going to fall to his death in someone's back garden in Bath. He fought the urge to look down, knowing well enough that he was unlikely to survive a fall from this height. His instincts told him to climb down again, to where the pipe was still strong, but the window ledge above seemed so close; almost close enough to touch.

He edged upwards, trying to keep his weight flat against the pipe. When his hands were level with the window ledge, he inched slowly higher. A bead of sweat ran down from his forehead, stinging his eye, distracting him, but still he continued. When he was close enough he reached out with one arm, gaining a tenuous hold on the bottom of the window-frame. Then he pulled himself onto the ledge, feeling the pipe judder and shake with the sudden movement. He held his breath, fearing the pipe would come away from the wall and fall to the ground below, but it held. Once he got his balance he reached out and pushed the fixing back in place.

Removing the wedge of wood that James had put there to hold the window closed, he slid the window open and climbed in. John wanted to get to work and to get out of there as quickly as possible, but he could not shake off his concerns with the loose gutter-pipe. He looked out of the window. The pipe would never take his weight again and it was a good twenty or so feet down to the kitchen roof below and thirty or more to the ground. If he fell, all hell would break loose. If he didn't kill himself he was unlikely to be able to walk away, let alone run, and though Harcourt might not call the police, the servants would summon them at the least little noise. He tried to shake off his concerns and concentrate on the job in hand.

His eyes were used to the darkness now and he felt his way slowly to the door and bent down at the keyhole; the key was still in the lock. Riding his luck, he tried the door handle; it was unlocked. John smiled to himself and eased the door open.

The candle in the hallway spluttered in the draught of cool air from the bedroom and he stood still, willing it to remain alight as he lit his own candle stub from it, and opened the next door along, the door that led to Harcourt's bedroom. He listened for any sound of movement in the house. It was still silent.

In the dancing shadows of the room he made out the shape of the safe. Bending in front of it he tried the key that Charlie had made. It turned without a sound and he pulled the door open, staring, disbelieving for a while, at what he saw within. Then he took the bag from his pocket and filled it.

Pulling the looped rope tight, the neck of the bag closed and he took off his jacket and slipped the rope over his shoulder before putting his jacket back on. The rope cut into his flesh from the weight of the coins he had taken and he knew that the risk of climbing down the loosened gutter-pipe was now even greater.

Closing the door of Harcourt's room, John descended the stairs slowly, stopping and listening every half dozen steps or so. It wasn't until he reached the first floor that he heard their distant voices, two women talking. By their loudness and raucous laughter he guessed that they'd had more than a bit to drink. He could hear their loud exchanges clearly on the ground floor through the closed door to the basement.

He tiptoed slowly to the front door. The key was still in it and the door was unlocked, though bolted. Looking up he could see that the bolt had not been slammed home properly. It had barely engaged with the edge of the poorly drilled and worn hole in the top of the doorframe above. There was no point in risking the noise of pulling the bolt when he could avoid it.

He put a chair beside the door and taking the knife from his pocket he reached up, picking carefully at the worn wood of the bolthole until the bolt was completely free. He put the small splinters that he dislodged carefully in his pocket, then licked his fingertip and dipped it in the dust on top of the door frame. He smoothed the dark paste into the newly exposed wood until its shaved surface was indistinguishable from the dark wood around it. There was no sense in alerting them that anyone had been in or out of the door until Harcourt came home. He would know soon enough that he had been robbed. John smiled to himself as he returned the chair to its customary place by the hall table and tentatively eased the front door open. Let Harcourt figure that one out, he thought.

Chapter 28

The heavy hand James felt on his shoulder took him by surprise. He had not seen or heard anyone on The Gravel Walk for almost quarter of an hour. Turning instinctively he raised his fists, ready to strike. Then he found himself grinning uncontrollably as John backed away with a grin. 'You always were light on your feet, John,' James said. 'I kept watching Harcourt's house and yet I saw no sign of you.'

John laughed. 'It seemed a waste of energy, climbing a wall, so I used the front door instead.'

'Did all go well?' James asked.

'Better than we could ever have dreamed,' John said. 'Now let's be away from here.'

When they returned to the house they found Charlie slumped in a chair in the dining room, a glass in his hand. He struggled to his feet as they entered and lurched towards the whisky decanter and glasses on the dining room table. 'How did it go?' he asked.

'It went well,' John replied.

'Have a drink,' Charlie said, topping up his own glass, then pouring large measures into the other two glasses that stood in readiness. He left the glasses sitting in a puddle of spirit and collapsed back into his chair. 'So nothing went wrong, this time?'

'I had to use the front door to get out because the gutter-pipe was coming away from the wall,' John said. 'I had a slice of luck there. Perhaps Father Brennan had put a word in for me.' He removed his jacket and swung the bag off his shoulder and onto the dining table.

Then he proceeded to take from it bundle after bundle of banknotes and handful after handful of sovereigns. 'We've cleaned out Mister Harcourt, and I've got the letters too.' He tipped the bag and a host of coins clattered and rang as they fell onto the polished wood and spilt onto the floor.

Charlie got up again and went and sat at the table. He put his glass down with such force that half its contents were lost on the polished wood.

'I thought you never touched spirits?' John asked.

'Tonight's different,' Charlie said. 'I was worried for you, and now we've got something to celebrate. I want to enjoy it.' He spread the notes over the table and began counting them, between swigs of whisky. 'Harcourt obviously don't trust the banks with his business, there must be over three thousand pounds here.'

'There's more than I've ever seen, and I found this,' John said, tossing a small leather-bound notebook on the table. 'I thought it might be of interest, seeing as it was locked away.'

James picked up the notebook and began thumbing through its pages. The book spanned several years, itemising Harcourt's income, month by month, detailing the amount paid by various people and businesses and the date on which it was received. He was obviously a meticulous book-keeper.

Scanning the pages, names appeared and then disappeared with new ones taking their place. He could only guess as to why they should be paying Harcourt. Then towards the end of the book and starting about eighteen months ago a new name appeared and the sums paid were large and frequent. 'I cannot believe this,' James exclaimed. 'Nathaniel Caine is paying Harcourt.'

'Well it won't be blackmail,' Charlie said. The sight of all the money seemed to have sobered him a little. 'Anyone who tried blackmailing him wouldn't live for long, and besides Nat Caine's proud of every wrong deed he ever did.'

There were names in brackets next to some of the payments. James read some of them out.

'All robberies,' Charlie said. 'He's paying him for information, more likely than not. Harcourt's a snitch, telling Caine who to rob and what to steal.'

James scanned through the entries in the book. The payments seemed too much and too regular just for the passing of information. Then it hit him, what an arrogant fool he had been. He had asked

John to leave his visiting card on Frank's open safe. If Frank was in league with Caine, then Caine would soon know he was in Bath. What if Caine worked out that Charlie was involved? He tried to shrug the thought off. 'We should return this money to some of those named in the book,' he said.

'Bloody lunatic,' Charlie said. 'We can't go round these people saying, "We think you might have been robbed or blackmailed by Frank Harcourt." How der we know they didn't pay him for some dirty favour he did them? Anyways, there's not enough here to pay everybody, so who would we choose? Return the letters and we'll have done our bit.'

James noticed that Charlie was not stumbling so much now over his words and nor was he slurring, but there was little humour in his sarcasm. 'If we can't return it, then the money should go to Sean, so he can do some good with it,' James said, sensing the change in atmosphere instantly. Charlie's expression was one James had never seen before. He looked over towards John, seeking some sort of confirmation.

John's expression seemed to signal back that he understood, but that they should let it drop. 'We all took risks getting this money,' he said, with a peace-maker's tone. 'And Charlie used his skills to help and to train you. We're all entitled to some payment. There's Belle as well, and Tom, and Billy, as well as Sean.'

'Why should the priest benefit when he's done nothing,' Charlie spat.

'It's not Sean who would benefit,' James said, looking to John for some support. John turned away, as if he had had enough of the argument, but James could not let it end like this. 'Sean would get the money to the people who need it. This is dirty money and we should try to do some good with it or we're no better than Harcourt or Caine.' There was no response from either of them as they went on counting, and James wondered if they had even heard what he had said. 'Where are the letters?' he asked.

John fished in his coat and took out three bundles of letters, each tied in a differently coloured ribbon. He smiled and threw them to him. 'I didn't want to waste time going through the letters by candlelight, but these were the only letters in the safe. I guess that since your friend was concerned enough to lock them away, then they must be what you were looking for.'

'I would appreciate it if no one in future referred to Harcourt as my friend,' James said as he took the bundles of letters over to the writing desk, all too aware that the atmosphere between them had changed. It saddened him that it should happen now, just when everything seemed to be going so well, and he consciously fought the darkening in his own mood, knowing that they couldn't afford to be diverted from the plan now.

As he shuffled through the packages of letters, the shock hit him almost physically. The third bundle was smaller than the rest, three letters only and he recognised the handwriting the moment he saw it. Putting them to one side he took a deep breath and then another before looking at the letter again; there was no doubt in his mind. Taking out the first from the bundle, he read the opening paragraph; it was enough. James felt sick in the pit of his stomach and sensed his mood become sourer.

He refolded the letter and replaced it with the others, retying the ribbon before secreting the bundle under his jacket and holding it in place with his arm. He swallowed what remained of the whisky in his glass and exhaled more loudly than he had intended. 'What's wrong now?' Charlie asked. He sounded annoyed rather than interested.

'Nothing,' James replied, as he made for the door. 'I'll return in a moment.'

There was a writing slope on the table in James' bedroom. He put the letters in the bottom compartment and locked it, putting the small brass key on the silver chain around his neck. Sitting on the edge of the bed, he took a while to compose himself.

When he returned to the dining room, James made straight for the whisky decanter. It was nearly empty, he noticed. He topped up his glass before returning to the other two bundles of letters. He was more composed now; more dedicated to his purpose. Opening the first of the letters in the top bundle, he scanned its contents before rebinding the papers in the ribbon. He followed the same process with the other package before taking a pen and writing in the top left-hand corner of the first letter in each bundle. His writing was precise and deliberate, as he printed the names of the senders on both packages.

'Are they the ones you wanted?' John asked.

'Yes,' James replied, without looking up. 'Now I must return them as quickly as possible. The women who placed themselves in Harcourt's power and committed their feelings in these letters are sure to be at the ball this evening.' James turned to John, despairing of any meaningful communication with Charlie. 'I intend to free them from his hold at once.'

'It's too risky,' John said. 'You've been out tonight already. Let me take them.'

'You wouldn't be admitted to the ball and even if you got in, you wouldn't know the women concerned and nor would they speak with you. I must go. No one will expect me to show my face, besides they still believe I am in London.'

'Then I will come with you,' John said. 'I can wait outside and at least watch your back.'

'Very well, if you are sure you can be parted from the money for a while.'

'Don't let the money come between us,' John said, looking first to James and then at Charlie, but Charlie was too busy with the money to take notice.

James found himself unable to take part in any meaningful conversation with John on the way to the Assembly Rooms, his mind was too busy with the letters. He had wanted to save the women from Harcourt's blackmail and at least in that he had been successful. When the letters were returned Harcourt would have no hold over them and James knew, or at least hoped now, that they would turn on him.

He knew the women only by name, but the fact that he knew their names spoke volumes for their position and power. If they acted as he believed they might, then their influence could be turned against Harcourt; and if society shunned him he would find it difficult to worm his way back into acceptance now that he was virtually penniless. He found himself pondering on the power that lay in those letters, and felt guilty for wondering if that power could be used to advantage.

By the time that they reached the Assembly Rooms the festivities were at their height. James made straight for the ballroom. The brightness of the room, lit by five enormous crystal chandeliers, festooned with tier after tier of candles, was dazzling. It was difficult to think in the throng of a hundred conversations competing with the music which drifted down from the musicians in the gallery, high above his head. Yet in the chaos of sound he felt the plan becoming clearer in his mind.

He knew where to look for those he was seeking. Every one at the ball knew their place and understood, without instruction, with whom they could, or could not speak, or dance. The places in which they stood, and the company they sought out, was dictated by the unseen power of social gravity, its laws unwritten yet fully understood. The higher orders moved with ease to preordained positions by one or other of the three ornate marble fireplaces in the room. Those who knew them well enough to converse would position themselves within earshot, whilst the majority patrolled the opposite side of the room, like ships in search of a friendly harbour, or they stood or sat in company always with acquaintances of their own class.

James found Richard and Charlotte in the Octagon Room. The shock was clear on their faces when they saw him approaching and Richard spluttered rather than spoke as James greeted them. 'Say nothing,' he said, nodding to Charlotte as he drew Richard to one side. 'You told me one of your patients was being blackmailed by Harcourt,' James whispered. Richard nodded, his face showing no emotion. 'I have letters to Harcourt from two women and I will return them this evening. I have written their names on the packages.'

He handed the letters to Richard, who looked quickly at the names before returning them. James watched him closely, waiting for a reaction, but none came. 'Is one of these the woman you referred to?'

'Yes, Mrs Mayhew, the wife of the banker,' Richard said, tapping one of the letters, 'but how did you get them?'

'It does not matter how I came by them. Do you know if she is acquainted with the other lady?'

'I cannot be certain, but I would think so,' Richard said.

'Very well then; you introduce me to Mrs Mayhew and I will have her introduce me to Lady Nayland. You must say nothing to Charlotte of this.' James turned; the annoyance was already clear on Charlotte's face, her agitation plain in the motion of her fan. She was not used to being excluded and made no secret of the fact.

'My apologies on Charlotte's behalf,' Richard said. 'She has not been herself of late. She seems detached, as though her mind were always somewhere else. I thought the ball would please her, but it seems not.'

'You need make no apology,' James said, 'but she must know nothing of what we are doing.'

'Of course,' Richard replied. He returned to Charlotte and took her arm, guiding her to the door of the ballroom. James could hear nothing of their conversation, but he watched as Charlotte's irritation grew more obvious.

When the next dance ended, Richard walked over and led him through the dispersing dancers and to a party standing at one of the central fireplaces. When he introduced him to Mrs Mayhew James heard the mutterings; saw the disapproving looks exchanged amongst the party.

James passed his card to the woman. Next to his name he had written, 'I have your letters.' She looked at the card and placed it in her purse before turning to her husband. 'You know Dr Wetherby of course, my dear,' she said, 'but I don't believe you are acquainted with Mr Daunton, the solicitor. I had promised him a dance.'

She took his arm, and he led her onto the floor. Their faces, he knew, were smiling masks, hiding the words they exchanged whenever the dance brought them within whispering distance. 'I have your letters to Harcourt,' he said.

'What is your price?' Mrs Mayhew asked.

'There is no price other than your discretion, but I would ask a favour.'

'Tell me,' she said, her anger showing through her smile.

'Write to the newspapers expressing concern at the growing levels of crime in the city and point to Avon Street as its source; speak about it to politicians, to the Watch Committee, question the integrity of the police at every opportunity and bring pressure to bear on the chief constable. Make corruption within the constabulary in Avon Street a topic of conversation at every social function you attend.'

'Is that all?' she asked. 'It seems little enough in return for the favour you have done me.'

'You and your family and friends have great influence in Bath and while this may seem a trifle to you, it will help a great many people.' His feigned smile was forgotten for a moment as he looked her square in the eyes, all deference gone from his expression. 'I am depending on your honour in doing what I ask.'

Her smile was easier now. 'It will be done, but can I do nothing more?' she asked.

James smiled. 'Perhaps you could include Dr Wetherby and his wife occasionally in your social circle.'

'That too shall be done,' she said, as the dance drew to an end. 'You are more of a gentleman than I anticipated, and you have my word.'

Her introduction to Lady Nayland was enacted easily and as she turned to leave, Mrs Mayhew executed a perfect stumble as they had arranged and James passed the letters to her, unseen as far as he could tell. He asked the same two favours of Lady Nayland and when he was done she slipped the letters into her purse and smiled her thanks.

Richard looked happier as they returned across the room. He smiled to Charlotte. 'Mrs Mayhew has asked if we would care to join her party for a while?' he said. Charlotte's delighted agreement needed no words.

'You must join them immediately,' James said. 'It may brighten Charlotte's mood.' He hesitated, waiting for her reaction, but she showed nothing but delight.

'Incidentally, have you seen Harcourt?' James asked. His question was to Richard, but his eyes were still on Charlotte. He thought he saw her smile diminish for a moment, but he couldn't be sure.

'No,' Richard replied, 'and I shall put distance between us if I do see him.'

'Best join Mrs Mayhew,' James said, 'I have to leave now.' He nodded to Charlotte and watched them walk together, arm in arm, across the ballroom. There was little sign of emotion on her face now, just a composed, cool demeanour and a look of fulfilled acceptance.

When he was sure that Richard and Charlotte were oblivious to his presence, James stood for a while in the doorway to the ballroom, mingling, he hoped un-noticed, on the fringe of the people entering and leaving the room. He wanted to stay, to watch the reception that Harcourt would receive; to see society beginning to turn its back on the man, but he knew he must leave. By the time Charlotte had reached Mrs Mayhew's party he knew she would have fully rationalised this sudden elevation in society. She would have no doubt that she was more than their match in both accomplishment and appearance.

When they returned to the house, Charlie greeted them in the dining room – a glass in one hand and the decanter in the other. James noticed that the decanter had been refilled. Charlie raised his glass in a toast, but the statement was largely unintelligible, so badly slurred were his words.

John took the decanter from him and poured a whisky for himself and one for James. 'We've some catching up to do,' he said. Charlie fell back into his chair as though the removal of the decanter from his hand had upset his equilibrium.

James looked at the table and the neat piles of money. 'I see you have shared it all out,' he said to Charlie, 'without feeling the need to discuss it with John or me.'

'There's a fair share for each of you expecting the priest,' Charlie said, failing to even notice the mistake in his words. 'My share's put away safe. So if you want some for the priest give it him yourself, or steal it from John, and Belle, and Billy's share.'

'You're drunk as a skunk, Charlie,' John said. 'Let's not fall out over this.'

'We are supposed to be friends,' James said. 'We decide together how the money is to be shared.'

'You tell us and we agree,' Charlie spluttered, 'that's what you mean. My opinion's not worth anything.'

'That's not true,' James said.

'We have to do what thur gentleman tells us,' Charlie slurred, and then muttered under his breath. 'Smug bastard.'

'Leave it,' John said. 'We can talk about it in the morning.'

'That's if he's here in the morning,' Charlie said. 'It's my house and I want you out of it. You're not welcome.'

'We will leave in the morning,' James said.

'Why don't you go to bed, Charlie.' John said.

'Why don't you go to hell,' Charlie spat back. Then he tried to grin. 'No not you, John, I didn't mean you.'

James looked towards John, expecting a reaction. He returned James' glance, but his face was impassive and betrayed nothing.

'Go to bed, Charlie,' John said again. 'We'll talk about it in the morning.'

'This is my house,' Charlie replied, 'and I take orders from no one in my own house.'

As Mrs Hawker entered the room to clear away the dinner table, the three men fell into silence. Charlie tried to smile, but it came out more like a leer.

'Charlie has asked us to leave and we will go in the morning,' James said.

'Not 'er,' Charlie said. 'She can stay.' He lurched to his feet and tried to take Mrs Hawker's hand. She pushed him and he toppled back into his chair.

'I'll not stay where Master James is not welcome,' she said. 'I've never seen you like this, Charlie ... ' her words petered out as though the emotions were too much for her. James put his arm around her shoulder and guided her out of the room, turning back only for a moment to look at John.

'Get Mrs Hawker to her bed,' John said. 'I'll sit with him.'

James looked over towards Charlie. He had passed out in his chair.

Chapter 29

Frank Harcourt did not sleep that night. He sat instead for hours on the edge of his bed, staring at the empty safe, turning James Daunton's visiting card over and over in his fingers. He knew the servants could never have kept up a lie to him during the interrogation he had put them through, reducing them both to tears, time and again. They hadn't let anyone in, though they'd obviously been drinking. He could be sure that they knew nothing about the robbery.

The thief must have got in and out through the window in the room next to his own bedroom, he thought. It had been left open yet the room hadn't been used in months and the window was never opened in the winter. That's how Daunton must have done it. He had climbed up the gutter-pipe and prised the window open.

Frank wondered, though, how Daunton had opened the safe when the key never left his sight. How had he even known about the safe, unless he'd told him about it on one of their drinking sprees, though he couldn't remember ever doing so. Perhaps Daunton had got hold of the key when he had been drunk one night and made an impression of it? Or had he hired some cracksman who'd picked the lock? Maybe he had recruited someone in London, if he'd ever been in London? But how could two get in unnoticed? He had tested the gutter-pipe outside the window. It was loose. It would never have supported a man's weight, let alone two, unless they had loosened it during their escape?

Frank pulled savagely at his hair, willing his mind to clear. If it was Daunton, and he had had a partner, who was it? No one worked in Bath without Caine's knowledge; unless of course it was with Caine's knowledge? Caine knew about his safe. It was Caine who got the safe for him when they first set up their partnership. Maybe Caine had done it? He might have kept a key to the safe. Perhaps Caine had robbed him and left Daunton's card to deceive him?

The questions went around and around in his brain until each possible answer contradicted the other, until he trusted no one but himself. All his money was gone and had to be replaced somehow. Even the letters were gone; another source of income lost. That in itself was strange, he deliberated. It was as though the women at the ball had already known he no longer had the letters. Lady Nayland and Mrs Mayhew had both cut him dead; treated him like dirt, ignored him. And others had ignored him too, as though the whole of Bath society was suddenly turning against him.

He had to focus his mind, concentrate on the future, stop his head aching; stop dwelling on what had happened. There was enough, he calculated, in his bank account to cover one or two small payments and he had a modest amount of cash and saleable trinkets in the secretary desk, sufficient for a few days' expenditure, which was still there, untouched. Other than that he had only his clothes and some silver plate – he could sell them, but if he stooped that low then he was finished – all that he had worked for would be lost.

He focussed his hatred on Daunton, as if that would clear his mind. He despised him and his class, now more than he ever had in the past, and he'd hated them well enough all his life. Yet he had to be accepted. How else could he demonstrate his superiority and show them up for the fools they were? He could not let them win and yet he could not win, if they excluded him from the game.

He would cut his losses, he determined and set up in some other city where he was unknown; but to do that he needed money. Whether he stayed or left he had to have money and quickly, and he knew, as he had known from the moment he discovered the robbery, that his only remaining source of income was Nat Caine.

Frank wished that he had had more faith in the banks, but he had always mistrusted them, always been wary of investing in speculative ventures where he might be cheated, or lose everything through some market foible; besides, so many banks had failed and left their investors penniless. He much preferred to hold his wealth in cash and to hold it nearby, ready for a fast escape. But he had never countenanced someone having the audacity to rob him. He still had one asset though that no one could steal, the ideas and knowledge he kept locked away in his mind. The shame of it was that at the very time that he needed Caine most, he was least sure how much he could trust him.

Placing the writing box on his bed, he threw open the curtains and began drawing out the plans of the first of the houses he had in mind for Caine to rob. He marked the access points, the locations of the valuables to be taken, noting what should be taken and what should be left, and listing who might be in the house. He checked in his diary for any social events that might draw the residents away from their homes, but nothing came to mind.

He had planned so meticulously in the past, but there was little time for finesse now. The break-ins would have to be late at night. They would have to take the chance that the households would be abed and asleep. But he would have to plan his strategy carefully; Caine would not like the idea of carrying out three robberies so close together. He would have to appeal to his greed, and provided Caine did the three jobs as quickly as possible, a lower cut might be acceptable.

Then he remembered it; the next big event of the season. Lansdown Fair was due in a few weeks time. Yet Caine always made money at the fair. It was where accounts outstanding were always settled. After the fair Caine's coffers would be full and his greed would be more difficult to appeal to. Frank knew that he would have to demand that the jobs were done before Lansdown Fair. They would dissolve their partnership and he would take his share while Caine had his mind busy, preparing for settlement day.

A few hundred yards away in The Paragon, the household was very quiet on the morning after the robbery. James had slept little and came down early to the kitchen to speak to Mrs Hawker. He found the kitchen table already set with plates of bacon and eggs, kidneys and mushrooms. John broke off from eating and pulled a chair back for James to sit. 'I've been talking with Mrs Hawker,' he said.

'And will you come with us when we leave?' James asked.

John ignored his questioning stare and carried on eating. 'We've decided,' he said, talking between mouthfuls, 'that there are friendships at stake here, friendships worth fighting for. Let's see how Charlie is this morning.'

'Perhaps I was too quick to judge him last night,' James said. 'I knew he was drunk, but I've never seen him like that before.'

'Neither have I,' Mrs Hawker said. 'He needs caring for and a little guidance; someone to help him. He's not really like that.'

'You have to understand what Charlie was trying to say,' John replied. 'Forget his drunken rantings. Neither he, nor I, nor any of the others have any money to speak of. Charlie's getting older and he knows nothing but thieving. If he goes back to it, he'll end in prison without doubt.'

'But it's dirty money and if we keep it we are as tainted as Caine or Harcourt,' James said, trying to engage John's eyes. 'I believed we had a nobler purpose.'

'There's truth in what you say,' John said.

'What we do determines who we are and I will not become like Caine,' James replied. 'Sean could do so much with that money.'

'Sean's a good man,' John replied. 'Not because he's a priest. It's just how he is with his people.' He stopped eating and stared back, his eyes unblinking and intense. 'But you're not the only one with a conscience. What we do, we should agree together. I've spent too long taking orders. Just bear in mind, we never talked about what we'd do with anything we took from Harcourt.'

It was true – John and Charlie had asked for nothing. It was he who had held out the prospect of further booty like a carrot before them after they had cheated the silversmiths, and now he was proposing to take everything from them. He had brought them together and because they had accepted him as their leader he had blindly assumed that they would accept his decisions without question or reason. But there was more than one way of descending to Caine's level, James now recognised. John and Charlie had risked their lives for him and he had taken it for granted.

John was still looking at him, expecting some response. He was about to speak when the kitchen door creaked open. They all looked up as Charlie shambled into the room and shut the door behind him, avoiding every set of eyes upon him. He pulled back a chair and sat, knotting the fingers of both hands together on the table in front of him and staring at the floor between his legs. The room fell silent. James saw the shake in Charlie's hands as Mrs Hawker parted his arms and placed a plate in front of him. His eyes were sunken and his lined face looked older and intensely vulnerable.

'What have you to say for yourself?' Mrs Hawker said.

'I apologise with all my heart,' Charlie said. 'I don't remember much of what I said or did, but I know I caused pain. I should never have drunk; it is like a sickness with me and I know it. The priest should have half of the money,' he said, his eyes still rooted to the ground. For a while there was silence and then he looked up uncertainly, and held out a still shaking hand across the table towards James.

'I have one proviso,' James said. 'Whatever else we take from Caine, even if it is ten times what we took from Harcourt, the lion's share should go to Sean and we agree it together, now, or we go our separate ways.'

'You have my word,' Charlie said, without hesitating. 'And you have my word that I'll never drink again.' He offered his hand and James took it in his own and shook it firmly.

'You can pay off your debts, James, with your share from Harcourt's house,' John said. 'There'll be more than enough.'

'My debts are largely of my own making,' James replied. 'I'd rather get some good out of Harcourt's money and perhaps ease my conscience a little in the process. My share will go to help my brother and pay off the debts of the tenants. My borrowings can wait until I can pay them by my own endeavours. The last thing I want is to profit from this.'

Charlie turned to look in Mrs Hawker's direction and James could tell that he still found it difficult to look her in the eyes. 'You won't be going now, will you, any of you?'

'You left the dinner plates in the dining room,' Mrs Hawker said to him, 'so I brought them down and put them in the sink. When you've finished your breakfast you can wash and dry them and your breakfast dishes and stack them on the kitchen table. I'll put them away after I've had a sit down. We'll talk then.'

When James and John returned to the dining room, all of the money that Charlie had taken as his share had already been returned to the table. James sat reflecting for a while. They had each done what was called for day by day, yet they shared no common plan other than the desire to destroy Caine; a desire that had grown from a simple fight for survival. Now it was about honour, a different type of honour for each, but honour nevertheless. He looked over at John thumbing through the newspaper. They could never have got so far without him, and yet he still gave away so little of himself.

John must have noticed his glance. 'Where would you have gone if Charlie had thrown you out?' he asked.

'I have a bolthole,' James replied. 'Richard rented a house for us in Walcot Parade and I have the key. It was a safeguard on the chance that Charlie's hospitality might run out, or that Caine might discover our whereabouts.' He hesitated, watching John's reaction. 'I think the time is rapidly approaching when we should use it.'

'Charlie would be hurt,' John said.

'He can come with us,' James replied. 'We can't hide here indefinitely. Caine will track us down eventually. It would be safer to keep on the move.'

'Don't say anything to Charlie yet,' John said. 'He'll think it's because of last night.'

It was almost two hours before Charlie joined them. 'Today is a new day, Charlie,' James said, 'and anything that happened last night is forgotten.'

Charlie smiled. 'You mentioned taking more from Caine,' he said, 'so I take it we are going to rob his house in Hucklebridge's Court.'

James massaged the life back into his face. 'It's still too early. We agreed at the outset that we would never defeat Caine with brute strength,' he said. 'We have been victorious against Harcourt, more by luck than judgement. Now we must put chance aside in favour of sound preparation.'

'Robbing Caine's den needs careful planning,' Charlie said. He seemed enthused, as though he was now on more familiar territory and felt he could contribute, put right the offence he had caused. He was smiling, with new energy, and the last thing James wanted to do was to squash his spirit, but he knew it was too soon to meet Caine head-on.

'You have done a good job, Charlie,' James said. 'We know all the ways in and out of Caine's house thanks to you and John.'

'The best way in is through the back door,' Charlie said. 'But there's allers two guards outside the door and the street is not much used. We couldn't get near them without being seen and they'll 'ave pistols cocked and aimed by the time you reach them.'

'And then we don't know who we'll find inside,' John interrupted.

'There are too many problems and risks,' James mused. 'We need to consider other options. We cannot allow ourselves to be trapped into a single course of action. How else might we strike at Caine?'

'There's his old haunt in Cockroad,' Charlie said.

'There's nothing there but grief,' John said. 'Diarmuid's been staying at The Blue Bowl in Hanham and he knows all the comings and goings in Cockroad. Caine keeps it as a bolthole, but there's no money there and the village is like a fortress, they're all loyal to Caine. Even the peelers daren't go there.'

'Bring Diarmuid back to Bath then,' James said. 'He'll be of more use here and it seems there is little more he can learn where he is. Is there any other way that we could strike at Caine, Charlie…? Think!'

Charlie looked lost in thought for a while and then he smiled. 'Well there's Lansdown Fair. I should have thought of it afore.'

'Tell us more,' James said.

'It's a Cockroad tradition that goes back long before the gang moved to Bath; before Nat Caine was their leader,' Charlie replied. 'Lansdown Fair is the settling day; most of those who the gang extorts protection money from pays up at the annual fair and they take a cut from the pickpockets, card sharps and con men.'

'So he is sure to be there?' James asked.

'Caine has to be there in strength or he'd lose all reputation,' Charlie replied. 'And they're running the Bath Races this year for the first time in years. That's going to bring even more money to the fair. Caine will be looking to take a cut from the bookmakers. He won't give that up if the devil himself was there and if we hit him there, he'd go down. But we'd need to hit him hard.'

'That sounds more promising,' James said, 'We can face him down in the open where he has nowhere to hide, but we'd need help, we'd be outnumbered.'

'But we have money now,' John said. 'We can get more men. And besides, I get the feeling that there's plenty in Avon Street who'd side with us now, without pay.'

'We decide nothing for now,' James said. 'It will take careful planning, but there must be a way.' For a while he was lost in his thoughts, almost forgetting that the others were still in the room. 'We don't have very long,' Charlie said. 'The fair's in three weeks time.'

'That's long enough, for what I have in mind,' James said. 'In the meantime we must weaken Caine as much as we can.'

'What's your thinking?' John asked.

'Caine has built a wall around himself, thicker than the walls of any house,' James said. 'He has the local constabulary in his pay and they protect him. He seems invincible to those whom he bullies and exploits and their fear protects him. We need to break down the walls he hides behind. We have to sap his strength before Lansdown Fair, make him and his men feel vulnerable. Make the people he exploits believe that they can stand up to him; that he can be defeated.'

'And how do we do it?' John asked.

'I've set some events in motion, now we need to build on them,' James replied. 'I asked the ladies to whom I returned Harcourt's letters to use their influence and bring pressure to bear on the politicians and the chief constable.'

'How will that help?' Charlie asked.

'Society may not react to a problem largely confined to Avon Street,' James replied, 'but when the upper echelons begin complaining, the council and chief constable will have to be seen to respond.'

'That's true,' Charlie said. 'They'll listen to lords and ladies where they won't to real folk.'

'I need you to get me the names of the constables in Caine's pay, Charlie. When the chief constable's been whipped into action, an anonymous letter written in a gentleman's hand, listing the corrupt officers, is bound to have an effect. We must try to ensure that Caine has no friends in the constabulary by the time that Lansdown Fair comes around.'

'I can get you the names,' Charlie said, smiling with obvious satisfaction.

'Only the bad ones, Charlie,' John interrupted. 'No settling old scores. We don't want the innocent to suffer. We may need the peelers.'

Charlie laughed. 'Don't worry; the peelers will be out in force for the fair.'

'What can I do?' John asked.

'Get Brendan and the others together and begin picking off one or two of Caine's collectors again. They should have relaxed their guard by now. It will worry and distract Caine, and more importantly it will make him seem less invincible to the people of Avon Street. But take no risks and cease the moment he responds – no more than three days.'

'I'll take no risks,' John smiled. 'We'll start against Caine's men tomorrow, and I'll bring Billy in this time. He's got money in his pocket now and if he's not kept busy he drinks too much of it away.'

It was clear from John's face that he had realised what he had said almost as soon as he had said it. James and he looked at Charlie almost simultaneously, but Charlie looked away.

Belle was alone in the room when she heard the knock on the door. She was apprehensive, calculating who might be calling, nervous that Harcourt might have sought her out. Hesitant at first, she opened the door a little. When she saw Charlie's grinning face she allowed herself to smile. 'I'm alone, Charlie,' she said, as though the words were everything that needed to be spoken between two conspirators in crime.

'It were you I came to see,' he replied, 'though I brought a gift for all of you.' He fished underneath his coat and held the object out towards her. 'It's a pineapple,' he said. 'Some folk use them as table ornaments, because they're so dear, but I'm told as they make very tasty eating. You skins 'em and cuts out slices and they're very sweet. I thought it would help the littl'un get stronger.'

The pineapple probably cost as much as would have fed all three of them for a week, Belle thought, yet she found herself loving him for the ridiculousness of the gesture, and he seemed strangely vulnerable today. 'It's a very kind thought, Charlie,' she said, smiling, 'but they're very expensive.'

'Aye, I know that, but we're all quite well to do now.'

'Were you successful . . . I mean at Harcourt's house? I was worried. No one was hurt were they?'

'No one was hurt, except Harcourt, and he were only injured in his pocket and his pride. It weren't a success that night, but it laid the grounds, and we did the job proper last night.' It was then that he took out the money wrapped in a handkerchief from under his jacket and offered it to her. 'This is yours, your share for helping in the robbery,' he said, thrusting the small cotton sack into her hand. She could feel the weight of the coins, hear them jingling together. She opened the cloth on the bed; there were more gold sovereigns than she had ever seen, and banknotes too.

'It wasn't for money that I gave what little assistance I could,' she said, stumbling over her words. 'I am happy that Harcourt has been punished and even more pleased that no one was hurt.'

'But we are all agreed that you earned this money,' he said gripping her hand and placing it on the money.

She looked again at the money, scared to estimate how much was there. 'I cannot take all this,' she said, 'all I did was provide a diversion.' Her mind would not be still – thoughts of freedom – what she could buy – a house for them all – schooling for Molly – everything she could ever want. Then the nagging doubts took form. Stupid doubts, but yet she could not make them go away. Charlie was watching her; she could see he was confused and possibly offended by her reluctance.

'It was you got James in, and besides you're one of us now,' he said. 'Half of the money is going to help people in Avon Street and those in debt to Nathaniel Caine. Say you will take your share of the rest.'

She recognised Caine's name instantly. It was the man that Jenny had borrowed from. 'But Charlie . . . ' she said, her thoughts still jumbled and her words failing. She retreated into the room, away from the bed, trying to compose herself, to make some sense of what was happening. 'Yes, I'll take the money.' She let herself laugh and he smiled in response. 'But where can I keep it safe?'

She watched as Charlie picked up the handkerchief of money and walked around the perimeter of the room, apparently lost in thought. Then he dropped to his knees, pulled out a penknife and prised away at a small floorboard near the chest of drawers. 'Do you have a tin or box?' Charlie asked. Belle emptied some buttons from a tin and handed it to Charlie. He placed the money inside and put it under the floorboard, easing the chest of drawers over one end. 'We don't want the mice eating your nest egg, do we?' he said. 'Put the money in a couple of the banks in the city. You don't want to put all your trust in one bank. And move the money in, a few notes at a time, so they don't get suspicious. There won't be any trouble though, the notes are well used.'

'Thank you, Charlie,' she said. 'I need time to think what I am going to do with so much money.'

The smile returned to Charlie's face as he took the two gold sovereigns that he must have already removed from the stash and handed them to her. 'At least enjoy this,' he said, stuffing the coins into her hand. Then hearing footsteps on the stairs he went to the door.

'Hello, littl'un,' he said as Molly wrapped her arms around his legs. He picked her up and carried her into the room. 'Look what I've brought you,' he said, picking up the pineapple from the bedside chair.

Chapter 30

Belle had chosen a dress of black and grey, patterned in large silken squares, with a matching bonnet, to visit James at the house in The Paragon. It was old, and she wondered if the ensemble made her appear too dowdy and matronly, but she had no others suited for visiting that she had not already worn; besides she liked the outfit, or so she kept telling herself.

Mrs Hawker showed her up to the drawing room, where Belle endeavoured to sit composed and elegant on the sofa, but when she looked down she found herself arranging and rearranging the leather gloves folded on her lap. When James entered the room he also seemed uneasy, uncertain as to where to sit and what to say or do. She wondered if he was embarrassed by her visit, but the warmth of his smile seemed to say otherwise.

James flitted from topic to topic, as if searching for common ground and Belle gradually felt the easiness grow between them. The more it grew, the more playful his eyes became and the more she felt herself slipping into the game they were playing. For a while it seemed that games were all that mattered, and life outside the room was merely an annoying distraction.

'I wanted to thank you,' she said, 'for what you did to Harcourt and for the money. It was very kind.' As soon as she had said it, she felt a change in his mood. All it had needed, it seemed, was the mention of Harcourt's name for the games to be set aside. 'I considered for a while refusing the money,' she said.

'Charlie told me,' he replied. 'But they would not have allowed it. You earned the money.'

'How can anyone earn that amount of money?' she asked. 'Do you realise how so much money can change a person's life?'

'Of course,' he replied.

'You reply easily,' Belle said. 'But you have had money all your life. You are used to what it can buy. I cannot even begin to think how having so much could change me, and the others about me.' She saw a difference in his expression, and wondered if the spell was broken. She thought perhaps she should leave. 'Perhaps our business is concluded,' she said, as she made to rise from the chair.

'Please stay,' he said. 'I've not yet told you about the robbery, or thanked you properly for all that you have done.' His voice was gentle, almost pleading.

Belle smiled and remained seating. 'Knowing that the robbery has helped others makes it easier for me to accept so much. But please know that the money . . . I didn't only take it for me. It buys security for Molly and Jenny and it buys freedom for us all.'

'I see now that the money will help a great many people, and in ways I never contemplated,' he replied.

She wondered whether she was justifying her actions to him or to herself. When she had mentioned 'freedom' she thought his expression had changed, but he said nothing. 'I will stay a while longer. Tell me about the robbery.'

He seemed to relax and sat in the chair opposite her as if about to tell an after dinner anecdote. Once he had begun, James told every bit of the tale, dwelling on her own small role and emphasising his own ineptness as a housebreaker. She could tell he enjoyed the telling and he watched for her every reaction. His brown eyes were so dark and warm and reassuring. She felt she should look away, but his eyes wouldn't let her. She felt compelled to provide the occasional gasp of amazement, yet it felt quite natural to do so, and when she laughed, he laughed with her.

Then, almost without her noticing it, the room grew quiet. The silence seemed to draw her in, with all of its potential for misunderstanding. It should have felt comfortable to her, the peace between two people, but instead it felt uneasy, the reality and illusion of the moment blending in the nothingness of silence, until the one was indistinguishable from the other. She tried to recognise his emotions from his face. He glanced back at her, his expression registering the same uncertainty, the same nervousness. She smiled and again he smiled back, but the silence was there again.

Belle strolled over to the piano by the far wall, drifting her fingers over its gleaming polished keys. Then she sat on the stool and began playing, wondering if he truly understood her.

'Do you read music?' he asked.

'No,' she replied, 'though I can learn a melody relatively quickly, provided it's not too complex.' She remembered her mother playing, teaching her how to listen and to feel the movement of the music through her hands.

'What is the name of the piece you're playing?' he asked.

'I really don't know,' she replied. 'It's a piece my mother taught me and I always find it calming.'

He walked towards her, standing by the piano, watching her play. 'How strange it is that music has no objective meaning, yet speaks so eloquently. The language of notes, and beats, and chords, and rhythms, defies translation. We cannot say that these notes say this, or that sequence means that, and yet it speaks to us sometimes better than any spoken words.'

'I know little of composition or purity of form,' Belle replied, 'but I envy those who can create music, with such passion, and without the need for niceties and polite trivialities.'

His answering smile felt so warm. 'If we had met under different circumstances, we might know each other better by now,' he said, as though leaving a question hanging in the air between them.

'A well born solicitor and an actress,' she replied. 'Not the most auspicious basis for a lasting relationship. We would hardly be the most sought after couple in Bath society.' She felt her nervousness show in the tempo of the piece, but he didn't seem to notice.

'Perhaps that would not be important, and besides Bath can be an understanding city.'

'I would not want to be tied to Bath,' she replied. 'My work requires that I travel and it is important to me to pursue my career.'

'You misunderstand me,' James stuttered. He was obviously embarrassed by her comment. She had not meant to be so forthright. 'I merely meant we might have been friends,' he said.

Belle stopped playing and walked around the room, feigning interest in the paintings and ornaments. His face seemed very gentle and capable of understanding. What prompted her to say it she did not know, but the words appeared from her lips, 'There is something I did not tell you, concerning Harcourt.'

'What is it?' he asked.

'He sent the note telling me to go to Queen Square that day for a reason.'

'The man is malevolent,' James interrupted. 'He knew what was to happen. He wanted you to see me shot for some malicious reasoning of his evil mind.'

'No that's not all of it,' she said, 'it was meant as a warning to me, but not because I had slapped him. It was because I know more about him than I should. He took me into his confidence to break down the barriers between us and he achieved what he wanted. You see, we were lovers.'

She was surprised at the shame she felt in saying the word 'lovers' and yet she needed to tell him. 'To use the word love in connection with Harcourt now feels abhorrent, but I was taken in by him.' She tried to gauge his feelings from his face but it was like a mask. 'I'm not sorry I told you,' she said. 'I did not want to deceive you in any way. Please do not judge me.'

'Harcourt is a convincing liar,' he said. 'He made a fool of me and he has a way with women.'

His answer was too quick, she thought, too dismissive. It hurt, to be considered as one of the women Harcourt 'had a way with'. She had truly loved him or so she thought, but then so had the others, she supposed. Frank had the ability, when it suited him, to make you feel as though you were the centre of his universe; that all your faults were endearing and your virtues unique and beyond compare. He would listen as though nothing else mattered, every conversation an exercise in flirtation and manipulation.

It hurt that James now thought less of her, but that was the risk she had taken. He would undoubtedly deny it, if she was to ask him, but how could she ask? Such a simple word, 'lovers', yet its simplicity hid so many complexities, so many different stories and interpretations, understandings and misunderstandings. She did not know what to say, so she said nothing and the silence became a wall between them for a while.

It was James that first spoke. He began telling her how Harcourt was tied in with Nat Caine and how the gang were money lenders and extortionists and she struggled to keep her mind in check, to listen to his words. When he began talking of how they were at war with Caine and how they planned to bring him down, she realised how badly the odds must be stacked against them and forgot her own concerns for a while. He had obviously wanted to change the subject and she saw no reason to deter him. He described Caine's lair: its entrances and exits, fortifications and guards, and she found herself drawn into the situation as though it were the staging of a new play. He told her about settlement day at Lansdown Fair and how Caine used it to exert power. When he had finished he looked at her and smiled, and she knew that he understood, all too well, that it was unlikely they would succeed.

'I will help in any way I can,' she said. 'I know the pain that Caine inflicts. I've seen the fear he creates.'

'You have already helped enough,' he replied.

'Getting into Caine's house,' she said, 'I can help with that as I did with Harcourt.' She started to outline an idea. He cut her short.

'It would be dangerous,' he said, 'besides it may never come to that.'

'Shall I visit again?' she asked. 'We could discuss it further, or perhaps I can help in another way.

'No,' he replied. 'While Harcourt remains in Bath you may still be in danger. Don't come again, unless I send word that it is safe.'

Nat Caine allowed himself to feel content for the first time in days. It was some time now since the last attack on his men. They had been going about their business in groups for a while, just to make sure. He had readied himself for war, against whoever might be setting up in opposition, but then the trouble had died away. Most likely it was some band of vagrants or gypsies, with ideas above their station, he thought. There were enough of them passing through the city on a daily basis. But this had seemed too organised, as though there was someone behind them, planning and controlling; someone who wanted to challenge his power.

Caine had toured Avon Street that day with Harry Wood and a few of the lads, visiting some of his better customers and some of the more difficult ones. The respect was still there, but not what it had been, as though they sensed he was not the man he had been. Perhaps they thought he was getting soft. He'd have to disabuse them of that idea.

'That Harcourt's waiting for you downstairs,' Jeb said as he opened the front door. Caine smiled, seeing Jeb's displeasure at Harcourt's presence. Divide and conquer, he thought, it's always the best way, always leave them guessing where they stand. He put his arm around Harry's shoulder before leading him down to the kitchen.

Harcourt turned as they entered and some of the papers that he had spread across the table in front of him spilled onto the floor. He bent and picked them up, replacing them on the table, careful of their order. There was something different about him, Caine thought. He'd never seen Harcourt edgy before, but the man was nervous, there was no mistaking it.

'How bist?' Caine asked.

'Not well,' Frank replied, 'I've been robbed.'

The news came as a shock. Nothing seemed as it had been any longer. 'Who were it?' Caine asked. 'I've heard nothing.'

'Probably Daunton,' Frank replied. 'He left his card.'

Caine laughed as he let the news sink in.

'So he's back in Bath?' Harry said. His expression worried Caine, as though thoughts of Daunton had driven everything else from his mind. Harry always seemed to have a short fuse these days, and Caine knew this news would be more than enough to set him off.

'That's if he ever left,' Frank said. 'He took everything I had. I need money, Nat, and quickly.'

'Didn't you keep your money in the safe I got you?' Caine asked.

'Yes,' Frank replied, 'he picked the lock, or got in somehow.'

'Then he had help,' Caine said. 'That were a good safe.'

'I don't know,' Frank replied. 'I think he was alone, perhaps he got the key off me one night when I was drunk and made a copy. I don't know.'

'There's only one or two in town with the skill to get into that safe without a key,' Caine said. In truth there was only one name that came to Caine's mind: Charlie Maggs. He was the only one capable of getting into that safe, unless Daunton had brought someone down from London. But there was something wrong, Caine thought. Harcourt was being evasive, as though he knew more about the robbery than he was letting on.

'How did he get into the house?' Caine asked.

'Does it matter?' Frank replied. 'Perhaps through a second-floor window, but I'm trying to put it behind me. Can we get on with making some more money?'

It couldn't have been Maggs, Caine thought; he couldn't have climbed up to the second floor. Yet he was the only one capable of picking that lock. Still, it would do no harm to put the word around; find out where Charlie was living these days and what he was up to.

Caine was suddenly conscious that the others were watching him. He smiled. 'I can lend you money, Frank,' he said.

Frank laughed. 'Borrowing's for fools,' and then as though it was an after-thought he added, 'kind though your offer is, Nat. Besides I may well decide to leave Bath and I'll not leave owing.'

Caine watched him, trying to fathom the truth. 'I've plans for a house that's begging to be robbed,' Frank said.

'I suppose it's about the right time to do another big house,' Caine replied, shuffling through Harcourt's papers. 'But what was it you said about leaving Bath? How would that leave our business arrangement?'

'All good things come to an end,' Frank replied. 'Besides, it may not come to that.' He hesitated, as though judging his words. Caine studied his face and wondered why he was lying. There was no question. Harcourt was intending to leave; he just didn't want to discuss it. But he had another thing coming if he thought he could just walk away as easily as that, it was disrespectful.

'And it's not just one house we're robbing,' Frank resumed, 'it's three. My parting gift for you; provided they're all done before Lansdown Fair.'

'We agreed three or four each six month, enough to bring the money in but not too many as would stir up the law,' Caine said. 'Three in as many weeks is too many.'

'Needs must, where the devil drives,' Frank said.

'I don't like it. It's too many and too rushed,' Caine replied. The doubts began gnawing at his mind and at his guts, and he wondered if Harcourt had been robbed at all, or if it wasn't some ruse he had dreamed up. He could have invented the robbery to force his hand or to get out of their partnership. Caine looked at Harry, wondering if he too was uneasy with what Harcourt was saying, but he was staring into space, his mind somewhere else. He kicked him. 'Get your mind off Daunton. We've more pressing business.' For a moment Harry seemed more attentive, but Caine could tell his mind was still elsewhere.

'These plans are for the first house and the poorest,' Harcourt said, shuffling nervously through the papers on the table. 'If you don't want to do three then the plans for the other houses go with me.'

Frank paused. Caine knew why, and said nothing. It seemed to unnerve Harcourt but he kept up the same line when he resumed. 'The last I had in mind is all cash; more than we've ever taken before;

one I've been saving for a rainy day. You'll have the plans on the day we do the job or not at all.'

Caine leapt to his feet. 'This is blackmail and you know damn well it is. I'd be taking all the risks.' The thought kept going through his mind that Harcourt was setting him up for something; maybe he was trying to take the gang away from him. If that was it then Harcourt was a fool. The men would never follow him. Yet the thought of the money wouldn't leave him. Eventually his curiosity got the better of him. 'What's the last job?'

'A shopkeeper,' Frank replied. Caine laughed, watching his reaction, but the man just smiled in reply. 'He's a shopkeeper with three stores, and two of them in Milsom Street. There'll be a week's takings from all three in his house if you go in on the right day.'

It was tempting, Caine thought, too tempting to pass up, and Harcourt had known that from the start. But if he believed he could set him up, then he had another thing coming. 'We will have to share the risks though,' Caine said, with a grin. 'It's only fair. You will have to go along on all three jobs.' How would he take to that idea he wondered, having to put his own neck on the block? Caine watched for Harcourt's reaction, waiting for the argument.

Frank just smiled. 'Very well, I've nothing to fear,' he said.

'Tell me about the first job then,' Caine said, pawing through the drawings and plans. He could almost smell the money. These three jobs might make enough for him to bow out too, and then he could leave them all to it. Let them fight it out between them, he was getting tired of it all. Besides he'd already decided that Harry would be the winner, but it would be good watching Jeb and Harcourt put in their places.

Jeb let him out of the front door of the house in Hucklebridge's Court and slammed it closed behind him. Frank laughed; another chapter of his life was drawing to a conclusion. He wondered if he'd given it away that he half suspected Caine might have had a hand in the robbery. There was no point in making accusations; what could be gained by that? He couldn't take Caine on. All that mattered now was laying his hands on enough money and getting away.

As Frank strode through the streets of Bath, he found himself whistling. He would still have to settle with Daunton, but there was time, and he was in no hurry. He felt purpose in his stride now and a new vigour as he approached his house in The Circus. He found himself picturing that doctor's wife, Charlotte Wetherby; so beautiful and refined and confident, yet so married. She was a prey worth stalking, a delicious feast worth taking time over and savouring. With a woman like her, half the fun was in the chase, and the other half in the capture, but for now that particular treat would have to wait.

Still, the prospect of what lay ahead brought a smile to his face. He had dismissed the older maid that morning and the younger girl, Emily, would now, he knew, be in the house alone. The older one had been pleasurable to a degree, and only too willing to earn an extra few pennies, but her features were hard and her body worn. He thought of Emily's pathetic obsequiousness; a pretty girl, but born to be a servant. He had offered her money in the past, but she had always refused; all she had was her prettiness and she didn't even know what to do with that. Now he was going to enjoy it without having to pay. The thought excited him and he felt his optimism returning.

As Frank stepped into the hallway he called out, 'Emily, come here my little butterfly. I have something for you.' He waited for her answering light footsteps on the stairs, but there were no responding sounds, no answering voice.

He searched the house from basement to attic and found no trace of the girl. Instead, in the drawing room he found the secretary table open, its lock prized apart and its contents scattered across the floor. Emily had gone, and she'd taken everything of value she could lay her hands on. He laughed; the girl had more spirit than he had credited her with.

Sweeping aside what was left in the secretary desk he pushed the small button hidden in the drawer next to the panel, checking the hidden compartment. It was intact and he breathed a sigh of relief. No longer trusting the safe, he had put a small pile of banknotes in the compartment. The money still lay there on top of the letters. He took out the letters and undid the red ribbon they were tied in. He had kept them so they must have meant something to him, he thought. Yet as he scanned the scrawled, childish handwriting he realised that they now filled him with disgust.

Frank took out the letter from the top envelope. It opened with 'My dear son' and was signed 'Your loving ma,' and was full of the usual pathetic sentiment in between. His parents fitted even less comfortably in his life now than they ever had before. He could remember being happy when he was young; an only child and spoilt as much as they were capable of spoiling him, yet they had tried to push him into servitude, and the same empty life as their own.

The childhood memories were still there, and yet it was as though they were part of a story that someone had told him. He could not feel any happiness, looking back. All he remembered was their incessant bowing and scraping to their so-called betters. They had put him in service as soon as he was old enough, and he still recalled their pathetic ambitions for him. Still, that's how he learnt to be a gentleman, and how quickly he had learned. It was so easy to ape his lords and masters.

He had told Belle where he came from, but he was glad he had not told her how he had got his start in life; how he had blackmailed the man who employed both him and his parents. He wondered if the man's wife had yet discovered that he preferred the company of boys to her own. Probably not, he thought. He had honoured his word to the man, never returning, never asking for more. In return the man had also honoured his side of the deal. His parents would never want for employment, or a home, while the secret remained between them.

He thought of the person he might have been and smiled to himself. The past was best buried, he thought, as he tossed the bundle of letters on the dying embers of the fire. Only Belle had ever seen them. Why had he shown them to her? Had he really wanted her to understand, or was it just a manoeuvre to lure her into his bed? Whichever, it wasn't worth worrying about now.

When he had composed himself, he felt compelled to check the doors and windows yet again. He bolted the front door and stood in front of the mirror in the hallway. For a moment he thought he saw Belle's reflection, as though she was standing behind him, and the memories of that night flooded his mind.

She was the only one he had let near him in years. For one short night she had made him imagine that he could change, made him confess to a weakness he had never shown to others. If she'd still been there in the morning, perhaps things would have been different, but in the cold light of day he knew he could not change, did not want to change. She would have made demands and altered the way he lived; who he was.

How could he have allowed himself to become so vulnerable? He could never be tied down and subdued like some tame pet. He smiled, admiring his appearance for a second, before lashing out with his clenched right fist, smashing his reflection into a thousand slivers of broken, useless glass. He licked the blood from his fingers.

'You've made me bleed, Belle,' he said to the empty hallway.

The room was crowded but Jeb was, as usual, standing alone at the bar when John walked into The Fountains Inn. John was never sure if Jeb chose to drink here because the other gang members never did, or whether the others avoided the place because Jeb drank there. Whichever it was, his isolation had proved useful.

Jeb had not seen him enter and John reconsidered for a moment. The man might still be valuable, but he knew he took a risk each time he met him. The hours he had spent in his drunken company had left him in no doubt as to what Jeb was capable of. The pleasure he took from the pain of others was never long out of his conversation and the closer John got to him, the more intensely he disliked the man. He had had to listen, night after night, to his boasts of whom he had beaten and why; whom he had robbed and how; bragging about what he had done to Belle, and cursing the fact that he hadn't taken the pleasure in her that he had wanted. But it was too late now. Jeb had seen him.

John smiled, there was no option but to comply as Jeb motioned him over to the bar. It was obvious he was drunk again; his unsteady stance and slurred words left little doubt of that, and it took no effort on John's part to turn the conversation gradually to Caine and to begin picking at Jeb's insecurities. 'So what's Harry Wood up to these days?' he asked.

'Harry's the blue-eyed boy now and no mistake,' Jeb said.

'But Caine would be no one without you,' John replied.

'He don't realise that though,' Jeb said. 'He treats me like dog shit on his shoes and expects me to be grateful. Wood gets an arm round his shoulder and I get pushed into whatever dirty job's going. It's all down to Harcourt, is too thick with Caine.'

'You reckon it's him that's poisoned Caine against you?' John asked. 'I've heard no good of him myself.' Jeb looked suspicious. He had to follow up, somehow, put him back at his ease. 'It's only that I've heard his name before and how he cheats at cards.'

Jeb laughed. 'That's him, a cheat and a bastard; except now he's a bastard who's been robbed.'

John laughed. 'Just deserves; I hope he lost a lot.'

Jeb smiled. 'Lost everything, I reckon.'

'Did you do it?'

'No, he's too close with Caine,' Jeb said. 'Not that I couldn't have if I'd wanted to put my mind to it.' He stopped and leant towards John, grabbing his collar, pulling his face closer. John could smell the foulness of his breath, but he smiled and bent forward towards him. 'We'll see what he's made of now,' Jeb whispered.

'How d'yer mean?' John asked, speaking quietly and looking slowly around the room.

'He's set up some break-ins, big houses. The first is tonight, but I don't know where. They don't tell me nothing. Caine says Harcourt's got to do them himself.'

'What, just him?' John asked.

Jeb laughed. 'No he's too much a gentleman to know anything about housebreaking; there'd be lads with him and maybe Harry or maybe Caine. But they won't send me out with him. They know what I think of him. I'd be happy to see the bastard caught.'

'You wouldn't rat on him though?' John asked. He was pushing now and he knew he might be pushing too far, but Jeb looked interested, as though it were an idea he had already toyed with.

'Never,' Jeb said. 'It's too dangerous, and besides you never rat on your own.'

'I would,' John said. 'For a friend – and if there was something in it for me.' He realised he had committed himself now. There was no pulling back as he watched Jeb's face. There was no reaction for a while, as though he were thinking, lost in his own small world. John thought he had pushed him too far.

Then Jeb grinned. 'You'd need to know when and where though, to do that.'

'That's true,' John said, hoping he was not reading too much into Jeb's reaction.

'I'll need time to find out the wheres and whens of the other jobs,' Jeb said. 'Give me a few days to find out. Meet me back here, a week from today.'

Jeb held out his hand and John shook it. 'There'd be a place for you if I was to take over,' Jeb said.

'And I'd take it if it was offered,' John said. 'You know that, Jeb.'

Chapter 31

John had been in Avon Street for three days. He could smell the place on his clothes and his skin and in his hair, as though he had become part of it, or it of him. The lodging house wasn't so bad though. In fact it was one of the better ones at fourpence a night. Until lately he might have thought it quite acceptable, but he had become used to a better life and now longed to be back at Charlie's house.

He had slept badly that night. The same thought that had disturbed his sleep was still troubling him when he woke, just as it had been nagging away at him for days now. He needed to speak to James and Charlie, to put things right and clear his mind or it would just keep haunting him. They had accepted him almost without question as if he'd ridden to their rescue like Paul Revere, but he had allowed too many half-truths to form between them.

Perhaps he hadn't trusted them at first, but he had let it go on for too long until the secrecy didn't make sense to him any more. Perhaps he had begun to enjoy being the person they thought he was, the person he knew he was not. They deserved to know the truth though, just as he needed to be true to himself.

Someone grunted, half asleep, half awake, interrupting his thoughts. There were six beds in the room and that morning four were still occupied. The room was as cold as the street outside and stunk of unwashed bodies, damp over-worn clothing, and the animal stench of urine left standing in the penny piss pots beneath the beds. The draught through the window blew like a true winter's wind, but the air it carried from Avon Street was just as foul as that within.

The only furniture other than beds was a wash-stand, with a bowl and two cheap candle-holders. He poured some of the contents of the jug that stood beneath the wash-stand into the bowl and brushed aside the fine film of grease and soot covering its surface, before cupping his hands and dousing his face with icy water.

He shivered and wondered if it was the cold or the thought of another day in Avon Street, trying to pick off Caine's men, dodging and hiding, never knowing if one of them would be alert enough to pull a knife or get off a shot, for most of them seemed to be carrying pistols now. If it was just him it would have been all right, but knowing there were other lives involved, and that those lives depended on him, made it all so much more difficult. He stared down into the bowl as the oily rainbow scum reclaimed its dominance of the surface.

James and Charlie thought he was fearless; that he could do anything. Perhaps he'd let them think it, though he knew that it wasn't true. And it seemed important to him now that they understood it, recognised him for who he really was. He resolved that he would tell them everything when he got back to the house.

He smiled to himself, feeling his conscience ease, as he shook the water from his face and smoothed his hair back with wet hands. Looking around the room, he realised how quickly he had grown soft, remembered the 'shake-down' he had stayed in once, with straw and rags laid down between the beds and rats running over you. He had only spent one night there, but he still shivered at the thought.

As he made for the door, he reflected on the three days. The first had gone well and they had got two of Caine's men, both in the morning. No one was hurt and no one was recognised. But Caine was quicker to react this time, yesterday they had caught only one man on his own, the others had been in twos and threes and looked too alert to tackle. Perhaps he'd just had enough of skulking in alleyways and running the risks. Perhaps he'd seen too much of Jeb and come to realise all too clearly what he and Caine were capable of.

James had been right though. Rumours of Caine's men being beaten and robbed seemed to spread through the streets faster than the wind. John had listened to the exaggerated gossip in wonder; how another gang had beaten half of Caine's men and threatened to burn him out of his house; how Caine was packing to leave the city. Let them dream, he thought, one day it might be true.

Today it might be safer if they left off the robberies altogether. Still, he'd see what was happening before he decided. He wanted to get back to the others; needed to get back to tell them about his talk with Jeb. He wondered what Charlie would think of the idea of informing on the brotherhood of thieves. It all seemed too easy, or perhaps too much of a risk. After all James' planning, it was hard to imagine that it might all be resolved at the end of the day by something as simple as informing on Caine.

When Jenny and Molly returned from their morning walk, Belle found it hard to believe that this was the same little girl who had been so ill such a short while ago. Her cheeks were now as red as a ripe apple, her complexion healthy and her energy boundless. Belle took her from Jenny and sat her at the table with her beloved Dolly. 'You sit here for a while and play with Dolly,' Belle said. 'I need to speak to your mother for a while.'

'Molly and Dolly,' Molly said, and laughed to herself at the rhyme. Within seconds she was in another world, chattering away to the doll and nodding its wooden head in agreement, as if she was unaware that it was her own fingers that were making it move.

'This money I've come into,' Belle said, rejoining Jenny, sitting on the edge of the bed.

'I suppose it means you will be moving away soon,' Jenny said.

Belle took Jenny's hands in her own. 'Not necessarily, but I must go to where the work is and seek out the opportunities where they exist. The money has made me realise that acting is much more to me than a wage. I would be lost if I gave it up, but I want to invest the money in you.'

The look of shock on Jenny's face turned to disbelief and then concern. 'What do you mean?' she asked.

'Is it so shocking?' Belle replied. 'You are the finest seamstress I know and your eye for detail and your designs and the way you use material all set you apart from the others. We will open a dress shop as partners. I will put in the money and you the skill. That way I will have an investment; you will have an income, and we will have a home that we can share whenever I am in Bath.'

'But the risk,' Jenny said.

'What risk?' Belle said, as dismissively as she was able. 'There is demand in the city for quality gowns, and you know the women who have the best dressmaking skills, and where the best materials can be bought at least cost.'

'But I know nothing of running a shop, or of accounts.'

'Then we shall employ someone to run the shop and the salesgirls, and someone to keep the books. You take charge of the fittings and the dressmaking and the designs. In time, I'm sure you will master all the skills necessary, when the ladies begin beating a path to your door. Will you do it?'

'Does it mean you will stay?'

'No,' Belle said, 'but if I were to take large enough premises there would be room for a shop and fitting rooms and workrooms and living quarters. You could keep a room for me and then, if I do go, I will stay with you whenever I return.' It seemed enough to persuade Jenny. Belle could see that she was already busy with her thoughts.

'What of Molly?' Jenny asked. 'Who would care for her while I was working?'

'You could employ someone, perhaps another mother bringing her child up alone. Then she would have someone to play with.'

'I know other women who would work if there were someone to care for their children, but it wouldn't be a sweat shop. I'd make sure that our place was the best place for women to work in Bath. I'd pay good wages and there'd be somewhere clean and warm to work.' Belle remembered Jenny's stories of the places she had worked when she was apprenticed, and later when she was an improver; the filthy ill-lit hovels where girls paid to be trained and were used as slave labour.

'But I'd take only the best women,' Jenny said, as though she were justifying a good heart. 'And we'd teach apprentices properly, not just take their money and treat them like dogsbodies.'

Belle said nothing, but simply watched the transformation. Jenny's excitement was obvious now, as though in her mind the shop was already there; the fitting rooms occupied, the workroom busy and productive, bolts of material being delivered. 'I take it you are in favour of the idea?' Belle eventually said.

'What if I make a mess of it?' Jenny asked. 'I'm no businesswoman.'

'You could estimate the price of any dress on sale in Milsom Street without reading it first, and you know what to pay for any piece of material, and how to cut it to produce the most, and how to use every last remnant.' Belle said, but she still felt Jenny's nagging uncertainty and self-doubt. 'Besides,' she went on, 'what would I lose if it failed; six month's rental of premises, the cost of the materials and the cost of a few months' wages. I have that now, and if you succeed, which you will, we would both stand to make a great deal more. I'd rather risk my money on you than on investments that I do not understand, and that go towards making someone else rich.'

Jenny had that faraway look again, planning and thinking and dreaming; any thoughts of failure were dispersing in a flurry of excitement. When she eventually spoke it was as much to herself as to Belle. 'We would not be a first-rate house, not at the beginning,' she said. 'Court dresses and outfits for the very rich means having them looking down on you, and buying expensive materials, and having more girls in the shop than we have making the dresses. But neither would we be third- or fourth-rate common shops. Our dresses will be silk, not cotton and they will be finished as finely as any court dress. We will buy in the skirts; making them takes little skill and yet a great deal of time – but we will make the bodices and sleeves and do all the fitting and alterations ourselves. We shall sell to the doctors' and lawyers' wives and the daughters of wealthy shopkeepers and factory owners; and our dresses will be so fine that the rich women will come begging us to serve them.'

'I take it your answer is yes?' Belle said, aware that she was interrupting Jenny's reverie.

'Yes, yes, yes,' Jenny said.

'Then you stop taking in work from today,' Belle said. 'You must make contact with the girls you plan to employ, and plan your designs, and then we need to start looking for a shop. We will buy outfits suitable for ladies of business, and they will be the last dresses we ever buy from anyone but ourselves.'

Drawn by the insistent sound of knocking on the front door, James ran to the drawing room window. John was expected back at any time, but looking down he saw that it was Sean Brennan that Mrs Hawker was admitting. James smiled as he ran to the stairs.

He felt in an optimistic mood and seeing Sean made his spirits rise further. Monday's paper had contained letters from Lady Nayland and Mr Mayhew complaining that the city was no longer safe for women. Both blamed the attitude of the constabulary and both hinted at corruption in the force in Avon Street. James had penned his anonymous letter to the chief constable, listing the names of the constables in Caine's pay earlier that morning, and Charlie had already had it delivered.

By the time Sean had removed his coat James had run down the stairs to join him. 'Come into the dining room,' he said, trying to hide the pleasure he felt at the prospect of presenting Sean with the money.

Sean's face was serious and he barely glanced at the money on the table. 'I had a visit yesterday from Harry Wood,' he said.

'Were you attacked?' James asked.

'No, he came into the confessional, as if he was a parishioner. He made no threats, not at first. He claimed he was acting alone, without Caine's knowledge.'

'I presume he had not come to confess his sins,' James said, his stomach tensing.

'He said that he knew I was your friend and that since you were in Bath, I would know where you were hiding. He asked me to deliver a message to you. But how did he know you were in Bath?'

'I made a stupid error of judgement,' James said, 'but never mind that now. I'm worried for you, Sean. You must be alert. If Wood can get to you, then so could Caine, now that he knows I am in Bath.'

'Caine has always known how to get to me. I don't hide from him. But he knows me well enough to understand that I would never reveal your whereabouts. Besides we're two different problems to him. You, he wants to kill. Me, he only wants to intimidate.' He laughed, but there was no humour in the sound. 'At least for the moment, he's scared to take my life because it might start a war. I just hope he doesn't know that I'm as afraid of causing a war as he is. Bad people always seem to think that everyone else thinks as they do.'

'You know your enemy well, but take care,' James said. 'What was the message Wood left?'

'He said he would meet you on the path beneath Pulteney Bridge at dusk, in three days time. He wants to meet you face to face, to fight a duel with you.'

'It might be a ruse,' James said, 'a way of tracking us down.'

'That's why I left it for a day,' Sean said. 'I know I was not followed here; I've been around Avon Street long enough to know if I am being followed. I believe he wants this kept between you and him. He's not interested in the others.'

'We should have moved,' James said. 'I knew it, yet I did nothing. Caine will track us down eventually and I cannot let Mrs Hawker and Charlie suffer for my stupidity.'

'Will you leave Bath?' Sean asked.

'No,' James replied. 'We will leave this house though. We have been here too long and there have been too many comings and goings. But Wood will have his duel.'

'He said you should bring duelling swords, so that he should end your life in the same way as you ended his brother's, and that you should bring a second with you, as witness, and no one else.'

The challenge felt inevitable to James, as though he had always sensed its coming. There was only one way in which his fight with Wood could end. 'Your visit was fortuitous, Sean,' he said, crossing to the dining table. 'This money is for you. At least some good can come from all of this.' He smiled as he watched Sean's bewildered gaze.

'I could buy half of Avon Street with this,' Sean said. 'Where does it come from?'

'We robbed Frank Harcourt. It was he who betrayed me to Caine,' James replied. 'Charlie and John and I want you to accept half of what we took from him, so that you can do some good with it. It's dirty money. Harcourt's been in league with Caine for some time now. The other smaller pile on the table is my share from the robbery and I want you to get it to my brother. He can use it to make good the tenants' debts and invest in the estate.'

'So you are a robber now?' Sean said, smiling. 'I won't pretend that the money isn't welcome, because it is.'

'It's all blood money, but hopefully you can wash it clean. I have tried not to act like Caine in fighting him, but it is difficult.'

'You should go to Ireland, James,' Sean said. 'Take the money to your brother and stay there for a while. I can loosen Caine's grip on Avon Street with this, but I don't want to see you die for it. Go while you still have your life.'

'What time did he specify we meet?' James asked.

'He said at dusk, but I wish now I had never told you.'

'What else did he say?'

'The rest was just ranting; threats and name calling.'

'Did he threaten you?'

'No,' Sean said.

His response was too quick. 'You never could lie to me.'

'I can look after myself.'

'I know,' James said. 'And I will do the same. I'll not run and leave this mess for everyone else to clear up. It was you who reminded me of who I used to be. I've found a sense of honour again, and I do not intend to lose it.'

'God might not approve of this type of honour. Turn the other cheek, James.'

'Wood won't let me turn the other cheek, and if he can't get to me, he will take it out on others.' James did not wait for a reply for fear that Sean would counter. 'Do you think Caine is involved in this?'

'I can't be sure, but I believe Wood is acting on his own behalf.'

'Fetch your coat,' James said, 'I'll bundle this money for you to take, and I'll write the address we are to move to. Take care of Mrs Hawker, if you do not find me there after my meeting with Wood.'

'I'll pray for you, James.'

'Just make sure you're not robbed going through town and get this money safely into a bank and be watchful.'

'Please thank the others,' Sean said. 'This is more money than I ever thought I might have. It will be put to good use. Do not doubt it. And please think again of going to Ireland. You do not have to do this. It is wrong.'

It was some time before John arrived back at the house, later than James had expected. Charlie joined them in the drawing room and James was glad of the company, hoping they might free him from his thoughts, though he knew they would not like what he had to tell them. He relayed quickly what had happened and asked John if he would act as his second. John agreed as he knew he would.

'You can get out of this, if you wait,' John said. 'Caine's got some housebreakings planned with Harcourt. It's likely that Wood or Caine himself will lead them, and Jeb is willing to rat on them. All we need do is inform the peelers.'

James laughed. 'If only it had happened sooner,' he said. 'I never thought we could get to Caine as easily as this.'

'We shouldn't trust Jeb,' Charlie said.

'We can in this,' John replied. 'Jeb wants to be free of Caine and Harry Wood and he hates Harcourt. This is his way of getting rid of them and taking over the gang.'

'I don't much like it,' Charlie said. 'I've never ratted on anyone to the peelers.'

'Caine had no honour when he left your apprentice to the hangman,' John said. 'Or in the way he's treated others.'

'I suppose not,' Charlie relented, 'and if it gets James out of having to fight Harry Wood then it's worth it.'

'No, Charlie,' James said. 'It's worth doing it if it puts Caine behind bars, because he deserves justice, but I'll not put off the duel in the hope that Harry Wood is caught. It's a coward's way out; another way of running. I caused all that has happened and I will finish it.'

'Caine rarely does his own dirty work these days,' Charlie said. 'He'll not go out on the job.'

'If he doesn't have Harry Wood, then he might have to,' James said, 'and if Wood wins, then you must continue the fight against him without me.'

'We will,' Charlie conceded. 'We'll tell the peelers, but let's have no talk of you dying young 'un.'

'There is something else we need to do.' James paused, cursing his own stupidity, knowing that what he was about to suggest would hurt Charlie. 'We need to move from here, before the duel.'

'You told me you'd put the other night behind you,' Charlie said. 'I promised you would never see me drunk again. I swore it, and I meant it.'

'It's not because of you, Charlie,' James smiled. 'That incident is forgotten and I would prefer it to remain so. The truth, as you can see, is that Caine knows now that I am in Bath, and it's through my own stupid arrogance that he knows it. I asked John to leave my visiting card at Harcourt's house.'

'But we weren't to know that Harcourt was in league with Caine,' John interrupted.

'Nevertheless there is only one day before I meet Wood,' James said. 'For your sake, Charlie, I will not risk Caine finding me here on that day.'

'What's a day matter?' Charlie asked.

'We should have left straight after robbing Harcourt,' James replied. 'What if Caine should link your name with the robbery, Charlie? And if I survive, then won't Caine double his efforts to find me and link our names in his search? It would be best that we were away from here. I will not put you in danger, Charlie, for my stupid error.'

'I should have thought of it myself,' Charlie said, 'when we realised as Harcourt was in it with Caine. You're right; Caine will think of me.' The realisation was clear in his face, but whether his reaction was fear or anger was hard to tell. 'But Caine knows I don't work anymore,' Charlie resumed. 'You're worrying for nothing.'

'Perhaps so,' James replied. 'But if we leave I will feel safer for us all.'

'I'll not be pushed out of my home by Caine,' Charlie said.

'I half expected you might say as much, Charlie,' James replied. 'The decision must be yours. I would like you to come with us, but if you don't, at least you will be safer with us gone. There will be nothing to link you to me or to the robbery. If I survive the duel then we will still go on to fight Caine together, but not from here.' James paused, trying to assess his reaction, but the man's expression gave little away other than his determination. 'Mrs Hawker and I will move tonight. We will take provisions with us and we will not leave the new house until I attend the duel. In that way Mrs Hawker will be safe and so will you, Charlie.'

'Where will you go?' Charlie asked.

'Richard's taken a house for us in Walcot Parade. It's not as prominent as The Paragon and new tenants will raise little interest in such a busy street. Will you both come with us?' James asked.

'Of course,' John replied, 'I'm your second. We'll need to prepare for your meeting with Harry Wood.'

They both looked at Charlie. 'It doesn't sit easy with me,' Charlie said, 'none of it. I'll not move from my own house. I can see why you're doing it, but I don't care for the idea at all.'

'Think it over, Charlie,' James said. 'Tom's coming for us with a cab in about two hour's time.'

Chapter 32

James slept badly that night, his dreams full of death. Faceless bodies mocked him from every nightmare, contemptuous laughter ringing in his ears as he ran, or tried to run; his legs always weak, his feet sucked down in a quagmire from which he could not escape. He kicked out and punched in his sleep, but his every movement was slow and drained of energy. The sheets and blankets wrapped themselves around his limbs in dream knots and shrouds. Each time he woke, he was glad to leave the dreams behind him, and yet each time he dozed it was only to relive his death again.

In the end he gave up and dressed and went downstairs. The house in Walcot Parade was comfortable enough, though not expensively furnished. He sat in a chair in the drawing room between bouts of pacing. The room was freshly decorated and the smell of fresh paint still hung listlessly in the air.

John joined him an hour or so later. He smiled and looked around the room. 'This will do us for a while,' he said, stretching out on the chaise longue.

'Assuming I'm still here,' James said.

'Of course you'll still be here,' John replied.

James rose and crossed to the window. He found himself thinking of Belle and that he might never see her again. She had looked hurt when they last parted, when he told her not to return. Yet he could not ask her to risk her life for him. He pictured her face, smiling and comforting, and he wished that things were different, that he could somehow re-shape the past, but what was done could not be undone.

Then despite himself, he thought of them together; Belle and Harcourt. He did not want to, but the thought kept returning and each time it came back, it hurt a little more. He wanted to write to her, to tell her how he felt, but each sentence he composed in his mind led to others that he knew would only cause her sadness. It was best left like this. He wandered out of the room without a word to John and went down to the kitchen.

Downstairs a smiling Mrs Hawker greeted him, by now used to seeing him there, though he had rarely visited the kitchen in his own home. He had told John and Charlie that she should know nothing of the pending duel. James walked over and hugged her large frame.

'What's all this about?' Mrs Hawker asked, smiling whilst freeing a hand to pinch James on his arm. He knew then that she suspected nothing.

'You've been a better mother to me than I could ever have hoped for,' James said.

'And will continue to be so for a good time yet, God willing,' she replied. Small diamond tears glistened at the corners of her eyes. She turned away and dabbed at them with her apron. 'Now stop this silly talk and sit yourself down and I'll make you breakfast. It's lonely in the kitchen without Charlie. I miss the old fool.'

'I tried to persuade him to come with us,' James said.

'I know it,' Mrs Hawker replied. 'He's a stubborn old fool and set in his ways, but I still miss him, for all that.'

James went back to his room and took out the letters; the last of the three bundles that John had taken from Harcourt's safe, the only ones he had not returned. It was too late now to deal with them properly. If he survived then he would deliver them; if not then they should be destroyed.

He decided that he would leave them for John to deal with and bound them in a sheet of paper, writing on the front, *'To John – I apologise for leaving this task to you, but on your honour I ask that you burn these letters unopened, should I not return.'* He sipped his coffee with a momentary sense of relief and then took the silver chain from around his neck. He lowered it slowly into his palm like a gentle waterfall of quicksilver, feeling the links cascading together. Letting it slide into the package he added a postscript to the note. *'Please deliver the enclosed chain to Miss Bennett and tell her that I hope it brings her good fortune and that she will think of me from time to time.'* Outside he heard footsteps approaching. He placed the package inside the desk and closed it quickly.

After a short interval there was a knock on the door and John entered before he had time to reply. 'I wondered where you'd gone. I went out this morning to purchase the weapons,' he said. 'I've put them in my room. We should practise now.'

The words chilled James to the core of his being. 'I know how to use a sword,' he said, 'besides the noise would alarm Mrs Hawker.'

'She's busy in the kitchen. You may have some skill at fencing, but Wood will not fight as you are used to fighting.'

James followed him upstairs. John produced the swords from beneath his bed and the two men began sparring. John could use a sword almost as well as James, though his technique was very different. Whilst James had the greater finesse, John was much the stronger. On the first occasion that the blades locked diagonally, John began pushing him back with his sword arm and shoulder. 'Wood will always try to get in close, where strength counts more,' John said.

'Then I will sidestep or draw him on,' James said, momentarily resisting the force John was exerting.

'And how will you counter this?' John said, producing a knife from his boot with his left hand and holding it under James' chin. John laughed. 'Don't forget I will be your second. I'll make sure as best I can that he has no weapons hidden about him before the duel, but you must watch his other hand as much as his sword arm. A punch may be as effective as a knife and a handful of dust can blind you for vital moments. He may try to kick you, or head-butt you in a clinch, use his elbows and forearm or sweep your legs. Harry Wood is no gentleman.'

He sparred with John for the rest of the morning and they resumed practice again in the afternoon. Gradually James began to anticipate John's strategies and ruses. 'I can't teach you everything in a day,' John said after several hours of sparring. 'But you learn quick and you're good with a sword. Rest now and get yourself right for tonight.'

Belle stood in the wings, looking out on a full and silent house; a sea of faces held spellbound by one man's performance. At that moment she knew she was probably the only one who was not watching Mr Macready. Instead she watched the audience's wrapt stares, following him as he prowled the stage like a hungry predator, demanding their attention, sucking them into another time and place, commanding that they forget where and even who they were, and to accept that he was for that moment Macbeth. The audience was mesmerised, as though each one of them were alone; a privileged bystander in Macbeth's cold castle, watching the dark tale unfold, watching the man who would sacrifice everything to be king.

The rumours that had preceded him left little doubt as to Macready's nature. Touring in America, he had argued with another actor and it had led to a full-blown bloody brawl between hundreds of their respective followers in which several had died. It was also common knowledge that he regularly fought with his manager, though it was equally well known that his manager was a rogue.

Belle was still unsure as to whether or not she actually liked the man. He was moody and given to sudden fits of temper, but it did not matter what she thought of him as a man, for as an actor he had already changed her life. From the moment of his arrival he had taken command of the theatre and everyone in it and reminded her of what it was possible to aspire to as an actor.

Cauldfield had managed to stand up to Macready for all of thirty seconds. He had greeted him on arrival in his usual way, introducing himself as the leading man, blustering and shouting in what he obviously believed was a convivial, but commanding manner. Macready had ignored him and when his blustering faltered he turned to him and told him he would not be required until rehearsals on the following day. Arrogance had met its match, in greater arrogance. When Cauldfield replied that he never rehearsed with the minor players, Macready said, 'If you do not rehearse with the full company, then you do not share the stage with me.' Cauldfield had been very quiet at rehearsals.

It was the words that mattered to Macready and what lay deep within the character. Even when they were rehearsing and the theatre was empty it might well, as far as he was concerned, have been packed to the gunnels with the most appreciative audience possible. Belle watched his every movement and hung on his every word for days. She gradually felt her understanding grow and with it her sense of presence on the stage.

The first night had been well enough received, but the audiences had grown more clamorous on each succeeding night and she had felt her confidence grow. So great was the demand that on the closing night they had put on an extra performance. It sold out within hours of being announced.

Yet as she looked over now towards the stage box, a sudden dread swept over her; the theatre was packed but that box was empty and she had begun to think of it as Harcourt's box, even though she had not seen him since the night of the assault.

As the door at the back of the box opened she waited, half expecting to see Harcourt emerge and begin his mocking. She felt her confidence weaken. But when the door opened it was Mrs Macready that she saw, smiling encouragement. Then as she waited for her cue she felt as though someone else was watching her, yet she felt no fear but only comfort. The sense of being observed was so strong that she looked over to the opposite side of the stage, turned to look behind her. It felt almost as though her mother and father were there, willing her on. Then the feeling left her as she stepped out from the wings.

James hugged Mrs Hawker for the second time that day. He told her he was going into town for a while. She seemed uneasy and he wondered if she suspected that something was wrong, but when he told her that John would be with him she looked decidedly more comfortable with his going out.

They left the house before the sun had begun setting. John had reasoned that a walk through the city would help settle nerves and loosen limbs for the contest to come, and James was glad to be doing something other than waiting. He paid little heed to the comings and goings around them as they walked through still-busy streets and the sprawl of market stalls which seemed to increase and spill everywhere at that time of the evening.

The normality of life took James aback, as if a part of him expected ordinary activities to be suspended in deference to his circumstances. But his own life, he realised, no matter how real its problems, was largely a matter of indifference to the world in general. He might well be at the centre of his own universe, but he was forced to accept that he was largely irrelevant in the lives of even this small pocket of humanity. Yet at that same moment his sense of being was never stronger and the value he placed on his own continued existence had never been greater.

The noise of the factories backing onto the river by Pulteney Bridge fought and fused with the sound of the weir below. As he and John walked on, across the bridge, neither of them even glanced at the shops that lined its sides, staring straight ahead, oblivious to their surroundings. At the beginning of Argyle Street they reached the entrance to the narrow winding steps which tunnelled beneath the buildings lining the road to the river beyond. Brendan was waiting for them.

'Are they there?' John asked.

'They are so,' Brendan replied. 'And they've kept to their word, as far as I can tell. There's two of them and Diarmuid's been keeping a watch on Caine's house. If there was any sign of more joining them then he was to let me know, but I've heard nothing.'

'Get back home now,' John said.

'Please watch out for Father Sean, and tell Diarmuid the same,' James added. 'I have an uneasy feeling about Caine.'

Brendan shook hands with them both. 'We'll watch his back and God be with you.'

The passageway down to the river was dark and damp and James hesitated as he led the way, allowing his eyes to accustom themselves to the sudden darkness after the glow of the gas lamps in the street above. The steps were slippery and the smell of damp and urine heightened the pressure of the grimy sweating walls.

Feeling his way cautiously, step by step, James emerged from the tunnel and came out on a half landing where the remainder of the steps straightened before descending to the riverbank below. The light was better now, and he could see the way more clearly. James was turning to speak to John when the lead ball shot past his ear like an angry wasp, the sound of the blast echoing almost instantaneously in his head.

He ran down the remainder of the steps and along the riverbank in the direction he judged the shot to have come from. A second gunshot rang out, muffled by the sounds of the factories and the weir. He heard John stumble and fall behind him and turned to check if he had been hit, but John was already getting to his feet, waving him on. James ran towards the sound. He could now make out the shapes of two men standing in among the trees which lined the riverbank. 'You killed my brother!' one of the men shouted.

As James reached Harry Wood, the man was desperately trying to reload his pistol. James launched himself at Wood's waist and they both went crashing to the ground. From the corner of his eye he saw John Doyle making for the other man, Wood's second. The man turned and fled down the riverbank and John set off in pursuit.

James had winded Harry Wood as he tackled him. He knew at least for a moment he had the advantage. But they were wrapped too close around each other and James' punches made little impact on Wood's torso. Then Wood tore his arm from beneath his body and raised his pistol. He only caught James with a glancing blow to his head, but the shock of the blow was enough to stun him momentarily. He felt his strength draining, and his grip on Wood's body loosened.

Wood leapt to his feet and began kicking him in the stomach and chest and legs. James curled instinctively into a ball to protect his head and reached out with his right hand to grab Wood's leg. He managed to throw him off balance, pulling him crashing down on top of him. Struggling to hold Wood down, he could already feel the man tearing himself free, getting to his feet again.

As he looked up James saw Wood pull the long knife from the sheath at his belt. He felt strangely calm, almost resigned to what was about to happen. Then he heard the shout. Wood turned, distracted for a moment. James brought his right leg back and kicked him in the groin, sending him reeling back towards the river, doubling with pain.

By the time Wood had recovered, John Doyle stood facing him, his own knife drawn. The two men circled, each waiting an opportunity to strike, then Wood lunged forward with a loud cry. John brought up his left arm and caught hold of the wrist of Wood's knife arm with his right, but dropped his own knife in the process.

Both men were strong and struggled for control of the knife. John brought his knee up into Wood's stomach, but as the man went down his weight pulled John after him. The two men rolled across the ground and John turned the knife towards Wood's chest. James watched, unable to move, not knowing how to intervene as their bodies locked together.

Wood let go of the knife and left it behind them. James fought to regain his breath as he struggled to his feet and picked up the knife. The two men were now rolling away from him with increasing speed towards the riverbank. By the time James reached them, they had plunged over the edge and into the deep waters of the river below.

He could see the two bodies in the river now; the undertow from the weir was pulling at them, throwing them around like wooden dolls.

Wood was hanging onto John, neither man able to raise their heads
above the waters for any length of time. Then both of them were
sucked under the thundering dark chaos of the water.

James fought the impulse to dive in. There was nothing he could
do from here other than to be pulled into the current himself. The
pain of the kicking he had received wracked his body as he struggled
to move. He ran as fast as he was able down the path at the side
of the river. His chest felt as though every breath of air had been
sucked from it. He took a deep breath and the pain knifed through
his expanding lungs.

As the evening drew on, Caine tried to shake himself from his
melancholy. He was in the foulest of moods as he had been for days
now. Everywhere he looked there seemed to be problems. He was
back to having to send the men around in twos again, after three of
them had been attacked in two days. It seemed to have stopped now,
but he couldn't take chances and yet everything seemed to take twice
as long to plan and organise.

Then there were the housebreakings that Harcourt had set up. The
first of them had gone well enough and they'd carried away a tidy
amount of silver plate, but the second had been a fiasco. Harcourt
had knocked a saucepan from the kitchen table on their way in and
all hell broke loose. They got away all right and without injury, but
the house had supposed to have been empty and it wasn't. Some
flunkey had raised the alarm and they had ended up taking nothing
and having to run. And there was still the worry of the third job. He'd
put it off as long as he could, but Harcourt was still demanding it be
done before Lansdown Fair.

Caine wanted to hit out at someone; to get rid of his frustration.
He realised there was no one now he could rely on to do anything.
Harcourt was leaving and Harry Wood could think of nothing but
taking revenge on Daunton. He couldn't trust Jeb anymore, either;
he always seemed to be sneaking around sticking his nose where it
didn't belong.

He found himself thinking about the robbery of Harcourt's house
and the safe being opened. There was only one man who could
open that safe without a key and that was Charlie Maggs. He was
a cunning one, that Maggs. It's strange how he hadn't seen him for

months and then he turned up on his own doorstep, in The Pig and Whistle. There'd been something odd about him that day, and that stranger with him.

Caine tried to compose himself, taking up the newspaper and sitting in his favourite chair by the fire, but he had barely sat when Jeb burst into the room. 'There's a pick-pocket at the front door, someone we've done business with, says he has important news, but he'll only speak to you.'

Caine stormed up the stairs and opened the door. The man took one look at him and for a moment Caine thought he was going to run, 'Well, what have you got for me?' Caine said.

'Beg pardon, Mr Caine,' the man said, 'but there's a little Irishman up at The Pelican in Walcot Street. He's drunk and telling everyone who'll listen that he's got a gang.'

'What's his drunken talk to do with me?' Caine asked.

'He says he's robbed your men and driven them into hiding.'

Caine pushed a sovereign into the man's outstretched hand and turned to Jeb. 'Fetch Harry Wood.'

'Harry went out a while ago with one of lads . . . Lem, I think,' Jeb replied.

'You'll have to do then,' he spat. 'Send the men out to find Harry and lock up and come after me. You've faster legs than mine so make sure you catch me afore I get to The Pelican.'

Below the weir James saw the two bodies emerge from the pounding waters. He dived in, striking out towards the nearest of them, hoping it was John, the shock of the cold water momentarily numbing his pain.

John's body was limp and motionless when he reached him. James grabbed hold of the collar of his jacket and began swimming back to the bank. For a moment he thought he felt him responding, but it was only the current dragging at his body.

As he dragged John's lifeless body through the mud of the riverside, James heard a cry and looked back across the river. Harry Wood's arm was raised above the surface for a second or two. James walked back to the river's edge, feeling the mud dragging at his legs, draining the last of his strength, the stench of the river effluent driving the last of the air from his lungs, but when he looked up again the surface of the river was unbroken and Harry Wood was nowhere to be seen.

James wrapped his arms around his chest to ease the pain and made his way back to John's body. He was lying on his front, his head to one side, his face to the ground and his mouth and nose barely clear of the mud. Seizing hold of his jacket collar again James dragged him clear of the mud and up to the path, laying him on his back.

It was as though the movement had rekindled some life in John and seconds later he began coughing and spluttering. James feared he was choking. Kneeling closer to him he pulled his arms forward forcing John's body into a sitting position. John struggled for a moment, gulps of river water spewing from his mouth as he struggled to breathe.

'You're alive!' James said.

John punched him weakly on the shoulder, still coughing. 'And it must be thanks to you,' he said. 'All those years at sea and I never learnt to swim.' He was smiling now. 'Where's Wood?' he asked.

'Drowned, there was nothing I could do.'

'It's as well,' John said. 'There was a powerful amount of hate in the man. He'd not have rested till he'd killed you.' John struggled to his feet.

'You should stay still for a while until you're recovered,' James said.

'No, we need to be away from here as quick as possible and take away any trace that we've been here. I owe you my life, James.'

'You owe me nothing,' James replied, 'I have only repaid a little of what I already owed to you.'

The two walked down the pathway, each with an arm around the other, though neither was capable of providing much support. They retrieved the two swords and picked up Wood's pistols and knife that lay at the side of the riverbank and replaced them in the velvet bag. There would be no evidence that any fight had taken place that night, save for the body in the river. Wood's body would be badly bruised, no doubt, but he bore no wounds to indicate anything other than a drowning.

'What happened to the other man?' James asked.

'I left him up the path.'

'You didn't kill him?' James asked.

'No,' John replied. 'We faced up to each other and then he looked like he was going to run. I couldn't have him fetching Caine, so I caught him and hit him. I don't know if it was the blow or the fall that knocked him out, but he's still alive.'

With what little strength they had left the two returned to the road and made their way home.

Jeb had caught up with him before Caine had gone more than a couple of streets from Hucklebridge's Court. Caine resented the fact. Jeb was light on his feet whereas he was beginning to feel his age and weight. He felt worse by the time they reached the inn.

One of the barmaids in The Pelican recalled a small, very loud Irishman leaving about an hour ago and described him well. He had got into an argument with one or two of the locals and the landlord had thrown him out.

Caine was losing patience and growing even more tired as the two of them retraced their steps down the road. At The Saracen's Head they went in through the door from the stable yard off Broad Street. As he looked he saw a man on the other side of the bar in the far room, and it was plain from the fear on his face that this was the one he was looking for. He stood transfixed for a moment before he dropped his tankard and began pushing through the crowd.

Before they could get to him the Irishman ran through the other door onto Walcot Street. Caine was trapped in a sea of bodies. By the time he got out of the place the man was disappearing into the slaughterhouses on the far side of the road with Jeb a little way behind him.

Caine could see neither of them as he threaded his way through the network of passageways between the buildings. When he emerged onto the wasteland beyond he could still see nothing. Then he heard movement down by the river. He slowly followed the sounds, slipping and sliding on the muddy sloping path. When he reached the bottom he could just make out the shape of a man kneeling, bent over on the ground.

Caine called Jeb's name and the shape turned. As he grew nearer he could see Jeb taking the pocket watch from the man lying in front of him. He held it up by its chain, watching it spin. Closer still and he saw Jeb's knife lying on the ground at the side of the body. Blood was pumping from the Irishman's neck. Jeb stood and put the watch in his pocket. 'I got him, Nat,' he said.

Caine slapped him across the mouth with the back of his hand, sending him tripping backwards over the inert body at his feet. Jeb tried to stand again. Caine kicked his knife out of his reach and bent forward, grabbing him around the throat.

'I couldn't do nothing else, Nat,' Jeb stuttered, his voice half strangled by the pressure of Caine's hand. 'There was no holding him. If I'd waited for you he'd have been miles away and besides, I thought you wanted him dead.'

Caine let go his grip and turned and walked away. 'Did he say anything?' he asked over his shoulder.

'No, he was out of breath when I caught him, that's how he give hisself away,' Jeb replied.

'Now we'll never know what he could have told us,' Caine said

'I tried to hold him, Nat,' Jeb said, 'but he kept struggling, nearly had me in the river, so in the end I give him a taste of me knife.' He picked up his knife, wiped it on the Irishman's body and returned it to its sheath.

Caine bent down to check that the man was dead, and then pushed the body into the river with his foot. 'Another job well done,' he spat. 'Am I the only one with a brain between me head and hands? You know we've no friends in the peelers up this end of town.'

'It's all right,' Jeb replied. He was grinning now, as though he had found some silver lining to the black cloud. 'There's nothing to even say we knew the Irishman. He was drunk and he'd been arguing with folk all night.'

'Well that's summat, I suppose,' Caine said. 'Now let's get away from here before we're seen.' His mind was in turmoil. The peelers would already be stirred by the robberies, and now there was a killing for them to sniff around; worse than that, the Irish would be baying for blood. The murder would bring them together and they would fight; they had nothing to lose. Somehow he had to get things back in order or he would have to lie low for a while and there was no respect in hiding.

When Caine got back to Hucklebridge's Court the men were all gathered in the kitchen. They all stood as he entered, congregating nervously at one end of the room. He watched them, knowing something was wrong as they pushed and shoved one of their number

to the front, as though they expected him to speak. It was Lem, one of the few that he had any time for. 'Speak then,' Caine said.

'Harry fought a duel with James Daunton,' Lem said. 'I got knocked unconscious and when I come to Harry was gone. I think he's dead, Nat.'

Out of the corner of his eye Caine saw Jeb's reaction. He looked as concerned as the others now, but for a split second he had seen him grinning. 'Get out, all of you,' Caine shouted as he collapsed into the nearest chair, but he knew he couldn't just sit there, doing nothing. 'No, wait,' he said. They turned, waiting for orders.

Caine knew it wouldn't take much more to have them deserting like rats from a coffin ship now, with everything that had gone bad. He would have to work to keep them together and work even harder to keep the Irish in their place. Let them rampage around Avon Street until they'd spent their anger, if it stopped them breaking apart. And perhaps it was time to do something about the priest; may as well be hung for a sheep as a lamb. 'How about getting even for Harry tonight, lads?' he shouted. It was exactly what they wanted to hear. They were smiling now and shouting their agreement, keen for revenge. Violence was something he knew they understood.

'Why don't we go up Avon Street and lay about the Irish,' Caine said, 'nothing permanent, just pick a few out and give 'em something to think about. Break an arm or two and we'll get the priest. But first of all, let's pay a visit to my old friend Charlie Maggs.'

Chapter 33

'Stop pacing up and down, or you'll wake Molly,' Jenny said. 'You've been like a puppy dog chasing its tail these last few days. Whatever is wrong with you?'

'It's Macready,' Belle replied. 'It has been so exciting working with him, and tonight he told me that he has found me a position in the company at the Haymarket Theatre in London. I would be a fool to pass up the opportunity. It's all I've ever dreamed of.'

'So you will leave us?' Jenny said, as though she already knew the answer.

'I'm torn,' Belle replied. 'I truly don't know what to do. Even when it's kind, life can be cruel. I feel pulled in opposite directions. I know anyone would be grateful to choose either path, but having to choose is so difficult. I hate the thought of leaving you and Molly, but the chance of working in the Haymarket with Macready is too good an opportunity to reject.'

'And James,' Jenny said. 'Do you hate the thought of leaving James? Perhaps it's not only Macready that's opened your eyes.'

'It's true,' Belle said. 'I do care for him, and yet I hardly know him, and one minute I think he really cares for me, and the next he seems to be pushing me away. I don't know what to believe.'

'Perhaps you more than care for him,' Jenny said.

'You know how I feel,' Belle said.

'I know what I see,' Jenny replied. 'I've watched you mooning about the place like a lovesick puppy; and I've seen you return from visiting him, one minute like the cat that got the cream, and the next like the cat that got a kicking. What is it that attracts you to him? Is he so handsome?'

'Of course he is handsome, even with his silly crooked nose,' Belle giggled. 'As handsome as a peacock, but not nearly as vain and he is very caring and not a bit snobbish.' She paused, picturing him, that concerned look on his face, trying to cope with events that seemed likely to engulf him. 'He willingly carries the weight of the world on his shoulders, yet at the same time looks for all the world like a lost little boy. Sometimes I want only to hold him.' Then she smiled. 'He makes me laugh when I'm sad, and there is a trust between us that I know is real.'

'And has he told you how he feels about you?' Jenny asked.

Belle hesitated, wondering if she truly knew what he felt. If she did it came not from his words but from his eyes. Perhaps she saw something that was not there, but she knew that was not true. His emotions were rarely spoken at all, but they were in his being and his manner as though he spoke without words. It was when they talked of other things that she felt she understood him. She smiled. 'He has not told me in so many words, though he told me that I was beautiful and that he would like to know me better.'

'Much as Harcourt did,' Jenny said.

Belle laughed. 'Ah, but Harcourt didn't tell me that he admired my teeth and then blush from telling me. And I never saw in Harcourt's eyes what I see in James' eyes. But you're right, perhaps it is all in my imagination, I have heard nothing from him for days. I don't even know if he is still in Bath. When I'm with him, sometimes I feel awkward, and yet when I'm not I want only to see him again.'

'Harcourt you kept locked away,' Jenny said. 'Like the guilty secret he was. I think Master James must be very special. I can see how you would be torn. I wish I could advise you, but all I can say is listen to your heart.'

'But it is my heart that pulls me in both directions,' Belle said. 'I love acting and if I am to progress then I have to leave. Yet the thought of leaving Bath hurts more now than I ever thought it might. It's my mind I must rely on to decipher my heart.'

'Look at the state of you,' Mrs Hawker said, as she threw her arms around James and hugged him. 'And now you've got me all wet. What have you been doing?'

He leant over and kissed her on the cheek, tasting the salty stream of tears coursing from her eyes. The pain in his chest from her embrace was intense and he wanted to fight free of her arms, but the happiness and relief on her face were more than worth the discomfort.

'Don't try to deceive me now,' she said.'I know what has happened. I'm just so happy you're alive and walking; and you too, John,' she said, reaching out and pinching John's arm.

'But how do you know?' James asked.

'Because we have a visitor,' Mrs Hawker replied.

James looked up the stairs in time to see Charlie's grinning face appear from the drawing room.'What are you doing here, Charlie?' James called, as John closed the front door of the house in Walcot Parade.

'I couldn't abide the thought of her being here on her own,' Charlie said, 'not knowing if you would return or what state you might be in. She needed company and someone she could trust. What about Harry Wood?'

'He won't bother us again,' John said.

James looked at him. His words seemed so cold and dismissive, and yet he could not deny the relief that he felt himself. He said nothing and looked up at Charlie.'And how long did it take Mrs Hawker to get the truth of what was happening out of you?'

'Not long,' Charlie said, coming down the stairs.'We don't let secrets come between us anymore.' Charlie threw his arms open wide and closed them as tight as he could around James and John.'You need to rest,' he said, 'and I'd best be off home.'

'A man has died, and yet all I feel is relief,' James said.

'He was a man who would have happily killed us both,' John said, 'Stay, Charlie, we'll tell you all that happened.'

'No,' Charlie replied, 'I'm happy that you are well. The details will keep for another day. I'll leave you to it.' Charlie pulled on his coat and kissed Mrs Hawker on the cheek before leaving.

In the drawing room Mrs Hawker sat them down and fetched a decanter and two glasses from the sideboard. She must have noticed James wince as he sat, because she began fussing around him, trying to ascertain if he was injured.'Shall I send for Dr Wetherby?' she asked.

'Not at this hour,' James replied.'I just need to sleep.'

'A bit of sustenance wouldn't go amiss though, Mrs Hawker,' John said.

'I'll get you both something now,' Mrs Hawker said, smiling. The thought of doing something practical seemed to ease her concerns, if only temporarily.

He and John sat in silence, letting the decanter of brandy gradually do its work. By the time Mrs Hawker appeared with a tray of food, James was ready to eat. They were about to begin when the loud knocking at the front door sent them both to their feet. John leapt from his chair and grabbed the swords from the velvet bag. 'Someone must have followed us,' he said, passing James a sword as he ran to the window. 'It's too dark to see.'

'Don't answer it,' Mrs Hawker said.

'I'll light candles in the morning room,' James said. 'We should be able to see then who's there. Who ever it is they already know we are in.' John ran down the stairs and James summoned all his strength to follow.

By the time James got to the bottom of the stairs John was leaving the morning room, smiling. 'It's Charlie,' he said. 'I can see him plain as day from down here.' James opened the door and Charlie came in, checking over his shoulder.

'What's happened, Charlie?' John asked.

'There were two of Caine's men outside my house. Caine's either been there or he's on his way,' Charlie said, bolting the door behind him. 'I'm pretty sure they didn't see me and they certainly didn't follow me, but let's not take any chances.'

'You two go upstairs and I'll watch from the window for a while,' John said.

Mrs Hawker met them at the top of the stairs. 'You look frightened, Charlie.'

Charlie sighed. 'I had a bit of a scare, Angela, but I'm fine now.'

'I'll make some tea, and you both sit down and rest, neither of you look well. You'll stay here tonight, Charlie.'

'Yes, Angela,' Charlie agreed, 'but I've nothing but what I'm wearing.'

'I'll sort something out,' she said.

'There's no sign of anyone outside,' John interrupted as he walked into the room.

Charlie collapsed into an armchair. 'No, I'm sure I wasn't followed. You were right, James; Nat Caine must have added things up.'

'You need to stay here for a while, Charlie,' James said.

'Can he get in your house?' John asked.

Charlie smiled for the first time. 'I knows my trade too well for that. The house is well protected. He wouldn't find it easy. Even if he does, the money's well hidden and nowhere he could find it, but I've nothing with me, a few sovereigns and no change of clothes.'

'We have money,' John said. 'We can buy what you need.'

'Caine's closing in on us,' James said.

Charlie leapt to his feet and punched the back of his empty armchair sending it rocking. 'It's me Caine wants now; he won't be bothered with you.'

'Do you think we would stand by and see him harm you, Charlie?' James said. 'We are all in this together ... and always have been.'

James had not drawn the curtains in his room but the first light of day still failed to wake him, as he sat in the chair where he had fallen asleep. It was half-way through the morning when he finally awoke. Adjusting his body the wave of pain swept through him and he felt his mind swimming between dreams and reality, as though he was about to lose consciousness again. He lifted his shirt gingerly and immediately saw the purple and yellow bruising on his rib cage. He struggled to the door and called out.

It was Charlie that helped him to wash and shave and dress. He almost carried him to the armchair in the drawing room after supporting him in his long and painful journey down the stairs. James asked him to explain to Mrs Hawker that he was tired and would take a light breakfast on a tray in the drawing room. It was an elaborate charade concocted by them, to reassure Mrs Hawker that all was still well in the household, but when she brought the tray to James it was clear the charade had not worked. One look at his face was sufficient for her to announce that she would be sending immediately for Dr Wetherby.

It was some hours before Richard arrived, and when they were alone, he examined James thoroughly. Most of his injuries, Richard determined, were muscular bruising, but he also had damage to his ribs. Richard bound his chest in swathes of tight bandaging that hurt intensely when they were applied but allowed him to breathe largely without pain when they were completed. He ordered him to rest as much as possible over the next week and to inform him should his breathing deteriorate in any way. At the end, he smiled and told him that he had been fortunate, and that he should make a complete recovery.

'It would be as well if Charlotte went away for a few days,' James said.

'I'm sure it can be arranged,' Richard replied. 'Is there danger?'

'I don't believe so, but it's too early to say,' James said. 'Keep her away until all this is over. It would be safer.'

'Very well,' Richard replied, 'if you think it prudent.'

Whilst Richard administered to him, James told him of his duel with Harry Wood and watched as his face became increasingly animated. When he told him he had seen Wood's body disappear under the water, Richard interrupted. 'The reason I was late arriving today, James, was that I was called this morning to the morgue in the Mineral Hospital, by the police. There were two bodies taken out of the Avon last night, a man who had had his throat cut and a drowning. The drowned man's body was badly bruised from the weir, but the police had already identified the man as Harry Wood. He was well known to the police and as far as I could ascertain they are treating the death as an accidental drowning or possibly suicide.'

Sean arrived an hour or so after Richard had left and Charlie brought him up to the drawing room. James could tell immediately that something bad had happened. 'I'm glad to see you still alive,' Sean said. 'I take it you did not proceed with the duel.'

'I take no pride in it, but Harry Wood is dead.' James replied. 'He drowned.'

'That explains everything,' Sean stuttered.

'What's wrong, Sean?' James asked.

'Billy is dead. His body was recovered from the Avon this morning. His throat had been cut.'

James felt suddenly cold. 'Are you sure it's Billy?'

'I went with Mary, his wife, to identify him,' Sean said.

The room fell silent. James looked at Charlie, struggling to find something to say. It was obvious that neither of them wanted to be the first to speak. 'Do they know who did it?' James asked eventually, reluctant to use Billy's name as though by naming him it would confirm his death. The same stupid thought went around and around in his head; Billy and his dreams of going to Ireland.

'As soon as I said it was Billy and confirmed where he came from, they decided right away it must have been a drunken brawl,' Sean said. 'The peelers are bringing the body to the church at three.'

'It was Caine,' Charlie said. 'It must have been.'

'I'm certain too,' Sean said. 'Caine took his revenge last night on every Irishman or woman he found. The whole of his gang were out throughout the night, breaking into people's houses; anyone they took a mind to beat and rob. He even tried to get at me, but Brendan and Diarmuid must have been keeping watch and they ran and warned me. Caine broke into the house and wrecked it, but I used the tunnel and got into the church and away.'

'Billy had children,' James said, remembering snatches of random conversations that now felt so much more important than they had at the time.

'Yes, Mary has three little ones to care for now,' Sean said.

'Well she won't go wanting,' Charlie said. 'I'll see her right and so will we all.'

'I have no money,' James said.

'Let's not worry about money,' Sean said, 'no money will put this right.'

'I'll come to the church,' James said. 'What are they doing now, the gang?'

'They've all lain low today,' Sean replied. 'It's not them I'm worried about, it's the people. They're so full of hate for Caine and his men that anything might happen. I must get back and do what I can to still them.'

When Sean and Charlie left, the room felt very empty. Alone, with his memories and his guilt, James' imagination filled the room with Billy's laughter. The sound was in his head, he knew that, yet the pictures in his mind seemed almost real. He saw Billy walking behind him that night on the way to The Circus, saw his grinning face for a moment and then he stilled his mind and the ghost vanished, but the thought still remained. If it was not for him then Billy would still be alive.

When Charlie returned he thrust a purse of money into James' hand. 'That's a share of my money from Harcourt's. I want it to go to Billy's widow and I'm sure John will do the same. Should I take it down there and pay my respects.'

'We will both go,' James said.

'That's risky,' Charlie said, but his expression showed that he already understood that argument was pointless.

'If it were not for me Billy might still be alive,' James said. 'On second thoughts, Charlie, wait for John and tell him what has happened.'

'We all have his blood on us,' Charlie said, 'but we did not kill him and we cannot bring him back by wishing it. Take care going through town and be sure no one follows you back, or there will be more blood spilt.'

'John was the closest of us to Billy,' James said. 'He's sure to take it very badly. Tell him with as little hurt as you can.'

Chapter 34

The rain was coming down heavily as James hailed the hackney cab at the top of Walcot Street. The wind howled and whipped the raindrops into biting, horizontal, needle-sheets of icy water. His cab soon overtook Sean and the priest clambered on board. The two travelled together to the priest's house in silence.

When they arrived, Sean went to the church, leaving James in the house. 'I will send for you when Billy's body is laid out. Brendan will show you the tunnel entrance. It's best you spend as little time as possible in the open, though there's no sign of Caine's men about now.'

The morning stretched relentlessly long into the afternoon as James waited, alone with his thoughts, until Brendan came to fetch him.

After the darkness of the tunnel, the church was a sea of candlelight. The smoke of incense hung heavy, as though the emotion of the place clawed the scented smoke back to the ground each time it tried to rise. James looked at the walls rather than the faces; at the pictures of the Stations of the Cross, sanitised scenes of suffering, their garish colours over-bright. Billy's makeshift coffin stood raised on builder's trestles in front of the altar. He wanted to look away, but stood transfixed as the stream of people slowly filed past Billy's body, paying their last respects.

Mary, Billy's widow, he guessed it must be her, sat on a bench at the front, a long black shawl draped over her head and shoulders and wrapped around the baby in her arms. To one side of her sat her son, and, on the other side, her daughter. As each of the mourners passed the coffin they crossed themselves and came over to whisper to Mary, pat the boy on the head or pinch his cheeks and kiss the young girl. Some gave small amounts of money to the wife, some gave only tears.

James filed past the coffin with the others and like them he made the sign of the cross before stopping for a moment to look at Billy's grey, soulless face. His lips were slightly parted as though he was about to speak, but there was no longer anything to say, no funny stories to tell. Loosely draped around his neck was a brightly coloured woollen scarf tucked into a freshly ironed waistcoat, but there was no sign of the watch John had given him.

James took out his own pocket watch, the one his father had given him, and leaning forward, placed it unseen under Billy's waistcoat. As he did so, he disturbed the scarf and saw the edges of the ugly jagged scar on the white skin of Billy's neck, sewn closed with a few makeshift stitches. The sight was enough to bring tears to his eyes, but he held them back and before moving away he adjusted the scarf to re-cover the wound.

'You don't know me, Mary,' he said, as he approached Billy's widow, 'but I was a friend of Billy's.' The children at her side, made so small by the rituals of death, gazed around the church as if numbed by the waves of emotion that engulfed them. James remembered his own feelings of loss and confusion when his mother had died and wanted to tell them that he understood.

'My name is James Daunton,' he went on. 'I am very...' He got no further.

Mary rose quickly to her feet at the sound of his name and slapped him hard across his left cheek. Her shawl fell down off one shoulder, trailing down to the ground, leaving the baby's head exposed. The little boy stepped forward, standing between his mother and James. 'You were no friend to Billy,' Mary said. 'You used him as it suited you and it cost him his life.'

'I understand your feelings,' James replied, 'and I would do anything to bring him back if I could.' He stood still, waiting to be slapped again, hoping that it might diffuse her pain and give expression to his own. He wanted to pick up the shawl and put it back around her shoulder, but he couldn't move.

'You understand nothing of my feelings,' Mary spat back. 'And now you'll start a war to save yourself.'

'I will help you and the children in any . . .' James started to say, but he got no further.

'I want no help from you. Keep your blood money,' Mary interrupted.

He struggled to find words again, but none came. People were staring at him now, the church silent. He kept wanting to replace the shawl around Mary's shoulder, as though it was all he could think of to do. Sean rushed forward and shepherded him to one side as Mary collapsed back to the bench, weeping. 'Now is not the time, James,' he said.

'I want to help,' James replied, 'to somehow make amends.'

'Your needs are not important now, James,' Sean said. 'Mary will need help. She has no family. Without help her future is in the workhouse, separated from her children. Do you think she will let that happen? She would give her life before splitting her family.'

'I don't want her to lose her pride. I have nothing left now, but Charlie is bringing money and probably John too, will you make sure she gets it,' James said, 'and if she needs more tell me.'

'I'll do it, James,' Sean said. 'Mary's family will never see the inside of the workhouse, but let it be for now. There are more pressing problems.'

'I can feel the people's anger,' James said. He wanted to look at Mary, feeling her eyes still on him, but he looked away. When he turned to see her again, she was staring at the coffin and trying to smile for the children. He no longer existed as anything of any importance in her life.

'Their anger's not aimed at you,' Sean said. 'For most of them, you and Billy are heroes. You took on Nat Caine and worried him for a while. It's him they blame for all that's wrong in Avon Street. You and Billy and the others have made them believe for the first time that Caine can be beaten.'

'What are the constabulary doing concerning Billy's murder?' James asked.

'He's just another Irishman to them, and the peelers have little interest in an Irish death,' Sean replied. 'Besides, Caine has too many of them in his pocket. But the people are angry and my fear is that they will take the law into their own hands.'

James looked around the room. The men had begun congregating at the back of the church, uncomfortable in their Sunday suits, but this time they were not exchanging whispered jokes and muffled laughter or waiting to sneak out to the nearest ale house. They were gathering in small groups and their voices were getting louder despite the solemnity of the occasion; their movements jagged with barely contained emotions, their expressions cold with hatred. Sean pointed out one of them to him, a man called Dempsey; a great ox of a man. James watched him as he moved from group to group, gradually gathering a crowd around him.

Sean moved away, over to the altar, behind Billy's coffin. He stood silent for a while then brought his fist down hard on the corner of the altar, three times. 'I will not have this occasion made foul in the sight of God by talk of revenge, and the assemblage of a mob,' he shouted. The church was silent for a moment.

'We'll have justice, Father,' Dempsey called back, 'and if the law don't give it to us, we'll take it for ourselves. It's time the Irish were heard in this city, be Jeesus.'

James walked up the steps and joined Sean by the altar. He looked down the length of the church to the crowd of men at the back. The door was open and more men were joining the swelling crowd from outside. The people around Dempsey were nodding their approval and then, there by the door, standing motionless, arms folded before them, James saw Charlie and John.

'I'll have no profanity in the house of God!' Sean shouted. 'Billy will have justice, but it will come from the law, and if not from the law, then from God. We do not even know who is guilty of his murder.'

'We know Nat Caine's behind it,' Dempsey shouted. 'His men were beating every Irish soul they could lay hands on last night. Let's see how he feels when we outnumber him. Sure, there's enough of us to do for them all, they're all guilty of something.'

'And if you do for them, how many more widows will there be?'

'There'll be more Caine widers than Irish,' one of the men shouted, accompanied by calls of agreement.

'Do you think the authorities will stand by and watch?' James shouted out above the noise of the crowd. 'Nothing would please them more than to see every Irishman driven out of Bath. All they need is an excuse to act. The dragoons are stationed outside the city. Do you think they will stay there while you march through the city?' The crowd fell quiet for a moment.

'Then we'll fight the dragoons!' Dempsey shouted. There was a chorus of approval.

'And who is it will care for your widows and children?' Sean answered at the top of his voice.

'We will have vengeance,' Dempsey replied, looking around him as if he could feel the crowd slipping from him. 'Who's wid me?' he called as he turned to lead the men out of the church.

Charlie kicked the church door with the back of his heel and it slammed with a bang as loud as a musket shot. John stood in Dempsey's path, his back to the door. 'Listen to the priest,' he said, 'now's not the time. We'll get whoever killed Billy in good time.'

'What's it to do wid you?' Dempsey said, moving towards the door. 'We'll take justice now!'

John stood stock still, staring into Dempsey's eyes, blocking his route to the door. And Charlie stood beside him..

'I'll not have talk of violence in God's house!' Sean shouted.

Dempsey looked round for support, but the crowd now looked less certain and he must have sensed his control fading.

'You can all avenge Billy,' James called at the top of his voice from the stage. 'You can all help defeat Nat Caine. But do it from cold courage, not from the heat of anger. Those of you who are willing to fight Nat Caine, give your names to Father Brennan now and I promise you, you will have justice. But wait until the time is right and respect Billy's life.'

'Listen to him.' It was a woman's voice. James turned. Mary had risen to her feet, the children at her side again. 'No more deaths,' she said. She looked towards James, but as he returned her look, she turned away.

The men began shuffling forward. One or two lined up to give their names to Sean. 'Form a line,' Sean called, 'and I'll take all your names.' He turned to look at James. 'Thank you,' he said, his voice now quiet. 'I think the mood is broken for now, but I'll not see you use these men as your army.'

'I know,' James replied.

'Well, how do you intend using them?' Sean asked.

'I need to plan,' James replied, 'but for now at least, they're not taking to the streets. They need time to cool down and I need time to think. Look after Mary. I will do nothing without speaking to you first. Walk with me to the door and take the money from Charlie.'

They made their way to the door, acknowledging the faces of those who had joined the line to give their names and those standing, less certain, at the back of the church. Their progress was hampered from time to time by people clapping James on the back and pledging support, though it did little other than to increase his feelings of guilt. At the church door John and Charlie passed the money to Sean, 'Make sure she gets it,' Charlie said.

James turned. Mary was sitting, her arms around the children, alone with their grief. He wanted more than anything to speak to her, but he knew he had no words that would make any difference to her life. He wished Belle was with him. She would have known what to say, how to comfort Billy's widow and the children; compassion came so easily to her.

Chapter 35

Caine sat at the head of the table with the five bags of sovereigns, staring in turn at each of the faces of the five men sitting in front of him. They were nervous and they couldn't hide the fact. He looked around the kitchen, at the dozen or so of his men scattered around its perimeter, their faces stony and impassive. He waited, sensing the tension growing, then, when he felt the time was right, he spoke. 'I see new faces now, around Avon Street, wearing peelers' uniforms . . . and they'm unfriendly faces, brought in from other parts of the city. Some have even come from Bristol. And then I see you lot, not wearing uniforms. Can anyone tell me why?'

'Because we've lost our jobs,' one of the seated men replied.

'And why did you lose your jobs?' Caine asked.

'The chief constable said he had information as we were taking money from you and turning a blind eye to what you were up to, said he was replacing us.' The man hesitated, thinking what to say next, wondering if he had said too much. Caine could see the beads of sweat on his forehead. 'He asked us questions about you and about things that had happened and . . . '

One of the others interrupted him, eager to demonstrate loyalty even if it was too late. 'He's seen all of us, one by one.'

'And how did he know all your names?' Caine barked.

'He didn't say, but he knew them all right, and that we were somehow mixed up with you. But we didn't tell him anything, none of us.'

'And how do I know that?' Caine asked.

They all looked at each other, each reluctant to draw attention to themselves. Then the second man spoke again. 'If we'd ratted we'd be inside now, and he'd be a hammerin' on your door. We know better than to cross you, Nat. He's no proof, but he sacked us anyway.'

'But you're none of you any use to me now,' Caine shouted, 'not without your uniforms!'

'We could come and work for you proper,' one of the men said.

'I don't need you. If you can sell out once you can do it again. Besides, I've got enough men. Men as I can trust.'

The room fell silent for a moment as Caine's gaze shifted from one to the next. 'There's one of you not here today,' Caine said.

The men looked around the room. 'Aye, Dawlish ain't here.' It was the first man who had spoken.

'Aye, Dawlish,' Caine said. 'Constable Dawlish came to see me yesterday and told me all six of you had been given the boot.'

'But like Harris said, we haven't said anything.' This time it was one of the others that spoke.

'That's what Constable Dawlish said too,' Caine replied. 'Only he wanted paying to say nothing and he wanted paying a lot. That's why he's not here today.' He stopped speaking, letting their imaginations work for a while. 'Do you know where Constable Dawlish is today?' Caine looked at the faces, watching the fear grow in the silence. No one spoke and he let the silence build again. 'Well I'll tell you, shall I?' He hesitated, knowing the tension would take hold, knowing no one would interrupt. 'Constable Dawlish is resting in the woods on Lyncombe Hill, buried good and deep, where no one will find him.'

One of the men made to stand. Caine gestured to two of his own men who rushed forward and restrained him. He lifted one of the bags in front of him and dropped it back with a bang on the table, smiling inside as he saw two of the men jump. 'In each of these bags is fifty sovereigns,' he said, 'fifty pounds for each of you. You can take them now and walk out of the room, with one condition.'

'We won't talk,' one of them said.

'Oh, one of you would talk if you stay,' Caine said. 'I don't doubt it, or you'd try what Dawlish tried. Besides, the chief constable will be watching you, waiting for you to put a foot wrong. One of you'd get caught doing something, and he'd offer you a lighter sentence to spill your guts. Someone's put a bee in his bonnet. He's after me now and you're his way in.'

'But we'd never talk,' one of the men said.

'Maybe not, but I can't be sure of that. Then there's the Irish. They'll be after you with scores to settle, and no uniforms to protect you.

It's best you leave Bath. That's the condition. If you take this money you leave the city today and you don't come back. If I find any of you in Bath tomorrow you join Constable Dawlish on Lyncombe Hill and don't think the chief constable will protect you. I'd get to you in time. I'm a patient man. And if I can't get to you, I'd get to your kin. Of course you can ask for more, but that's all that you'll get; fifty sovereigns a piece – or Lyncombe Hill. Think about it for a while if you must.'

'I'll take the money,' one of the men said, without hesitation. The others quickly nodded their agreement.

Caine threw a bag to each of the men and turned to Jeb. 'See these gentlemen out,' he said.

When they were gone Caine summoned his own men to the table. 'Watch each one of them and make sure they leave the city before the end of the day. If they don't, I want to know.'

It was all starting to go wrong, Caine thought. He could feel it on the streets when he walked around. He had half-expected the Irish to react, but they had not. The money lending was drying up. People were paying off their debts, thanks to the priest. Now the peelers were sniffing around and the chief constable was after him, brothels and gambling dens getting closed down or moved on. He was almost a prisoner in his own house. At least, he thought, there was still Lansdown Fair. A chance to show them all that Nat Caine was still a name to be respected.

On his way to The Fountains Inn, John couldn't put Billy's death out of his mind. The last thing he wanted to do was spend time in Jeb's company now. So many things had happened in the last few days. There had been no time to think, or talk. Last time he'd met Jeb he'd vowed to tell James and Charlie everything. But James had only just received Harry Wood's challenge and the time hadn't seemed right. Then they'd been preparing for the duel, and then Caine went after Charlie, and now Billy's death. There was never a right time. He knew the truth had to be told and soon, but the longer he said nothing, the harder it got to speak.

John half expected Jeb not to be there when he walked into the ale house, but he found him already at the bar, a quart tankard in front of him, standing alone as usual. He smiled; the same ugly, loathsome smile that John had got to know so well.

'So you're here,' Jeb said, his grin growing broader. 'Harry Wood's dead, you've probably heard, drowned in the river.'

John tried to act surprised, 'I heard someone had drowned, but I didn't know it was Wood. Was it an accident?'

Jeb leered, 'Maybe, or maybe I got rid of him. There's no one now between me and Caine except Harcourt. You know what that means?'

'You're in line for taking over from Caine.'

'More than that,' Jeb said. 'Caine will have to go with Harcourt on the next break-in, himself. If neither of 'em comes back then I take over.' He looked to John for acknowledgement and John smiled. 'Like I said,' he went on, 'there'll be a job for you. I'll need someone I can trust and you'll make more money than you've ever dreamed of.'

'I can see it now,' John said. 'We'll be unbeatable.'

'But I'd be boss,' Jeb said. 'Don't go getting ideas.'

'I've no ideas,' John said, 'but we need to deal with Caine first.'

'The house they're doing's in Queen Square – belongs to a man called Etheridge.'

'When?' John asked.

'Three nights before Lansdown Fair,' Jeb replied. 'Now if someone were to tell the peelers ... '

'I won't let you down,' John said. 'Let's drink to it.'

Caine looked through the window of The Fountains Inn. Inside he saw Jeb and another man deep in conversation. He tried to make out who he was, this man who was so obviously friendly with Jeb, but there were too many people in the way to see him clearly. Each time he caught a glimpse of his profile the man turned away, or someone obscured his view, but there was definitely something familiar about him. If only he could remember.

When he saw him make a move towards the door Caine hid in the alleyway opposite and watched him leave, his cap pulled down over his forehead, his features masked in the shadows cast from the light of the opened doorway. Caine watched him walk up the road and then ran over to the window. Jeb looked settled in for the night and he decided to follow the other man.

There was something about the man's face. He knew he had seen him before, but for the life of him he could not recall where, and the where was important. It wasn't too long ago, but how long? He had been with someone, someone he knew, but the more Caine thought, the more the man's face faded into a hundred other faces until he could no longer picture him.

Caine tried to catch up with him, without giving himself away, but the faster he walked the more distance the man seemed to put between them, as though he were playing games with him. He turned a corner, seeming to glance back, but Caine could not make out anything of his face and when he turned the same corner the man had disappeared.

Caine made his way back to The Fountains Inn, checking first through the window that Jeb was still there. It was then that the sudden realisation came to him. He could picture him perfectly now, even remember their conversation. The man he had just followed, the man who had been talking to Jeb, was the same man he'd seen with Charlie Maggs that day in The Pig and Whistle; the one Maggs had said was his nephew. He'd been right all along; Charlie Maggs was mixed up in all this.

Throwing open the door, Caine waited for the silence which always followed his entrance to a room. He had not been to The Fountains Inn for months, but it was still Jeb who looked the most shocked to see him; taking those few too many seconds to find the uncertain smile that he eventually affected; the all-important seconds that proved he was guilty.

'What brings you here, Nat?' Jeb said. 'I'll get you a beer.'

'I saw this chap leaving just now,' Caine said. 'He were a stocky man. I'm sure I've seen him before. Do you know who I'm talking about?' He watched Jeb's face; the guilt was plain beneath his mask of indifference. His eyes always gave it away.

'There was a chap, just left. He's in here a lot, but I don't know him.'

'It doesn't matter,' Caine said. 'It was you I was looking for. What time is it?'

Jeb took out the pocket watch on the end of its silver chain. 'It's just before ten,' he said. 'Where's your watch?'

'That's the point,' Caine whispered, leaning in towards Jeb's scarred ear. 'I can't find it anywhere. I think I lost it the other night scrabbling around down the riverbank where you did for the Irishman.'

'You've probably mislaid it,' Jeb said. 'It'll turn up.'

'I can't take the chance,' Caine said. 'It's got my name cut proper on the back. If they find it they'll put me in the frame for the killing.'

'But they'd have found it by now.'

'Well they haven't yet, as far as I know, and I don't want someone else stumbling on it. Best we go and look for it now.'

'We won't find it in the dark,' Jeb said.

'Well we can hardly go rooting around there in the daylight,' Caine snapped back. 'It's gold. We'll find it sure enough if it's there. It may be on the path down to the riverbank, I fell over there when I was looking for you. I can find the spot easy enough.'

Caine led the way out of the ale house and back up to Walcot Street. On the slope down to the river he found the clump of brambles near the spot where he had fallen. He pointed out to Jeb the now worn impressions his feet had left on the muddy path when he had slipped, and they both ferreted around in the brambles until they were satisfied that nothing could be found. 'It must be down by the river,' Caine said, 'where we had our little disagreement.'

The steepness of the path down to the river propelled them at a rate of knots and Caine tumbled at the bottom almost ending in the water. Jeb helped him up.

'What did you tell that man in The Fountains, Jeb?' Caine said. 'It weren't to do with my business were it?'

'Why would I tell him anything to do with you, Nat? Besides, I don't know anything.'

'That's right old friend,' Caine said as they walked along the path. He stopped when they came to the spot where the Irishman had died and looked around. Then he pointed to a spot in the oozing mud at the river's edge. 'It's there – look.'

Jeb looked at where he was pointing. 'That's just a pool of water, Nat, catching the light.' He bent over to get a better view of the spot. Caine grabbed the collar of his jacket then and kicked him at the back of his knees, sending him sprawling forward. He planted his knees in the small of Jeb's back with all his weight, and pushed his face into the river-slime. Jeb struggled for a while, arms and legs thrashing the ground, but Caine kept him pinned, hands around his neck until his body finally went limp.

It was as though someone else was taking Jeb's life, acting for him while he watched. Caine held him there for a while after his struggles had stopped. Then, when he was sure he was dead, he reached under his lifeless body until he located the watch chain. He pulled it free and the Irishman's watch along with it and fastened it tight around Jeb's wrist.

'No loose ends, Jeb,' he said. 'Now they've got someone for the Irishman and who's to say you didn't do for yourself out of remorse. I warned you enough times old friend, but you wouldn't learn.' He waded a few steps into the water, pushing Jeb's body in front of him and watched as the river took it.

It was almost ten thirty when John got back to the house. He found James alone in the drawing room and the words burst from his mouth without thought, 'I think Caine saw me with Jeb. He followed me from The Fountains Inn.'

'He followed you here?' James asked, rushing to the window.

'No. He's not as fast as he's strong. I lost him soon enough, but he may have recognised me. If he did and he remembers seeing me with Charlie, then he knows we're all in this together.'

'Thank God we moved from Charlie's house,' James said. 'What did Jeb tell you?'

'Three nights before Lansdown Fair, Caine and Harcourt are going to rob the house of a man called Etheridge in Queen Square.'

'Then I will have to write tomorrow to the chief constable, in the same fine copperplate as my last letter and inform him of the facts.'

'But what if Caine knows what Jeb has told me?'

'Then we will have to deal with him in some other way.'

'There's something I have to tell you,' John said, pausing, 'something I should have told you long ago.' He looked at him, almost expecting an interruption, but James said nothing. 'I know you've wondered at times why I was so eager to help you. Perhaps you put it down to bravery or kindness, I don't know. But in truth my fight with Caine began before I met you. I haven't been kind, nor brave.'

'I don't understand,' James said.

'That night in Avon Street when I helped you, I wasn't there by accident. I'd been watching Caine's men for days, off and on; following them from place to place.'

'But why?' James asked.

'I'll get round to that,' John said, 'but there's something you need to understand first. I'd followed Caine that night to kill him. You being there and him being after you gave me the perfect chance, or so I thought.' He looked James full in the eyes, needing him to understand. 'Do you see?' he asked, not waiting for a reply. 'I wasn't bothered about what happened to you; I just wanted to kill Caine. I wasn't even bothered what happened to me.'

'Why didn't you do it?' James asked. 'Why didn't you kill him?'

'I don't know,' John said. 'I've been over it a thousand times in my head. You think nothing scares me; that I can do anything, but Caine is the man I hate most in the world, and I couldn't kill him.' He hesitated, reliving the night, trying to remember the thoughts that went through his mind. 'I came up behind him with my knife. No one heard me. I could have done it then, while he was watching you, but I wanted him to know I was going to kill him and why. When he turned round and I saw his grinning face, I wanted to kill him more than ever, but I couldn't do it. I couldn't take his life.'

'So you hit him instead and saved my life,' James said.

'I wasn't being noble,' John said. 'I hit him because I lost my nerve, because I wanted to get away from there as much as you did. All I had in my mind was the need to run.'

'It doesn't matter why you did it,' James said. He looked sincere. 'What matters is that you stayed. You didn't have to and how many times have you helped me since?'

'I've done no more for you than you have for me,' John said. 'But you're a friend now and I want no more half truths between us.'

'Then tell me why you hate Caine so much.' James said.

'I told you once that a woman I knew had made me think about my life and the things I'd done,' John replied. 'I said she looked at the world as Sean does.'

'I remember,' James replied. 'It was when you were talking about the Opium Wars.'

John nodded. 'Her name was Isabella; her father was Spanish. We met up each time I was in England, and we wrote to each other. I'd tell her all the ports on the voyage ahead, and there would always be letters waiting for me wherever I docked.' John paused, remembering how much those letters had meant to him, read time after time, each reading a reminder of a softer life. 'She was the gentlest person I've ever known, and yet so strong with it. I don't think I even realised how much I loved her until it was too late.'

'She lived in Bath?' James asked.

'Her father had a wine shop in Bristol and she worked for him. In her last letter, she told me that they were moving to a better shop in Bath. She was excited and looking forward to living here, so full of plans. Then I heard nothing.'

'Where is the shop?' James asked.

'It doesn't exist,' John said. 'I tracked it down easy enough, but it was derelict. I asked the neighbours what had happened. They said there'd been a fire.'

'Was she killed?' James asked.

'The neighbours said Isabella and her parents got out alive, and they'd moved to London, to stay with her mother's brother. I tracked them down eventually, but it was too late, Isabella never recovered from breathing all the smoke. She died a few days after they moved.'

'I'm sorry,' James said, and John knew that he truly meant it.

'Her father told me Caine had threatened him, wanting payment for the privilege of running a shop so near to Avon Street,' John said. 'He'd refused to pay of course; the Spanish are a proud and stubborn people.' He hesitated, as though struggling for the strength to go on talking. 'Isabella was always proud and knew her own mind. I suppose that's one of the reasons I loved her.'

'So Caine set fire to the shop,' James said.

'Caine, or one of his men,' John said, 'it doesn't matter who did it; Caine was behind it and I couldn't even kill him for it. I was going to, but now I remember . . . ' He hesitated. 'When I grabbed the knife I kept thinking of Isabella, and what she would have thought. That's why I couldn't do it.'

'There's no shame in that, John,' James said. 'There will be justice in the end for Caine. We will make sure of that.'

'Will you tell Charlie all this, about Isabella and what happened?' John asked. 'I couldn't go through it again.'

'Of course,' James replied. 'Charlie needs to know, he thinks a great deal of you. Caine will have his just deserts. Believe me, John.'

Chapter 36

Belle took off a white glove and ran the index finger of her right hand along the mahogany shop counter. It was fine quality timber, wood that her father would have enjoyed working with. Her finger had left a faint trail where the polished wood glowed, fiery dark against the slight peppering of dust. 'The landlord spoke true when he said the shop was not long vacant,' she said. 'We should decide quickly if we are going to take it.' She turned around, looking to where Jenny had been a moment ago, but found herself alone in the room. Smiling, she listened to the sound of footsteps on the bare floorboards above her head and pictured Jenny flying from room to room again, her mind busy with plans and her eyes full of the future.

Belle looked out of the shop window. The man who had been standing in the shop doorway opposite was no longer there. For days now she had felt as though she was being watched everywhere she went. Yet each time she thought she had identified her watcher it was as though they were a ghost, able to appear and disappear at will. It rarely seemed to be the same face, but there seemed to be eyes on her wherever she went. She shuddered as the cold feeling ran up her spine. Harcourt was still in Bath as far she knew, and she had heard nothing from James. His parting words of warning kept running through her mind.

Belle looked at her watch again. They had been in the shop for nearly three hours; climbing up and down the stairs over and over again, wandering from room to room. She felt tired, but Jenny's energy seemed to grow as if she gathered strength from every cupboard and recess she inspected, in every room.

She had felt from the moment they had opened the shop door that this was the right place. Any doubts she had regarding their venture had died with the first step across the threshold. She wrote in the dust of the shop counter 'We will succeed', as though the words were a magic spell she was casting on the fabric of the building. When she turned again, Jenny was standing by the shop window, her smile filling her whole being.

'It's all so perfect,' she said, 'we need do nothing with the rooms or the decorations, but we will need furniture and curtains and so many other things. Are you sure you want to proceed?'

'No,' Belle replied, frowning. She wiped the words from the counter and watched the dismay on Jenny's face for a few seconds, but that was all she could bear. Then she laughed. 'Of course I'm sure. This will be our new home and the first of our shops. Are you certain it is large enough?'

'I'm certain,' Jenny replied. 'There is space for a window display and a seating area.' She pointed to the rear of the shop. 'Where the stock rooms are now, we shall have two fitting rooms.' Then she whirled around like a ballerina. 'On that wall we will have shelves with materials and drawers full of decorative finishes.'

'And the location,' Belle asked. 'Is Green Street suitable?'

'It's perfect,' Jenny replied. 'It's close enough to Milsom Street to attract the customers we need, but not so expensive.'

'We will have to budget carefully,' Belle said. 'We have enough for six months' rent and a few alterations and the materials you will need. With what is left and what I will be able to send from London we should be able to pay wages for the staff for the first few months, but the shop will need to start bringing in income quickly.'

'Have no fear,' Jenny said. 'When they see the quality of our clothes and our fine gowns, the customers will come.'

'Have you spoken to the women that you intend to employ?' Belle asked.

'Yes,' Jenny smiled, 'the girls are all eager to begin, but you will need to help me selecting staff for the shop.'

'We will find a manageress and she will select her staff. You need to sketch out the alterations you will require and we will select a carpenter as soon as the lease is signed.'

'I can't believe that this is real,' Jenny said. 'It still seems like a dream.'

'It won't be easy,' Belle replied, 'but it is real. I'm sure we shall encounter set-backs, but for the time being everything is good.' She hesitated. 'Before I leave I shall speak to James and Dr Wetherby and ensure that they are available to advise you on business matters if you need help.'

'Do you have to leave Bath?' Jenny asked.

'I must,' Belle replied. She was certain now. She had heard nothing from James in weeks and it was for the best that she sought out a new life.

'If you have decided then you must go,' Jenny said. 'Molly and I will miss you, but you must go.'

'As you must pursue your dream,' Belle said, throwing her arms around her.

James found John Doyle sitting alone in front of the fire in the dining room that afternoon. John did not look up when he entered the room, but sat poking the coals listlessly, watching the sparks taking to the air and burning out in flight. James paced around the room for a while, neither of the men speaking or even particularly acknowledging each other's presence.

'I have had some news,' James said, sitting opposite John and trying to engage his attention.

'What news?' John asked.

'Jeb is dead,' James said.

'Was it the Irish lads that killed him?' John asked.

'Sean thinks not,' James said. 'He called an hour ago. Jeb's body was found in the river this morning. Billy's watch, the one you gave him, was tied around his wrist.'

John plunged the poker into the fire, his face full of anger and hatred. 'I wasn't even sure it was Caine's men who had killed Billy. I feel guilty for it now, but I thought he might have just talked his way into a fight. I should've guessed it was Jeb,' John said, thrusting the poker over and over into the fire. 'He was evil and deserved to die, whoever did it.'

'I'd put my money on Caine,' James said. 'He followed you that night when you'd been talking with Jeb. Caine must have seen you together. God knows if he's worked out who you are.'

'What do we do?' John asked.

'We have to proceed on the basis that Caine suspects nothing,' James said. 'Sean's having the letter delivered for me to the chief constable, with all the information you gleaned on the intended robbery.

Diarmuid and Tom will come and stay here for the next few nights, and Brendan and Patrick will stay with Sean at all times.'

'Do you think Sean's in danger?' John asked.

'I think we all are,' James replied. 'The sooner this is over, the better. I feel more wary of Caine now than I did at the beginning.'

'Because you now know what he's capable of,' John said. 'I've never doubted it and neither has Charlie.'

'Sean gave me a list of the Irish lads who volunteered to follow us against Caine after Billy's funeral. There are almost forty names on it.'

'We could wipe the Cockroad gang from the face of the earth with that number,' John grimaced, 'that's if we need to.'

'For the first time I believe it's possible,' James said. 'But we must not act hastily. We might defeat Caine in an open battle, but how many would die? I want no more widows on my conscience.'

'I just meant that for the first time we could more than match Caine in strength,' John said.

'I know, John, and we will,' James said. 'If the constabulary don't catch Caine in the robbery, we'll finish him at Lansdown Fair, but I have promised Sean that no one else will be hurt and I intend to keep my word. I have been through the plan with him and he knows exactly what to do and when, but I would be happier if you were by his side.'

'I'm sorry,' John smiled. 'It's just the thought of Jeb killing Billy. I won't do anything hasty, but before I can help Sean I'll need to know what you have planned.'

'It may not be needed if the peelers take him, but we will be ready if they do not. First I need to write to Belle and Richard,' James said, halting momentarily to gather his thoughts. 'I'll give you letters to take to them. Wait for their response and when you return we will sit with Charlie and go through the whole plan, until we are certain it is as near flawless as possible. In the meantime let's pray that the constabulary catch Caine without the need for any confrontation.'

Chapter 37

Nat Caine had been anxious all day and Harcourt's arrival in the early evening had done little to reassure him. Harcourt was too sure of himself, Caine thought. Normally his certainty seemed to breed confidence, but this time it made him nervous.

Caine watched him as Harcourt laid out the plans of Etheridge's house on the kitchen table. 'I'll get the two men we're taking with us tonight,' Caine said, walking to the stairwell and bellowing out their names. He returned to the table and sat facing Harcourt, resenting the smug smile fixed on his face.

'Why so quiet?' Harcourt asked.

'I've got a bad gut, and I still think it's too soon after the last one,' Caine said. 'The peelers are like wasps about the place, as though we'd just stoned their nest.'

'They won't expect us to do anything then,' Harcourt replied. He paused, raising a quizzical eyebrow. 'I understand Jeb's no longer with us? Took his own life I hear.' He laughed and looked towards Caine as though he expected him to share the joke. 'I never took him for a man with an over-active conscience.'

'It ain't funny,' Caine said, 'Jeb had been with me for years afore I met you and he never used to be trouble. I'm only glad I told him nothing about tonight, he'd developed too loose a tongue.'

'Well, may the devil find rest for his tongue and his soul,' Harcourt said, laughing again, 'because God won't have much time for him.'

'Shut yer mouth and get on with it,' Caine said, as the two other men walked into the room. They gathered around the table and began examining the plans Harcourt had drawn of the ground floor of the house in question.

'You'll be pleased with this one,' Harcourt said. 'Etheridge is a bit of a miser, though he'd never admit it. He has no manservant, only two maids and a cook, and he's a weedy character, and not in the best of health.'

'What about the safe?'

'The safe is in his study and that's where his miserliness suits us well. It's old, and more like a tin box than a safe. If you can't pick its lock, we can turn it and cut through the back. Failing that we get him out of his bed and make him open it. He'll not put up much of a fight.'

'I still don't like it. How do you know so much about the place?'

Mr Etheridge is not as righteous a man as he would have the world believe. I befriended him, and did a favour for him a while back; or rather you did, on my behalf – a competitor of his who you persuaded to shut up shop. Etheridge must not see me if we have to wake him.'

Caine insisted that they went through their preparations time and time again; planning the entry, escape routes, what was to be taken, the layout of the rooms and who was to do what. Then it was just a matter of waiting.

Belle read the letter from James a third time as Jenny hovered around her, giggling. 'Is it a love letter?' Jenny asked when she could no longer restrain her curiosity.

'Would that it was,' Belle replied, 'but no, James has simply asked if I will do him a further favour regarding Caine.'

'Is it dangerous?' Jenny asked, the concern clear in her voice. 'Please say it isn't. Not now; not when everything is going so well for us.'

Belle folded the letter as though she were finished with its contents. 'No it's not dangerous,' she lied. 'It was an idea . . . my idea. I thought he'd dismissed it, but obviously not.'

'What do you have to do?' Jenny asked.

'He simply needs my help with a little charade. Don't worry yourself.'

Jenny went back to her drawing and Belle unfolded the letter again. It was plain from James' words that he too understood very clearly the risk entailed in what he was asking. She read the last sentence over and over. 'I do not ask this lightly and will understand if you do not feel able to help this time, but please accept my assurance that I would willingly sacrifice my own life to preserve yours.' He had signed it, 'With all my love, James.'

The prospect of what lay ahead frightened her but there was no choice and she had already sent her answer. She would do it for him and then it would be done. She looked at his signature one last time before carefully folding the letter and placing it in her trunk.

It was half an hour after midnight that Caine announced they should make their move. Frank was glad. He'd never seen Caine look apprehensive about anything before, yet the longer the evening had gone on, the more nervous Caine seemed to become and it was clear that his nervousness was affecting the others.

All Frank wanted now was to put the night behind him and to get as far away from Caine as was possible. He wondered what had affected the man like this. Perhaps it was because the last job had gone wrong, or because it was the third robbery in under a month; more likely he thought it was because he no longer had Harry Wood and Jeb to rely on. Caine had grown soft, too old, too used to giving orders. He'd forgotten what it was like to take the risks himself. Frank could see it in his face. Caine the hardened criminal, feared by half of Bath, was scared at the thought of a simple burglary. Perhaps he should stay in Bath, he thought; make a bid for the gang himself, now that Jeb and Harry Wood were out of the way. He knew he could do it. Even on the last job when things had gone wrong, he hadn't panicked. The escape had been better than the break-in. All those hard men had gone to pieces, but he had stayed cool as a cucumber and led them out of the house.

As they walked up to Queen Square, Frank had to keep stopping to let Caine catch up. They'd split into two parties so as not to draw attention to themselves, Caine's men carrying the tools in case they were stopped, but Caine seemed reluctant to stay with him. 'It's very quiet,' Caine said when he finally caught up.

'That's good,' Frank replied. 'And better than that, there's no peelers about.'

They looked up at the front of the house. It was all in darkness and Caine signalled to the men to make their way to the lane at the back of Queen Square. There, at the back of the house was a stable yard and a number of outhouses. Frank took the lead and tried tentatively to open the tall gate leading into the yard, but it was bolted. He motioned to one of the men who crouched beneath the wall, interlinking his fingers ready to take his weight. Frank placed one foot in the stirruped hands and scrabbled to the top of the wall. There were no lights at the back of the house and all was quiet. He let himself back to the ground. 'Are we ready then?' he asked, smiling.

'You go in,' Caine said. 'I'll check the front again. Leave the gate open for me.'

'That's not what we planned,' Frank said.

'I just want to be sure.' Caine said. 'Don't waste time jabbering. Get on with it.' He turned and walked away.

Frank cursed Caine under his breath before clambering over the wall and letting the others through the gate. At least Caine had chosen men who knew their jobs well and they needed no instruction. The first opened the window catch with his knife and eased the window open wide, while the second slipped the small jack between the middle two bars of the window. A couple of minutes of careful cranking and the bars bent apart as gently and silently as though they were made of wax.

Frank quickly realised he was the only one slender enough to slip between the bars, but he got in easily enough. The moment he set foot inside the dark hallway he slipped back the bolts on the back door and turned the key in the lock. Caine's men entered silently and shut the door behind them.

The second it was shut, the other two doors leading into the hallway flew open. Uniformed bodies filled the room. Frank knew instantly that there was no escape. He offered little resistance, grinning in the faces of his captors and holding out his hands to show he had no weapon. In their lamp lights he could see at least a half dozen if not more of them. Two of the peelers grabbed his arms, one on each side of him and began leading him into the stable yard. He watched over his shoulder as the others wrestled Caine's men to the floor. Still he did nothing as they pushed him out of the back door into the yard. He knew Caine would be outside and he knew that he would be ready.

Caine had walked slowly back to the front of the house, trying to calm his mind, to dispel the nagging feelings inside him. His throat burnt as though he had drunk a pint of vinegar, and the cramps were sweeping through his stomach again in great wrenching waves of pain. He had felt the ache growing all through the day. His body would not be stilled now, reacting to a fear that seemed to increase by the minute, as though this were the first job he had ever done. Every instinct in his mind shrieked warnings. Something was wrong and his whole body sensed it.

He looked around him. There was always a peeler patrolling around Queen Square at this time of the morning – why not now and why did it seem so quiet? He stood in front of the house and closed his eyes, letting them adjust to the blackness. When he opened them again he saw it. He thought he had imagined it at first, but he could see it plainly now. There was a small glow in an inner room of the house, like a single shielded candle, or a lamp set very low. Then the light became brighter.

His first instinct was to run back and warn them, but if he was right, then it was probably too late. He began running, but he could already hear the shouting from the rear of the house. He stopped outside the back wall and stood in the shadows of the yard gate that had swung open into the lane.

The two peelers on either side of Harcourt were chattering to each other as they led him out of the house. Frank looked directly at him, as though he had been expecting him. Caine watched them. Neither of the peelers had seen him yet. Harcourt was staring at him, as he cocked and aimed the pistol. He began trying to shake his arms free from the peelers, still staring towards Caine, his face pleading. Despite his efforts Harcourt could not shake himself free and instead he shouted, 'Shoot; what are you waiting for?'

The pistol sounded like a cannon in the stillness of the night. For a fraction of a second, Caine watched as Harcourt's body slumped lifeless between the two peelers. Then he slammed the gate closed and propped a rock at its base before running down Princes Street. By the time he heard the pursuing footsteps drawing near he was already approaching the maze of Avon Street alleyways, and soon the footsteps faded into the distance.

Only when he was sitting alone, back in the house, did the thought of what he had done truly hit home. The calm and control he had felt when he pulled the trigger were gone now, but he had no regrets. His men could be relied on not to talk – but Harcourt? Harcourt would have told them everything in exchange for his freedom, or a lighter sentence. The man had no honour. Caine knew he couldn't take the chance.

Yet he kept seeing Frank's face in the shadows of the room; hearing his voice like a muffled cry in every creak and groan of its timbers. He grabbed the bottle of brandy from the table and spitting out the cork, drank half its contents, swallow after swallow.

Sean brought the news of the robbery to the house in Walcot Parade on the afternoon of the following day. James felt strangely emotionless when he heard of Harcourt's death. His revenge could not be more complete, and yet for a while he could remember none of the wrong the man had done, but only the times they had laughed together. He looked at Charlie and John, strangely silent, perhaps because they understood his mixed emotions, or perhaps they simply respected his need to come to his own understanding of what had happened.

'We have only two days to prepare for Lansdown Fair,' James said, addressing them all. 'Caine has to be finished then, whatever it takes to do it.' He felt a strange coldness inside, as though his conscience had at last fallen silent and granted sanction for him to act in whatever way he could to achieve his objective. Perhaps the others sensed it, because no one responded.

Chapter 38

John stood on the rich, broad, upland pasture of Lansdown Hill. The River Avon snaked its coils around the city below, and from the top of Lansdown Hill the sky stretched out like an endless waveless ocean. From here, high above the cityscape, the dazzling golden buildings that lined the wide parades appeared like nothing more than building blocks in a child's playroom.

John turned his back on the scene, switching his attention to the pleasure grounds laid out in front of him. The fair occupied a wide sweeping loop of the hilltop, with sideshows and exhibits, booths and tents encircling the livestock market. He'd watched from early morning as cattle and sheep were herded into makeshift pens, and horses were trotted around the circumference to show their gait to best advantage. Deals were already being struck and money exchanged, on the shake of a hand.

The racecourse, further out along the hill, had been abandoned for four years, its rich ground lying fallow; good grazing for sheep and cattle. Now it was to be used again. The track had been laid out, and marquees were dotted to the north of its perimeter. By first light the carriages had already begun pulling up around the course to claim the best views, and the bookmakers had set up their stalls.

The spring air blew free and clean and rich with country smells on Lansdown Hill, its customary quiet tranquillity lost in a sea of barking, bellowing and bleating, all blending with the chatter of the fair-goers and the raucous calls of the traders and entertainers. Those whose business was already done or yet to begin, and those whose business was pleasure, made their way around the tents and fairground booths.

Wombwell's Menagerie made up much of the entertainment with its human anomalies; the wonderful Scottish giant, the mountain creature, the living skeleton, and Madam Osiris, the seer of the future. Carnival girls strolled between the booths in their costumes made of delicately layered silk handkerchiefs. The wild animals from Africa and India were displayed some distance away in their own area, so as not to disturb the less exotic livestock. The tents were full of games of skill and chance, lucky dips and shies, and the tog-tables with their crooked dice and magnificent prizes, only ever won by the lady dice thrower's accomplices.

Nat Caine arrived in a landau just after nine in the morning. He ordered the driver to tether the horses in one of the fields set aside for wagons and coaches, as near as possible to the fair to occupy a vantage point, but avoiding the prominence of a place by the racecourse. Under the seat of the coach he had stowed a tin box for depositing the monies to be collected that day, together with an array of flintlock pistols of varying age and specification.

Caine sat for a while in the coach with one of the men, loading, priming and setting the pistols in readiness. He would never ordinarily have felt the need of such an armoury. Settlement day at Lansdown Fair normally proceeded without trouble, yet today felt different, and he was uneasy about the task ahead. The Irish troubled him in particular. He had expected them to react to the night of beatings and to the death of the little Irishman, but nothing had happened. Yet the talk on the street was of them coming together at Lansdown Fair for a fight.

Caine watched as the gang assembled. Apart from his own men, almost all of whom were there, he had hired a further half dozen or so local bruisers for the day. He felt more secure when he saw their number. Yet he still felt nervous as he took a swig out of the flask of brandy on the seat beside him. He looked around searching for anything out of the ordinary. His stomach was knotted with pain again. The laudanum was all that seemed to keep it in check these days, but today he needed his wits about him.

Caine stepped down from the coach and addressed the gang. Six of the best men he designated to guard the coach and to accompany him on his occasional forays into the fair or the races. Some of the others he split into twos and threes, and dispatched with their specific orders to sniff out the unlicensed games of chance and other activities that the law might frown upon, scattered around the fields, crouching behind walls and hidden between the canvas tents. The tricksters and card sharps were always vulnerable to the persuasions and intimidation in which the Cockroad gang specialised and could be expected to yield a reasonable toll. The rest of the men he dispatched to collect the annual fees from those who enjoyed his protection; the farmers and trades people, innkeepers and shopkeepers. He told them to leave the fairground people alone. They could not hope to match them in numbers or strength.

Caine decided he would personally collect the dues from the bookmakers on the course, knowing that they might require persuading as to the value of his particular insurance. He knew most would find it preferable, after a little personal persuasion, to the risk of being robbed of their takings by some cut-throat on their way home.

Leaving two men to watch the coach, he felt in a better mood as he commenced his first tour, cutting a wide swathe through the crowd. The respect was still plain in people's eyes, though at second glance it seemed less certain and more questioning than it used to be, as though his appearance at the fair was almost viewed with some degree of disbelief. 'Something ain't right, Jeb,' he said, turning to the man next to him. Almost before the words were out of his mouth he had corrected himself. 'I mean Lem,' he said, looking again at the man's face.

'What's wrong?' Lem asked.

'Nothing I can lay my finger on,' Caine replied. 'But I know something's wrong. I think we may have trouble today.'

'What do you want me to do?' Lem asked.

'Pass the word amongst the men. Tell 'em to come down hard on any who shows any reluctance in paying. But tell them to mind they're watchful too, there's something not right.'

Sitting at a makeshift table between two tents, a man was challenging passers-by to find the pea, which he shuffled between three thimbles. From time to time one of his confederates would appear and win quite easily. The small crowd of farm labourers gathered around him were obviously captivated by the ease of the game, and eager to stake their wages on a sure thing. Caine pushed his way past them.

'Let's have a go then,' he said as the man looked him in the face for a moment and took note of who he was.

'I've already paid, Mr Caine,' he said.

'Well let's call this a bonus,' Caine said, slapping a sovereign on the table. 'I hope you've trimmed your fingernails this morning.'

'You'll break me, Mr Caine,' the man said.

'Well you'll have to work harder then,' Caine replied. 'I'll have the thimble in the middle.'

'But I haven't shown you yet which one the pea's under, nor shuffled the thimbles.'

'It don't matter,' Caine said. 'I'll have the middle one.'

The man raised the thimble on his right, showing the crowd the position of the dry, wrinkled, nut-hard pea. As he replaced the thimble on the table, even Caine couldn't see him trapping the pea under the long fingernail of his index finger and removing it from the table. He shuffled the thimbles in wide circular mesmeric sweeps of the polished wood and as he lifted the central thimble he deposited the pea, again unnoticed, on the table, beneath it. The crowd gasped in admiration of Nat Caine's skill as the man handed back his sovereign together with one of his own. Caine tested both with his teeth and walked away as the crowd of labourers pushed forward, eager for some easy money, having just witnessed almost a month's wages changing hands.

John suddenly became aware that he had been out in the open for far too long. He made his way towards the ranks of tents at the far side of the fair, near the wild animal cages. They were pitched side by side for the sale of beer and wine and liquor. Next to them were a number of stands selling tea and coffee and a row of less garish, less busy tents selling baked potatoes and pies and other foodstuffs.

All of the tents had their entrances open to allow the customers a view of the goods and to help the cooking scents to percolate through the crowd and whet their appetites. Only one tent, set-back a little way from the others, had its front flap closed and tied shut. It was this one that John made for, careful to keep his cap pulled down over his face, watchful at every step.

Sean Brennan stood inside the tent, checking the rota of assembled men against the list of volunteers. He looked at first startled and then relieved when John stepped through the opening. The men stood chatting and smoking; some helping their wives, busy assembling a long row of trestle tables, stretching for almost the full width of the tent. Each of the tables was covered with cheap white calico cloth that stretched down to the floor at the front. The tables were laid with bread and cheese and bowls piled high in waiting for the rabbit stew kept simmering in a massive pot at the back of the tent.

'I think everyone's here that should be here,' Sean said to the assembled men. He turned to John. 'I make it to be fifteen in all, with another twenty or so around the fair keeping an eye out for Caine's men and waiting for orders – and there's more on their way.'

'That should be more than enough,' John replied, with some satisfaction.

'Now you lads stay here and have a drop of stew while Brendan takes me round to show me who we're dealing with,' Sean said. 'And if any of you men have any weapons other than your fists . . . ' He looked around at the men. His voice had been loud and authoritative and when he hesitated the tent fell totally silent. 'Well, you can put them behind the table now, for the women to watch. I'll be checking you all when we get back and you can be sure of that, if nothing else. I'll have no killing or accidents today. You women sort your men out, now.'

'Make sure you find where Caine is based,' John said to Brendan, as he made to leave. 'Charlie says he always has a coach where they keep the money and meet up during the day. We need to know where he will be.' He watched through the closed tent flap as the two men set off across the fair.

It seemed to John that they were gone for hours, but in truth it could not have been more than twenty minutes. Sean explained the exact location of Caine's coach and then he and Brendan took up their positions at a small table outside the entrance to the tent, barring admittance. John pulled the canvas flap back far enough for Brendan's twelve-year-old son to step out of the tent and stand at his father's side.

The boy already looked older than his years, John thought. Brendan always kept him near, now. It was less than a year ago that he had been imprisoned for a month's hard labour for stealing a chicken. It had been the first meat the family had had in weeks. Locked in a cell, he had turned the crank for hour after hour, in pointless, back-breaking labour every day, to pay for his offence. Brendan had kept him close by since then. Today the boy desperately wanted to help his father and though Sean had objected, Brendan had relented, provided the boy agreed in turn to attend Sean's school in the mornings until he had learnt to read.

John took a grey scarf from the pile of coats and passed it out to Sean. 'Here's your scarf, Father Brennan,' he said, smiling. 'We wouldn't want anyone to recognise you as a priest.' The priest returned his smile and tied the scarf around his neck. They had little time to wait before one of the groups of Caine's men drew near. Brendan's son knew what he had to do and his father duly dispatched him to talk to them.

As the boy spoke, he pointed at the tent and one of the men held a coin out to him. The lad snatched the coin away quickly and disappeared into the crowd. Sean and the others stood, as Caine's men approached the tent. John signalled to the men inside to make ready.

'What's amiss, lads?' Sean asked when they were within earshot.

'There's a game of chance in here,' one of the men said as he pushed past and untied the tent flap. He entered of his own accord. Brendan propelled the second man through the entrance with the assistance of his right boot. Once inside a dozen Irishmen fell on the men, forcing them to the ground with a minimum of noise and resistance. The two were quickly bound and gagged and deposited, out of sight, behind the calico cloths which covered the trestle tables.

During the course of the morning more of Caine's men joined those already stowed behind the tables. Each man was gagged, then trussed like a chicken, with hands and feet bound and with a rope securing the knots around their arms to those around their legs, to prevent them kicking out or moving. By noon, seven of Caine's men had been subdued and restrained.

'I'll get word to the lads around the fair to start the trouble,' Brendan said. 'We'll draw them as far away from the coach as we can and quiet one or two of them.'

Lem leant on the door of the coach where Caine was sitting. 'Something's definitely not right, Nat,' he said. 'Some of the lads haven't been seen for hours and there's fights breaking out everywhere, usually with one or more of our lads involved. The peelers are chasing around like mad things. They get to one fight and it breaks up and then another one starts up somewhere else.'

'I've felt uneasy all morning,' Caine said. 'Get all the men back here and then ride into town, Lem, and get more men. Anyone you can lay hands on. Leave a couple to watch the house, but fetch everyone else and hire anyone you see that's worked for us before. Get them here quickly. If they want a battle I'll give them one they won't forget.'

Chapter 39

The streets of Bath were deserted on the day of Lansdown Fair, and the area at the back of Nat Caine's headquarters was no exception. Belle made her entrance to the lane in the middle of the afternoon as they had planned. She knew the others were close, but still she was afraid. The cold air and her own fear conspired together until she was uncertain as to which was the cause of the trembling in her legs.

The thin dress clung to her body as though it was moulded to her skin, as it was meant to; just as Jenny had fitted it for her. Bought second-hand, she tried to imagine who had worn it before, feeling for a character to play, as though some vestige of the spirit of its previous owner still existed in the fabric of the dress.

Belle was to all intents and purposes a common barmaid now, and walked with an affected, teasing laziness; moving, she hoped, like a cheap seductress. It was a part she had played on stage many times before, but never had her life depended on how well she played the role.

In her right hand she carried an earthenware jug that steamed in the cold air, and two tankards swung from her left hand. The burdens rose and fell with each contrived step, as though her arms were measuring scales, dipping and counterbalancing each other. She used the rhythm of her movement, fighting each nervous impulse that might make her appearance less languorous, or show any sign of the fear that was gnawing at her.

As soon as they saw her, the men guarding the back door of Caine's house began shouting and gesturing. Their words left little doubt as to their opinion of her charms, and likely morality. She felt her fear receding; she was an actress again and her performance was going well.

'What've you got there?' one of the men called.

'Just a hot toddy for a customer, who's sickly in his bed,' Belle replied. 'I'm hoping to warm him up a little.'

'You could warm me up,' one of the men shouted. 'Bring yourself over here.'

'But it's already paid for,' she said, as she drew nearer to the men. 'You wouldn't want to get me into trouble, would you?'

'You'll be paid, if I like what you've got,' he said, turning to his companion, laughing. Belle placed the jug and tankards on the floor near their feet. The scents of the nutmeg and cloves spread through the air, damping the stench of the street for a moment. As she squatted down on her haunches to put the tankards on the ground she spread her legs wide, making sure that the thin cotton fabric clung as tightly as possible to her thighs.

She bent forward and a tangled mess of hair fell across her shoulders and her shawl slipped far enough down to show her cleavage to best advantage. She sensed rather than saw the men leaning over her body as she filled the tankards; felt their gaze crawling over her as she licked imagined drops of the liquid slowly from the ends of her fingers.

'Here you go, gentlemen,' she said, standing and handing a tankard to each of the men.

'Will you have a drink?' one of the men asked.

She stood close in, her legs touching his and stroked his matted beard with her fingertips. She could smell his breath, like rotten meat. 'It ain't ladylike to drink from a tankard,' she said. 'You take a drink for me and keep it warm in your mouth.' As he took a deep draught, she leant forward and kissed him open-mouthed, sucking a small quantity of wine from his eager wet lips, letting it run down her chin.

As she broke away from his grabbing arms she spat the liquid, unseen, to the ground and wiped her lips on the back of her hand. She felt his clumsy hands rough against her body, but offered only mock resistance. 'You're an eager fellow,' she said, tossing her hair back. 'There's only one way I'll satisfy your appetite, but I ain't doing it here, not in front of your friend. What sort of girl do you take me for? We'll go somewhere – and I'll want paying.' She hesitated, watching his reaction; sensing his eagerness. 'Why don't we go in the house?' she asked.

The man's expression changed. 'If I gets caught taking you into the house, it's more than my life's worth,' he said. His face was suddenly serious and she sensed she was losing the initiative. Her nerves threatened to get the better of her for a moment. She sensed all too well that she had made her move too soon. If only she had waited for the drugs to take some effect. She needed another plan before it all went wrong.

'Well I know a place,' she said, pointing back to where she had come from. 'If you feel like I do we shouldn't be gone too long.' She suppressed the shudder she felt and took his hand before turning away. It was a gamble. She could feel the sudden resistance in his arm. She let go, letting her own hand trail to her side as she walked away. Only then did she sense him following her; felt his hand taking hers. She began running across the road, pulling him with her, sensing her power.

'There'll be hell to pay if Nat Caine shows up!' the other man shouted, behind them. She looked over her shoulder and saw him filling his tankard again.

'Tell him I've gone for a piss,' her companion shouted, without a glance behind them.

'There's a good place up the end of the alley,' Belle whispered to the man.

As they reached the top of the alleyway, she felt the shockwaves through the man's hand as the cosh came down on the side of his neck. He sank to the ground, without a word, like a dropped sack of potatoes. 'Thank God,' Belle said, shuddering. She scrubbed at her mouth with a handkerchief, trying to erase the taste of the man.

'I am sorry you had to endure that, Belle,' James said, placing an arm around her shoulder. He kissed her on the cheek and his lips were warm and dry against the cold of her skin. 'Why did you change the plan?'

'He wouldn't open the door, so I thought I would at least draw one of them away.'

'This might be better,' James said. There may be no need to rush the door. 'If I put on his cap and coat we can get up close to the other one.'

Belle smiled at Charlie who looked concerned. James gestured to one of the other men, 'Diarmuid, get his pistol, search him for the door key then get his coat and cap off him, while I gag him and tie his hands. That bump I gave him should keep him out for a while. Did he drink much of the wine, Belle?'

'No, I think his mind was on other things,' she replied. 'But the other one is already on his second tankard.'

'Richard said the drugs he gave me would act quickly,' James said. 'They should be taking effect by now, and the other one should be easy to deal with if we can get up close to him.'

James put on the man's coat, pulling up the collar to cover his beardless chin. 'Pass me his cap.'

'Your man here hasn't got the key,' Diarmuid said. 'The other one must have it.' He passed the man's tattered cap to James.

There was still no one about in the alleyway, but Belle felt suddenly more conscious of the group's conspicuousness. It was as though James felt it at the same time, as though they were communicating without speech. 'Tom, don't leave him lying on the floor,' James said, gesturing to the unconscious body of the guard. 'Help Diarmuid prop him as though he were drunk; and try and hide these,' he said, kicking one of the empty carpet bags into a doorway. Tom and Diarmuid dragged the body to its feet and held him up between them like drunken friends.

'We've waited long enough,' Belle said, turning towards him. 'Are you ready?'

'Yes,' James replied.

Belle wound her right arm around James' waist. 'Pull the cap further down to cover more of your face,' she said. 'We don't want him shooting you now, do we?' Her laughter was forced and did little to exorcise her fear.

'Take a pistol with you, James,' Charlie said.

'No!' James said, turning to face him, 'I'll not carry a gun and put Belle's life at risk.' She felt the concern in his voice and words and her nerves receded for a moment. 'Don't worry,' he said turning to her, 'I'll not let them harm you, whatever happens.' He put his arm around her shoulder as though it would protect her, perhaps a futile gesture, and yet she felt stronger for it.

As they set off down the alleyway, their bodies pressed close together, a single dark shape, she sensed rather than heard him whispering words of comfort to her. As they emerged from the other end of the alley, they tried to relax into their respective poses. The guard in the doorway opposite saw them immediately, but she could see he was finding it difficult to focus his eyes and his stance was already unsteady. 'Bring your face closer to mine,' she whispered to James, 'lest he see you.'

'Were she as tasty as she looks?' the guard called, his words slurring together, 'only I wouldn't mind giving her something to remember me by.'

James bent closer to Belle's face and kissed her. She knew it was a subterfuge to avoid having to reply, but the kiss felt good and she offered no resistance. She felt her eyelids closing, forgetting for a second where they were; then she turned away. James had also turned and she felt his warm breath as he buried his face in the crook of her neck. She looked around; there was no one else in the road.

There was a moment, she thought, as they drew up to him, when the guard's expression showed a sudden realisation that the man approaching was not his friend. She disengaged from James and lashed out with a kick to the man's groin. It felt good. At the same time, James swung the cosh back with his right arm and brought it down on the man's head. As his body fell to the ground, the others sprang from the alley and ran to join them, dragging the other guard between them. Charlie reached down and pulled the key from the man's pocket.

Within seconds Belle had opened the door and ushered everyone inside. They dragged the bodies of the guards with them. James handed his coat and cap to Diarmuid. Tom took the fallen guard's pistol and passed it to Charlie, while James gagged and bound the unconscious body.

'We'll have no further trouble from these two,' James said. 'Now you stand outside, Diarmuid, and watch the street. Tom, you go and fetch the gig.'

Belle handed the key to Diarmuid.

'Any sign of trouble, get in, lock the door and we'll get out through the front,' James said. The two lads went outside, Diarmuid standing on guard by the door as though nothing had happened, whilst Tom ran down the street.

'You'd better get away now, Belle,' James said. There was urgency in his voice and hastiness in the kiss he planted on her cheek.

'Take care, James,' she said quietly. She took his hand for a moment in hers then she broke her gaze and let his hand fall. 'Take care, all of you,' she said as she left and Diarmuid closed the door behind her.

James and Charlie made their way slowly and carefully down the passageway to the main house. Things had gone better than they could have expected, he thought, thanks to Belle. Charlie grabbed his arm, 'Let me go first,' he said, 'I'm used to this.' The door of the room next to the front door was open. Charlie put his head tentatively around its frame and sighed with relief. 'Empty,' he said. The key to the front door lay unguarded on the table and he placed it in the lock of the front door ready, should they need it.

Charlie led the way down the stairs to the basement, the pistol ready in his hand. If there were any number of men in the kitchen all they could hope for was that a shot might delay them long enough to run to the back door and lock it behind them. Charlie kicked the kitchen door open and they burst into the room. The kitchen was empty and James felt the relief sweep through his body. 'We've done it,' he shouted. 'We've bloody well done it.'

'Not yet, we haven't,' Charlie said, making his way to the safe. 'But it must have gone well at Lansdown. They've managed to suck all of Caine's men out of Bath, like you said. Come and help me with this, James.'

James was mesmerised for a moment by the sight of the clock and the pair of silver Georgian candlesticks on the mantelpiece. 'These are mine,' he said, 'and I'm taking them back.' He took the empty carpet bag they had brought with them over to the long mahogany table in the centre of the room and placed the objects lovingly inside it. Charlie opened his tool-bag and began work on the lock of the safe with a range of picks and skeleton keys.

After about ten minutes Charlie sat back on the floor. 'This one's got the better of me, James. We're going to have to use the peter-cutter and the sooner we start the better.' He took the drill from his bag and fitted its clamping grip in the keyhole of the safe. James had practised with the cutter before and knew that it took time and effort to do its work.

Using the grip to create leverage, Charlie applied as much pressure as he was able in engaging the cutter. He was strong and the cutter was the finest that money could buy, but he soon tired and James took over. The steel door shrieked its resistance at each grudging millimetre that the cutter dug into its surface, but still they continued. At last, taking it in turns, they created a small hole and James reached in, pulled the lock bolt back and opened the safe door.

A glance inside was enough to confirm that the contents were well worth the effort. Charlie began taking handfuls of gold sovereigns and bundles of notes from the safe.

'Leave the notes,' James said. 'Remember what we agreed. Anything that might be traced we leave.' Charlie pulled a deep drawer from the safe and emptied its contents on the ground. It was full of watches, rings, necklaces, bracelets, silver card cases and snuff boxes.

The snuff spilt out of some and filled the air with its heavy scent, causing Charlie to sneeze. 'I could sell these easy,' he said, grinning.

'We might not get what they're worth, but it'd be well worth having.'

'We take nothing but the gold sovereigns and coins,' James said.

'I know,' Charlie agreed. 'I was just dreaming for a while, but what about the silver that's been smelted down?'

James thought for a while. 'I suppose its origins cannot be traced. Take it.'

Charlie began loading the small bars of silver into the other carpet bag. 'I've got old coiner friends in Bristol what'll give us a good price for they bars,' he said. 'All the gold can go safely to Sean and we can each take our share from the silver when I've sold it.'

James retrieved a bundle of papers from the back of the safe. He unfolded them and began reading them. 'Look at these, Charlie,' he said, 'these are plans for the three houses Nat Caine burgled with Harcourt.'

'Well they ain't worth having now,' Charlie replied, tipping trays of gold sovereigns into the bag, delighting in the noise like a young child.

James laid the plans out across the kitchen table and then left them where they lay. Frank's handwriting was still so recognisable. It was still hard to believe that he was dead.

'Sean will like this,' Charlie said, tossing an old leather bound book in James' direction. James thumbed through the pages, scanning the names of the people and the money they owed to Caine. He threw it into the bag. 'You're right, Charlie,' he said, 'it's the best gift we could give to Sean and all the ones listed in its pages, all those debts cancelled.'

'We'd better go,' Charlie exclaimed, 'we've already been here too long. Shall we have a bit of that silver plate?' he added, pointing to a pile in the corner of the room.

'No, leave it,' James said, picking up the carpet bag. 'Make sure you've packed all your tools away, Charlie. We must leave nothing that can be traced to us.'

The streets of the city were still deserted and James hunted in vain for a passing constable. Eventually he gave up and made instead for the police station in Grove Street. Opening the door, he found two uninterested constables and placed the key on the desk in front of them. 'There's a robbery going on in the big house in Hucklebridge's

Court,' he said, his voice muffled by the scarf pulled up around his mouth. 'I've locked them in but you'd better fetch help.'

'Who are you?' one the constables called as James ran towards the door.

'It doesn't matter who I am,' he said. 'Get down to Hucklebridge's Court.' By the time the first constable had reached the door of the police station, James was boarding the waiting gig and Tom was urging the horse into a gallop.

Caine's uneasiness had grown as the day grew older. More men had been brought from Bath and yet he still felt vulnerable. He had kept the men with him since they arrived and sent no one out in parties of less than four at a time. Yet still they came back beaten and bedraggled. By late afternoon he had had enough and sent out orders that everyone was to come back with whatever they had collected. When they had assembled in front of the Landau they looked like a defeated army, and so many were missing.

'There's something happening,' one of the men said.

'You don't need to tell me that,' Caine spat back.

'No, I mean something's happening in Bath. Half of the peelers have already disappeared back into the city.'

It was then that Caine saw them; a crowd of forty or so men and women converging on the coach. The nearer they got, the more their numbers grew. He reached instinctively for the pistols under the seat and began passing them out.

'There must be sixty of 'em,' one of Caine's men said, 'we can't kill them all and besides there's as many women as men. I don't kill women.'

As the crowd grew nearer, one of the men at the centre of the crowd signalled for the others to stop. They fanned out in a crescent around the coach, still some distance away. Caine recognised the figure. 'It's that bastard priest, Brennan,' he said. The men looked uneasy and one of them made to break for the fields. Caine jumped down from the coach and grabbed the man by his collar, 'Make a move and I'll drop you before you've gone a yard,' he said, pushing the barrel of the pistol into the man's back.

'How many of your flock are ready to die?' Caine shouted, staring directly at the priest. The priest said nothing. Caine brought the pistol up to eye level, taking aim. The priest raised his arm and the crowd began to disperse. Caine laughed. The gutless Irish were running. Soon all that was left was the priest and half a dozen men. 'Go on; run!' Caine shouted. 'You can't take me on face to face, can you?' He lowered the pistol, beckoning them to come nearer.

The priest smiled and so did the man standing next to him. Then they too turned and ran. The realisation was like a slow fuse being lit in his head. The man with the priest was the same man who was with Jeb that night; the one Maggs had called his nephew that time in The Pig and Whistle. But if he was here, where was Charlie Maggs?

Suddenly Caine understood what was happening. 'The house,' he said, 'there's only two men at the house. Get me a horse. I need to get back to Bath.' He turned round. The priest, and the man, and all of the Irish were nowhere to be seen in the crowd of Lansdown Fair. He turned to his men. 'You three come with me, the rest of you take the money we've collected back to Cockroad and wait for me there.'

When Caine reached the house in Hucklebridge's Court it was swarming with peelers. He watched, powerless, as they loaded the wagon outside with silver plate and everything else of value, taking from him in hours what he had spent years in acquiring and building; filching the very respect he had created for the name of Caine.

Chapter 40

Charlie poured whisky into three tumblers and took them round in turn to James and Sean and John. Then he raised his own mug of tea in salute and proclaimed to the room. 'We beat him! Raise your glasses, gentlemen. We beat Nathaniel Caine.'

James looked at their faces; each seemed older since the beginning of their time together, or perhaps it was simply that he had got to know and trust them so well. Each was an old friend now. He raised his glass, wanting to celebrate, like John and Charlie, yet part of him felt weary. The deaths played heavily on his mind – Billy, and Harcourt, and the Wood brothers and even Jeb. And perhaps he was too used to living in fear to now let it go so easily. 'But can we be sure that he is beaten?' he said, to no one in particular.

'Caine's nowhere to go but Cockroad now,' Charlie said. 'The law is after him, his gang's in tatters and he's lost his fortune. I don't think we'll see him in Bath again for some time to come.'

'But he knows each of us now,' James said, 'and understands what we did.'

'And he'll want to get even,' Sean interrupted.

'I knows him well enough to know that his first thought will be to keep away from the law and rebuild,' Charlie said. 'He won't bother us for a while, and I've got friends who'll keep a watch on him.'

'Let's not forget in our celebrations,' Sean said, 'that people have paid with their lives for this victory.'

John raised his glass again, 'To Billy,' he said. They all joined in the toast and the room was silent for a while, each of them alone with their thoughts. None willing to break the silence until John spoke again. 'I feel as guilty as any for Billy's death, but it was Caine who killed him. Let's not forget that. We did what we had to. Don't go making sinners of us all, Sean. How many others would have suffered if we had not stopped him? How many others would have paid with their lives? We did what was right.'

'We are all sinners,' Sean said. 'I too feel the guilt for Billy's death, yet I believe we have all tried to do what was just, and to act not simply for ourselves, but for the good of others. Perhaps we have even found some justice for Thomas Hunt and his daughter in what we have done.'

James felt his conscience pricked at the mention of Hunt's name. Over the weeks he had forgotten them; forgotten Hunt's dead daughter and his wife and children. 'What has become of his family?' he asked. 'Can anything be done for them?'

'I have found that Imelda Hunt has a sister in Ireland,' Sean said. 'But she has two children of her own and her husband has lost the tenancy of their farm. They are at present in the workhouse and cannot take on more mouths to feed.'

'Some good must come of this,' James said, 'some putting right for Hunt's death and some justice for his daughter. What of Imelda Hunt? Is she recovered?'

'There are times when she is lucid,' Sean said. 'She at least recognises me now, but she still cannot face the children, and she talks at times about her daughter and husband as though they were still alive. When she remembers their deaths, she blames herself and is as ailing as before.'

'Some of the money should go to help Imelda Hunt and her family,' James said. 'Write to my brother, Sean,' James said. 'There must be vacant tenancies on the estate. Imelda Hunt's sister can go there with her family and take in Hunt's children. We can use some of the money to pay their rent and make sure that they have enough to live on.'

Sean nodded his agreement. 'It was already in my thoughts to do so.'

'If they should ask where the money comes from, Sean,' John interrupted, 'could you tell them it comes from Isabella, a Spanish lady.'

Charlie nodded. 'Aye, John, that's fitting. Let it come from Isabella, not us.'

'Of course,' Sean agreed, as he fished in his pocket and produced some papers. 'I have received a letter from your brother, James. The news is good. He thinks the blight has passed on the estate and in many other parts of the country. 'Here,' he said, handing James the letter.

James began reading. 'Michael thanks me for the money I sent. He has invested in the land, with new drainage systems and new machinery. The signs, he says, are very promising for the year to come and he has invited me to visit and see what has been accomplished.'

'Will you go?' Sean asked.

'I will,' James replied. 'If you are all in agreement I want Sean to have the money we took from Caine,' James said.

'That's what we agreed,' John said.

'I thank all you gentlemen,' Sean said. 'In all this you have bettered the lives of a great number of people. There are more signs of hope now in Avon Street than I have seen before, and now that Caine has been driven from the city, it will feed that hope more.' He stopped for a moment, turning to Charlie, 'and not just Catholics, nor only Irishmen.'

Charlie smiled. 'What about the silver?' he asked. 'I'll need to sell it.'

'We should repay the silversmiths we robbed,' James said, 'and the rest we share amongst us, if you are all in agreement.'

Charlie coughed loudly. 'Take a little over and above for yourself,' John said, smiling, 'to pay for our board and lodgings.'

'Do you think me as tight as I'd charge my guests?' Charlie asked. 'I'll get the money back to the silversmiths, if it will ease your consciences, though it goes against the grain. The rest we share equally for all those involved.'

'I will need to set up a properly administered charity with all of the money you gentlemen have donated,' Sean said. 'Will you serve on its board, James?'

'Of course, together with Charlie and John,' James said.

'Not I,' Charlie replied, 'I'm not one for paperwork and giving money away. Besides I intend to fill my life in a different way.'

'Nor me,' John said. 'I'll be moving on soon.'

'But why?' James asked.

'I have some money now, and I'd like to set up somewhere in business, but I don't think it can be here.'

When James awoke, early the following morning, he made straight for John's room. The room was empty; the bed made and at its foot, neatly folded, was the manservant's uniform Mrs Hawker had altered for him when he had first entered the household, the one he wore when they had cheated the silversmiths in Clifton. Pinned to the front of the jacket was a piece of paper, on which was written simply, 'Thank you'.

James opened the chest of drawers and found it largely empty; John's few clothes and possessions had gone, along with the canvas bag he had been carrying when he had first met him in that alleyway in Avon Street. As he was closing the drawers, he heard a loud cough and jumped as he became aware of the dark shape in the doorway behind him. He turned and saw John. 'Stealthy as ever, John,' he said. 'I thought you had gone without saying goodbye.'

'Maybe I would have at one time,' John replied, 'but not now. I was waiting for you before setting off.'

'Why do you have to go?' James asked.

'It's for the best,' John replied. 'I have a chance at a new life and I have to come to terms with the ghosts of Bath in another place.'

James shook his offered hand. 'Will you take breakfast with me one last time?' he asked.

'With great pleasure,' John replied.

'I would offer to walk down to the station with you when we've eaten, but I must see Belle, and as soon as possible.'

'It's best I say my goodbyes here,' John said. 'Besides I'd like a little time with Charlie and Mrs Hawker. We'll have breakfast and then you find Belle. Follow your heart, James. If I had followed mine sooner, Isabella might still be alive and we would be together.'

As they walked down the stairs together, one thought filled James' mind. He almost spoke it, but then thinking of the hurt it would cause, stilled his voice. If John had saved Isabella, then he would not have been there that night in The Pig and Whistle; would never have come to his rescue or helped in the fight against Caine. Would he even have survived without John, he wondered? Yet living was full of 'ifs', and each choice bore the potential of another possible life. If as a young boy he had looked the other way when Sean was being bullied, if he had remained in Ireland, if Thomas Hunt had never borrowed from Caine, never killed himself and his daughter, if he had never met Harcourt, nor defended Charlie in court, if Richard had not given him the swordstick, if he had run from the fight with Caine. It was like a dam bursting in his brain; a flood of events and happenings, choices and decisions each leading it seemed to some different destiny. Yet it wasn't destiny; nothing was preordained, the choices were all there to be freely made. Inheritance and upbringing might make us who we *are*, but it is the decisions we make that determine who we *become*.

More than anything now, Belle wanted to be away from Bath. She felt confused, she had heard nothing from James since the robbery; did not even know whether he was alive or dead. It was best she was away from here, yet she wanted to hear he was safe.

Deciding to occupy her last day in the city with setting Jenny up in the shop, she felt pleased, knowing that she would now have a reason to return to Bath whenever she wanted. Mrs Macready had been very understanding when she had handed in her notice. The company's season was coming to an end and she already knew she was moving to the Haymarket, yet she could still have been difficult. Instead she had offered only encouragement when Belle asked to leave early, telling her what a wonderful theatre the Haymarket was, and how much she would learn from Macready.

When Belle had told her about her venture into the dressmaking business with Jenny, Mrs Macready had raised an eyebrow as though momentarily taken aback by the announcement, but if she was shocked she did little else to show it. If she wondered how the two of them had acquired enough money to invest, she did not give voice to her thoughts. She promised instead her custom and said that if their work was of sufficient quality and was offered at a suitable discount there may be work available from the costume department. Belle assured her of the finest quality of work, extolling Jenny's capabilities, and said they would of course give a discount if the work was of sufficient quantity.

When she told Jenny about the potential business from the theatre she was delighted. 'I might be tempted to watch a play if it were my costumes on stage,' Jenny said, but it was obvious she had other things on her mind. From early that morning they had been interviewing women for the post of manageress at the shop. At first it had been Belle who asked all the questions, but gradually Jenny had found her voice. By the time they interviewed the last woman it was Jenny asking most of the questions. And it was Jenny who made the appointment, pleased that they were in fact poaching the woman from one of the finest dress shops in Milsom Street. She was a little taken aback at the salary the woman requested, but met her request in full.

Belle left her that afternoon working in the shop with their new appointment, discussing the shop fittings and meeting with carpenters. Any uncertainty in Jenny had long since disappeared and she was already every inch the businesswoman, as she re-interviewed the new appointee on what customers she might be able to tempt from her previous employer. The lack of confidence was forgotten and no observer of the discussion would have been in any doubt as to who was employer, and who employee.

Belle was glad to leave them to it, but when she returned home her nervousness returned. The feeling of loneliness at leaving Bath hit home. It was the end of one life and the beginning of another. She tried to conjure up the excitement and magic she had felt at the prospect of working in the Haymarket Theatre, but it would not come. The thought of a new job, new friends, a new home no longer thrilled her when she thought of what she was leaving. It was as though a part of her was dying. She was leaving behind those she loved, and life in Bath would continue without her.

John took the breakfast things down to the kitchen. Mrs Hawker and Charlie were as usual ensconced in chairs side by side in front of the kitchen range. Charlie was holding Mrs Hawker's hand and showed no sign of loosening his grip when John entered the room.

'I'll be off soon,' John said.

'Shall we walk you to the station?' Charlie asked.

'James has already offered, but I'd rather say my goodbyes here.'

'Where is James?' Mrs Hawker asked.

'In pursuit of love,' John replied, grinning. 'Just like the two of you.' Mrs Hawker began fussing around the kitchen, her face flushed. 'James can look after himself you know, Mrs Hawker. Isn't it time you let him go and found some happiness of your own?'

'I keep telling her that,' Charlie replied.

'Listen to him,' John said. 'I've never met a couple more suited than you two. You've been like a mother and father to me.' Mrs Hawker walked over to him, pinched his arm, and then threw her arms around him.

'What about the money you have coming?' Charlie asked.

'I've written out an address in Boston where you can find me,' John replied.

'You've helped us through difficult times, John, and for that I'll always be grateful,' Mrs Hawker said.

'And you trusted me and welcomed me into your home when you had no reason to do so,' John replied. 'It's you two that gave me the courage to write to my family. I've decided to go back to Boston and visit them, and now I have the money to travel in style rather than work my passage.'

'Will you come back?' Charlie asked.

'Of course,' John replied. 'My closest friends are all in Bath. How could I stay away? It may have been chance that brought us together, but I'll not see it part us again.'

When James knocked on the door of Belle's house, he heard her footsteps running in answer. Throwing open the door, she did not give him time to speak, 'So you are come at last!' she said. She turned her back to him and walked quickly up the stairs, saying nothing. He followed her, sensing from her demeanour that she was annoyed.

'What has upset you so, Belle?' he asked as she led him into the room.

'You, it is you that has upset me!' Belle retorted. The anger was all too clear in her voice. She sat on the bed and he on the chair facing her. 'I hear nothing from you, I have no knowledge of whether you are alive or dead and then you appear as though nothing had happened. You did not even have the good grace to send a note to tell me how you were.'

'This is my fourth visit this morning,' he said. 'I have walked round and about the city so many times I have lost count, and each time I called you were out.' She said nothing. He felt uncertain in his words. When he had rehearsed their meeting in his mind it had been so very different. 'I am sorry. I should have been more considerate, but I did not wish to see you in any danger. I needed to be sure it was over.'

'But I have been at risk for weeks and I was alone.'

'No, you were never alone. You were watched constantly by our friends in Avon Street. If they had suspected any immediate danger to you, we would have plucked you from the theatre and taken you to a safe place.'

'I felt you had used me to suit your purpose,' Belle replied, 'and having served my purpose I was of little importance to you.'

He leant forward, taking her hand in his and she did not resist. 'You helped so much and asked so little in return, but I could never use you.' He stopped, searching for words that did not come easily. 'I was foolish to accept your help and put you in danger.'

'I gave my help freely,' she said. 'Because I wanted to – Because I was concerned for you. I did nothing that I did not choose to do of my own free will.'

'You will have a share from the robbery,' James said. 'Most of what we took will go to Father Brennan to help in his work in Avon Street, but there will be something for you.'

'Do you think I did what I did for money?'

He sensed her anger rising again as she snatched her hand from his grasp. She stood and walked over to the window.

James followed her to the window. 'Nothing could be further from the truth,' he said. 'Are you so unaware of how highly I regard you?'

'And what feelings *do* you have for me, Mr Daunton?' Belle asked. She kept her back to him for a moment and he could not see her face.

When she turned she seemed less certain in her rage, but he thought he saw tears against the redness of her cheeks. He wondered if it was embarrassment, or simply anger. He paused before replying, searching for the right words. 'I feel as though I have known you all my life and yet you are a mystery to me. I want you never to be hurt, never to feel pain, and yet I know I have already hurt you.' He placed his hands on her shoulders and stared into her eyes. 'I need you.'

She pulled away, as though unable to look into his eyes. 'I could have wished that you would have said something of such feelings before,' she said. 'I leave Bath this afternoon for London.'

'But do you care for me?' James asked.

'Of course I care for you,' she said, turning back, staring this time directly into his eyes. 'Were you so blind that you could not see how I felt? After Harcourt I thought I could never trust a man again, but I found myself trusting more in you than I have ever trusted before. Now I am confused. I do not want to lose that trust, and yet I do not feel ready to put it to the test.'

James hated the sound of Harcourt's name; the thought of him being with Belle. He could see the pain of betrayal now in her eyes and understood her confusion and uncertainty. He took her in his arms and kissed her gently. It was not how he wanted to kiss her, but a tentative, searching kiss. He felt her soft complicity, unresisting in his embrace and cradled the nape of her neck softly in his hand, drinking in the scent of her being. The kiss seemed to last so long and yet was over almost as soon as it had begun and she rested her head on his shoulder and he felt her tears on his neck. 'You should stay,' he said, as though the words were more important than the kiss.

Belle broke away, 'I have to go,' she said, 'I have to pack and say my goodbyes. You should not ask this of me so suddenly. I have commitments and a profession I love.'

'So you will still leave, knowing how I feel about you?' James said, only half questioning.

'You say it as though it was a decision lightly made,' Belle replied. 'Do you not understand the pain that leaving gives me? If I was to stay I know I would be happy; that you would make me happy. But in years to come the decision would haunt me and would come between us. I have to go.'

'Then will you allow me to visit you in London?' he asked.

'Yes,' she replied. 'But more than allow. I would expect it.'

'Even if you are a famous actress and courted by the whole of society?'

'Even then,' she smiled. 'But it is better we part now, before I change my mind.'

'And will you return?' James asked.

'You have my promise,' Belle said. She smiled. 'Besides, I have a business in Bath that will require my attention.' She took the card, already written, from her purse and gave it to him. 'Perhaps you will call occasionally on my partner, Jenny, and give her any assistance she might need.'

'Nothing would give me greater pleasure,' he smiled.

She led him to the door. 'Be patient with me,' she said. It was as though they both understood that nothing more could be said. He wanted to stay longer yet he knew this was not the time. On the front doorstep he turned to her. 'I saw your performance as Lady Macbeth and you were truly magnificent.'

'But you were in hiding,' she interrupted.

'The others did not know, but I stole out one night and watched you. You taught me well how to disguise myself, and I mingled with the crowd in the stalls, but I saw you clearly; heard every word. You were magnificent.'

They kissed again in the shadow of the doorway, softly and warmly, and he turned to leave. Then he reached behind his neck and unfastened the silver chain. 'Will you wear this?' he said, reaching forward, placing and fastening it around her neck. 'It was my mother's and means more to me than all we took from Nat Caine.'

'I will be wearing it,' Belle said, smiling, 'when you see me next.' Then her face became serious, her expression intense. 'I am not deserting you, James.' The words were slow and measured and then she laughed. 'I understand there is an exceptionally efficient rail service between here and London. I hope you will take advantage of it soon.'

Chapter 41

As soon as they had packed their belongings, James returned to his house in South Parade with Mrs Hawker. On his arrival he found a fernery on the cupboard in the drawing room, the exotic plants creating their own small jungle world under the protection of its large glass dome. At its side was a small card which read, 'Welcome home. Please visit soon,' and it was signed, 'Charlotte,' not 'Richard and Charlotte' or 'Mrs Wetherby', but simply 'Charlotte.' One glance at the gently looping strokes had been enough, it hadn't really required a signature; he could have picked out Charlotte's handwriting amongst a thousand forgeries.

The following morning James woke early, and, as soon as he was dressed, took up a position on the ottoman by the drawing room window where he could observe the Wetherby's house; waiting to see Richard depart on his rounds. When at last he saw him leave he went immediately around to the house.

Charlotte was alone in the drawing room as he had hoped. It had been some time since he had seen her and her beauty took him by surprise, as it often did, as though each time he saw her it was for the first time. She seemed so accepting of her appearance, but he knew she understood the effect it had on others.

She smiled at him and he knew it was not a smile she would have bestowed if Richard had been there. Charlotte used her beauty to confound; her mouth, her eyes, the way she held herself, all said, 'Look at me, I am defenceless and I want only you.' He knew she was playing to his uncertainty; that the moment he responded she might change, become angry and reject him, tell him she was a happily married woman, that he had misread their friendship for something else.

Yet there was always that ambiguity in her manner, as though she might equally accept an advance. Whichever way she chose, he knew it would be her choice and that she would be in control.

She sat on the chaise-longue, patting the seat next to her with her left hand, 'Come sit here beside me,' she said.

'I prefer to stand,' he said. 'There is something I need to discuss with you.' She frowned, with an affected hurt expression and lounged back against the cushions.

'I feel hurt, James,' she said. 'Have I offended you?'

He took the package from his jacket. 'I found your letters in Harcourt's safe.'

Her smile had disappeared now, and there was a barely concealed anger in the frown that replaced it for a moment; but only for a moment. 'Richard told me you had found some letters in Harcourt's safe and returned them. I guessed that you would have also discovered the ones I wrote. Have you told Richard?' she asked.

'Not yet,' James replied.

'Three innocent letters, that's all they were,' she said. 'Nothing happened between us.'

'Harcourt's dead you know,' James said, studying her face. If she felt anything she did not show it.

Her expression changed again, as though she was a little girl, being scolded for a small misdemeanour. 'I was very foolish,' she said. 'I should never have written them, but they don't amount to much. Nothing came of them.'

'You forget that I have read them,' James replied. 'It troubles me now to think that I was used in this. I remember Harcourt trying to find out from me when Richard was likely to be out of the house. Perhaps nothing did happen between you, but if you hadn't gone away and if Harcourt hadn't had more pressing matters on his mind, then something would have happened, I have no doubt.'

'You cannot know that,' she replied. 'Please give me the letters and promise you will say nothing to Richard. It would hurt him dreadfully and I could not bear to lose him.'

'You should not have betrayed him then,' James retorted. 'How could you have done this to him, when he loves you with all his heart?'

'I love him also,' she replied, 'yet he cannot always give me all that I need.' She rose from the chaise-longue and walked over to him, her movements as delicate and precise as a cat. He thought he could see tears forming in her eyes as she encircled her hands behind his neck pulling him towards her.

James wanted to push her away, yet he could not. Her lips felt hard against his and though he resisted at first, her kiss became more urgent, her mouth open, her body pressing hard against his and he gave way. He put his arms around her, the letters falling to the ground. For a time he felt as though he were drowning, incapable of thought and then the memory of Belle's kiss came back to him and the thought of Richard's friendship. The realisation of what he was doing hit him like a shower of ice and he pushed her away more roughly than he intended.

She stumbled momentarily. Then she stooped down and picked up the letters and threw them to the back of the roaring fire, standing resolutely, until she was satisfied they had caught, barring his way to the fireplace, grabbing the poker from the hearth. 'There, it is done,' she said. 'We need say nothing of this to Richard.'

'And if I tell him what you have done?' he asked.

'Then I shall tell Richard that you are acting from spite, because I rejected your advances. You have no proof otherwise.' She was smiling, composed again now.

He turned his back towards her. 'You have burnt only two letters,' he said, 'I still have the third.'

Her anger was plain now. 'You're a liar,' she spat, her beauty lost for a moment in her spite.

'You cannot know that,' he said. 'You will never know if you burnt them all and if I have the slightest doubt of your fidelity in the future I will give the proof to Richard and you will lose everything.'

Charlotte said nothing as James left the room.

It was in the afternoon of that same day that Richard called on him. If he had any suspicion of what had happened that morning James could not detect it in him. He seemed happy at first, as he set out the chessboard, as though everything that had happened in the last few months was forgotten or had never occurred. Then as if it were a matter of little consequence he asked, 'Where is the other letter?'

'What letter?' James said, almost without thinking.

'Charlotte told me everything,' Richard replied. 'She said you had called on her this morning and told her that you knew about Harcourt and her.'

James felt his cheeks redden and wondered if it was obvious to Richard. 'What did she tell you?' he asked.

'She told me that Harcourt had been flirting with her for some time and wrote repeatedly before she answered. I knew that even if she hadn't been unfaithful to me, there was someone else in her thoughts. I think I must have half suspected it was Harcourt, and yet I pretended it was imaginings, and did nothing. At times I even suspected that it might be you she was attracted to.' He spoke the words as though he were more contemptuous of himself than condemning of Charlotte. 'She said you had shown her two of the letters and allowed her to burn them, but that you had kept another to be sure that she did nothing like it again.'

'What else did she say?'

'She told me she was truly sorry and that it would never happen again.'

'Do you believe her?' James asked.

'Yes,' Richard replied. 'She did not have to tell me what she did. She also told me that she tried to coax the letters from you and that you rejected her. She told me you are a good friend, and that she wants nothing to spoil our friendship. For my part I am sorry that I ever doubted you.'

'Can you trust her again?' James asked.

'I love her so much that I have little choice in the matter,' Richard replied, 'but things will be different in the future. Please give me the other letter and let us not speak of the matter again.'

'It is forgotten,' James said, 'and there is no other letter. They were all burnt this morning.' Instantly he resolved to destroy the last letter as soon as Richard had gone. He could not bear the thought of his friend reading its contents, and he knew that Richard would never have been able to destroy it without first reading it. He knew it would not change his mind, and yet would hurt him even more.

'Can I ask a favour?' Richard said.

James instantly felt apprehensive, but said, 'Of course you may after all that you have done for me.'

'These have not been the easiest of times for my daughter, and Charity has grown much attached to the dog, since he has been with her.'

James smiled. 'Then she shall keep him, for I believe Mrs Hawker has someone else on whom to lavish her affection now, and as for me, it will be yet another reason to visit your home more often.'

Over the next few months, James gradually rebuilt his practice as a solicitor. His reputation grew, particularly in criminal cases, and though many of the cases he took involved residents of Avon Street, he was able to subsidise them from the more lucrative fees he charged to his wealthier clients. Eventually he reached a stage where, despite the long hours he worked, he found himself having to turn work away. His social life was now, of course, far less demanding and expensive than it had been, and he surprised himself at the comparative speed with which he was able to repay his debts.

James contrived at every opportunity to have business in London, and when he could find no other excuse he went regardless. He found himself needing Belle's company more and more, and though he felt she reciprocated his feelings, he also felt for a time that her career was drawing her further away with each success. He resolved to ask her to come with him when he visited his brother in Ireland, only half expecting that she might agree, but agree she did, despite having to cancel several engagements.

Needless to say, Sean could always be relied on to generate new projects which required an input from him. James often found himself called to attend the Orchard Street Church, on charitable matters, or to help someone who had fallen foul of the law, and whom Sean believed was at heart a good person. Try as he might though, and his efforts seemed to increase in those first months, Sean never managed to persuade James to attend a service there; yet the strength of their friendship grew.

For all Sean's work, Avon Street remained much the same, though the lives of many became more tolerable. Some managed, with Sean's help, to escape from the place and make new lives, or at least to ensure that their children could get away, but they were inevitably replaced by others.

Richard remained a close friend, but never spoke again of Charlotte's infidelity, or of Harcourt. Though a regular visitor to James' house, it was some time before he invited James to his own home. The visit, a dinner party just for the three of them, felt uneasy for all concerned, at first, but they gradually settled into a comfortable politeness. Charlotte thanked him for coming at the end and seemed sincere. It was clear to him that both Richard and Charlotte were working desperately to rebuild their relationship.

Imelda Hunt was discharged from the mental hospital and took her family to live close by her sister's family on the farm in Ireland. James made sure that they would never struggle for money. It was plain to all, however, that she was unlikely ever to fully recover the spark of life that she had once had. On more lucid days she remembered better times, before life had become such a struggle, and when they had all been together. But she would never be able to forgive her husband for what he had done, in taking the life of their daughter.

Billy's wife, too, took her family back to Ireland, where Billy had always dreamed of settling. James never saw her, before her departure, but he made sure through Sean that she had enough money to secure her future. She told Sean that she would use the money to set up a lodging house in Kenmare, where she had family.

John returned to Boston and made his peace with his family, but realised from the start that this was no longer his home. He had been rootless for too long, experienced too much, to go back. He decided to travel again, with the hope one day of making his home in England, where he could be near his friends. This time he would at least part on good terms with his family.

Charlie Maggs also became a regular visitor at James' house. It was rare now for James to find Mrs Hawker sitting alone. She of course had more free time once staff had been engaged to help her, and she was the first to admit that she was anyway far less interested in domestic matters now. It came as no surprise to James when one morning, in August, dressed in his best Sunday suit, Charlie asked him for his permission to propose to Mrs Hawker. He gave it with pleasure.

Epilogue

In the early hours of that October morning in 1850 Nat Caine sat, resting in a chair, in the kitchen of his cottage in Cockroad. October had been a brutally cold month and that night there was a thick frost on the ground. It had not seemed worth the effort of taking himself off to bed for another cold, sleepless night. It was much warmer down here by the fire and besides, his stomach was less painful when he was sitting.

He rarely slept for long now, even with the brandy and laudanum. The dead faces were never far away, awake or asleep; Jeb, and Harcourt, and the Wood brothers, and all the others, over the years. Yet the nightmares seemed less frequent, less terrifying, when he dozed in the chair. Here he could keep most of the unwanted visitors at bay for a while, but not Thomas Hunt and his daughter. For some reason it was their images that most plagued his thoughts when he tried to sleep. Though in truth he could barely remember what Hunt looked like and he'd never seen the girl. Yet he knew it was them, she, lying in her father's arms, her face almost featureless, except for her eyes. She would never let him sleep for long.

And when he did sleep, the slightest noise would wake him. This time it was the sound of movement in the village. He listened again. He had not been mistaken. There were sounds of movement; not livestock, nor fox, nor badger, but people; trying to approach without noise. And in their self-conscious stealth, their movements disturbed the order of the night; the pattern of more natural, nocturnal sounds. He knew at once that they were coming for him.

He went to the window and pulled back the edge of the curtain. They thought they were so clever; thought they had done nothing to give themselves away, but he had heard them, clear enough. He could see them now; dark shapes moving from cottage to cottage. He wondered how many there were? It was hard to tell, but he knew almost instinctively that this time there would be enough.

He rehearsed his ending in his mind. He would die with a pistol in his hand, defiant until the end, and people would remember his dying, remember Nathaniel Caine. There'd be no trial, no mocking testimonies against him, and no jeering crowds. He'd not give them the chance to disrespect him. They'd not see him dancing for them on the end of a rope, as his father had done.

He unbolted the door in readiness and moved to the deal table at the centre of the room. Shuffling in the wicker-backed chair, he moved its angle quietly so that he was facing square to the door. He lit the candle stub that sat in the middle of the table, straightening it in the pool of wax at its base. It seemed important somehow to have everything neat and tidy. He adjusted the two pistols on the table, straightening them too, so that they lay exactly a shoulder width apart, pointing towards the door. Knowing it would not be long now, he readied himself, sitting upright, resting both hands on his lap, his eyes trained on the doorway.

When the door burst open there were only two of them, each with a brace of pistols. He smiled and said nothing, made no movement, his hands steady, held immobile on his lap. They seemed nervous; taken aback at his ease and lack of surprise. Then the tall one at the front spoke.

'Nathaniel Caine, I am Police Sergeant Hazell and I have come to arrest you. Surrender your weapons.'

Caine studied their eyes, enjoying their fear. He laughed at them. It's me that ought to be afraid, he thought, but look at them. They still respect the name of Caine. Then the thought shot through his body like a bolt of lightning. There were only two of them and he had two pistols. Outside the night was dark and he knew the lay of the land better than any of them. The sound of shots would create confusion; feed the fear of his pursuers. If the others were even half as scared as these two, he could make it. Perhaps he had dismissed the idea of escape too quickly, he thought. Yet it could still be done. Besides, if he failed, he would at least die fighting.

'Curse you, Caine,' Hazell said. 'Don't make me fire.'

It was easy, Caine thought. All he had to do was grab the pistols on the table and fire. He wouldn't miss, he was sure of that. It was only then, with the thought of escape, that he felt the first slight tremble in his hands. He looked down and saw his hands begin to shake, first one and then the other. He flattened them, slowly, against his thighs, but the shaking only worsened.

'I have a company of militia with me,' Hazell said. 'There are men in every house. There is no one to come to your assistance.'

'There never was.' Caine spat out the words, and the words took hold, and he found himself repeating them again, this time more quietly, as though talking to himself. 'There never was anyone.'

Caine urged his hands to move, but they shook worse than ever and he felt the fear grow stronger in his mind. He didn't want to die, not here, with only the militia as witnesses. While he was alive there were a thousand ways of cheating the hangman. And if they hanged him, he'd give them a show like no other, let them see how a true Caine dies; not like his father, but with pride. It didn't need to end like this, unseen and alone.

Caine smiled and began to get up from the chair, keeping his arms at his side, so they should not see the shaking. The trembling now had spread through his body. He wondered if his legs would carry him. He reached out instinctively to support his weight against the table.

For the shortest of moments, Caine was conscious of the pain as the sound of the shot reverberated against the cottage walls. Just for that instant he felt the questions forming in his mind. Then the darkness took him.

The room filled with noise and smoke as the shot that hit Caine sent him backwards into the chair and then onto the floor. Police Sergeant Hazell ran over to him as he fell, but he could already tell, before examining him, that Caine was dead. He crouched on the flagstones beside his body and closed his lifeless eyes with a thumb and forefinger.

'Why did you shoot?' Hazell asked, turning to the young militia-man, standing in the doorway, his pistol still smoking.

'I thought he was reaching for the guns,' the young man replied.

'Perhaps he was,' Sergeant Hazell replied. 'Perhaps he was.'

❖ THE END ❖

What Really Happened in Bath in 1850?

On Sunday 6th February 1850, in the early hours of the morning, Thomas Hunt drowned himself and his daughter. Suicides were relatively common in that stretch of the River Avon at the time and rarely merited more than a mention in the local paper, but the deaths of Hunt and his daughter were reported in *The Times*. The Coroner's Court found her father guilty of murder.

It was in a newspaper archive that I first read of Thomas Hunt and his daughter. There was nothing in the newspaper records to indicate that he was in debt, but debt and loan-sharks were a way of life for the working class at that time. I had intended to use the story as an anecdote somewhere in the book, but gradually, as I wrote, the deaths of Thomas Hunt and his daughter became the link that bound the story together, though I never discovered his daughter's name.

In 1850, Bath was one of the largest and most prosperous cities in Britain. The fine Georgian buildings, the spa waters, the fashionable shops in Milsom Street, and the annual round of concerts and balls still drew wealthy visitors for the *season*. The wealth of this transient population was the bedrock on which the city had been built and grown.

Most of the better houses in the city were rented, as were the accoutrements that went with them; the horses and carriages, furniture and bedding, table linen and crockery, cutlery and silverware, cooks and servants. If you had the money and the manners, you could be whoever you wanted to be in Bath. Yet by 1850, the nature of the city was changing and its popularity as a fashionable resort was declining.

In truth, the grandiose Georgian façades hid buildings that were often poorly finished and viewed from any other angle quite unsightly.

And the city, too, hid its uglier aspects behind an illusion of opulence. By 1850 industry was thriving in the city – corset makers, furniture and coach-making, brass foundries, printing, tailoring, shoe-making, breweries and stone quarrying. Bath did its best to keep the factories and sweat-shops largely out of sight and as far away as possible from the minds of visitors and wealthy residents. The cholera outbreak in the previous year (largely confined to Avon Street) had been the second largest in the country, yet it too was kept out of the public eye.

The Avon Street area had grown by 1850 into a sprawling, disease-ridden slum and was subject to frequent flooding. It was bounded to the east by a complex of courts and lanes leading off Southgate Street, one of the main thoroughfares of the city. To the north of the area lay Lower Borough Walls and Westgate Buildings, the latter referred to in Jane Austen's *Persuasion* in which Sir Walter says to Anne Elliot, 'Upon my word Miss Anne Elliot, you have the most extraordinary taste! Everything that revolts other people, low company, paltry rooms, foul air, disgusting associations are inviting to you.' The western boundary of Avon Street was Kings Mead Terrace (now Kingsmead East) and the wasteland beyond and to the south was the River Avon and the Quay. Avon Street itself cut through the western part of the area from Kingsmead Square in the north, in a straight line down to the river in the south.

In all, the Avon Street area occupied a relatively small part of the city geographically, but by 1850 it was home to 20 per cent of Bath's population, largely Irish and other immigrant minorities, and itinerants looking for work. It was abhorred and for the most part ignored by the city and its visitors, but provided a convenient source of cheap labour for the factories and hotels, and domestic servants for the fine houses. When disreputable behaviour spilled out into the city, it was usually put down to the ethnic origin of the *sinner,* or the influence of alcohol.

By 1850, evening outings by the wealthier classes to the theatre, concerts and balls had, to a large extent, been superseded by dinner parties and entertaining at home. Despite the introduction of street-lights and police, the streets were neither a pleasant, nor a safe place to be after dark, though there was plenty of *alternative* entertainment for the *gentlemen.* Prostitution, gambling and other vices were well catered for in the city, and largely centred around Avon Street.

The Theatre Royal in Bath had been in decline for several years and Mrs Macready is widely credited with saving it. The more famous Mr Macready appeared there in 1850 in the role of Macbeth, though it was towards the end of the year. Mr Macready remains famous for an incident which occurred during his American tour in 1849, when he played Macbeth at the Astor Place Opera House in New York. His fierce American rival Edwin Forrest as an open challenge, decided to play the same role, on the same night, in the same city, but at the Bowery Theatre. Many of Forrest's fans went to Macready's performance and pelted him with rotten fruit. Crowds began converging on the Astor Place Opera House. The police and militia were called out. Rather than retreat, the mob turned on them. In the ensuing battle, twenty-two people were killed.

In 1850 the constabulary in Britain were still at a formative stage in their development and the various forces were riddled with corruption. Since their primary duty was often perceived as minimising inconvenience and distress to the wealthier classes, they were largely resented by the working class. Crime was rife; thieves were known as *Maggsmen*, which is where Charlie got his name. The confidence trick that Charlie carried out on the silversmiths of Clifton in Bristol was a *con job* well known by criminals, and was recorded by Henry Mayhew at the time, in his chronicles of *London Labour and the London Poor*.

Bath Races were one of the earliest horse-racing meetings in England, but they were suspended for a number of years. They resumed at Lansdown in 1850. A fair was also held at Lansdown every year and was notorious for an event in the 1839 when, as the day was drawing to a close, and the fair-men were packing away, a gang of drunks from Avon Street led by a notorious local character known as *Carroty Kate* converged on the fair and began smashing up the stalls.

The riot grew in intensity as the band looted every available source of alcohol and started setting fires, before eventually returning to the city. Thirty or so fair-men pursued them and captured the ring-leaders, including Kate. They were taken back to the fair, tied to the wheels of the wagons and flogged. Kate was the last to receive summary justice, and was held over a trestle table as two young women flogged her with canes until they were too tired to continue. As the beaten rioters returned to the city, they were met by the police and another skirmish ensued. Several were arrested and later transported. One of the rioters severely injured a policeman with an iron bar and was later tried and hung, for wounding with intent to murder.

Nathaniel Caine is a fictional character, but the *Caines* family did exist. They were notorious throughout the West Country for being connected with, and sometimes leading, a gang of thugs based in the village of Cockroad. Abraham Caines was hung for stealing at Gloucester jail in 1727. Francis Caines stole a valuable consignment of cloth, was caught, confessed, and was hung at Ilchester jail in 1804. Benjamin Caines was hung in 1817 for robbing a young woman. His father had his corpse brought home and charged people to view the body laid out in the parlour to help pay for his funeral. In 1842, Edward Caines, defending the honour of the family name, drew a knife in a fight and was transported for seven years.

The Caines' Cockroad gang were largely petty criminals, but exercised substantial power, extorting money from farmers and publicans, stealing from houses, and robbing coaches and travellers on the highways. There is no evidence for them being money lenders, though they were involved in various protection rackets, and though they never established a meaningful presence in Bath, they did collect their dues each year at Lansdown Fair.

The gang was one of the last bands of highwaymen to operate in England. They were finally subdued and arrested by Sergeant Hazell in 1850. So great was their strength and the fear they generated that he required the support of a troop of militia to enter the village of Cockroad. Even then they had to approach with stealth, at dead of night and pick off the gang members, house by house. The last highwaymen were not romantic figures, but violent thugs who terrorised those around them.

I have tried to be scrupulous in reconstructing the Bath of 1850, but on a few occasions have resorted to a little literary licence to assist in conveying a scene, or to help the plot along. The free public fountain at the end of Bath Street (since demolished) where James and John drank when fleeing from Caine was not erected until 1859, and the County Club outside which James was shot (now the Bath and County Club) was not developed as a gentleman's club until 1858. I hope the reader will forgive an occasional bending of the truth in the interests of story-telling.

Most of the Avon Street area is now occupied by Bath Spa University, various commercial properties, bus depots and sundry car parks. The past and its people and their stories lie buried. Yet their struggles deserve to be remembered.

The past makes us who we are. The choices we make determine who we become.

Visit our website and discover thousands of other History Press books.

www.thehistorypress.co.uk